"In Hannah Grace, the first book in Sharlene MacLaren's newest series, Shar's writing style is as spunky and spirited as her characters! Truly a great read!"

—Jean E. Syswerda
Coauthor, *Women of the Bible*
General Editor, *Women of Faith Study Bible*

"A cozy fire and some buttered popcorn will lend warmth to an already heartwarming tale. Hannah Grace is a riveting story filled with contagious characters and a few hidden surprises."

—Debra Ullrick
Author, *The Bride Wore Coveralls*

"Sharlene's fresh, unique voice brings a delightful story full of romance and intrigue. Her characters are multidimensional and quickly make their way into readers' hearts."

—Lena Nelson Dooley
Author, editor, and speaker

Hannah Grace

Hannah Grace

A NOVEL BY SHARLENE
MacLaren

WHITAKER
HOUSE

Hannah Grace

First in The Daughters of Jacob Kane Series

Sharlene MacLaren
www.sharlenemaclaren.com

ISBN: 978-1-60374-074-6
Printed in the United States of America
© 2009 by Sharlene MacLaren

Whitaker House
1030 Hunt Valley Circle
New Kensington, PA 15068
www.whitakerhouse.com

Library of Congress Cataloging-in-Publication Data

MacLaren, Sharlene, 1948–
Hannah Grace / by Sharlene MacLaren.
    p. cm.
    Summary: "Feisty, strong-willed Hannah Grace Kane strikes up a volatile relationship with the new local sheriff, Gabriel Devlin—a relationship that turns to romance, thanks to a shy orphan boy and a little divine intervention"—Provided by publisher.
    ISBN 978-1-60374-074-6 (trade pbk. : alk. paper) 1. Fathers and daughters—Fiction. 2. Domestic fiction. I. Title.
PS3613.A27356H35 2009
813'.6—dc22
                                                        2008038642

2 3 4 5 6 7 8 9 10 11 12 𝖂 16 15 14 13 12 11 10 09

Chapter One

Sandy Shores, Michigan • August 1903

The minute hand on the nickel-cased Waterbury clock ticked away the seconds as Hannah Grace Kane primped in the mirror. She leaned back and squinted with displeasure when her unruly, rusty-colored curls refused to cooperate, poking out all over like a bunch of broken bedsprings. "Aargh!" she muttered, throwing down her comb and watching it bounce off the wood floor with a ping before landing on the braided wool rug.

"Supper's almost ready!" wailed the youngest of the Kane sisters, Abbie Ann, from the foot of the stairs.

"Abbie Ann, you'll damage my hearing," Jacob Kane muttered.

Even from the upstairs bedroom, Hannah heard her father's newspaper rattle and sensed that his tone bordered on brusqueness. She pictured him sitting in his plush blue velvet chair, as he always did at six o'clock, the *Sandy Shores Tribune* spread in his lap, his reading spectacles perched low on his longish nose. "Why is it that at seventeen, you're still screaming like a banshee?"

"Seventeen, Papa? Have you forgotten that I turned eighteen in May?"

There was a lengthy pause. "Eighteen? Are you sure?"

Her high-pitched giggle drifted upward. "Of course I'm sure, silly. A lady never forgets her age."

"Well, then, all the more reason to cease with your howling."

"Sorry, Papa."

"Besides, Hannah Grace isn't even eating at home this evening."

"Oh, how could I forget? That ol' Stuffy Huffy's coming to call. I suppose they'll take a long stroll in the moonlight. Blechh." Her voice danced with unrestrained sarcasm, and Hannah could only imagine the look of disapproval on her father's bearded face. "I don't know what she sees in him, do you, Papa? If you ask me, he's boring and unfriendly."

The newspaper crackled. "Abbie." He heaved a breath, which echoed up through the register. "*Doctor* Van Huff seems like a nice enough gentleman. There is no call for judging him. And besides, your sister seems to like him."

"I'm not judging. I'm merely expressing my view on things, which I happen to think is more fact than opinion. Personally, I suspect she just likes him 'cause he's just about the only eligible bachelor around."

Hannah bent down to retrieve her comb and sighed in the process. Everyone knew sounds carried faster than a windstorm in this two-story, foursquare structure. Was there no respect? Why, had she wanted, she could have walked to the twelve-inch heat vent in the floor and peered through its narrow slats to give her sister a snarling glower, but she wouldn't, for that was exactly what Abbie wanted her to do. All three Kane sisters had played the "spying game" through that heat register as children, but Abbie seemed bent on continuing it till kingdom come.

"Abbie Ann, you mind your manners. Hannah will hear you."

Well, it's about time someone thought of that, Hannah mused, thankful for her grandmother's scolding tone. Helena Kane, Jacob's mother, had tirelessly tended to the entire family since shortly after the girls' own mother had succumbed to pneumonia and died just days short of Abbie's second birthday. "Ralston Van Huff is a fine, upstanding citizen, and you had best show your respect." Even after all these years in Michigan, her British accent still lingered like a fresh aroma.

"I do, I do," Abbie insisted. "But he's always talking about himself and that stupendous medical practice he runs. After a while, one grows downright weary of it."

Jacob snapped his paper and exhaled noisily. "The man is doing his best to make a success of himself. I would think taking on the task of town physician would require a bit of ambition...speaking of which, shouldn't you be out in the kitchen helping your grandmother and sister?"

"I'll second that," said Grandmother. "Take the napkins out of the bureau, Abbie."

"Do you suppose he's a true Christian, Papa?" Abbie asked, ignoring his inquiry.

"Well, I would hope so. Hannah Grace wouldn't settle for anyone who didn't claim to have a faith of his own. May I please read today's news now, Abigail?"

Keeping one ear to the conversation downstairs, Hannah picked up her comb and resumed her hair-styling task.

"I, for one, think Dr. Van Huff is charming." Maggie Rose spoke up for the first time that evening. From the kitchen wafted her habitually melodious voice—melodious in that she spoke in pleasant tones rather than melodious from a musical standpoint, that is. Sadly, Maggie thought she could carry a tune quite well, but after years of sitting beside her in church, Hannah knew otherwise. "He picked two roses from our garden last week and gave one to Hannah and one to me. I'd call that rather sweet."

"Oh, poke me with a stick!" Abbie whined. "He should rather have picked flowers from his own garden—or bought some at Clara's Flower Shop."

"Abbie Ann Kane, stop being so persnickety," Grandmother said. "My goodness, what side of the bed did—?"

A deafening scream sounded through the house when something metallic made clanging contact with the linoleum floor.

"My giddy aunt, what a gobblin' mess we have here! Don't burn yourself, Maggie!" Grandmother screeched. "Abbie, come in here this minute and lend a hand. Noodles are everywhere."

"What's happened?" Jacob asked.

"It looks like a pig's breakfast just landed on our kitchen floor. Oh, forevermore and a day! Supper will be delayed, I'm afraid."

Abbie's uncontrollable giggles lent to the clamor of rushing feet, running water, Grandmother's stern orders to stop laughing and fetch some rags, and Maggie's pathetic verbal attempts to vindicate her clumsiness.

From her cushioned bench in front of the vanity, Hannah stifled a smile, glad to be upstairs and away from the commotion. She leaned forward to study herself in the mirror. After this close scrutiny, her slightly upturned mouth curled into a pout. Grayish eyes, neither true blue nor clear green, stared back at her as she viewed her thin, longish neck and narrow shoulders, pointy chin, square jaw, and plump-ish lips. To top matters off, she had a skinny frame with very little up front to prove her womanhood. As a matter of fact, she'd thought more than once that if she wanted to pass as a boy, she could pile all her hair under a cap, if ever there was one big enough, don a pair of men's coveralls, work boots, and a jacket, and no one would be the wiser.

She thought about her sisters' attractive looks—Maggie's fair-haired beauty and Abbie's dark eyes, olive complexion, and flowing, charcoal hair. Assuredly, they both outshone her pasty features by a country mile, Abbie's assets originating from their mother's Italian heritage, Maggie's coming from their Grandmother Kane's long line of elegant features. To be sure, Helena was an aging woman in her sixties, but anyone with an eye for beauty could see that with her high cheek-bones, perfectly set blue eyes, well-chiseled nose and chin, and remarkably smooth skin, she must have been the picture of youthful elegance and charm.

But where did she, Hannah Grace, fit into the picture? Certainly, she'd inherited her grandmother's curly hair, but where Helena's lay in perfect, gentle waves, gathered into a tidy silver bun at the back, Hannah's crimped and frizzed atop her head like a thousand corkscrews. And nothing she did to tame it seemed to work. She'd even lain her head on an ironing board some years ago, like a sacrificial hen, and allowed her sisters to straighten it with a hot iron—until they came too close to the skin and singed her scalp. The silly rec-ollection made her brow crinkle into four straight lines.

She pulled her shoulders back, dipped her chin, and tried to look dignified in her ivory silk afternoon gown with the button-down front and leg-o-mutton sleeves.

"Hannah Grace Van Huff," she whispered, testing the name aloud and wondering how it would feel to say it for the rest of her days.

Tonight, they would dine at the Culver House in downtown Sandy Shores, and, afterward, perhaps walk down to the harbor to watch the boats come and go. Along the way, they would pass the closed shops on Water Street and probably do some window gazing. Ralston would speak about his practice and tell her about the patients he'd seen that day—the broken bones he'd set, the wounds he'd wrapped. He would tell her about his dreams of constructing a new building—one that would allow him to relocate his practice away from his residence. Not for the first time, he would mention his hopes for a partner with whom to launch this undertaking, someone who shared his passion for medicine, of course, and had the financial wherewithal to pitch in his fair share. There would be a placard above the door and maybe a more prominent sign in the front yard. They would hire a nurse, of course, and, down the road, a bookkeeper to keep the multiplying records straight.

He would ask Hannah about her day at Kane's Whatnot, her father's general store, and inquire as to how sales had gone. She would be vague in her answer, knowing that the details would bore him to tears. Nevertheless, he'd smile and nod, appearing deeply interested, but then quickly resume speaking about his medical practice.

Perhaps Abbie was right in calling Ralston stuffy and boring, if not a trifle selfish, but he had ambition on his side, and Hannah admired that. Even Papa recognized it. Besides, she'd reached the ripe age of twenty-one, and hadn't Grandmother once said that when a woman reached her twenties, her chances of finding a genteel fellow slimmed considerably? It was best not to listen to Abbie's foolish musings. What did she know about the subject? Dr. Ralston Van Huff would make a fine catch for any woman.

"Hannah wouldn't settle for a man who didn't claim to have a faith of his own."

Her father's words circled in her head, almost like a band of pesky mosquitoes out for blood. Well, of course, Ralston had an active faith. She'd met him at a church gathering, after all. *True, he rarely speaks about the Lord, but these things come with time and practice,* she told herself. *One doesn't grow strong in faith overnight.*

As the racket continued downstairs, Hannah proceeded to pile her mass of red curls on top of her head, using every available pin to hold them in place.

"Thank heaven for hats," she muttered to herself.

⟋K⟍

Gabriel Devlin tipped his dusty hat at the woman he passed on the narrow sidewalk, then scolded himself for stealing a glance backward after she passed. What was he doing? He was done with women! And he had Carolina Woods to thank for that. *No, I can thank the Lord for bringing our impending marriage to a halt,* he rephrased in his head.

A horse whinnied and kicked up a swirl of dirt as it galloped by, carrying its rider through the street, a barking dog on its heels. Since stores closed at precisely five o'clock in this small but thriving community of Dutch settlers known as Holland, Michigan, the dog and horse were about the only sounds he heard as he made his way toward an open restaurant, stepping down from the rickety-planked sidewalk and crossing the heavily trodden, dirt-packed street in the middle of town. He removed his hat and slapped it across his leather-clad thigh, letting loose a cloud of dust he estimated was almost as big as the horse's. Setting it back on his head of sandy-colored hair, he stepped up onto a slab of newly laid concrete and saw that one entire block of sidewalk looked freshly poured. Evidently the town council had started a beautification project, at least on this side of the street. He surmised the other side would follow, perhaps before the first blast of winter weather.

He passed several storefronts, glanced in a few windows, and then saw something out the corner of his eye that brought his steps to a halt as his gaze fell on the object of interest. Across the street and another block over, a young lad was crawling out from under a tarp that was stretched over the back of a wagon. He put his hands on his hips and twisted his body from side to side, stretching as if he had just awakened from a long nap. Then, he rubbed his neck and looked at the trees swaying overhead. The horse that was hitched to the front of the wagon turned and granted the boy a disinterested glance, then swished its mangy tail.

Wondering what the boy was up to, Gabe feigned interest in a window display, embarrassed to discover that it was laden with feminine wares and frilly garments. Still, he kept up the façade so as not to miss the boy's next move. With deft hands, he was plundering through the items under the canvas, stuffing things into every pocket, front and back.

Instinct told him to yell at the lad, for surely he was steal-ing from some unsuspecting citizen, but something held him back—the tattered clothing hanging off his skinny shoulders, the uncombed mop of black hair, the spattering of dirt and grime on his face and arms, and those shoddy-looking boots.

When the little vagabond had filled his pockets with who knew what, he took off on a run down an alley between two buildings, disappearing within seconds like a fox daunted by daylight. Gabe shook his head, vexed at himself for not caring more but feeling too exhausted after his long day's ride to muster up much indignation. Maybe once he crammed his stomach with beef stew and bread and gave his horse and mule a period of rest at the livery, he'd go looking for him to see if he could figure out his story.

Pfff! Who was he kidding? After a quick bite and a bit of respite, he planned to finish his trip, following the path along the railroad tracks to Sandy Shores, his final destination. There'd be no time to look for a tattered boy who couldn't have been a day over nine years old.

A few restaurant patrons cast him curious looks when he found a window seat in the smoke-filled room, but most kept to themselves, faces buried in newspapers or hovering over their suppers. They were likely accustomed to summer tour-ists, although, by all appearances, he probably resembled a bum more than anything else.

Certainly not Sandy Shores' newly appointed sheriff.

"What can I do for y', mister?"

He gazed into the colorless eyes of an elderly woman whose hard-lined face, slumped shoulders, and pursed mouth denoted some unnamed trial of the past. Gray hair fell around her stern countenance, straight and straw-like, reminding him of a scarecrow—the kind whose expression would chase off the meanest bull.

"I'll have a bowl of beef stew and a slice of—"

"Plumb out."

"No beef stew?"

"You hard o' hearin'?"

"Chicken noodle?"

"No soup atall." With hooked thumb, she pointed behind her. "Menu's back there."

His eyes scanned the chalkboard behind the counter where someone had scrawled several words with creative spellings: "Chikin liver and onyuns – 50¢; potatos and gravy on beef – 75¢; cheese sanwich – 25¢; pork sanwich on toasted Bred – 35¢; Ted's specielty – 50¢"

"What's Ted's specialty?" He had to ask.

"Fish. You want it?"

"Is it cooked?"

She gave him a scornful look. "What kind o' lame-brained question is that? 'Course it's cooked."

"I don't know. Some people eat raw fish."

"Not 'round these parts they don't. Where you from?"

"Ohio. Columbus area."

She sniffed. "Long ways from home, ain't ya?"

He grinned. "It's taken me a few days' ride."

Lifting one brow as if to size him up, but keeping her thoughts to herself, she asked, "You want the fish? It's fresh out o' the big lake, pan-fried."

His stomach had been growling ever since he walked through the doors, and, in spite of the grit and grime beneath his feet, the dark and dingy walls, and the fetid odors of burnt onions and cigarette smoke, he had a feeling this Ted fellow could cook.

"I'll try the fish." He smiled at the killjoy, but, as expected, she just nodded and turned on her heel. "Can I have some coffee, too?"

Another slight nod indicated she'd heard him.

"Ohio, huh?"

From the table next to him, a man sporting a business jacket, string bow tie, and white ruffled shirt, lowered his newspaper. A half-smoked cigar hung out the side of his mouth directly under his pencil thin moustache. He removed the cigar and laid it on an ashtray. "What brings you to these parts?"

Always wary of shysters, Gabe examined the fellow on the sly. Experience had taught him not to trust anyone until he'd earned that right. "Work," he replied.

"Yeah?" The man massaged his chin, and Gabe knew he was getting equal treatment, a careful scrutiny. Suddenly, the stranger reached across the four-foot span that separated their tables and offered his hand. "Vanderslute's the name. George."

Gabe stuck out his arm and they shook hands. "Gabriel Devlin. Good Dutch name you've got there."

Vanderslute chuckled. "You're definitely in Dutch territory. Pretty near half the town, I'd say. Maybe more." He looked out over the small, dimly lit eatery. "Not Ted, though. He's English, through and through. That there was Eva, his

aunt. She owns this place, has for thirty years." He leaned
forward. "She comes across as an old crank," he murmured
in hushed tones, "but on the inside, she's nothing but mush.
Known the two of them since I was this high." He stretched
a palm out level with the tabletop. "Used to stop by here on
my way home from school. Depending on her mood, Aunt
Eva—that's what everyone calls her—would pass out free
cookies. On good days, that is."

Vanderslute took a sip of coffee, then took a giant drag
off his cigar and placed it back on the tray. Gabe felt the tension roll off his shoulders. He glanced out the window and
spotted the little ragamuffin again, his lean frame bent over
a barrel as he rifled through the garbage within. "Who's that
little waif over there?" he asked.

"Huh? Where?" Vanderslute pitched forward to peer out
the smudged glass.

"Oh, him. He's been hanging around for a few days. He'll
move on. 'Spect he jumped the back of a train coming from
Chicago area. Vagabonds do that from time to time."

"Vagabonds? He's just a little kid. Hasn't anyone tried to
help him?"

"He runs off every time. Like some wild pup. Some of the
ladies leave bowls of food on their doorsteps, and he'll run
and get them whilst no one's watching, providing some mongrel mutt doesn't beat him to it." He laughed, as if what he'd
just said was unusually funny.

Just then, Eva brought a steaming cup of coffee to the
table and George slid back in place. When Gabe looked out
again, the boy had vanished—like some kind of apparition.
He blinked twice and shook his head.

Silence overtook the two for the next several moments as George dug into the plate of roast beef and potatoes Eva had dropped off at his table when she'd deposited a mug of coffee under Gabe's nose. Gabe's mouth watered, his stomach grumbled. He sipped on his coffee and ruminated about the boy.

"What's your trade, anyway?" George asked between chews.

Gabe took another slow swig before setting the tin mug on the table. "You ever hear of Judge Bowers?"

"Ed Bowers, the county judge? 'Course I have. I work the newspaper. I'm a line editor, not a reporter, but I read the headlines before anybody else does. I hear he just appointed a new interim sheriff up in Sandy Shores—someone from…" A light seemed to dawn in his eyes. "Ohio." Gabe grinned. "You wouldn't be…?"

"You should be a reporter," Gabe said. "You've got the nose for it."

"You learn, you know. Well, I'll be. Too bad about Sheriff Tate, though. He was a good man, honest and fair. Heard his heart just gave out." George shook his head. "The law business is hard on the body. Good thing you're young. What are you—twenty-four? Twenty-five?"

"Twenty-eight."

George nodded, as if assessing the situation. "You can handle it. Most of what happens in these parts is petty crimes, but there's the occasional showdown. Not often, though," he added hastily. "You watch yourself, young man. You'll do fine."

"Thanks. I appreciate that."

Not a minute too soon, Eva returned, this time plopping a plate of pan-fried fish in front of Gabe. On the side were cooked carrots drizzled with some sort of glaze and a large helping of applesauce. The most wonderful aromas floated heavenward, and his stomach growled in response. "Eva, you are an angel." He smiled at her and felt a certain pleasure to see one side of her mouth quirk up a fraction and the tiniest light spark in her eyes.

"Pfff," she tittered. "Go on with you." She swiveled her tiny frame and hobbled off toward the kitchen, still looking like a scarecrow, but with a little less severity.

As he always did before delving into a meal, Gabe bowed his head and offered up a prayer of thanks to God. Then, he draped a napkin over his lap, knowing George Vanderslute's eyes had taken to drilling holes in his side.

"You're a praying man, I see."

Gabe took his first bite. "I am. I pray about everything, actually."

"Huh. That's somethin'." Seeming stumped, George forked down the rest of his meal in silence, the smoke from his cigar making a straight path to the ceiling.

As much as he would have liked taking his sweet time, Gabe wolfed down his plate of food, thinking about the miles of road that still stretched out before him. If he didn't arrive before nightfall, he'd have to camp alongside the tracks again, and the thought of one more night under the stars didn't set well with him.

The image of the mysterious little imp who'd stolen from the back of a wagon, rummaged through a waste barrel, and disappeared down an alley materialized at the back of his mind. Would he be shivering in some dark corner tonight, half starved? Gabe swallowed down the last of his coffee, determined to chase him out of his thoughts.

Protect him, Lord, he prayed on a whim, suppressing the pang of guilt he felt for not taking the time to search for him.

Sandy Shores came into view at exactly a quarter till ten, three hours after he left Holland. It had been the slowest, steepest, and most precarious leg of the entire trip, requiring him to navigate gravelly slopes in the light of the moon. Not for the first time, he thanked the Lord for his sure-footed mule, Zeke the Streak, who could not run if his life depended on it but still had strength enough to pull a redwood from its roots; and for Slate, his dapple-gray gelding, calmly bringing up the rear but possessing the speed of a bullet if the situation called for it.

A cool breeze was coming off the lake, bringing welcome relief from an otherwise long, hot day on the trail. Gabe cast a glance out over the placid lake, amazed once more by its vastness. At first glimpse, one would never suppose its distance across to be a mere one hundred miles; it seemed more like an ocean. Gentle waves licked the shoreline, making a whooshing sound before ebbing back into the chilly depths. The Sandy Shores lighthouse, sitting like a proud mother at the end of the pier, flashed her beacon for incoming fishing boats and steamers.

Electric streetlights lit the way as Gabe turned east off the railroad path onto Water Street, which led to the center of town. On the corner to his right stood the three-story Sherman House, the hotel he would call home until he found permanent housing suitable for his budget, if not for his taste. According to Ed Bowers, who had made all his room arrangements, he had a view of the Grand River Harbor and the big lake from his third-floor window. *Nice for the interim,* he thought, *but not a necessity for my simple lifestyle.* He'd grown up in affluence and decided he was ready for humbler circumstances. His father's money had been well-earned, and it had reaped him warranted respect in the community and surrounding areas. Even so, Gabe couldn't live off his father's wealth and still respect himself. Besides, he'd had enough of women pursuing him for his family money—Carolina Woods, for one—and it was high time he moved away from Ohio, where the Devlin name didn't make such an impact every time folks heard it mentioned. Furthermore, a smaller town meant smaller crimes, he hoped—the kind that didn't require gunfire to resolve them.

Boisterous piano music and uproarious laughter coming from a place called Charley's Saloon assaulted his senses after two hours spent with nary a sound, save for Zeke's occasional braying, some sleepy crickets' chirps, and a gaggle of geese honking from the lake. Gabe wondered if he should expect a run-in or two with a few of Charley's patrons.

His eyes soaked up the names of storefronts—Jellema Newsstand, Moretti's Candy Company, Hansen's Shoe Repair, DeBoer's Hardware, Kane's Whatnot—and he wondered about the proprietors who ran each place. Would they accept him as their new lawman, particularly since the late Sheriff Watson Tate had held the office for well over twenty years?

When he spotted Enoch Sprock's Livery on the second block, he pulled Zeke's reins taut. Slate snorted, his way of exhaling a sigh of relief for having reached their destination.

"I know what you mean, buddy," Gabe muttered, feeling stiff and sore himself. He threw the reins over the brake handle and jumped down, landing on the hard earth.

"You needin' some help there, mister?"

A white-bearded fellow with a slight limp emerged from the big double door.

"You must be Enoch."

"In the flesh." The man extended a hand. "And who might you be?"

"Gabriel Devlin."

"Ah, the new sheriff. We been expectin' ya. Hear your room's waitin' over at the Sherman." They shook hands. "Nice place you're stayin' at."

Gabe grinned. "News gets around, I take it."

Enoch snorted and tossed back his head. "This ain't what you call a big metropolis." He took a step back and massaged his beard even while he studied Gabe from top to bottom. "Awful young, ain't ya?"

Is this how folks would view him? Young, inexperienced, still wet behind the ears? He supposed few knew he'd been responsible for bringing down Joseph Hamilton, aka "Smiley Joe"—a murderous bank robber who wielded his gun for goods throughout Indiana, Ohio, and parts of Kentucky. His last spree was on February 4, 1901, when Gabe received word in his office via telegraph that undercover sources determined Smiley Joe had plans to rob the Delaware County State Bank at noon that very day.

It hadn't made national headlines, but every Ohioan had the best night's sleep of his life after reading the next day's headlines: GABRIEL DEVLIN, DELAWARE COUNTY SHERIFF, TAKES DOWN NOTORIOUS MIDDLE-WEST BANK ROBBER!

Having watched the entire robbery out of the corner of his eye while pretending to fill out a bank slip, Gabe, who had placed two plainclothes deputies at the door in case the villain tried to escape, confronted him while the deputies aimed their guns. "Smiley! It's the end of the line for you, buddy," he said coolly. "Drop the bags and turn around slowly, hands in the air."

At first, it appeared Smiley would comply. His shoulders dropped and he started to turn. "Drop the bags!" Gabe yelled. "Hands to the sky!"

Other deputies, all placed strategically around the bank, surrounded him. The bank stilled to funeral parlor silence as customers scattered and backed against all four walls, terror pasted on every face.

But Smiley Joe wasn't one to surrender, and, in a rattled state, he went for the eleventh-hour approach: he drew his gun. *Wrong move.* Shots were fired, and, when it was over, one wounded customer lay sprawled on the floor, groaning and bleeding from the shoulder, while Smiley Joe Hamilton lay dead, Gabe's gun still hot from the bullet he shot through his head.

"That's all right by me, you bein' young," Enoch was saying. "Time for some new blood 'round here. 'Sides, any friend o' Judge Bowers is a friend o' mine." A slight accent from the British Isles colored his tone.

"I appreciate that."

"Want I should take your rig inside and tend to your animals?"

"That'd be mighty nice of you."

Gabe made a move to retrieve his money pouch, but Enoch stopped him. "You just get what you need out o' your rig, and we'll settle up in the mornin'."

"You have no idea how good that sounds." Gabe reminded himself to retrieve his carpetbag from the back of the wagon. All he needed was a change of clothes for tomorrow, his shaving gear, a bar of soap, and some tooth powder. Right now, nothing sounded better than a soft bed. *Shoot, I might even sleep through breakfast*, he mused. Ed Bowers didn't expect him in his office until mid-afternoon.

Slate sidestepped the two as they went to the back to remove the tarp. When they did, they got the surprise of their lives.

"Wull, I'll be jig-swiggered. What is that?"

Gabe stared open-mouthed at the bundle of a body curled into a tight ball.

"Looks to be a sleeping boy," he murmured.

Chapter Two

The bell above the door sounded a new customer's entry into Kane's Whatnot. Hannah ceased refolding the towels Mrs. Mayworth had completely undone in her quest to find the perfect one for her newly painted, yellow kitchen. She smiled at the elderly Edwin Fisher as he entered, his cane hooked over one arm. He carried the thing more than he used it.

"Good morning, Mr. Fisher. Have you come to check out some new books?"

Under his other arm, he lugged three large volumes. Ever since losing his wife back in February, he frequented the town library, which was stationed above the general store. Hannah figured that reading provided an escape for the retired postmaster, who had to be approaching eighty years of age.

"That I have, my dear."

"And did you read all of those?" she asked, nodding to the books under his arm.

"For the most part," he said with a twinkle in his eyes. "These, yes." He held up two volumes of Mark Twain's works. "This, no."

Hannah leaned forward and read the title. "*The Strange Case of Dr. Jekyll and Mr. Hyde.* I've not read that one yet."

He scowled. "Too strange for my taste. Hence the title, I suppose. A bit on the dreary side, actually. I waded through the first half of it before giving up on it altogether." He leaned forward and whispered, "If you want to know the truth, I read the ending to determine if I wanted to keep going."

She gasped. "Reading ahead? That's a mortal sin!"

"And you've never done it, I suppose," he teased back with a chuckle.

"Never—well," she said, dipping her chin in feigned shame, "all right, I'll admit that I did peek at the last page of *Brewster's Millions*, but that's the only time I've cheated. I simply had to know if he would manage to spend all that money by the given deadline and gain an even larger sum as his reward. I do so hate a story with a sour ending."

A flash of amusement crossed his wrinkled face, his white moustache quivering. "I understand. By the way, who's tending the library post today?"

"Maggie Rose." The Kane sisters took turns staffing the library. "I know she'll be happy to see you. She's set aside another of Twain's volumes that she thought you hadn't read yet."

"Ah, how you fair ladies do look after my interests."

She flashed him a smile. "We wouldn't do it for just anybody, you know."

"I can't believe that. Everyone knows the Kane sisters are a notch above the rest, helpful, kind, generous—and pretty, to boot."

She dropped her gaze to the unfolded towels. *Pretty?* Maggie and Abbie, to be sure. Endowed in all the right places, they were. To cover her insecurities, she took up again the task of refolding towels and sought to change the subject. "Shall I call Maggie to bring down the book, or are you of a mind to navigate the stairs today?"

He pulled back his curved shoulders and stuck out his chin. "What do you take me for, my dear? An invalid?"

She giggled. "Well, the least you can do is leave the books with me. Tell Maggie I'll bring them up later."

"I'll not argue with you there." He handed them over, then hobbled toward the stairs, hooking his cane over his wrist, as usual.

"You be careful now," she called after him, smiling to herself when he waved a backward arm at her, mumbling something under his breath.

A handful of customers came and went over the next half hour, forcing Hannah to give up straightening linen so that she could fill customers' orders. A lull in busyness allowed her to resume folding linen in the back of the store, so she wasn't at her post by the counter when the door opened again, this time admitting the first unfamiliar face of the day. Hannah stayed concealed behind the shelves of jam and preserves, peering out at the new patron.

At his heels was a young lad, skinny as a fence rail and looking like a flea-infested ragamuffin with his torn shirt, his too-short pants, his soiled toes that poked through his worn boots, and jet-black hair that looked like it had seen neither drop of water nor ounce of soap since spring. His tanned, burnt-umber skin showed signs of having spent hours in the sun. Did the man work him in the fields from morning till night? Her immediate reaction to the situation was revulsion—not at the poor lad, but at his neglectful father. What man could show such disregard for his own offspring, especially when he himself looked to be reasonably wealthy?

Instead of going out to greet them, Hannah remained hidden. She couldn't explain the indolence that had come over her, keeping her from giving a gracious welcome to the newcomers. She thought that if Mr. Fisher could see her now, he would certainly take back those words about every Kane sister being helpful, kind, and generous. Normally, she would have bent over backward to be gracious, especially to a new customer, but some strange sense of perturbation had started in her chest as soon as the pair entered the store. Perhaps it was the way the lad had eyed the candy counter with particular interest, and the way his father had so pointedly ignored it.

The boy remained as closemouthed as a clam while scuffling along behind the strange man, who had taken to looking at men's vestments. After picking up a flannel shirt and examining it quickly, he set it back on the top of the stack and sauntered past the candy counter, the women's hats, the brooms and dusters, and, finally, the apothecary jars and toiletry products at the rear of the store. Hannah watched him turn down another aisle and stop in front of a twenty-five pound sack of stone-ground meal, mumbling something to the boy, who said nothing in return. When the man glanced around the store, Hannah ducked behind a stack of grain sacks, careful to avoid his notice.

The man resumed moving about the store, his tiny companion acting as his shadow. At closer range, Hannah could make out a few of his features—his clean-shaven face with its square-set jaw that clenched and unclenched every few seconds, his broad shoulders, his strong yet lean physique. But that was all the time she would allow herself to examine the brute, who hadn't the slightest apparent concern for his son.

Hannah noticed that the man appeared to be seeking assistance, so she finally emerged from behind the counter. "May I help you find something?" she inquired.

The man looked almost startled, focusing on Hannah for a few seconds before removing his hat with a sweeping gesture. "You carry much in the way of kids' clothes?" His voice, though deep, rang crisp and clear. "I'm looking for something that would fit this little mud puppy."

What a strange way to address one's child, Hannah thought. *Crude, uncaring man.*

She found her voice hidden in a distant part of her throat. "It's—you'll find the children's clothing against that far wall there."

"Oh, I guess we didn't get over there yet." He put a hand to the boy's bony shoulder and pushed him in the other direction. With his back to her, she was able to glimpse his straight, fresh-cut hair, still tickling his shirt collar but a stylish length, the color of beach sand. If he had the time and resources to visit a barber, why couldn't his son go, too?

The fellow picked up a pair of boy's overalls and held them up against the lad's body, checking for size and length. "You think this'll fit you?" No response. He looked frustrated, if not distracted.

Hitching her skirt past her heels, Hannah made her way across the room. "He can try them on in that back room, if he likes."

At the sound of her voice, the man whirled and gave her the first hint of a smile. To say he had a pleasant face would be insufficient. Abbie Ann would call him infinitely divine, heavenly, a marvelous creation…she was wordy with her descriptions. Maggie Rose would concede his good looks but remain more subtle in her word choice. And she, Hannah Grace, would keep her thoughts entirely to herself. After all, what woman, nearly betrothed to the town doctor, for mercy's sake, would give another man's looks the slightest thought?

"We might do that, although these appear fine, don't you think? A little on the big side, maybe."

Hannah stood back to study the lad with the overalls tugged up under his chin. It was then she discovered several bruises along his arm and another on his forehead. Closer inspection showed that the hand most visible bore several scratch marks. Her stomach roiled in horror. What was this? She leaned forward to get a better look, but the boy jumped out of view faster than a monkey and skittered behind the man's thick thighs, sticking out his head so that all she saw were his big-as-the-moon brown eyes.

"What have you done?" she hissed at the man, daring to eye him with the menacing gaze of a livid lioness. Her flesh prickled with dread. "If you have so much as laid a hand to this boy, I'll—"

"Hush up and leave him be," ordered the stranger, his tone an authoritative, husky whisper. "It's not what you think."

"I'll—I'll report you to the local authorities," she finished, pulling back her proud shoulders.

His mouth spread into a thin-lipped smile as one blond eyebrow quirked. "Is that so?"

"Yes, that's so, and you can wipe that smug look off your face this instant."

She could handle most any kind of injustice by chalking it up as sin and reasoning that God would deal with the sinner, but the maltreatment of children? She simply couldn't abide it.

"Well, you go right ahead and report me, lady. In fact, word has it the new sheriff just arrived in town last night—he opened his office this very morning."

"Fine!"

"Fine!"

His cockiness bore a hole through her side, and the notion he didn't seem to take her seriously galled her even more. She'd heard about the new sheriff's arrival, and if this man thought she was kidding about reporting the senseless abuse of this tiny little slip of a boy, well, he could just—just—put forks up his nose.

Forcing out a calming breath, she leaned forward to make eye contact with the boy. "Are you all right?"

The impertinent man blocked her with his palm, and her resentment rose higher than a spring kite. "You can talk to me," she said to the child, trying her best to ignore the gargantuan hand that looked ready to seize a fistful of her hair if she so much as moved an inch closer. "Are you...?"

Quick as a hiccup, the boy made a mad dash for the door. An oil lamp was in the way, and it crashed to the floor, erupting into a million pieces. Shocked, Hannah straightened and merely watched the action, the young soul throwing wide the screen door, pursued closely by the man.

"You come back here, you little…!" At the door, he paused just long enough to glare back at Hannah. "I told you to leave him be!"

When she would have offered a retort, he plopped his hat on his sandy head and vanished from view, the screen door bouncing shut with a loud whack.

"Hannah Grace, what is all the racket?" Maggie came rushing down the stairs, skirts flowing. Mr. Fisher forded down after her, moving faster than she'd ever witnessed, albeit breathless once he reached the bottom.

"I've just been visited by a tyrant."

Maggie frowned. "What are you talking about, a tyrant?"

"An awful man who beats his son. I'm sure of it. When I tried to talk to the child, he sped out of here faster than butter melts on a hot griddle. I'm going straight to the sheriff's office."

"Now, just—wait—a minute," Mr. Fisher huffed. "You must have proof—before you make such an accusation, my dear."

"Oh, I have proof!" she blurted.

"What sort of proof? Did you—actually witness him— manhandling this—child?"

"Well, not exactly, but…"

"You need to sit down, Mr. Fisher," Maggie ordered, running to retrieve a folding chair by the door and hurrying back to prop it under him.

With assistance, he sat down with a thump, snagged hold of the curved handle of his cane with both hands, and leaned forward on it, looking up at Hannah. "Now then, who was this man?"

His tall, rawboned physique materialized in her head—and then that handsome, square face, giving her a chill despite the warm, August air filtering through the door and open windows. "Quite frankly, I don't know. I've never seen him before. That doesn't mean anything, though. We get tourists through here all summer long."

"True," Mr. Fisher said with a thoughtful nod. "Can you describe his looks?"

"His looks?" Frustrated that the man might now skip town before she even had a chance to file a complaint against him, she shrugged impatiently. "I don't know. It's hard to describe him. Big. Yes, big and—tall. That's about all I can say. But the little boy—oh, he couldn't have been more than seven or eight, with bruises running up and down his arm and smattered on his forehead. Not only that, but I saw a mess of scratches on his hand."

"Oh, dear," Maggie murmured.

"I'm going to see that new sheriff."

"But are you positive he's even there yet?" Maggie asked. "I thought he wasn't to start work till next week."

Mr. Fisher shrugged, indicating he hadn't a clue.

"Oh, he's there all right. I heard he showed up first thing this morning."

"Really?" Maggie looked slightly interested. "Who told you that?"

"I don't..." She paused to think for a moment. "*He* did!"

"*He*, who?" Mr. Fisher asked. "The fellow making all the racket?"

The pair wore equal looks of confusion, which Hannah had no way of easing, for her own head reeled with uncertainties.

She moved to the door. "I'm sorry that I don't have more time to explain. Maggie, will you please mind the store for me?" she asked. "I shouldn't be long."

"But what about this huge mess of glass? We can't have customers coming in here until we clean it up. You have to stay."

Hannah's eyes traced a path to the pile of shattered glass, which had, no doubt, scattered several feet in every direction. Annoyance rushed like water through her veins.

She sucked in a monstrous breath of air and let it out slowly. "Oh, all right. I'll clean it up. But then you'll have to watch the store till I get back."

"Oh, fine."

"Fine, indeed."

Gabe sipped on a cup of coffee that was set kindly on his desk by Kitty Oakes, the one accounts clerk in the City Hall building who appeared to be offering him the most assistance.

"Here. Drink," she said. "And try to relax. He's sleeping now." Standing on the other side of his desk, she cast him a sympathetic eye.

"Thanks. Go ahead and unlock the cell, but keep your eye out for the rascal. He'll likely try to run again as soon as he wakes up. The boy's easily spooked. As far as I can tell, he doesn't want anyone coming too close." An overwhelming sense of responsibility gripped him from the inside. "I need to get to the bottom of this thing, figure out who he is."

Kitty winced. "I wouldn't unlock that cell just yet. He'll shoot out of here like a cannonball, I'm afraid, and he's just too little to be out on his own."

Gabe considered her words, too tired to think. He'd thought he had the kid all settled down until he'd taken him to that store for some supplies—and then *she* stepped in. It vexed him anew to remember it.

"Whatever you say. I can't keep him locked up forever, though." They'd had no choice but to put him in a cell like a caged bird until he quit kicking, biting, and flailing. "How old do you think he is?"

Kitty shrugged. "Seven, perhaps."

Gabe nodded. "I thought he was closer to nine."

Her brow crinkled. She folded her hands and put them to her plump waistline. "If he is, he's underweight and sickly. You should probably take him to see Dr. Van Huff. He might need to check him over real good. There has to be some reason he won't talk. Maybe he's got no tongue."

Gabe shot her a look that could only portray his disdain for her remark.

"Well, a lack of a tongue would surely keep one from talking," she insisted.

"He's got a tongue."

"How do you know?"

"He stuck it out at me last night in the hotel room."

"Oh."

He groaned and closed his eyes, pinching the bridge of his nose with his thumb and forefinger at the first feelings of a headache. This was too much. He'd accepted the job as sheriff, not guardian to some homeless brat.

Lord, forgive me for this attitude, he prayed silently. *Tell me what to do.*

"I need to get him some clothes and boots, and he needs a bath. Who's that woman who works at Kane's Whatnot?" What he'd meant as mere thoughts came out of his mouth.

"Depends on which one you're referring to. There are three of them."

Three? He couldn't imagine three of *that* particular woman.

He must have thrown her a questioning look. "Jacob Kane has three daughters. They all take turns working the store, but I'd say Hannah's there most often. Was Mr. Kane in the store?"

"I didn't see any man about, just a tall, slender girl with red, wild curls on her head and a—"

"Oh, that's Hannah Grace, all right. She's such a sweet thing. So pretty, too. 'Course, all those girls are lovely. I imagine Mr. Kane was over at his office. Besides running the store, he runs a little insurance business with Leo Perkins. You might have seen the placard across the road from the Whatnot—Kane and Perkins."

"No," Gabe responded absently. He was still digesting the part about Hannah being sweet and pretty. *Are we talking about the same woman?* Oh, she was pretty, for sure, but sweet? Maybe if you poured a pint of maple syrup down her throat.

"Well, I'll let you know if that tyke wakes up." Kitty started to turn, then paused. "I'm going out for some lunch soon, if you don't mind. I shouldn't be gone long. Is there anything I can get for you, Sheriff?"

"No, I'll be fine, thanks. I'm just wading through some paperwork Sheriff Tate—uh, God rest his soul—left behind." He took another deep swig of the black brew in his mug and settled back in the leather chair with the squeaky roller, surveying the office that had belonged to Watson Tate just two weeks ago.

Kitty's round, weathered face took on a faraway look. "Truth be told, that man should've retired long ago. If he had, he'd probably be out fishin' right now. He had a weak ticker, and word has it he had a couple other heart spells before this last one took him. He just wasn't one to give up or give in." She shook her head and walked to the door, then quickly turned and buoyed up her shoulders. "At least we got a young, spry one this time." She grinned, and Gabe thought he detected a dimple amidst the creases of her cheeks. "You should outlast us all."

"Well, we'll see about that. You have yourself a nice lunch now, Mrs. Oakes."

"Oh, merciful heavens! Call me Kitty, please."

He nodded. "Fine, but only if you call me Gabe."

Her hand spread over her ample chest. "Oh, well, I guess I could do that." Pushing a lock of silver hair off her forehead, she held the door. "It'll seem odd, though. I never called

Sheriff Tate by his first name. 'Course, he was my elder. You're more like…well, you could be my son, I s'pose."

"Never. You don't look a day over thirty."

Now, Kitty clamped a hand over her blushing face. "Oh, my soul and body! I can tell already you're just going to be the berries."

She was still giggling to herself when she closed the door behind her.

Gabe folded his hands in his lap and leaned back, crossing his legs and propping his feet up on the marred desktop. Staring at the ceiling, he watched a spider weave its web in the corner above the door. A jagged breath blew past his mouth. *Fine way to start my first day on the new job*, he thought, *bringing a rapscallion along with me to the office because I don't know a single soul in town on which to pawn him. Who would want to take care of a mute child who refuses to stay put, anyway?*

"Lord," he muttered into the quiet office, "I need a big batch of wisdom."

K

Hannah lifted her skirts, and, with quiet determination, climbed each step leading to the double doors of the entrance to City Hall. She reviewed the morning's events in her mind so that she might give the new sheriff an accurate account. When questioned, she would say the stranger was tall and dangerous…no—in fairness, she couldn't say "dangerous." The sheriff would call it—what? Supposition? *Stick to the facts*, he'd say. *I want details.*

Details. In her head, she began to imagine again. The man stood tall and broad shouldered, with a commanding presence. His blond hair tapered at the neck, a nice style, you might say, the sort that…facts. He had a square-set jaw and fine nose, and, well, symmetrical face. And those blue eyes of his, why, one might call them shimmery and iridescent.

The sheriff would be leaning forward now, pencil in hand, perhaps even tapping one end of it on his imposing desk, impatient for the particulars.

She would finally concede that she had no way to adequately describe his physical features, but if he would kindly produce one of those books that featured all the criminals' faces, she would most certainly spot him straightaway.

The solid door swung open when she used all her strength.

"Kitty?" she called. "Are you about?" On the desk at the front of the office stood piles of papers, thick volumes of information, a Mason jar containing pens and pencils, a wilted flower in a vase gone dry, and a couple of ashtrays. At present, Kitty's little desk in the middle of the room, also piled nearly to the ceiling with paperwork, appeared unoccupied. Several plaques framed in dark cherry wood hung from the walls, as did a large painting of President George Washington. A United States flag graced one corner, its six-foot pole jutting out from the wall so that it hung at a nice angle.

She knew that the sheriff's office was down the hall, first door on the right, but to get there, she needed someone on the other side of the counter to unlock the gate and let her through. She couldn't imagine why the sheriff's office, or the other rooms down the hall, for that matter, had to be so inaccessible to the public.

From one of the back rooms emerged Nathanial Brayton, Sandy Shores' community treasurer. In his fifties and of medium height, he wore a perpetual smile. Round-faced and bulbous-nosed, he also sported a bushy gray moustache. Hannah remembered standing beside her father as he talked with Mr. Brayton in the churchyard after the Sunday service when she was a child, feigning interest in their conversation while staring intently at Mr. Brayton's bobbing moustache.

"Wull, hello there, Miss Hannah. Kitty's out t' lunch, I'm sorry to say. What can I do for you?" With hooked thumbs, he held his brown suspenders—an accessory that didn't seem to serve its purpose, if one compared where the waist of his pants was supposed to fall and where it actually wound up: below his protruding belly.

"Oh." She stretched to her full five feet and seven inches and stepped forward. Why did she suddenly feel like shrinking? She'd hoped to find Kitty at the counter. Kitty would have bolstered her reasons for coming.

Beads of sweat pooled on her neck and trickled down her back. She removed her hat, a foolish thing to wear on a day pushing ninety degrees, and laid it on the counter. Its absence left her russet-colored curls to fall in complete disarray. "I've come to pay the new sheriff a visit."

Something happened to Mr. Brayton's perpetual smile. "Um, now might not be the best time, miss."

"But I insist on seeing him."

"He's had a bad morning."

"Already? It's his first day on the job."

"That it is—but, well, let's say better first days have gone down in history."

Hannah lifted her chin ever so subtly, her stubborn persistence mounting.

"That may be, but I've an important crime to report."

This got his interest. His eyebrows twitched and flickered. "A crime, miss? What sort of crime are we talking about? Was the Whatnot robbed?"

She shook her head. "I think it would be best if I dispensed with matters of the crime in the sheriff's private quarters, Mr. Brayton."

His chin dropped and he prepared to argue, but he clamped his mouth shut at the first sounds of a door creaking open.

Both heads turned to face the source. One mouth remained closed; the other gaped in disbelief.

Chapter Three

"Y ou!" Hannah's breathing seemed to come in short spurts, her otherwise pretty face assuming a sour expression. "What are you…? What, exactly, is the meaning of this?"

Gabe smiled, enjoying this other-side-of-the-fence feeling. "Was there a problem?" he asked.

She made a grumpy, disdainful noise—not at all of the ladylike variety, as it wound up coming out both her mouth and nose. Steely eyes shot him a look that was piercing—no, murderous. "Problem? Of course, there's a problem." With every word, her voice rose in minute decibels. "And you know exactly what I'm talking about, Mr.—Mr. Deluder, Mr. Deceiver, Mr. De—"

"—lightful?" he supplied.

"Aargh!" Another unbecoming growl came from somewhere deep within her skinny frame. He stepped forward to lift the gate, then proceeded into the lobby area, where he hoped to be able to calm the waters of misunderstanding.

"No need to scream."

"I am not screaming," she screamed. Mr. Brayton, appearing completely bewildered, had not yet made one move to speak.

"First of all, my name is not any of those 'D' words you mentioned; it's Gabriel Devlin, Gabe to my friends." His eyes made a quick pass over her mop of rust-hued hair, then moved on down to her dusty shoes peeking out from the hem of her full-skirted yellow calico. Clearly, she didn't intend to shake the hand he held out, so he dropped it. "And whom do I have the pleasure of addressing?" he asked, knowing full well, thanks to Kitty, that her name was Hannah Grace Kane.

"You are a beast. An abusive beast."

A good deal of throat clearing came from Mr. Brayton. "Miss Hannah, you are speaking to our new sheriff."

"Hannah. I like that name. I'm Gabe," he repeated.

Her face looked near the popping stage, red and silky with perspiration. "If you are who I think, you have no business holding the sheriff's title."

He smiled. "More likely than not, I'm not who you think, then."

She nearly sucked the air out of the room, then slowly gave it back. "Where is that child?"

"He's sleepin' in the cell," offered Nathanial, suddenly all eager about jumping into the conversation. "Little whippersnapper, he is. Don't mind saying I'll take my leave when he wakes up. No telling what'll happen."

"In a cell, did you say? You're holding that poor, innocent child in a jail cell?"

If looks could kill, he'd be lying flat out on a board. "Innocent, you say? If he's innocent, I'll eat my socks for dinner. That boy's been—" But she whirled around, skirts flying, before he could finish and made a beeline for the gate he'd failed to lock.

He chased her through the office and down the hall. "Just a minute, there."

"Where is he?" she demanded. "And where's his mother?"

"Just hold on," he said, watching while she opened one door after another.

"Where did you put the jail?" she asked.

The question struck him as humorous, so he laughed. She turned and stomped her foot. He quickly sobered and put out a hand in much the way he would to calm a wild filly. "I did not put the jail anywhere, my dear lady. It is in the basement, where it's always been."

Stepping forward, he seized her by the arm.

"Unhand me," she ordered, viewing his hand as she might a snake.

Frustrated, he murmured into her ear, knowing Nathanial stood at the end of the hall watching the fiasco. "I've a mind to slap some sense into you. You're about as obstinate and willful as Zeke."

She blinked twice, and suddenly their eyes connected. "My mule," he explained, drawing close enough to pick up a lovely citrus scent.

"Everything okay?" asked Nathanial.

Snapping to attention, she threw up her arm and stepped back, glaring at him with the eyes of a woman who means business.

"If you'll settle down, I'll take you to the boy. How's that?" And to Nathanial Brayton, "Everything's fine. Go on about your job."

That curbed her little conniption. They walked to the next door, and Gabe pulled it open. Wooden steps led to a dimly lit basement. When Hannah meant to proceed ahead of him, he grasped her arm midway up, noting how his thumb and middle finger met behind her elbow. Slender as a cornstalk.

"Be forewarned," he whispered. "The boy does not speak, and need I remind you that the last time you talked to him, you scared the living caca right out of him."

"Mr. Devlin!" she exclaimed.

He grinned and let her go. "Just warning you, that's all."

She hesitated when he nudged her forward. "I asked you where his mother is," she reminded him.

Besides underfed, he could add persistent to her wonderful list of attributes. He sighed in spite of himself. "Well, there's the rub. I haven't a clue."

𝒦

Shocks of jet-black hair stuck out from the tattered quilt covering the little boy, who'd rolled himself up into a ball and lay sleeping on the narrow cot, his whiffing snores proving how deeply he slept. The twelve-square-foot jail cell with the bare cement walls showed signs of mildew, impelling Hannah to wrinkle her nose in disgust. Shivering in the dampness, she wrapped her fingers around the cool steel bars and peered through them. A chamber pot stood in one corner, as did a pitcher of water and a tin mug. Hanging from the ceiling, a dim electric lightbulb with a pull chain gave off a muted glow, indicating the glumness of the place.

Never had she felt such compassion for another human being. Oh, she'd always loved children, and she longed to have a few of her own someday, providing Ralston shared her enthusiasm—if she ever married him, that is—but this little fellow stole her heart, broke it in several places, tugged at the core of her emotions.

"Where did you find him?" she asked in a soft voice.

"Fool kid jumped under the canvas on the back of my rig while I was getting ready to set out from Holland last night. He must have overheard me talking to the fellow at the livery stable. Maybe he thought he'd be safe with a lawman—who knows?"

"I should think he'd have thought otherwise, especially if he's on the run. You could turn him in to your superiors."

"He doesn't know it, but I'll be forced to do just that in the next day or so. I'd like to get some answers first, though—figure out where he comes from, why he's running. Could be something as simple as him running away from home on a whim and then getting himself lost, and he's just too scared to talk to strangers about his predicament."

"He shows signs of abuse," she said, staring at the lump under the quilt.

"Or maybe they're just the natural bumps and bruises of a runaway. He looks like he's been in a scrape or two."

They stood in silence as if ruminating on one another's words.

"Got an appointment with Judge Bowers this afternoon," he put in. "I'll run the story by him. Maybe he'll have some ideas for me. Lord knows I don't have time for the little chump, but I can't just turn 'im loose, either."

In the span of a second, she glanced up at the strong, rigid profile of this Gabriel Devlin, noted again his compelling blue eyes, the firm features of his face and frame, the confident set of his shoulders. Mere moments ago, she'd come close to kicking him in the shins. Now, they were standing side by side outside a jail cell, contemplating the fate of a tiny boy.

"Any thoughts on what his name might be?" she asked, still holding her voice to a whisper.

He answered with a shrug. "There hasn't been a peep out of him, so I've no way of knowing."

More silence.

"Unlock it, please," she finally said. "So I can go inside."

"Huh?"

She felt her shoulders tighten in resolve. "Unlock it."

Gabe stared at her as if she'd lost a good piece of her mind, and maybe she had. After all, she had responsibilities at the Whatnot, and she had left Maggie Rose in a bit of an inconvenient place, having to mind both the store and the library.

Perhaps she could send word to Abbie Ann to cover for her, at least for the remainder of the day—or until they decided this child's doom or destiny. Surely Grandmother Kane wouldn't mind releasing her youngest granddaughter from her garden duties.

"I don't think…"

"Mr. Devlin, I am fully capable of defending myself against a mere child."

He slipped his hands into his rear pockets and rocked back on his heels. "You haven't a clue what you're talking about, miss. The little devil tried to bite me, and he took a swing at Kitty just before I nabbed him from behind and hauled him, kicking and spitting, down those stairs."

"Just the same, unlock the cell door, please."

He studied her for a full ten seconds. "You're a stubborn woman, you know that? You're not married, are you?"

A dratted blush crept up her face. "Not yet."

"Yet? Ah, so you're attached, then?"

She shifted on her pointed-toed, Prunella walking boots, feeling her arches go weak. "That is none of your business, Mr. Devlin. Kindly unlock this door."

He shook his head and chuckled under his breath as he dug into his side pocket and withdrew a ring of keys, his eyes glinting with merriment. "Have it your way, then. What are you going to say to him when he wakes up?"

She hadn't thought of that. "I will cross that bridge when I come to it."

"Okay." He gave a half nod. "You best prepare yourself for a battle, missy."

Missy? She bit back a retort.

"If you need anything, give a holler. One of my deputies will come down. You know Gus van der Voort?"

"Yes, but...you won't be here?" she asked, annoyed with her sudden feeling of ineptness. Surely a three-foot-something child posed her no threat.

His mouth curved into a boyish grin. "You hardly know me and already you're missing me?"

She had half a mind to knock his pearly whites crooked. "Don't flatter yourself."

Still chuckling, he unlocked the cell. "Just joshing you." His apologetic tone did little to ease her irritation. "I'll be around. I have an appointment with Judge Bowers in…"—he looked at his watch—"…an hour or so. You need anything in the meantime?"

On a whim, she asked, "Would you mind sending someone over to fetch my sister, Abbie? She needs to fill in for me at the Whatnot."

"Where do you live? I'll go myself."

"What? No. Kitty knows where I live. She'll be happy…"

He threw her an irritated look. "Where do you live?" he repeated.

She made a huffing sound. "In a two-story foursquare off Water. It's within walking distance."

"Address?"

She felt foolish. It was his first day and she had him running an errand for her.

"Turn south on Third and go three blocks until you come to Ridge Street," she sputtered. "It's at the top of a pretty steep hill. The house number is 210 Ridge. It's right on the corner."

"Great. I'll deliver the message. Anything else?" Was that a hint of curtness? He shifted his weight as he stood there holding the door.

"No."

"Well, then…"

Hesitating, she stepped inside the cell and felt the cold grip of confinement. A silent chill ran from head to toe.

"Shall I lock it behind you?" he asked.

She glanced at the still-sleeping boy. An unlocked cell would give him opportunity to escape. She swallowed. "Yes, lock it."

"You sure?"

She raised her chin. "Absolutely."

But when the lock clicked into place, her confidence wavered. The boy stirred under his blanket, and when she turned to see what the sheriff's reaction might be, he had turned his back and was sauntering off.

K

Not only was Hannah Grace Kane mule-headed and saucy, but she was crazy, to boot.

What would possess a woman of her caliber—for she did appear fashionable, if not somewhat privileged—to care about some little savage? Gabe kicked a stone out of his path as he made the turn off Water Street onto Third. Classic two-story houses lined both sides of the dirt-packed road, as did giant oaks and maples, the shade of which provided relief from the penetrating heat of the sun's afternoon rays. An old man rocking on his front porch lifted a grizzled hand to wave at Gabe. He returned the gesture but kept up his pace. Were he not in a rush, he would have stopped, but with only minutes to spare before his meeting with the judge, he continued on his way to the Kane residence.

He found the two-story redbrick house numbered 210 at the top of a hill on the corner of Ridge and Third, its gaping front porch gracing the exterior; rocking chairs and wicker couches strewn from one end to the other made it a welcoming sight.

He climbed the steps and knocked on the door, glancing in either direction as he waited for the sound of approaching footsteps. Several potted geraniums bedecked the porch, and he imagined that many a pleasant conversation took place there between people relaxing on rockers or wicker settees.

The door opened as he raised his hand to knock again, and a woman who looked to be in her early sixties or perhaps midsixties greeted him. His first thought was that Hannah bore a strong resemblance to her—the creamy complexion, coiled hair, high cheekbones, and crystalline eyes.

"Who's there, Grandmother?" A girl with hair the color of coal, pinned back with matching barrettes, emerged from the kitchen. Her brown eyes sparked with curiosity when she spotted him standing in the doorway. *This must be Abbie Ann*, Gabe surmised, at the same time recalling Kitty's words about how lovely the Kane sisters were. She'd get no argument from him.

He extended a hand to the older woman. "Afternoon, ladies."

"If you mean to sell us something, we don't need it, young man," said the matron, casually lifting a hand to press her silver hair in place.

Not that she need have bothered. Every hair on her head was gathered neatly into a fancy knot at the nape of her neck, a pair of oval, wire-rimmed glasses hooked behind her ears. Wiping her hands on the yellow apron that covered her olive-colored cotton dress, she wrinkled her pert nose and sniffed.

"Sakes alive, I've bought enough chicken and fish to last me through the winter. You wouldn't be trying to sell me more, would you?" She angled her head to peek past him as if to see where he'd stashed his goods. "I don't see your wagon."

He laughed. "No, ma'am. I am not here to sell you anything." Hand still extended, he took a step closer. "I'm Gabriel Devlin, Sandy Shores' new sheriff."

Throwing up her hands, she gasped. "Oh, my London stars!" Then, startled into action, she took his hand, gave it a hearty shake, and hauled him inside. "Abbie Ann, put on the teapot!" she ordered. Abbie turned abruptly. "I'm Helena Kane," the woman announced, still pumping his hand.

"It's a pleasure to meet you, ma'am, but I can't stay." Abbie made a quick about-turn. "Thank you, though. I've stopped by with a message." He proceeded to tell them about the nameless, wordless boy and Hannah's dauntless decision to sit with him in a locked cell.

"That's my granddaughter for you," Helena said in her pronounced English intonation. "She's unreservedly zealous about certain matters—always has been, ever since she was a little thing. Why, I recall the time a scraggly cat hobbled into our yard. My son told her to leave the thing be; could have had rabies, you know. But would she listen?"

"Nope!" Abbie chimed. "She makes up her mind on a matter, and there's no stoppin' her. Take Huffy, for example."

"Abigail Ann!" Helena interrupted, dropping her chin. Abbie looked duly reprimanded, straightening her shoulders and pinning her mouth shut. Without even knowing the girl, Gabe dubbed her a rascal.

Helena Kane cleared her throat and took a steadying breath before angling Abbie with a stern look. "Go change out of those garden clothes and hurry over to the Whatnot," she instructed her.

"Yes, ma'am," Abbie said with clear excitement. She dashed upstairs, but not before flashing Gabe a bright smile and awarding him a slight curtsy. "Nice to make your acquaintance, Mr. Devlin."

Gabe tipped his head at her, then made for the door. "We'll be expecting you for supper one night soon, Mr. Devlin," Helena said, rushing ahead to hold the door for him. "After you've had a chance to settle in a bit. And bring that little boy with you."

"Oh, he'll be gone by that time, I'm sure. I'll be getting to the bottom of this thing real quick, and as soon as I do, I'll put him on the next train."

She cast him an incredulous look, as if she doubted his abilities. "Well, on the chance he is still here, you bring him along, you hear?"

He turned his hat in his hands before plunking it back on his head, pushing back the nagging feeling that finding the kid's family might be a little like finding a silver coin in a rock quarry. "Yes, ma'am."

"We'll invite Hannah's gentleman friend, and a few others from the town, too. We'll look at it as an opportunity for you to meet some folks."

"That'd be mighty fine," he assured her, touching the brim of his hat before taking his leave.

As he walked briskly back up Third Street, he thought about Hannah's so-called gentleman friend. "Must be a man of great composure," he muttered to himself.

And what, or who, is Huffy?

⌒*K*⌒

The boy woke up in spurts, turning over and pulling the blanket with him, opening his eyes for brief periods to stare at the four walls that surrounded him before drifting back to sleep. He hadn't spotted Hannah sitting on the floor in a shadowy corner, knees pulled up to her chin, while she waited for him to awake; otherwise, he surely would have scurried to the door, trying to escape.

Hannah wished she had more experience with children, that she understood the way their bright little minds worked; all she had to go on were her years of teaching Sunday school, and those hardly counted, as she only saw the children forty-five minutes a week. She tried to remember how it felt to be a child, but that didn't help much when it came to the unfortunate boy—most of her memories were happy ones. Even the loss of her precious mother to a case of pneumonia hadn't put a terrible dent in her psyche, as Grandmother Kane had stepped right into the role of caregiver, tempering her granddaughters' loss with huge amounts of love and attention.

In her head, the words to the hymn "What a Friend We Have in Jesus" played repeatedly. Did the boy have any friends? Did he know the love of parents, siblings, grandparents—or even God? How long had he been running? And, most important, was anyone looking for him?

Hannah leaned against the cold concrete wall and closed her eyes. *Lord, please lend Your wisdom and guidance to this situation. I ask for compassion beyond measure and the type of*

love that You would show to any one of Your lost sheep. May I be
a friend to this poor boy, and may he somehow find the courage
from deep within to tell us who he is.

⌒K⌒

Judge Ed Bowers sat behind his massive oak desk, reading spectacles perched low on his nose as he shuffled through papers. His assistant rapped on the door frame. "Sir?" the young man said. "The new sheriff's here to see you."

Judge Bowers looked up from his work, threw off his glasses, and rose to his feet, a colossal smile forming beneath his graying beard. "Come in, come in. I've been waiting for you." As was proper, his assistant left without a word.

"Good to see you, sir," Gabe said, unable to contain his pleasure at laying eyes on the old family friend. As children, his brother and sister, Sam and Elizabeth, and he had known the judge, then a lawyer, only as "Uncle Ed." He was their father's best friend, but age and the circumstances of his profession now put them on a different plane.

The judge extended a hand, but then withdrew it and went for a rough embrace instead. Gabe surrendered to it in the same way he always had as a youngster. When Ed set Gabe back at arm's length from him, hands on his shoulders, he perused him from head to toe. "I'm glad you've come, son. You have a trail of commendations following you. Your role as hero hasn't dimmed much, last I heard. 'Fraid I've made a few enemies by hauling you up to Michigan, though. I heard the county offered you a considerable raise if you'd stay."

Gabe felt a sudden warmth in his cheeks that didn't come from the heat of the day. As a matter of fact, the judge's quarters were plain comfortable, what with his electric ceiling fan circulating the air and the open windows in his second-floor office affording a cool blast of cross-ventilation. "You've been talking to Pa, I see."

A hearty laugh escaped the judge's bulging chest. "He's mighty proud of you, that man, and for good reason. That was no small feat you accomplished, bringing down Smiley Joe Hamilton back in '01." The judge shook his head and frowned. "Still don't know why we didn't read about it up here. I guess the press didn't get wind of it."

"I'm glad for that," Gabe said. "Killing a man isn't one of those things I want to be remembered for."

Ed put a hand on Gabe's shoulder and squeezed. "'Lot better'n being known for lettin' that reprobate get away. You might not like hearin' this, but somebody had to stop Joseph Hamilton, and you were the man for the job. I heard you were mighty fast with a gun even before Hamilton came along. Guess that encounter proved it."

Gabe patted his holstered gun even now, a rather obsessive habit he'd acquired to assure himself it was still there. Unfortunately, as sheriff, gun-toting went with the job, as did the occasional gunfight.

"I'm praying for no such encounters in Sandy Shores."

Ed smiled and pointed him to a chair. "It's a downright pleasant place to hang your hat, Sandy Shores. But enough of that. Take some weight off and tell me how you fared on your trip north. I trust you didn't run into any problems."

Hat in hand, Gabe felt himself relax as he plopped into one of the two leather chairs positioned in front of Ed's desk,

Ed taking the one adjacent to it. "No problems—that is, not until I arrived here safe and sound, only to discover that I had a stowaway."

The judge crossed a beefy leg over his knee and settled back, hands folded in front of him, a curious expression elongating his brow. "How's that?"

Gabe proceeded to tell him about the nameless, mute boy he'd unknowingly hauled from Holland, how he'd carried him up to his third-floor room, fed him a big hunk of bread and a slab of dried beef, and then tried to pump him for information. That had gotten him nowhere, so Gabe had pulled back the blankets, thinking the offer of a real bed would win him points, but the kid made a beeline for the door instead. Then, he got fighting mad when he found it locked, and the slide lock beyond his reach.

A battle of wills ensued for the next hour, Gabe trying to get the boy to talk, the kid crossing his arms in belligerence and proving several times he had a tongue by sticking it out as far as it would go. Sheer fatigue finally forced him into a fitful sleep—not in the bed, but curled up in the chair next to the window.

Next, Gabe unraveled the events of the morning—how he'd won a measure of the boy's trust by taking him to breakfast and allowing him to eat his fill in silence. Then, how it all went downhill from there after Hannah Kane had scared the boy spitless with questions about his cuts and bruises, resulting in the wild goose chase down Water Street, until Gabe had managed to nab him by the sleeve in front of Sandy Shores Bank and Trust and carry him back to his office, albeit kicking, thrashing, and biting.

The judge hadn't appeared surprised when Gabe told him Hannah had stationed herself in the jail cell with the boy, determined to win him over. "Sounds like something one of those Kane girls would do," Ed said. "They have spunk, every one of 'em. 'Course, they come by it naturally. I've known Helena ever since she and Simon arrived here from England with their boy, Jacob. He must've been about eleven or twelve at the time. Like so many others, the family wanted a new start in America, so when Simon inherited a good amount of money after his parents' passing, they landed here and started up Kane's Whatnot. Right from the beginning, Simon got little Jacob involved in the general store, and it's a good thing. In 1879, Simon passed on very suddenly from a bad cough, almost the exact same time as my Marian. Later, folks speculated diphtheria was the culprit. It sent a number of folks to their graves that year. It could be quite an epidemic in those days, sweeping through both small towns and big cities. Anyway, that forced Jacob into the retail business full time. I think he was just out of school. He and Helena braved things together, but times weren't easy for a lot of folks."

Gabe detected the hint of reminiscence in the widower's faraway gaze, but he bypassed the temptation to prod him. Ed Bowers was a man who could converse for long periods, given the chance, but right now, other matters occupied Gabe's mind. "Any idea where I might start looking for this boy's parents?" he asked.

"What's that? Oh, that lad who jumped on your rig? Well, now, might be he's on his own. No telling how long he's been fending for himself."

"You mean, you think he's an orphan?"

"Can't say for sure, but there's a good chance. 'Lot of lingering unrest what with the aftereffects of the Civil War still weighing heavy on our nation, not to mention the westward expansion. 'Lot of youngsters have been lost in the shuffle. From what you tell me, this boy's experienced some pain along the way, physical and emotional. You might better take 'im over to the doc to see if he can find anything wrong with 'im."

"You're the second one who's suggested I do that. Problem is, he's not my son. I don't have time for messing with him."

The judge's brow angled into a thoughtful frown. "I s'pose you could take him back to where you found him."

"And do what with him? Leave him in the street? Come on, Ed, is that the best you can do? Isn't there some sort of orphanage or holding place where I can take him? Do you know of anyone around here who would foster him—at least until I can figure out what to do with him?"

The man's frown deepened as he pinched the bridge of his nose with his thumb and forefinger and set his chin at a tilt. "There's no children's home in Sandy Shores, or anywhere in River County, for that matter, but I'll ask around to see if anyone would be willing to take him in. Don't go getting your hopes up, though. It's asking a lot to expect someone to take in a little rapscallion like the one you just described."

"What about the churches? There must be some family who'd have room for him."

The judge gave a pensive nod. "That's a possibility. I'll see what I can find out for you."

"What should I do with him in the meantime?"

Ed moistened his lips and fixed Gabe with a confounded stare. "Well, I guess that's something you and Miss Kane will have to decide together. Seems to me you both got yourselves into a pickle with this one."

Chapter Four

The boy had spent the last hour staring daggers at Hannah, refusing to move from the cot. *That's a good sign*, she figured, considering he could have been throwing his fists at her. She coaxed, prodded, and talked in a gentle voice, but he maintained his obstinate demeanor.

"Are you hungry?" she ventured. "My grandmother makes a fine chicken and vegetable stew. Does that sound good to you? I know it's stew night, because I saw her dicing up potatoes and carrots yesterday evening, and she had my sister slicing up fresh chicken."

He licked his lips but quickly covered the move by drawing the wool blanket up over his face so that only his big brown eyes peered out.

"There's nothing like a good chicken stew to fix what ails you. Don't you agree?"

Even with her long skirts tucked around her ankles, a chill from sitting on the cold, damp cement scampered up her spine. She heard scuffling noises on the floor above and wondered if *he* planned to come down anytime soon. So far, the door at the top of the stairs hadn't so much as cracked. From the dangling, dim lightbulb, she could see by her wristwatch that five o'clock had come and gone. Surely, his appointment with the judge had ended long ago. Did he have even more appointments to follow that one?

She eyed the boy with caution. They'd been playing this staring game long enough. There had to be some way to get through to him. "Sure is nippy down here. You plan to sleep here tonight?" She exaggerated her chill by hugging herself and forcing her teeth to chatter. Truth was, the air, though damp and musty, felt far better than the muggy heat of the past several days.

The boy eyed her with a critical squint. Slowly, he shook his head from side to side. A reaction—a milestone! Hannah tried not to show too much delight.

"That's good. It'd be a might lonely in here, don't you think?" How many nights had he spent out under the stars, or perhaps holed up in some vacant building? Surely, solitude was nothing new to him. "Besides, this is a place for criminals, and you're no criminal. Nor am I. Fact is, I'd like to get out of here and go have some of that stew I was telling you about." She played with a lazy, auburn curl at her temple and tried to feign nonchalance, sitting forward to take in his coffee-colored eyes. "'Course, if you'd rather stay here, I would understand."

Suddenly, his hands came out from under the blankets and he sat up, swiveling on the cot so that his short legs dangled over the edge, his stockinged feet peeking out, his worn boots meeting the floor like those of a tired little soldier. Again, his head gave a slow shake, and he took great care not to show any emotion. Still, Hannah considered this reaction another milestone.

His black hair pointed everywhere like dry sticks on a leafless bush, and his grimy hands, arms, and face, covered in scratches and bruises, looked like they hadn't seen a tub of hot, soapy water in over a month. Was there a mother somewhere who had taught him the importance of cleanliness? Was she frantic with worry over her son's whereabouts? What was he running from—or was it that he'd just gotten himself so lost and in his plight had forgotten what it meant to trust another human being?

A sudden rush of steps overhead and a familiar female voice, rather demanding in tenor, drew her attention to the stairs. "Please open the door," she was saying.

"I'm coming, I'm coming. Bloomed if you Kane sisters aren't an impatient bunch," the sheriff's voice sounded.

The door hinge squeaked when it opened. Hannah sprung up from the floor, then turned and shot the boy a reassuring glance when his eyes widened with apprehension. "It's okay. It's just my sister, Maggie. You'll like her. And, of course, you know the sheriff." He didn't budge; he just pulled back his bony shoulders and sat taller, training his eyes on the stairwell, as if he had some weapon hiding under his ratty overalls and meant to haul it out if needed.

The tantalizing aroma of roast chicken beat the pair down the stairs. "Hannah Grace? Where is she, Sheriff?"

"Straight ahead," came his cool reply. "Watch your step."

"Oh, forevermore, it's like a dungeon down here. Hannah?"

"I'm here," Hannah said into the dimness of the room. "No need to make such a clatter." She found herself clenching the cold steel bars and pressing her nose between them.

When Maggie Rose came into view, it was with her brown skirts flaring and her arms full of covered dishes. Trailing in her wake was Sheriff Devlin, looking not the least bit apologetic. If anything, put out probably best described his manner, and the notion that he'd forgotten all about them made Hannah want to spit nails through his ears.

"Oh, for crying in a bucket, Hannah Grace, whatever are you doing in there? I heard you'd gone and locked yourself inside a jail cell, but I refused to believe it till I saw it with my own eyes. And who have we here?" Her eyes flitted to the bedraggled boy who'd kept his body stiff as a poker. "Kindly unlock the door, Mr. Devlin. I need to make sure my sister is unharmed."

"Oh, she's unharmed, all right," he said. The slightest grin tipped the corners of his mouth as he stepped forward and turned the latch—without the use of a key. Both women stared, dumbstruck. "What—you think I would really lock an innocent woman in a jail cell?"

"You mean…? Oh!" Hannah sputtered, abashed. She found herself propping her hands on her waist and pushing out her chin. "What of this innocent child?"

He cocked his blond head and squinted down at her, a most disarming maneuver. "Innocent? The little whipper-snapper tried to bite me. He might be better to stay locked up for a while."

Hannah swallowed down a rejoinder when the young boy wriggled off the cot and walked across the room. Just when she thought he might utter the beginnings of a word, he pushed open the door, bypassed the sheriff, and walked up to Maggie. Wordlessly, she bent at the waist. Without a sound, he raised his soiled hand and lifted the towel on the casserole. Then, while peering under it, he inhaled loudly and gave the first hints of a smile.

Another milestone!

K

"I ain't shootin' no kid."

Wispy clouds drifted past a shiny half-moon, which, along with the starlit sky and blazing campfire, emitted enough light to read by—if anyone had a mind to read, that is. But none did. The stale stench of cooked bluegill and burnt beans carried through the air, souring everyone's dispositions.

"You will if I say so, jughead," groused Rufus McCurdy, father to the three deadbeats lounging close by. "I tol' you right from the start, if you was gonna work with me, you was gonna go by my rules. If y' cain't abide by 'em, y' best scat— and watch yer back on yer way out!" He spat a wad of chewing tobacco into the fire and watched his three boys, men now, go stiff as dead carps on hot sand. *I've still got the touch*, he thought; *I still have the say-so 'round here*.

"I ain't goin' nowhere," muttered the youngest, Luis, aka jughead. "But I ain't happy 'bout shootin' no half-pint."

"I'll do it—iffin' I catch 'im," said the oldest, Roy. "The squirt ain't easy t' catch, though. He been jumpin' from town t' town like a flea on a griddle. Thought we had 'im back in that town o' Niles, till he climbed aboard that train and rode clear t' St. Joseph. The kid ain't dumb. Seems t' sense we's chasin' 'im. I swear, when he climbed the ladder on that movin' train, he looked back at me as if t' say, 'You cain't catch me,' but, truth is, I don't know as he really saw me. All's I know is no li'l three-foot-high tadpole's gonna get the best o' me."

Rufus breathed a little easier, knowing he at least had the support of his oldest. Roy, twenty-two, had always been the most dependable of the sorry bunch. Luis, on the other hand, had a ways to go, being he was the youngest and not much more than a boy himself at fifteen. Reuben, the middle son— now, he was another story. Pigheaded and impulsive, for sure, but slow on the draw. Rufus worried that one of these days, Reuben would get them all killed.

"It's important we stick together on this," he instructed, coughing up a wad of spittle mixed with tobacco juice. "And don't go talkin' t' nobody else." He eyed Reuben in particular. "You already opened your big yapper to that harlot in South Bend, you fool. I don't wanna hear 'bout you pullin' somethin' as dumbheaded as that again. You understand?" Reuben moved his head up and down while he scribbled in the dirt with a stick.

Rufus cursed and leaned forward. "That scrawny little imp saw me do his folks in while we was robbin' 'em. Fools would still be alive if that idiot man hadn't pulled a gun on us." He paused for dramatic effect. "Nobody pulls a gun on a McCurdy and lives t' tell about it. Figured I'd teach 'im a lesson."

The boys did the smart thing—they kept their mouths shut.

Rufus tossed another log on the fire, creating an explosion of smoke and sparks. Reuben, sitting closest to the blaze, lurched backward, brushing off several sparks that threatened to ignite his shirt. "Where you think he went off to, Pa?" he asked, maintaining his cool.

"Pfff. If he's true t' form, he's followin' up the lakeshore. Roy thought he got a glimpse of 'im in South Haven when he saw 'im diggin' through garbage, but by the time he got close enough t' tell, the little goon up 'n vanished. I'll be cussed if he ain't part Injun, as sly as he is. He won't get much further, though. If he makes it out o' Holland, I'll be surprised. Ar luck's gotta change sooner 'r later. Cain't have 'im runnin' 'round with the image of ar faces in his head. He's bound t' tell somebody 'bout us."

An owl let out a mournful cry, and, in the northern sky, a meteorite shot a straight path toward earth, petering out within seconds.

Reuben picked up a piece of driftwood and cracked it in two. "We know fer sure he saw y' kill 'is folks, Pa? I mean, what if…?"

"You dim-witted schmuck, you're the one who spotted 'im watchin' through the winder 'fore he took off like a streak o' lightnin' 'cross that field. You said his eyes was bigger 'n a barn. If you'd o' run after 'im, you could've caught the little twig and done the deed right there!" Gall heated Rufus's veins until he felt near boiling. "Instead, what do y' do but stand there lookin' dumber than a bag o' nails. By the time Roy took out after 'im, the kid was up some tree or lyin' low in a ditch."

Rufus leaned close enough to see the whites of his boys' eyes. "Now, you listen hard, y' hear? For all I know, ar mugs is plastered on sheriffs' boards and in post offices. If it weren't for that little twerp, we'd ride out o' these parts fast as ar horses would take us, but him bein' a witness and all, well, let's just say we got us a job t' do first. And the sooner it's done, the quicker we move on."

"We still got money, Pa?" Reuben asked. "'Cause if we got money, we could jes leave the country and start over, say, in Mexico."

Rufus breathed hard and narrowed his eyes on his middle son. "Mexico, you say?" He looked from Roy to Luis, then back at Roy. "Hear that, boys? He wants to go to Mexico." Then, to Reuben, "What state y' think we's in, anyways?"

Reuben raised one dusty brown eyebrow and squinted. A feeble shrug of the shoulders showed he didn't have a clue.

Rufus scoffed and spat, and, without another word, grabbed his bedroll and laid it out next to the fire, his movements short and snappy, his breaths gruff.

His sons followed suit, sober as bricks.

K

Gabe and the boy walked up Second Street, their stomachs full of poached eggs and toast. It had been another breakfast eaten in silence, save for Lucy Watkins, the middle-aged waitress at the Lighthouse Restaurant, who was eager to chat up a storm with Gabe when she wasn't tending to other customers. He'd learned more from her in thirty minutes than he had all yesterday afternoon, poring over Watson Tate's piles of paperwork and criminal records and talking with Gus van der Voort and Clyde Oertmann, two of his deputies. There had been a holdup at Marie's Ice Cream Parlor two years ago, "in broad daylight, if you can believe that!" Lucy had exclaimed. "All they got off'n Marie was a dollar fifty, though, 'cause Merlin Rogers came walkin' in for his usual afternoon double-dipper and that scared 'em off.

Dumb tourists was jus' passin' through town. Never did see hide nor hair of 'em after that."

Gabe had learned that there'd been a fistfight at precisely 1:28 a.m. this past March at Charley's Saloon—precisely, because Lucy lived in the second-floor apartment above Isabella Peterson's Hat Shop, which happened to be adjacent to the saloon, and she'd been awakened by the ruckus.

He'd also discovered that someone had busted out the window in Minnie Durham's Dressmaker Shop last winter, Hansen's Shoe Repair was missing several pairs of shoes, and the bad meat that Thom Gerritt had sold from his market last summer had made a slew of people deathly ill. If that wasn't enough, someone had broken into the Third Street Church four weeks ago and rung the bell at four in the morning. A prank, of course, Lucy clarified.

"You plannin' to talk to me today?" Gabe asked the boy as the two turned the corner onto Water Street. His night shift deputy, Randall Cling, would be happy to see him, but first he intended to make some purchases at Kane's Whatnot. Hannah had promised to open the store early just for them.

"You sleep good last night? You could share the bed with me, you know. I don't bite, and it's a big bed." He gave him a sideways glance. "Or the chair is fine, too. Entirely up to you."

They passed shops he'd not yet had the chance to explore, all with "CLOSED" signs on the doors. The boy stared straight ahead, but kept his pace, apparently feeling secure enough for the moment. A full stomach sometimes did that.

"You like horses? I need to stop at Sprock's Livery later to check on Slate and Zeke. I imagine Enoch's got a slew of animals in there who wouldn't mind a rub on the nose. Zeke's my mule, but he thinks of himself as a horse. Slate's my dapple gelding. He's a beaut. Fast as lightning, too. Don't be settin' any fires under Zeke, though." He chuckled just to see if he'd get a rise out of the lad. Fat chance. "Hey, why am I telling you all this? You've already met my horse and mule, right?"

The boy tilted his gaze upward, his freshly parted, longish black hair still wet from the dousing it had taken before breakfast, when Gabe had forced him into a tub of hot water.

"We're going to see that lady you met yesterday—Hannah. It's time we put you in some decent clothes, and she appears to have plenty in that store she runs. You don't plan to take off this time, do you? There's no need for it. No one's going to hurt you."

Nothing.

Several riders passed, each pursuing his own destination. A couple of rigs carrying lumber and other supplies rumbled up the street, their drivers tipping a hat or giving a nod to the new sheriff. One stranger smiled as he drove by and called out a greeting. "Fine morning, Sheriff Devlin." Although Gabe had met a mere handful of people, it appeared that the news of his arrival had spread quickly. Of course, his newly pressed police uniform, a recent requirement in departments across Michigan, announced his identity.

"At some point, I have to figure out what to do with you. You thought about that?" he mumbled.

A gull swept down in front of them and snatched up what looked like a dry piece of bread. The two walked side by side, arms swinging, every so often making slight contact, until the boy moved to the other side of the boarded walk.

"It'd be real helpful if you'd talk to me, partner."

$\mathcal{K}$

Hannah lifted the window shade on the front door of Kane's Whatnot in time to see the sheriff and his shadow advance across the street in her direction, pausing for a second to allow a man to pass on horseback. The boy looked spiffed up, even though sporting the same torn shirt, holey overalls, and worn boots that he was wearing the day before. *He bathed. That's what made the difference. And his hair is combed, parted on the side. What a fine-looking little man*, Hannah thought.

And what a fine-looking new sheriff—all swank and stylish in his pressed police uniform, something he'd failed to wear yesterday, perhaps because he hadn't considered it his official starting day. Whatever the case, she gave her head a little scolding shake and put a hand to her throat where the brooch she'd pinned on that very morning suddenly felt tight enough for strangling—the brooch Ralston had presented to her on her twenty-first birthday this past June.

"Think of it as a promise," he'd whispered close to her ear, so close she'd feared he intended to kiss her neck. This was a needless worry, in the end, for Ralston was nothing if he wasn't stick-straight proper. Why, a peck on the cheek was the most he had given her since they began courting a number of months ago—that, and a bit of hand-holding.

"The kissing part must come after the betrothal," Abbie Ann had said just weeks ago, after pestering Hannah for a full hour to determine what—if anything—had transpired between her and Ralston. "I shall never let a man with a beard kiss my lips. Papa's beard I don't mind, but only because he's old and his kisses are quick and only on the forehead. I can't imagine Huffy kissing me. Ick."

"Papa is only forty-three, and don't call Ralston 'Huffy.' It's unfitting. He should be *Doctor* Van Huff to you. Furthermore, I find his beard makes him look quite distinguished." She dried her hands at the sink after washing the final supper dish, anxious to finish the foolish conversation and retreat to her room.

"And ten years older," Abbie mused, staring at her reflection in the shiny plate she held at arm's length. As usual, she took her sweet time drying the dishes.

"Perhaps he wants to look older," Hannah contended, despising herself for arguing the finer points of Ralston's facial hair.

"And what do you want, Hannah Grace? Do you want a man who looks more like he could be your—your uncle?" The question rankled her, but she held her tongue. "And something else. He's as serious and grave as a tombstone. Does that man ever laugh? I've scarcely seen him smile. I told him a joke once, while you were upstairs dawdling, just to see what he would say, and he actually *sneered* at me. Can you imagine? I thought my joke was quite humorous. What do you call ten rabbits walking backwards?"

"Oh, for goodness' sake, Abbie Ann, this is silly!" Hannah stopped her with a scolding look. She folded the dishcloth into a perfect square and laid it on the counter. Seconds passed. "Oh, all right. What *do* you call—er—ten rabbits—what are they doing, again?"

"Walking backwards, silly. What do you call them?"

She drew in a deep breath, shook her head, and scowled. "I don't know. What?"

"A receding hair line."

Hannah had quickly covered her smile and pushed past her sister. "You better finish your drying chore."

As she'd headed for the stairs, Abbie had called after her, "I don't think he appreciated it, because, if you'll notice, he's thinning a bit on top."

As the sheriff and the boy drew closer, the lawman lifted his gaze toward Kane's Whatnot and guided his charge onto the planked sidewalk. Hannah quickly moved away from the door and busied herself with one of the displays at the front of the store, arranging several pairs of men's wool socks that had arrived yesterday, along with a shipment of other fall items.

No need for him to know that she had been waiting for him.

Chapter Five

The bell above the door chimed when Gabe and his quiet companion entered. Gabe glanced around, hoping his second visit to the place would be a tad more pleasant than his first. *She* looked up from whatever she was doing and walked quickly to the boy, smile as bright as a harvest moon. Of course, to him, she merely nodded. *Good morning to you, too,* he greeted her silently. *Lord, what is it about this woman that tries my patience?*

"Well, as I live and breathe, would you look here, you're all bathed and handsome-looking!" She touched a finger to the boy's chin and tilted it upward. Gabe waited for the boy to pull back, but, if anything, he stood a little taller, almost welcoming her scrutiny. "I've laid aside a few clothes for you. Want to have a look? I think I have your size all figured out, but we'll have to try them on, just to make sure. How would that be?" *With that balmy, dove-like voice, she could quiet a roomful of tyrants,* Gabe thought. Where was that voice when she addressed him?

When the mute boy did nothing but survey the store, Hannah reached down and took his hand. "Come on, I'll show you." Skirt swishing and heels clicking, she led him across the worn, wood floor, bobbing her head of red curls as she walked. Gabe followed like an obedient pup.

To say she'd laid aside a few clothes for the boy was an understatement. A wagonload better described it. He wanted to argue that outfitting the child for the next year seemed extravagant, mainly because he planned to unload him on the folks responsible for his care just as soon as he could locate them.

But he kept his thoughts tucked away, thinking now wasn't the best time for bursting her bubble.

"Let's try on a couple of these shirts," she suggested, maintaining her gentle tone while showing him a long-sleeved, plaid cotton shirt. She reached for his top button, but he quickly wretched away and took a giant step backward, his brown eyes untrusting.

Standing at the ready, Gabe said, "No one's going to hurt you. Remember the talk we had on the way over here?"

The boy's dark eyebrows slanted downward as he looked from Gabe to Hannah. Then, dropping his chin, he looked at his big toe protruding from the hole in his right boot and started to unbutton his shirt of his own accord. He took it off and handed it to Hannah. His shoulder blades were peppered with bruises—bruises Gabe had seen that morning when he'd forced the boy into the tub. He gave Hannah credit for not mentioning them now, even though her mouth temporarily slacked open at the sight. Hannah tossed the old shirt aside and handed him the new one. At first, he eyed it with incredulity; then he rubbed his hand over the fabric, as if he'd never seen or felt anything quite like it.

Slipping both arms through the sleeves, he stood a little straighter as he fastened the buttons. *He looks half-pleased*, Gabe thought. When he was done, Hannah led him to a cracked mirror propped against a wall, where he gave himself a silent inspection, his lip twitching in one corner and looking ready to break into a smile. Gabe remained in the shadows, almost afraid to breathe for fear of ruining the moment.

Hannah's own smile bounced off the mirror as she stood there, hands folded at her skimpy waistline, moss-colored eyes never straying from the boy. One red lock fell forward on her face. "He looks very dapper, don't you think, Sheriff?"

Unexpected tenderness came welling up. Were they looking at a child who'd never owned a new shirt? "He looks mighty fine."

For the next fifteen minutes, Hannah assisted the boy in trying on everything from bib overalls to trousers to knickers, from denim shirts to woolen socks to dark, ankle-high, lace-up shoes. She even plopped a blue cap on his head, which she said would be handy for keeping out the sun. When they were finished, three piles of clothes resulted: the "too big," the "too small," and the "just right." Naturally, the "just right" rose higher than the rest.

The dark-haired urchin examined himself from head to toe, taking in his new cap, his white button-down shirt under his bib overalls, and his new socks and shoes. A long interlude seemed to pass while he stood there staring at himself, hands shoved into his pockets, outwardly awed by his own reflection.

Hannah and Gabe exchanged a fleeting glance, along with a glimmer of a smile. "You want to wear those?" she asked the boy.

His reply was a simple nod.

"How about we split down the middle—the cost, I mean?" Hannah said later as she gathered up the clothes that fit, folding each piece with care. The boy had wandered off to a table to look at an assortment of toy wagons and miniature farm equipment, all handmade from fine wood.

"Does he need all these?" Gabe kept his voice to a low murmur. "It's not like he's going to be here forever."

He watched her hands perform the folding task and noted her neatly trimmed fingernails, buffed to a glossy finish. He tried to recall what Carolina's fingers even looked like, berating himself for having forgotten so quickly.

Without glancing up, she said, "Whether he's here five days or five weeks, he'll still need clothes, Mr. Devlin."

"Well, that's true, but he's not exactly our charge."

"No, he's not ours; he's yours." She made a point to emphasize the last two words. "But because you've brought him to my father's store, I would like to share in the expense of outfitting him, if you don't mind. It's the least I can do. Naturally, we'll purchase them at cost, so the final total shouldn't be too extravagant."

"I'm not worried about the cost."

"Good." She moved to the "too big" pile and started folding, not missing a beat.

"And for your information, he's not *my* charge," he added, coming up beside her.

"Of course, he is."

He swallowed down a knot of anger. "The boy jumped on my rig and hid, miss. I had nothing to do with that. I don't even have a clue where he belongs, or to whom. I'm not a foster parent; I'm the sheriff. "

She made a curt, snapping sound with her tongue. "Precisely. And, as such, you will see, I'm sure, that the boy *is* your responsibility. Now, you can arrange for his care, I'll grant you that, but he is ultimately your liability until you figure out where he belongs."

He cocked his left eyebrow down at her, but she failed to look up. "You're a bristly thing, you know that?"

No words of retort shot out of her mouth as he would have expected. Instead, she lifted her face and made an abrupt turn, advancing to the table where the boy's old clothes lay in a heap. "I'll just toss these in the waste barrel," she stated.

"Fine, you do that."

She picked up the pants with two fingers, as if they carried some kind of deadly disease. Next, she went for the shirt, but when she tossed it over an arm and bent to pick up the boots, the shirt slipped to the floor. Bending to retrieve it, she let out a little gasp.

"What?"

She plopped down on her bottom, extended her legs straight out, pants tossed aside, and stared at the inside of the boy's shirt. "What are you looking at?" he asked, coming up behind her to peer over her shoulder, making every effort to dismiss her lemony scent. "What is that?"

"It's a tag—sewn into the back of his shirt—with a name and number on it."

"Tag? I never saw a tag." But then he hadn't looked, either. The boy had undressed himself that morning.

He hunkered down beside her, arms resting on his thighs, and tried to see around her mass of curls, but all he got in return was a glimpse of the small square cloth stitched neatly under the dirty, torn collar and that blasted feminine scent wafting through the air.

"What's it say?"

"It says—Jesse Gant, #47," she whispered. A full ten seconds passed before she lifted her head to gaze full into his face, a smile tripping across her lips. "Jesse Gant."

He bobbed his head in a slow nod, mouth pressed together as he let the name sink in. *Jesse Gant.*

Reaching out, he snatched up the shirt to see for himself. There it was, clear as anything. *Jesse Gant, #47.* Quickly, he searched the garment for more clues. But nothing surfaced, so he handed it back.

They stared evenly into each other's eyes, their faces only inches apart, as if to draw out some piece of wisdom from the other's gaze.

"Let's see what happens when I call his name," Gabe whispered. Hannah swept her tongue across her upper lip and nodded in agreement.

He pushed himself up and spotted the boy on the other side of the store, where he was surveying a fishing pole suspended from two hooks on the wall.

Gabe cleared his throat and gave a little sniff. "Hey, Jesse, come here a minute."

The boy glanced at him, beheld the fishing pole with one last wistful look, stuffed his hands deep into his pockets, and walked across the room.

K

Hannah kept Jesse with her the rest of the day, putting him to work with Maggie Rose in the library for the first two hours. He helped stack books in their proper places and listened to Maggie's prattle. Then, in the stockroom at the back of the store, he unpacked cartons and arranged the merchandise on the shelves. Between customers, Hannah checked on him, finding him busy most times, except for when he found a box of toy soldiers and lined them up all around him on the floor. It occurred to her then how little he'd probably played recently, and she decided to give him the soldier set later.

After some discussion, she and the sheriff had worked out an agreement of sorts. She would manage Jesse's care during the day, at least until Gabe could figure out where the boy belonged, and he would pick him up, either at her house or at the store, at the end of his workday. He balked, at first, but she convinced him that he needed help, a point he could hardly argue. They measured each other a while with narrowed gazes. "Didn't you just say he wasn't *our* responsibility?" he asked with quirked brow.

"If you'll recall, I said he is ultimately your responsibility, but you can certainly make other arrangements for his care. I'm merely offering my services."

He nodded. "Well, then, since he's my responsibility, I'll pay you."

"You'll do no such thing, and if you try, I won't accept it."

An amused glint splashed through his eyes. "You *are* a bristly woman, slightly bullheaded, to boot."

She'd been called a lot of things, but never bristly and bullheaded. Determined and dedicated, perhaps, but not bristly. Bristly meant headstrong, but with Ralston, she was happy to settle back and let him make all the decisions. She couldn't imagine Ralston ever calling her bristly.

It struck her that Gabriel Devlin had a way of bringing out a side she wasn't accustomed to seeing, and it rankled her, particularly since she'd only just met the man.

"Mr. Devlin, I don't consider myself a difficult person." She forced a smile so as to appear unflappable. "But I suppose certain people can bring out the worst in folks."

At that, he laughed outright. His was a most contagious laugh—one that forced her to purse her lips tightly to dodge a smile. "Now, look there, you're putting words in my mouth. Did I say you were difficult?" He leaned forward, caught her gaze, and folded his arms. "You are a handful, though, I'll grant you that. I would imagine you present quite a challenge for that doctor friend of yours."

Now, how had he heard about her association with Ralston? "You are a meddlesome man, sir."

His laughter slowed. "Why, Miss Kane, don't you know a sheriff's got to get his nose in where it doesn't belong sometimes?"

She sniffed. "Well, not in my case, you don't."

"And speaking of that doctor—Van Huff, is it?—I'm told I should take Jesse to see him for a checkup."

Hannah had to admit it was a good idea. With his expertise, Ralston would certainly detect any physical ailments Jesse might have, particularly anything to prevent him from speaking. Still, the notion that Mr. Devlin might intentionally bring up her name in the course of the examination filled her with the jitters.

"I'll be glad to take him to see Ralston," she stated.

"I'd just as soon go with you."

"But it's not necessary."

"I'd like to hear firsthand if there's anything wrong with him."

She opened her mouth to argue, but he turned on his heel. "I'll start digging into Jesse's identity as soon as I get to my office," he said at the door, placing his hat securely on his head. "My father has some influence. I'll start by placing a telephone call to him. He might have a few leads or suggestions. Knowing Jesse's name is a huge bonus. Maybe by the time I pick him up tonight, I'll have some answers." He lowered his chin and tapped the brim of his cap in a farewell gesture, his sandy eyebrows barely showing from beneath it.

He closed the door behind him, making the shade waggle in his wake, and Hannah stared after him, suddenly curious. What did he mean when he said that his father had influence? Just who was this Gabriel Devlin, and where did he come from?

Hannah's own father entered the Whatnot at two-thirty that afternoon, all ears about the homeless waif who'd ridden into town on the back of the sheriff's wagon. Word of mouth around Sandy Shores traveled much faster than the newfangled telephone systems cropping up all over the country.

"Josh Herman stopped in to renew his insurance policy and told me you've got the boy here. Says he won't speak. Is that true? Afternoon, Arvel." Her father nodded at the elderly Mr. Sikes, who stood at the counter, waiting for Hannah to ring up his order of work gloves, a garden rake, a sack of flour, and two chocolate bars.

"It's true, Papa. He's in that little room off the library now, but don't go up there. He's napping on a makeshift bed Maggie made for him. He's plain tuckered."

"A—bed?" Jacob asked. "What in the world? This isn't a hotel, Hannah Grace."

His expression was one of amusement, not irritation. "Next thing you know, we'll be running a home for runaways."

"Oh, Papa, don't be silly."

She finished her order, wrapped the gloves and chocolate bars in some paper and twine, and handed the package over to Mr. Sikes with a smile. He nodded, tucked it under an arm, and picked up the rake.

Jacob stepped forward and hefted the sack of flour over his shoulder. "I'll take this out to your rig, Arvel. You getting ready to rake some leaves?"

Nearly deaf but not willing to admit it, Arvel replied, "Raisin leaves? Never tried 'im. You boil 'em for tea or somethin'? Ain't raisins really grapes?"

Jacob heaved a sigh and looked to Hannah for help. She shrugged. "I asked if you were going to rake leaves," he repeated in a booming voice.

Mr. Sikes shuffled toward the door. "What's that?"

"Rake leaves."

"I said, I never tried 'em. You got 'em in stock? I'll think about it next time I come in. Thing is, don't know if Hazel would like the flavor."

Hannah couldn't stifle her burst of laughter. "Good day, Mr. Sikes," she called after him, not surprised when he simply strolled out the door.

Helen McCormick, who'd been waiting patiently in line, moved ahead to plunk her three items on the counter—a bar of soap, a bottle of salve, and a new teakettle. "Poor man's deaf as a rock. Here Hazel spent all that money on an ear trumpet last year, and he won't even use it."

"It's an awkward contraption," Hannah said in his defense. "I don't imagine I'd want to bother with it, myself. Perhaps he uses it at home."

Helen looked aghast. "To listen to Hazel's unending twaddle? She's probably the first reason he went deaf. I daresay, that woman could talk a limb off a tree."

"Mrs. McCormick, be nice."

"Well, you know it's true. She cornered me in the churchyard last Sunday after the service to tell me about Harriet Gurley's bad tooth, Lydia Foster's heart ailment, and Hester Graham's mental upset over that brood of hers. Lydia's took to her bed, you know, over that oldest one who lives in Nebraska. Or is it Kansas? I get them two states confused."

Hannah concentrated on ringing up the order. Outside, a horse-drawn rig created a cloud of dust, a couple of dogs started a barking contest, and Sandy Shores' citizens hurried busily up and down the city sidewalks. Across the street, Alden Lawhorn and Merlin Runyan took up their usual places on the cast iron bench in front of Kane and Perkins, smoking their cigars in the pleasant shade provided by the new awning her father had installed last spring.

"He's in jail, is what she heard," Helen continued. "Got in some sort of barroom brawl, which resulted in a gunfight. Thank goodness no one died. I declare, it's still an untamed place out in some of them Western states." She laid a finger to her chin and scowled. "Now that I think on it, it might have been Wyoming—or maybe Oklahoma. Anyway, it's because of her my roast burnt."

"That will be three dollars and seventy-five cents, ma'am," Hannah said while packing the items in a small box she found under the counter. "Seems to me the Grahams could use our prayers."

"Well, I suppose that's true enough," Helen conceded, clamping her mouth shut for the time being. She untied her drawstring purse and started digging through it.

Handing over a couple of bills, she drew her arched gray eyebrows into an inquisitive tilt and leaned forward. "So, how'd that boy come to belong to the new sheriff?"

Hannah blew out a little sigh, knowing anything she said would spread like a September wildfire as soon as Helen McCormick left the premises. "He doesn't *belong* to him, Mrs. McCormick. The child appears to have wandered here on his own. The sheriff will investigate all angles until he can determine where he comes from. Once that's accomplished, he'll return him to his family—if there is one."

"Your pa said he doesn't speak? That's strange. Little guy must've encountered a frightening experience. My cousin Alma Ball got bit by a big snake when we were youngin's. Some said it was a rattler, but that's doubtful, since she lived to tell about it. 'Course, they say Michigan rattlers aren't near as dangerous as the ones from down South, so I guess it could've been. Scared the speech right out of her for pretty close t' two whole months. She quit walkin' out to the outhouse, too—which posed an even bigger problem. Why, I remember her mama yellin', 'Alma, there ain't no call to keep goin' in yer pants now that snake season's come 'n gone.'"

"What started her talking again?" Hannah asked, impatient to know.

"Huh? Why, I don't know exactly. One day she was mute as a marble, and the next, you couldn't shut her up. I guess she just got tired of not giving out her opinions. Alma always was one to talk, you know, 'specially after that two-month rest she took in that summer of…let me see here…it was 1868. Yes, we were ten years old, Alma and me.

"Anyway, don't know where she got that gabbing gift from. Nobody else in the family seems to have it near as bad as she does. We go to family get-togethers and no one gets a word in edgewise." Helen shook her head and sighed, as if exhausted from her own bout of nonstop jabber. "It's somethin'."

The bell above the door jangled as her father and the entire Martin clan—Mr. and Mrs. and their four little ones—entered the store. Everyone always held his breath when the Martins came to town.

Helen McCormick cleared her throat dramatically and drooped her bosom over the counter. "I hope you have your stuff anchored down, Miss Hannah," she whispered with a dubious smile, gathering up her box of goods and straightening to her full five and a half feet, give or take an inch or two depending on which shoes she was wearing. "Those children have the manners of jungle monkeys."

"Mrs. McCormick."

The woman turned and headed for the door without another word, barely managing to dodge an airborne wooden toy soldier. She grumbled something under her breath and made a fast exit. On the one hand, it was a relief to see her go, but on the other, seeing the Martin family felt like exchanging one sour morsel for another.

"Billy, don't throw stuff. Stick that back in yer pocket," said his mother, even as he retrieved the toy soldier and threw it at his brother. This time, she merely shrugged her shoulders and drew out a paper from her pocket: her list. A long one, no doubt. The oblivious Mr. Martin wandered over to a table of assorted gadgets.

Across the room, Jacob Kane ran a nervous hand through his gray hair and watched as all four children took off in different directions. "I'll talk to you later, Hannah Grace," he said to excuse himself.

"Papa, you just got here." She waved her hand in a silent gesture of despair, hoping he'd take it as a supplication not to leave her in such a predicament. Surely, his presence in the store would act as a deterrent to the scallywags bounding up and down the aisles.

Instead, he walked to the door. "We'll talk at supper. You don't plan to eat in that jail again, I hope?" He had to raise his voice above the sound of screaming voices.

"No, Papa," she enunciated. "I'll be home, but—"

"Good." Giving a cursory look at the Martin children, all boys ranging in age from three to nine, he tossed her an apologetic smile. "I'm sure you can manage things."

She wrinkled her nose at him. He never had been one for confrontation. Even while raising his daughters, he'd given them most anything they wanted if it meant keeping the peace, leaving Grandmother Kane to do most of the disciplining.

"Ouch! Give me that, you big swine," said one of the younger Martin boys to the oldest. Every one of them had hay-colored hair and similar faces. Hannah never had learned their names. The boy wore a disdainful look as he faced up to his oldest brother and held out his hand, palm up.

The older boy lifted his upper lip at the corner to signal his scorn. "Go find your own toy, runt. There's a table full of them over there."

Oh, Lord, Hannah prayed silently while moving out from behind the counter to go protect the merchandise, *give me patience enough not to strangle some necks.*

Chapter Six

An entire week had passed since the discovery of Jesse Gant's identity. Unfortunately, it hadn't brought Gabe any closer to determining where, much less to whom, he belonged, and the child's lack of speech only made the job harder.

After a thorough examination, Dr. Ralston Van Huff had declared that Jesse was healthy and fit, aside from his rather scrawny physique, and said he found no physical explanation for the boy's apparent inability to utter even the simplest of words. He'd tried to coax him into it by offering him candy, bribing him with a ride in his fancy carriage, and tempting him with a crisp, new dollar bill—all things that appeared to interest Jesse, but not enough to convince him to express himself.

Gabe hadn't approved of the doctor's tactics, as they didn't get to the core of his problems. Jesse wasn't merely being stubborn and obstinate in his speechlessness. Bribing him was as futile as using fresh-baked apple pie to entice a man with a broken leg to walk. The issue had to do with trust. Without establishing trust, no amount of coercing would get Jesse talking. It seemed to him the doctor ought to know that, but then, Gabe hadn't been overly impressed with the man. While examining Jesse, Dr. Van Huff had paid more attention to Hannah's presence than he'd paid to his patient's.

"I see no need for both of you to stay," he'd said at the door to his examination room, and then to Gabe, "Please—feel free to go back to your town duties, Sheriff."

"Tending to this boy *is* one of my town duties, Doctor."

"Then I suggest you go back to the store, Hannah."

She'd actually started to turn, like a sheep going to slaughter, but Gabe seized her by the arm. "She needs to stay and hear the results of your exam. Since she's watching him during the day, I think—"

"Which seems a bit much, considering she already has the store to manage. What does your father say about all this, Hannah? In my opinion, it's not a healthy situation, you taking care of…"

Gabe couldn't believe it. "I'm not forcing her into this. In fact, she's the one who came up with the idea."

"Hannah." The bearded doctor swallowed hard and angled her with a fatherly look, certainly not the sort one would expect from a beau. "Let's be pragmatic here."

"Could we discuss this later, Ralston?" Hannah asked. She put her hand on the boy's frail shoulder. "He may not talk, but he is not deaf."

She speaks! Gabe thought.

That ended that, but not the doctor's censuring side-glances to him. By the time Gabe walked out the door with Jesse, Hannah staying behind so Ralston could walk her home after he closed his office for lunch, it was clear as glass why Ralston Van Huff was *in* a huff, and it had little to do with her taking care of Jesse. He didn't approve of her connection with Gabe, which was funny in itself. He dropped Jesse off in the morning and picked him up at suppertime, and, most times, few words passed between them, usually because Hannah appeared too busy and distracted with her duties at the store.

Gabe gave the cheerless skies a fleeting look and wondered if he could make it back to his office before the gray clouds let loose.

"Afternoon, Sheriff!" Gabe slowed and turned. Frank Portman of Sandy Shores Real Estate waved at Gabe, then strode briskly across the street in his direction. Gabe had met with Frank the day before regarding a house for sale on Slayton Street. Situated six blocks from town on an oversized lot with a barn big enough to accommodate Zeke and Slate, the compact two-story, shaded with massive oaks and maples, held great appeal. Gabe hoped that Frank was able to work out the details with the owner. It wasn't that he didn't appreciate the Sherman House and its fine view of the lake, but he needed a bigger place—something more suitable, homey, and permanent. Before checking himself, he pictured Jesse scampering around in the backyard, maybe a smattering of chickens pecking at the dirt.

He paused and watched the man's approach, trying to gauge whether he bore good news. "Got some good news for you!" Frank said, as if reading Gabe's mind.

"Really?"

Frank looked as tickled as a pup in a meat market. "The Bronsons accepted your offer. They're especially anxious, since they've already moved to Lansing. We should be able to settle matters in the next few weeks. I have to pass a few papers back and forth in the mail. After that, the place is yours."

"No kidding!"

They discussed business a bit longer before Gabe headed off again, his step a little lighter. *Lord, You seem to be working out every aspect of my life in Sandy Shores. I thank You for that. Now, if You could just lend some wisdom to this matter of Jesse Gant.*

Up ahead, two barefoot boys in worn knickers who looked a little older than Jesse scampered across Water Street, a little black dog at their heels. They were carrying fishing poles, and Gabe figured they were heading for the pier. He wanted to tell them to be careful, but he was sure their mothers had issued them warnings. He'd recently heard that grown men had lost their lives on that pier when gargantuan waves swept them off with about as much mercy as a lion has for a lame gazelle. At least today, the waters were eerily calm, the air as still as a Quaker on Sunday morning.

As he meandered east on Water, stomach still full after a lunch of vegetable soup and a thick pork sandwich from the Lighthouse Restaurant, he passed the Culver Hotel on his right and the Mineral Springs Spa and Resort on his left, both at the corners of Water and Third Streets. He'd wondered about the spa, but not enough to venture past its front gate. Most resort goers who visited the ritzy place came from Chicago, Grand Rapids, Detroit, and beyond. They raved over the healing waters from the artesian well, not to mention the therapeutic massages, the hot and cold baths, and the various recreational activities offered. Even Gabe's mother had expressed interest in vacationing on the grounds, but Joseph Devlin never had been much for travel, so Gabe doubted she'd ever see her wish come to fruition.

He crossed Third, kicking up dust as he went. *We could use a good rain*, he thought. The grass had withered and turned brown in many spots, flowers bloomed for shorter periods, and farmers complained that the corn harvest hadn't produced nearly what they'd seen in years past. He stepped up onto the wooden sidewalk and wandered past one of the town's three barbershops. Howard Madison waved the hand that held a razor, and Tom Blake, one cheek shaved, grinned behind a soapy face.

In the nine or so days since he'd been here, he'd made a few friends and acquaintances, memorized some names, learned his way around town, and patronized a good number of businesses. Utmost on his list of priorities was familiarizing himself with his environment, and, so far, the scant number of crimes in Sandy Shores had allowed him to do that. Minor offenses had run the gamut from a couple of verbal disputes down at Charley's Saloon, to a spat between two oldsters at the harbor over some stolen fresh-caught fish, to a group of youngsters seen splattering the windows of a vacant building with ripe tomatoes. He'd managed most infractions verbally, perhaps his size alone working in his favor—that or his gun, stored conspicuously in its holster. From what he'd heard, Watson Tate hardly bothered with a firearm, spending most of his time socializing on the streets and in restaurants and leaving any disputes to his deputies to settle. Sandy Shores had vigilant deputies, but while he was on duty, Gabe meant to do his own law enforcing.

He passed a newsstand and read the headline: POLICE STILL SEARCH FOR McCURDY GANG. The blood racing through his veins made it impossible not to backtrack. He picked up the paper, stepped inside the market, and laid a nickel on the counter.

"Afternoon, Sheriff," called Eben Markleby, owner of the little stand. Wearing an apron that came down to his ankles, he set down a stack of magazines that needed to be sorted and approached the counter. "Buyin' a paper, are you? How's business? I ain't seen much action around here since you come t' town. You must be layin' down the law pretty good."

Gabe chuckled and tipped his hat to the middle-aged man with the silver beard and bushy-browed, beady eyes. "Thanks, Eben. I've got no complaints."

"Wull, I ain't heard nothin' but first-rate reports about you, so things are good all around, I guess."

Gabe grinned and laid the paper out in front of him. "Let's hope it stays that way."

"You figure out who that little shadow of yours belongs to yet?"

"Not yet."

He shook his head in wonder. "That's somethin'. Somebody's got to be missin' that cute li'l guy, I'd think."

"You would think."

Eben leaned an elbow on the counter and angled his gaze down his nose where his reading spectacles sat, perusing the article alongside Gabe. "What you readin' there?" He had a distinctive wheeze that probably came with a nicotine habit, and he exuded the odor to prove it. "Hmm. That McCurdy Gang still on the loose?"

"Appears so," Gabe mumbled, studying the photo he'd seen innumerable times in police files back in Columbus. Rufus McCurdy, the brains behind a string of crimes that spanned several states, all the way from petty theft to attempted murder, and his no-account sons were now wanted for a more recent case. This time, they were wanted for murder. Unfortunately, the photo was a couple of years old, and anyone in law enforcement knew how quickly time changed a face. There was that one newer picture of Roy, the oldest son, taken on the sly by some sharp-eyed reporter in a Cincinnati saloon one year ago. Too bad Roy had split by the time the reporter could return with the police.

"I read the other day they're top suspects in that murder case down in South Bend," Eben was saying. "Some, er, fancy woman claimed to have spent some quality time with one o' them McCurdy boys after it happened. Apparently, he bragged about the whole business t' her. 'Course, who can believe a harlot, even if she did have a number of details right accordin' to authorities when it come t' describin' the crime scene an' all?"

Gabe kept reading.

"It's a shame. That man and woman wasn't doin' a thing but mindin' their own business when them McCurdys come bustin' through their door. If it was them, that is. I guess everybody's innocent till proven guilty, idn't that right?"

Still, Gabe read on.

"Must've caught 'em completely off guard. It say anything there 'bout them havin' any leads? "I heard the dead guy had a gun in his hand. Poor feller must've thought he could draw faster. Why d'you s'pose he took a chance like that? Why, if someone come in here with plans t' rob me, I'm going to give 'em the shirt off'n my back, besides what little cash money I got." He chuckled to himself. "Which isn't much, mind you."

Gabe half-listened as he scanned the rest of the article.

"Call me a chicken-liver if y' like, but I'm no match for a gun. What's them folks' names?" He leaned in for a closer look at the article, his winded, wheezy breaths a distraction. "Harley and Mary Littleton."

He made a ticking sound with his tongue. "That's a shame, ain't it? Article I read a couple days ago says they was nice country folk, young, too. Kept to themselves, but they was nice. Attended church real regular."

Gabe looked up and acknowledged the gabby merchant, suddenly sorry for his poor manners in ignoring him. He patted the man on his shoulder. "I best let you get back to work, Eben. I thank you for the newspaper."

"Wull, now that you've read the article, you may as well take back your nickel."

Gabe folded the paper and stuck it under his arm. "Thanks for the offer, but I'll read the rest of it tonight with my final cup of coffee."

On his way back to the office, while Gabe pondered the article and the thugs on the loose, the sky started spitting rain. It came down in intermittent sprinkles, at first. He hastened his steps, thinking he might beat the storm, but before he reached Fifth Street and Sandy Shores City Hall, the clouds let loose their rain. He took the stairs two at a time but got wetter than a dog paddling upstream before making it through the doors.

Kitty Oakes looked up from her desk and scowled. "You couldn't have holed up somewhere?" she asked. "You'll catch your death. I don't suppose you have a dry uniform hanging in the back?"

"They only issued me one, but another's coming in next week."

"A lot of good that'll do you now," she chided him sympathetically.

He removed his hat and shook off the moisture as best he could. Kitty slanted her gaze at him. "You better put that hat back on and run across the street. Judge Bowers said to send you over as soon as I laid eyes on you."

He sighed and made an about turn, plopped his hat back on, and pushed open the door to the raging elements.

"And you best not sit on his fine furniture," she called to his back.

Judge Bowers was standing at the window and watching the rain. He spun around at the gentle knock on the door.

"Gabriel, come in." Then, giving him a perfunctory look, he said, "Appears you just took a dip in Lake Michigan."

Gabe lifted his mouth in a short-lived smile. "Very funny. Kitty said you wanted to see me?"

"Yes, have a seat."

"I better stand."

"Pfff. Can't hurt this furniture any. It's been kicked at, thrown around, wet on, spat on, and, hmm, retched on."

Gabe raised his eyebrows in silent curiosity.

"Don't ask. I'm sure that, as an officer of the law, you can relate to the fact that not everyone is going to love you. Same holds true for me." His eyes glinted with humor as he gestured at the closest chair. "Sit."

Gabe did as told.

Rather than sit in the chair opposite Gabe, the judge dropped into the one behind his oversized oak desk, folding his hands on his big green ink blotter. "Now then, have you come any closer to figuring out that young boy's identity, other than discovering his name?"

Gabe shook his head, frustrated that all roads thus far had led to dead ends. In all their digging, even his father and brother, an attorney-at-law, had come up with nothing more than a list of missing children, the same list he'd found in his police files, none of whom bore the name of Jesse Gant.

"I put out a bulletin to several lakeshore towns, sent wires to their law enforcement agencies, but nothing positive's come of it. You'd think if a boy came up missing, there'd be an outcry over it."

"Not if he had no home to speak of or anyone to care about him. Might even be his people shoved him out of the nest."

"At his age? I'm guessing he's no more than seven or eight."

Something like disgust brimmed in the older man's eyes. "Some folks don't have the brains to raise a window shade, let alone a child. Could be they mistreated him. He looks malnourished. Maybe they starved him."

Gabe winced. As much as he hated to admit it, he'd grown fond of the lad. The idea of someone harming him gnawed painfully at his heart.

"Fact is, until he talks, it'll remain a mystery. Anyway, you wanted me to see about finding him a place to stay."

Gabe repositioned himself in the chair, his wet clothing clinging to the seasoned leather. Outside, a sudden crack of thunder shattered the last nerve that ran along his spine. Torrential rain fell in sheets now, slamming against the judge's windowpane.

"Yes?"

"You'll be happy to know that I found someone to take him off your hands. They already have six critters, all under the age of twelve, mind you, but they seem to think one more into the pot won't matter. He'll have to sleep on their living room sofa, though, as all the beds in the house are spoken for." He chuckled to himself and shook his head. "You might have seen them at the church service last Sunday. I noticed you sat about five or so rows behind them. They take up an entire pew, as you can imagine. Names are Herb and Lizzie Monroe. Can't tell you all their kids' names, though. Nice Christian family. He runs a dairy farm a couple miles out of town."

The judge kept up his description, but Gabe still stumbled over the first part of it, namely, "You'll be happy to know that I found someone."

This is good news, Devlin—good news all around. He tried to snap out of the instant slump in his spirits; worse, tried to picture the boy surviving in an environment filled with certain chaos.

"…tomorrow morning. You listening?"

"What? Yes. Yes, that's good. Tomorrow morning? Already?"

"Around ten, after they've finished the milking. I can give you the directions now if you like, or, better yet, since my morning schedule looks clear, I'll go with you—make the introductions, you know. That work for you? In the meantime, you keep your nose to the grindstone and figure out where this little fella belongs."

Gabe gave a slow nod and dragged up his wet frame, suddenly numb with stupor.

"If it's any consolation, the Monroes were happy to accommodate. I approached a few other families, but most said they couldn't manage another mouth to feed. You understand. 'Course, he'll have chores, as any young man should," Ed droned.

"Of course."

He picked up a pen and tapped its ink tip on the blotter. "You okay?" he asked, giving Gabe a scrutinizing gaze. "I thought you'd be happy about this. It is what you want, right?"

"What? Sure, yeah. I'll just let Hannah know she won't have to watch him after today. I best swing by there once the rain lets up."

"You told me yourself you didn't have time for the boy."

"Exactly."

The judge leaned forward, comprehension dawning after he had given his graying beard a few thoughtful tugs. "You're growing attached to that boy." His voice took on a low, fatherly tone. "Best not do that, son. He belongs to someone, and, eventually, he'll be heading back home. It's just a matter of time."

He spoke the truth, Gabe knew.

So why was it so hard to swallow?

K

"Here we go." With Jesse at her side, Hannah pulled out the hardcover book she'd been seeking. "Someone must have put it on the wrong shelf after looking at it. Have you ever heard of *The Wonderful Wizard of Oz?*"

She put the book at Jesse's eye level and watched him gaze at the cover with interest. He gave his dark head of hair a slow shake.

"Well, I'm not surprised. It just came out a couple of years ago, but I hear it's really catching on with children everywhere. Would you like me to read some of it to you? You'll love the pictures."

He nodded and took her hand, leading her to the table and chairs on the other side of the room. It was her day to staff the library, and, with the rain coming down in steady intervals, only a handful of people had visited, allowing her to catch up on bookkeeping, organize files, and spend time with Jesse. Lately, he'd been more responsive to her; he hadn't spoken yet, but at least he smiled more readily. Maggie and Abbie both noticed the subtle changes, too.

They each pulled out a chair and sat. The clock on the fireplace mantle struck half past five. The rain had slowed to a drizzle, and a light breeze billowed the curtains, cooling the room to a pleasant temperature. Before long, fall would be upon them, and children would be traipsing back and forth to school. Hannah wondered about Jesse. Had he attended school last year? If so, where? Should they attempt to send him to Sandy Shores Grade School if the school year started and Gabe still hadn't found Jesse's family?

"Hmmmm," Jesse whined, poking his finger on the first page, impatient for her to commence reading.

She laughed. "What?" Daily she asked him questions, as if she expected a verbal response, but every day, he said nothing in return. He stabbed at the first word again and frowned.

"Do you know that word?" she asked. "Did you learn to read last year? What grade were you in?"

To all three questions, he merely stared at her.

She sighed and touched her forehead to his. "I know you're listening, Jesse Gant. Why won't you talk to me? Don't you know by now you can trust Gabe and me, not to mention Maggie Rose and Abbie Ann?"

He pulled back and clamped his mouth in a tight line, then proceeded to shove his chair back. She seized him gently by the arm.

"Okay, okay, no more pushing." Removing a thick lock of hair that blocked his vision, she cocked her head at him. "You're a mystery, sweet boy, you know that?"

After a half hour, Hannah found herself engrossed in the lovely tale, whether Jesse was or not. He'd put his head on her shoulder midway through chapter two, and, at the close of chapter three, "How Dorothy Saved the Scarecrow," had closed his eyes in slumber. She angled her head slightly to study his profile—the pointed little nose peppered with freckles, the sun-bronzed cheeks, the perfect little mouth, and the long, black, sweeping eyelashes—and quietly closed the book.

With her back to the stairway, she hadn't even heard Gabe's entry, perhaps due in part to her drifting thoughts.

As soundlessly as possible, Gabe removed his hat and invited himself to sit in a chair opposite her, rewarding her with a rare smile before focusing his attention on the sleeping boy, whose head was fast sliding down her arm.

"He's tuckered out, I see," he whispered.

"He found a stray dog out back and played with him until it started raining. I kept checking on him, mind you," she added.

"Who, the pup?"

"No, silly. Jesse." A ridiculous flush crept up her face, starting at her neck. She thanked the Lord for the darkness of dusk and its concealment.

He chuckled. "I'm not worried about you slacking off, Hannah."

The way he said her name, like a whispered song, sent her stomach tumbling. His presence always did strange things to her—made her nerves jump around in confusion. Like the pause between lightning and thunder, there came that tiny bit of anticipation at seeing him every day, no matter how foolish it was. It wasn't as if they stood around for long periods and talked about their days. Most nights, he arrived at six o'clock sharp to pick up Jesse, and the two would walk out five minutes later. She studied his silhouette in the dimly lit room, observing how the shadows cast a soft darkness over the clear-cut lines of his face, transforming his azure eyes into gray, his profile into a hazy mask. In her edgy state, she swept at her hair—a wasted effort, as it never ceased to fall out from its bun before day's end. She sought to see where he looked, but the dimness of the room made it hard to know.

"Did you feed him?"

It seemed a foolish question. "Of course I fed him. I took him over to the Culver House Café for lunch."

She heard rather than saw the smile. "Nice. But I was referring to the dog. Did you feed the stray dog?"

A childish giggle shot out of nowhere. "Oh. Yes. Maggie Rose ran across the street and got some meat scraps. The last time I checked, the food dish was empty. I put out a bowl of water, and that's half gone."

A silence fell between them. Across the street, the piano music at Charley's Saloon started in full swing.

"I suppose he'll be wanting to keep it now—the dog."

"I suppose."

"We needed the rain," he said, apparently in an attempt to keep the conversation moving. "I got stuck in it after lunch. Nearly drowned."

"It came down in sheets."

Downstairs, Maggie Rose sang "Amazing Grace" at top lung capacity. As usual, she sang louder than necessary. It would have been one thing if she could carry a tune. "I can always tell when she's locked the store and hung the 'CLOSED' sign out."

Gabe chuckled. "She's not that good."

"She's terrible," Hannah breathed.

Jesse slipped farther down her arm and made a snuffling sound, his wet breaths pooling on her sleeve. Hannah adjusted herself in the chair and drew the boy's head to her lap. He never stirred, just snored louder.

Gabe leaned across the table and folded his hands, his face coming into full view. If ever she had wanted to run, it was now. He looked as solemn as a marble statue. "Someone's offered to take Jesse."

"What?" Her breath caught and held.

When he swallowed, his Adam's apple poked out like the head of a tortoise from its shell. "Herb and Lizzie Monroe. You know them?"

"They have about a dozen kids."

"Six."

"I don't care. It's too many. He'll get lost in all that chaos. He'll stay silent forever."

Their gazes locked. "Hannah, he's not our responsibility."

"Yes, he is," she shot back. "He's grown accustomed to us. If we abandon him now, he'll run off again, and probably just about the time you figure out where he belongs, too. Then what?"

He tipped his eyebrows up in a curious slant and studied her for several seconds. "So, now he's *our* responsibility? I thought you said…"

"I don't care what I said. We're sharing the load, and because of that, I ought to have some say." Jesse stirred, and Hannah pulled her fingers through his freshly cut hair until his deep breathing resumed. She heaved a long breath of her own. "He can't go out there, Mr. Devlin. They're a nice family, but they won't do Jesse any good. He has big needs right now. Putting him in an environment where he can't get a word in edgewise will make him shrink back all the more." Her heart felt near to collapsing as she pled her case. "If you can't keep him with you, then I'll take him to my house. If my father and grandmother put up a fuss, I'll—"

He put his hand out. "Shh. Okay, okay, it'll be fine."

Threatening tears stung the backs of her eyes. "How?"

He sighed and looked down at his lap. Had he detected her imminent tears? "As long as you don't mind watching him during the day, he can continue staying with me. I'll admit I didn't like the idea of sending him out there either. They may be wonderfully generous people, but they don't know him as we do. I guess I had to see if we were of one accord, you and I."

"Oh." She relaxed.

He started to stand. "Bear in mind, though, that he'll have to go once I figure out where he belongs."

"Well, of course, but only if he has a suitable family to go home to."

He seemed to consider that before standing and walking around the table to lift Jesse into his arms. "Oh—it looks like I'm buying a house." After some adjusting, the boy settled against Gabe's broad shoulders.

"Really?" She didn't know why the news should strike a chord of exhilaration in her, but it did. "Where?" She pushed back her chair and followed him to the top of the stairs.

He turned to face her. "Out on Slayton Street. Folks by the name of Bronson."

"I know them. They moved to Lansing to be closer to her ailing folks."

"That's them."

"It's a pretty house. We've ridden past it many times. Ralston always comments about the nice rose arbor in the side yard."

A shadow crossed his face. "Ah, Ralston, your gentleman friend. So, when do you plan to marry him?"

"What? I—no date has been set."

"But he's already proposed, right?"

The final verse of "Amazing Grace" echoed up to the rafters, and the distraction almost pleased her.

"Hmm?" he asked, leaning close enough for their breaths to mingle.

She stepped back instantly, but it took her the better share of a minute to collect herself. "No, he—he hasn't asked me—yet. But he will."

After hesitating a moment, Gabe said, "Well, I'm sure you must be sitting on pins and needles just waiting for him to pose that question, hmm?"

Flustered, she blew a wisp of hair off her forehead.

He grinned and nodded. "I'll see you in the morning, Miss Kane."

Chapter Seven

"Did you wash behind your ears?" Gabe and Jesse had readied themselves for a good night's rest, Gabe on the bed, Jesse in his usual spot—the chair in front of the window.

Jesse wagged his head and walked to the dresser, where an array of toys lay scattered in wait. Gabe couldn't think of one day since Hannah had started watching the lad that she hadn't sent him home with something from the store. First, it was a collection of toy soldiers; then, a miniature farm set; a few days later, a ball; and, today, a couple of children's books. The woman had a soft spot for Jesse, no doubt about it. *How will it be for her once we return Jesse to his rightful family?* Gabe wondered. *Shoot, how will it be for me?*

He thought about the events of the afternoon—how he'd came upon Jesse sleeping against Hannah's shoulder and discovered a deep-set ache to know her better. Then, the instant berating he'd given himself. Hadn't he just escaped a near-marriage to Carolina Woods? The last thing he needed, or wanted, was some woman putting expectations on him.

Besides, Hannah Grace Kane was betrothed, or close to it, according to her.

He stretched out on the bed with his newspaper before him and scanned the headlines. No sooner had he started an article about the country's sorry financial state than Jesse let out a sorrowful squeal! Gabe lowered the paper and looked into eyes filled with terror. "What's the matter?"

When Jesse just stood there, baying like a hound dog, Gabe leaped from the bed, knelt down on one knee, and grasped the child by his shoulders. "Jesse, are you in pain? Tell me what's wrong. You look like you've seen a ghost."

Jesse wriggled free of him and ran to the door, grabbing hold of the latch with both hands and giving it a couple of frenzied twists, but it was locked. "Jess, what are you doing?"

"Aargh," Jesse groaned in frustration, continuing to try the door.

"It's locked, buddy. I'm not letting you go. Come on, tell me what's wrong."

Suddenly, Jesse pointed at the bed. "What?" Gabe asked. "The bed?"

"Hmm," Jesse protested, shaking his head back and forth.

Gabe swallowed down a hard knot. He tousled Jesse's thick mop of black hair with tenderness. "Talk to me."

Jesse walked to the bed and pointed at the newspaper. By his terrified expression, one might have supposed he'd uncovered a poisonous snake camouflaged in the bushes.

Gabe snatched up the paper and scanned the front page, where he beheld the source of Jesse's distress: the photograph of Rufus McCurdy.

He looked from the photo to Jesse, his heart thudding like a rock. "Do you recognize this man's face?"

Jesse ran to the chair and buried his head under the hotel blanket. A clap of thunder roared in the distance.

A yawning sigh welled up and pushed past Gabe's chest. *Dear God, help him see his way through the blackness and into the safety of Your arms—and mine.*

He got back down on his knees and rubbed the boy's frail shoulders through the woolen fabric of his nightgown. Now was not the time to press.

Within ten minutes, Jesse drifted off to sleep.

K

Blasts of gunshots and banshee-like screams. Blood mingling with blood, redder than them roses Mr. Godfrey sold outside his store on East 22nd Street, oozing like beet juice out the lady's mouth and ears and pouring from the man's chest, changing his shirt color from tan to crimson.

Jesse covered his eyes from the worst of it, but he still peeked through his separated fingers, wanting to know what happened to the man and woman. Were they dead?

For a second afterward, no one moved, not even the bad guys. Everything went still as a March moon, except for a blue jay overhead that kept up its yapping. Suddenly, the man with the gun started barking orders. "Grab as much as you can. Don't just stand there looking stupid. Move!" Like slaves, the other three carried out his orders, stepping over the bodies to snatch up whatever goods they could. "Money! Look for money!" the mean man wailed. They started yanking out bureau drawers, tipping over furniture, tossing debris in all directions. One of them picked up Jesse's little black suitcase, opened it, and dumped its contents on the floor.

Through the tiny kitchen window, Jesse looked at the woman, who lay like a sun-dried fish, eyes open but not looking, mouth drooping wide, blond hair clumped and wet-looking. Something pinched and burned at the bottom of his stomach, and he had the sudden want to retch, but he didn't.

While surveying the parlor room, one of the bad men spotted him, and for a heart-stopping instant, their gazes held. "Hey, some bratty little kid seen us, Pa. He was watchin' through that winder." Jesse tried to move, but his feet refused. Even peeling his hands off the windowsill seemed a chore. Finally, he managed, and when he did, he took off like a horse with wings past the barn and across a big field, soaring past bushes and through tall weeds.

"Well, go get 'im, fool!"

Footsteps pounded at Jesse's back, gaining on him. He ran faster, glad for his boots, holes and all. With every ounce of strength, he made a running leap for a ditch behind a big, wide oak and buried himself under a felled log, counting each breath, wondering which one would be his last. The runner kept going, passing his well-hidden body. *It pays to be small*, he told himself, *small and quiet*.

Mustn't make a sound, he said inside his brain. *Can't trust a livin' soul.*

Vomit pooled in his throat, but he swallowed it, pinching shut his eyes, as if to block out the bad stuff.

Everybody leaves, he thought. *Everybody leaves and dies. First, Daddy; then, Mama. Even that lady who dropped me off in Do-wagi-ack, or however it's said—she left me sitting at a train* station with those—those strangers. *Those strangers who were now dead.*

He'd thought he could trust her, but he'd been wrong. *Can't trust anybody. No siree. Nobody.*

K

Jesse opened eyes that felt heavy and damp in the corners. He wiped them and sat up, wondering for a second where he was, thinking he might still be running. His chest heaved and pounded as if that were so. But then he saw the sheriff sleeping in the bed, and he knew he was safe—at least for now.

The picture of the bad man he'd seen in the newspaper shot a path back to his brain. It was *him*. He knew it was. He remembered that gray beard, that balding head, that big stomach that bulged over his belt, and that mean, gorilla-like face with the sunken eyes. Granted, the picture looked like a younger version of the man, but that didn't leave Jesse any less certain.

And something else he knew. That man and those others were hunting for him, and when they found him, they would kill him dead. One of them had chased him in a town a few weeks ago, up a street and down an alley, until Jesse outsmarted him by jumping in a waste barrel. "We'll get you yet, you scraggly little stooge, and when we do, you'll be a sorry little twerp!" he'd hollered into the night. "Don't think you can run forever."

He could not stop the loud patter of his heartbeat, nor the sweat, clammy and clingy, that trickled down his face and soaked his nightshirt. His stomach knotted into a tight ball, paining him so much that he feared it would burn a hole through his skin. How to stop this panicky, sickening feeling coursing through his veins?

Outside, the moon tried to peek through the thick clouds, shedding just enough light to reveal Mr. Devlin's—Gabe's— chest rising and falling in steady rhythm as he breathed.

Jesse knew he needed to talk to him and Hannah. He could trust them, couldn't he? Still, every time he tried to make his voice work for either of them, his throat locked up tight as a rich man's safe, the very idea of spilling out the truth of what he'd seen making him quake and shudder. In fact, some days, his chest felt near to exploding. He could never seem to forget the sight of that bright red blood, oozing and pouring out of the bodies of the man and woman.

He tore the blanket off his skinny frame and made a running leap for the bed, thinking the quicker he got there, the faster the bad pictures would go away. Gabe shifted his weight and made a snuffling noise with his mouth and nose. He was more of a snuffler than a snorer, Jesse noted, turning on his side so that he felt Gabe's warmth against his back. Not too close to wake him, but close enough to feel safe.

K

The final days of summer turned into the earliest signs of fall—cooler temperatures, shorter days, and the start of the school year. Gabe wanted to start Jesse in school, despite his refusal to speak; Hannah thought otherwise, arguing that plunking him into an environment of raucous children would drive him only deeper into his private little burrow of silence.

"You're spoiling him," Gabe countered. "He needs to come out of that shell, and putting him with other kids will speed the process."

"What if he decides to run away during a recess break because he can't cope? I don't think it's smart to push him, especially since he's making small gains."

"What if introducing him to other children his age gives him the desire to communicate? You know how youngsters talk while they're playing. Maybe he'll forget about being determined not to speak and, one day, start yapping while they're playing a game of tag or something."

Hannah squeezed her lips tight together and crossed her arms to show her staunch skepticism. "I highly doubt that would happen."

"He needs to socialize with children his age."

"And he will—but not until he feels safe."

"How's he ever going to feel safe if we don't give him a little push?"

"What? That doesn't make a bit of sense."

Her father, who'd been standing next to the cash register counting bills and studying the week's receipts, put down the papers and announced they sounded like a couple of old marrieds who couldn't agree on anything.

At his words, Hannah's cheeks heated up until she imagined they must look as red as strawberries. She made an about-turn and walked to the back room, leaving Gabe and Jacob alone. From there, she gazed out the back window at Jesse, who was playing with the stray pup. She tried to gather her bearings as she listened to the men speak in low tones.

"She's probably right, you know," Jacob said. "If he's not talking yet, putting him in a school situation where he's forced to conform will almost certainly do more harm than good."

"You think so?" Gabe asked.

"He's shy, at best. If he refuses to talk, the others might start teasing him. The tongue can be an awful weapon."

"That's true enough. Children can be cruel little beasts when they put their minds to it."

"No sense in causing further trauma."

"Is it your opinion we should hold off on the school notion, then?"

"Indeed," Jacob replied.

Oh, it angered Hannah that her father's words carried more weight in Gabe's eyes than her own. Had he forgotten who'd been watching Jesse Gant for the past several weeks—tending to his needs, feeding him, reading to him, soothing his hurts?

After some discussion, the *men* decided Jesse's fate. Things would continue as before, Gabe dropping the child off in the mornings and picking him up at day's end. "Of course, you'll probably want to school him yourself, whenever possible," Gabe inserted when Hannah reentered the room, her temper barely intact.

She forced back a biting word and nodded. "As I've been doing ever since I started watching him, Mr. Devlin."

"Gabe," he corrected her.

"Mr. Devlin," she snapped back.

Jacob Kane merely shook his head and went back to his bookkeeping, biting back a grin.

Hannah and Jesse moseyed up Third Street, heading for the Kane home, a dusky sun settling on their shoulders. "Listen. Do you hear that? It's a chickadee." She put out her hand to stop Jesse in his tracks. Together, they tilted their faces toward a cloudless sky. "Chee-dee-dee-dee, chee-dee-dee-dee," she mimicked. "Hear him? He's putting up a fuss, isn't he? What tree do you think he's sitting in?"

With all his might, Jesse seemed to ponder her question, gazing from one tree to the next, hands shoved deep into the pockets of his blue dungarees, black hair falling to one side with the tilt of his head. Finally, he pointed at the aged oak. Through the thick-leafed branches, one could see a rustling of leaves.

"Exactly!" Hannah agreed, clapping her hands. "Look, there he goes."

Wordlessly, Jesse pointed at its trailing mate and smiled. She loved his smile, the way it transformed his dour face into something quite adorable, showing off his two permanent incisors, only halfway in. The teeth revealed something about his age, according to Ralston. Most children had their second teeth, or at least a good start on them, by age seven, he'd said.

They set off again, her hand guiding his shoulder as they crossed over to the other side of the street, the foursquare house at 210 Ridge Street now in full view. "My grandmother is hosting a little dinner tonight, and you're invited. Did you know that?"

With a sideward toss of his head, he gazed at her through troubled eyes.

"Nothing to worry about, of course," she said, maintaining a nonchalant tone. "Gabe will be there, as will my sisters and my father, and you know them. And Dr. Van Huff, of course. Remember him?"

Jesse scowled with some kind of private thought. "Then, there will be a few folks from town," she hurried on to say.

"My grandmother wants to make certain people get the chance to meet Mr. Devlin—if they haven't already."

He seemed to be processing the information. She had purposely kept the party from him all week, knowing it would make him worry. But the time for secrets had passed.

"That's why Gabe didn't pick you up today," she continued, sensing his growing agitation, his slower gait. "We agreed it made just as much sense for me to bring you as him."

She gave him time to digest her words, preparing to nab him should he decide to bolt. While they were still half a block away from home, Maggie Rose stepped out on the front porch and waved at the two of them, looking pretty as a picture in her pale blue satin gown, long blonde hair falling in perfect waves around her face and neck, shimmery barrettes stationed at either temple. It struck Hannah afresh how God had played favorites. Secretly and without forewarning, she wondered how Gabe viewed her younger sister. "Probably smitten with her," she said aloud. "And why not?"

Ignoring her spoken observation, Jesse took off at a run toward Maggie.

"Hey, where are you going, young man?"

But he paid no heed to her question, running full tilt instead toward Maggie's waiting arms.

"Humph. Gabe wouldn't be the only one smitten," she muttered to herself.

Over dinner, the conversation ranged from the going price of beef to politics, from the upcoming community dinner at the church to the Wright brothers' foolish notion that they would one day fly over the trees like birds. Gabe mostly listened, offering comments from time to time, observing Sandy Shores' citizens with interest. Most of them he'd already met in passing, but the gathering tonight gave him a chance to delve deeper into their personalities. There were Peter Van Poort, who ran the grocery store; Simon and Anna Jellema, who owned the shoe store; Harvey Godfrey, the town's only dentist; and Grant and James Mulder and their wives, owners of Grant and Son Tailor Shop, to name a few.

Jesse clung tight to Gabe's side, as if there were something to fear in the friendly little gathering. Certainly, there'd been no sign of Rufus McCurdy in Sandy Shores, and he had no reason to suspect there would be, but he'd kept his eyes peeled anyway ever since the incident in the hotel room when Jesse had panicked at seeing the photograph. Obviously, he had witnessed something, but just what remained a mystery. Somewhere along the line, Jesse had encountered the man, and Gabe meant to discover when, where, and under what circumstances, just as soon as he could put the pieces together. Getting the boy to talk would solve a multitude of problems.

Helena Kane made the perfect hostess, as did her lovely granddaughters, all of whom worked the crowd with the greatest of ease, Hannah included. Of the three, he considered Hannah the most alluring, if not the prettiest—but she also took the prize in unshakable tenacity, perhaps because he knew her best. Maggie Rose appeared sweet and prim; Abbie Ann childlike, impish, and a trifle spoiled. Anyone could see, after watching Jacob for even a short time, that the baby of the family shone like a star in his eyes.

Of course, Ralston Van Huff stuck to Hannah like a barnacle to a boat, following her about the house and out onto the front porch where a few guests mingled after dinner, exuding his charm on everyone, entertaining them with his small talk. Gabe prayed that the bizarre envy boiling in his gut would subside. In the first place, he had no claim whatsoever on Hannah Grace Kane—the only thing they shared was the responsibility of Jesse's care. Second, a woman required time and effort, particularly one as prickly and impetuous as Hannah. Every day, Gabe thanked God for revealing the truth about Carolina Woods, that she amounted to little more than a money-starved socialite who was more interested in seizing hold of his family's wealth than in finding true love. Not that Hannah came close to comparing with Carolina, but she was a woman, wasn't she? And hadn't Gabe promised himself just weeks ago to wait a long time before looking at another one? Besides, anyone could see that the good doctor already had dibs on her.

"She's a fine woman, that Hannah Grace." A hand came up and gave him a vigorous slap on the shoulder, startling him out of his thoughts. Had he really been watching Hannah so close as to draw attention to himself? Ed Bowers grinned from one big ear to the other, looking all cocky, as if he were privy to some secret. "Yep, she's quality all the way, that one," he said, leaning close and whispering, "A far cry from that lady you nearly betrothed yourself to back in June."

Gabe tossed back his head and frowned. "What do you know about that?"

Ed laughed his usual hearty chuckle and his silver beard waggled. "Word gets around, my friend. Have you forgotten I went down for your folks' anniversary celebration in May? She was a beauty, all right, but you know what they say— looks'll go skin deep, but character drives clear to the soul."

"Is that what they say?" Gabe asked, suddenly irritated with his old family friend for knowing so much. As if on cue, Hannah's light laughter drifted in from the porch. He couldn't help but take a gander at her, and, when he did, it rankled him to see the doctor's arm around her shoulder—in plain view, even. Was he imagining things, or had she purposely put space between herself and the doctor when she sidestepped to allow a clear passageway for Isabella Peterson, owner of the hat shop, who wore a flowery concoction big enough for an eagle's perch atop her head to advertise her business?

"Fine Christian she is, too," Ed continued. "Won't find a more virtuous woman anywhere. Takes after her grandmother, she does."

His heart's desire, when he did go looking for a wife, was to marry someone who shared his Christian principles—who put Christ before all else and didn't look at possessions as more important than a person's heart. He'd watched Hannah with Jesse and found her selfless and kind. Just not with *him*. And, now that he thought about this, it irritated him plenty.

"Now, if I were you, I'd make my move, yes, I would."

"Ed."

The judge raised a hand to hush him. "Here's my opinion, for what it's worth. She's settling for that Van Huff character. He's not a bad person, mind you, but he lacks passion for the things that truly matter in life. I can't say I've ever carried on a conversation with him that didn't center on that practice of his. And then, there's the matter of his walk with God."

As little as Gabe wanted to discuss Hannah Grace's infatuation with Ralston Van Huff, Ed had managed to reel him in. "How do you mean?"

"Just something I overheard him say to Clyde Perkins a couple months back when I was sitting in another room waiting to get my ticker checked. He alluded that going to church wasn't really his cup of tea, but he did it for Hannah's sake. Just struck me that he lacks conviction, that's all."

Gabe winced inwardly but refused to show it externally. What Hannah Grace chose to do with her life mattered little. At least, that's what he told himself.

Ed was studying him, Gabe knew, looking for a clue that what he'd said had struck some chord.

Gabe avoided Ed's gaze and glanced down at Jesse. Still stuck to him like a duckling to its ma, Jesse showed no interest in wandering, save for the ogle he gave the triple-layered chocolate cake on the buffet table across the room, which Helena and Maggie Rose were even now cutting into serving-sized pieces and sliding onto elegant crystal plates.

Apparently, Ed noticed. "That cake looks mighty scrumptious, young man," he said to Jesse. "I bet Maggie would serve you a piece if you asked real politely."

Jesse's eyes sought Gabe's permission. He nodded and urged him forward with a gentle nudge. To his surprise, Jesse left his side to weave through the crowded room.

"You making any progress with that boy?" Ed asked, watching with Gabe as Maggie Rose smiled at Jesse and bent down to whisper something in his ear. The boy's face lit up, and he eagerly accepted a piece of cake. No "thank you" came from his lips, however. Gabe sighed, glad for the shift in topics.

"Not much." He gave a light chuckle. "Unless you consider the fact that he now finds me safe enough to share a bed with, sometimes even hogging it. That kid kicks and fusses in his sleep like nobody's business, and I've got bruises in the middle of my back to prove it."

"Nightmares?"

"Most likely. I wish he'd talk to me."

"He will when he's ready. You have any leads on that McCurdy gang?"

"Not a one. I was hoping you might." He'd gone straight to the judge's office the morning after Jesse had seen Rufus's photograph, eager to talk to someone about it. He figured telling Hannah about the incident would only cause her to fret. No point in enlightening her until he had something firm to go on.

"I did hear one thing."

Gabe straightened, raising his eyebrows.

"Someone reportedly saw the four of them in a St. Joseph Saloon a week or so back," Ed informed him. "The one called Roy, I believe he's the oldest son, asked a patron if he'd seen a little stray boy with black hair. Claimed it was his sister's youngest, and that he'd run off, worrying his sister sick. The fellow knew right off it was a McCurdy, because he'd seen a 'Wanted' poster nailed to the outside of the bank that very afternoon. He tried to act real casual, but apparently, they all picked up on his bad case of nerves and left the place ahead of him. By the time he reached the police station to file a report, the gang had skipped town."

Gabe listened intently, stuck on the part about the stray boy. "You don't think it's possible, do you? That Jesse is Roy McCurdy's nephew?"

"Roy McCurdy doesn't have a sister," Ed said. "Don't know how Jesse could be related. Far as I know, it's just the three boys, and none of them is married. Old Rufus raised them all after their ma passed on. Did a rotten job of it, too."

Something troubled Gabe, chewing a hole in his side. "So, why would Roy be asking about a runaway boy? You think there's any connection to Jesse?"

Ed shook his head. "Might be, but I don't know what it'd be."

The two ruminated for the next several moments, sipping punch and nodding at various guests.

"You move into that house yet?" Ed asked.

"Still waiting for a couple of loose ends to come together. I expect to sign the final paperwork in a couple of days. It's taken longer than projected, since the owners live in Lansing. Phone service isn't always dependable, and the post office is slower than a tortoise with its shoelaces strung together."

A slow chuckle came from Ed's chest. "All in good time, son. I would imagine you have furniture and such waiting to be shipped?"

"Some, but, fortunately, a lot of pieces came with the house." Gabe glanced across the room at Jesse, who was gazing up at Maggie Rose while she spoke in soft tones to the wordless boy. He appreciated the way folks accepted Jesse despite his issues. So far, the citizens of Sandy Shores had more than exceeded Gabe's expectations when it came to affability, the Kane family rising above the rest. Even though Hannah kept a safe emotional distance from him, she certainly lavished plenty of affection on Jesse Gant.

Someone made a clinking sound against a crystal goblet, silencing the guests. All heads, including those of Ed and Gabe, turned in the direction from whence it came. In the doorway separating the porch from the parlor room, Ralston Van Huff held a silver spoon in one hand and a goblet in the other. He smiled at the roomful of curious onlookers. "If I may have your attention, folks, I have an announcement I'd like to make." He looked down at Hannah with a wide smile.

An uneasy sensation coiled in Gabe's stomach, while across the room, a whispered hush fell like a misty cloud. Gabe's eyes sought Hannah's, but she stood next to Ralston, stiff as a frozen fence post, her face gone pale as a fish as she fixed her blue-gray gaze on the floor.

"Well, I'll be," murmured Ed out of the side of his mouth, giving Gabe a strong poke with his elbow. "Looks like he's beatin' you to the punch."

Chapter Eight

D id you see Papa's face when Huffy made the marriage proposal?" Abbie Ann paced back and forth in the upstairs bedroom until Hannah was sure she would carve a permanent path into the pine planks. "What on earth did Papa say to you afterward, Hannah? We're sisters, after all, and we keep no secrets, so you must tell us." Hands tightly clasped at her tiny waist, she heaved a dramatic breath. "Was he quite angry? Why, everyone present knew good and well Huffy bamboozled him. You're not truly going to marry that man, are you, Han? He doesn't bring out the best in you. Goodness, I'm not even sure he encourages you in your Christian walk. Does he, Hannah?" Abbie's pace quickened, her pretty face gone into a dark frown, her hands now wringing in worry. "And if you tell me he's perfect for you, why, I'll—I'll fry up my dirty stockings for breakfast."

"Oh, for goodness' sake, Abbie Ann, what kind of remark is that? And slow down, would you? You're turning me into a nervous Nellie."

"Well, good! You should be nervous. Huffy's proposal is nothing short of ridiculous. You've nothing in common with him."

Hannah lay sprawled across her bed, staring at her wiggling toes peeking out from the hem of her gown. "I read in *Ladies' Home Journal* that when searching for a mate, it's best to find one whose interests vary from your own. Otherwise, things tend to get boring. There was a similar article in *Vogue*," she replied.

"Hannah Grace, you should hear yourself," Abbie wailed. "I feel more grown up than you right now."

At that, Hannah sat up, ire rising faster than the price of milk. "Well, you're not, young lady, and don't forget it. You haven't even been on your first outing with a boy."

"And I'm glad for it. Unlike you, I don't need a man to make my life complete and fulfilling. God is all I need, and you should say the same. Why, just last Sunday, the Reverend Cooper spoke on the virtues of seeking God's divine guidance when making important decisions. Imagine seeking answers for your future in some silly magazine. What do those writers know about anything, anyway? You should be reading your Bible instead."

"What? I'll have you know I read my Bible every day, sister dear, and I have not run across one thing that has warned me against marrying Ralston. And another thing. I don't need a man to make my life complete, but that doesn't mean I'm longing for spinsterhood, either."

"Stop it, both of you." Maggie's stern tone from her perch by the vanity drew both girls to a halt. She was still dressed like a queen in her blue brocade gown, and her freshly brushed hair curved gently about her shapely shoulders. Ever the practical one, Maggie cleared her throat and swiveled on the seat until she faced her sisters. "Hannah's right; your pacing isn't helping matters," she said to Abbie. "Nor is your incessant squealing. You best settle down and allow Hannah to make her own decisions—with the Lord's guidance, of course."

Properly put in her place, Abbie sighed and crossed the room. Turning away from her sisters, she pulled back the lace curtain and gazed out the window, granting them a moment of pleasant silence. Hannah lay back down and sucked in several calming breaths.

"I think remaining single would be highly advantageous," Abbie said.

"Perhaps," Maggie agreed. "But only if God willed it."

"In fact, I'm seriously considering it. Katrina is simply not the same since she and Micah Sterling married, and neither will you be, Hannah Grace. We used to share so many secrets, Katrina and I, but since she married Micah, she seems so—so old. Oh, we still see each other often, but it's not the same. Micah forever hangs on her, or she on him. We can't even have a decent conversation most times."

"Why, Abigail Kane, you're jealous." Maggie turned back around to the vanity mirror and resumed her nightly hundred strokes to her glorious, gold mane with her horsehair brush, leaning forward to study her flawless complexion in the mirror. "Micah Sterling stole your best friend, and you're just plain mad as a hornet over that."

Abbie spun around, black locks bouncing, dark eyes snapping with newfound spark. "I most certainly am not. The last thing I want is a man to have to cater to and pick up after."

Then, to Hannah, she added, "Which is exactly what *you'll* be doing if you marry Huffy. Lots of catering. Doctors like to have their social gatherings, you know. You'll be forever hosting some function or another."

Hannah draped a weary arm across her forehead and peered at a spider's web just overhead. Abbie's banter fueled her exhaustion, making changing into her nightclothes seem like an impossible chore.

Ralston's proposal of marriage was rather shocking, she mulled. Why, he hadn't even kissed her yet, unless one counted a peck on the cheek, and even those came at rare intervals. Moreover, his failure to seek her father's blessing beforehand troubled her. Why ever had he thought it necessary to announce his wishes to marry her in a public setting? Had he expected immediate elation from everyone present, thinking she couldn't possibly turn him down in the presence of others? She winced as she recalled Papa's face—his look of surprise, then confusion and disapproval, and perhaps a hint of anger, albeit appropriately contained and controlled. To be certain, uncomfortable didn't come close to describing the general feeling in the room, particularly when she delicately withheld an answer.

After the party, Hannah and her sisters straightened up the house, washed every last dish and crystal goblet, shook out rugs and linen tablecloths, and folded and put things in their proper places, all with Grandmother's hasty orders and strict supervision. Papa stifled any talk of the wedding proposal the second Abbie brought it up, saying, "Hannah and I shall discuss this issue in private." His brusque tone had everyone scurrying about the house, Helena included. Within an hour, one would not have known a flurry of guests had filled every room. Without ado, everyone but Hannah and Papa escaped to her room, and Papa ushered Hannah to the library, pressing her gently into the settee.

"Now then, do you love this man?" he asked, wasting no time in getting to the point, dropping down beside her with a sigh and crossing one leg over the other. When he turned to look at her, his eyes penetrated deep into her core, and yet they held a tenderness that made her want to weep.

"Papa, I—I don't know for sure. He's a very fine man, and he has high aspirations. He would be a good provider, of that I am certain."

Papa nodded, raising his eyebrows a mere notch. He stole her hand from her lap and sandwiched it between his own. "And so you would marry him for these reasons?"

"No…well, I understand that love must play a big part."

"A big part?" Jacob gave her fingers a gentle squeeze and smiled. "My dear, it must play the biggest part of all—love, and a deep conviction within yourself that God has led you to this pivotal point."

In that moment, she felt the tiniest tweak in her conscience. What part, if any, had the Lord played in bringing Ralston and her together—or was that something she would sense with time? A tumble of confused thoughts scurried through her head, and she sucked in a jagged breath.

Her father must have sensed her inner turmoil, for he patted her hand. "I must confess, I haven't made much of an effort to know Ralston better, but what I've seen of him, I like. It's just that I had no idea your relationship had risen to such a level; I certainly had no idea of his intentions to propose marriage."

"If it's any consolation to you, Papa, I had no idea of Ralston's plans, either, and in the presence of so many guests. If you'll recall, I gave him no formal answer."

He exhaled a long sigh, accompanied by the first hint of a twinkle in his eye. "For which I am most grateful. I have never once doubted your sensible side, Hannah Grace. I know you will make this a matter of diligent prayer." Again, that needling sensation pricked at her soul.

Lord, forgive me for neglecting to seek Your wisdom.

Suddenly, Jacob leaned forward and kissed her on the forehead, then clasped her shoulders and studied her face. "It's hard to believe you've grown up so rapidly. When did this happen?"

She smiled and picked a piece of lint from his shirtfront. "Oh, Papa, I can't stay a child forever."

"Humph, I suppose you are nearing a marriageable age."

"Grandmother said anyone past twenty can't be too picky."

"Don't bring me into this," Helena suddenly chimed from the living room. When had she sneaked back downstairs? "I said no such thing—not in those exact words, anyway."

"Mother Kane, how long have you been lurking?" Jacob asked.

"I'm not lurking at all. I just came down to retrieve a book." Helena walked grandly into the library, her silken housecoat flowing behind her, and took down a volume from a shelf directly behind her son's mahogany twin-pedestal desk.

Jacob raised his eyebrows. "So, if you didn't say it in so many words, how did you say it?"

"What? Oh, well, I suppose I mentioned something at one point about the importance of finding a proper husband before, say, the age of twenty-five. After all, the older a woman gets, the narrower her chances."

"Ah." He combed his long, slender fingers through his thick beard. "It is all in God's hands whether one finds a lifelong mate, and a matter for much prayer and seeking God's Word for direction. I would hope you added that as an afterthought."

The normally intact, highly controlled woman grew pink with embarrassment, if not indignation. She drew back her shoulders. "I have always taught your daughters the truth of God's Holy Word, Jacob Stewart Kane."

It was one of the few times Hannah had heard Grandmother address her grown son with such sternness, and, for a split second, Hannah had to hold back a telling smile. What Grandmother said was true. Rarely had Helena Kane dismissed an opportunity to make a Sunday school lesson out of the minutest misdemeanor. Hannah's head filled with childhood recollections.

"Well, I wasn't questioning your Christian training, Mother, just your—oh, good grief, I don't know. I feel out of my element. This is something new to me, discussing matters of marriage with my eldest daughter." He suddenly rose to his feet, so Hannah jumped to hers, as well.

"If you don't mind, Papa, I'd like to go to bed."

He leaned forward to kiss her forehead and give her a warm hug. "It has been an eventful evening, hasn't it? We'll let the matter of the proposal rest until we're all a bit more clearheaded."

She sighed with relief and moved out of his embrace. "Good night, then." She blew her grandmother a kiss on her way to the door.

"It was a nice party, by the way," Jacob said. She turned to acknowledge his compliment. "Folks seemed to enjoy meeting Sheriff Devlin in a less formal setting. I must say, he's a most likeable fellow."

"And charming, too," Grandmother added in a wistful manner, pressing a hand to her throat, her book to her bosom.

For reasons unknown, a knot formed in the back of Hannah's neck. *Why must Gabriel Devlin's name come up when Ralston's should be at the forefront, even if the party was for the benefit of the new sheriff?*

Hannah forced a smile. "Good night, now."

On the way to the stairs, she'd caught her grandmother's final remark.

"To be sure, that Gabriel Devlin will make some woman a fine catch."

Oh, bother! With a great deal of effort, Hannah had dragged herself upstairs and dangled her feet over the edge of her high Jenny Lind bed, doing her best to rein in her tangled thoughts.

"Well, are you going to tell us what Papa said about the marriage matter?" Abbie asked, walking away from the window.

Hannah let out a labored breath. "My head's too discombobulated at the moment. Besides, tomorrow's Sunday, and I have to get up extra early, since it's my week to make breakfast."

"Hannah's right," Maggie said, rising from the vanity and stretching her slender arms toward the ceiling as she expelled a wide yawn. "Undo my buttons, Abs," she said, turning her back toward her little sister.

Abbie set about the task. "Let's talk about the very divine-looking Sheriff Devlin, then, shall we?"

Hannah groaned. "Let's not." She padded to the bureau drawer to find her nightgown.

"He is a handsome specimen," Maggie said dreamily, standing patiently as Abbie moved her hands meticulously down her back. "Why, if I were a wee bit older and didn't have my heart set on going to New York…"

"But you do," Abbie reminded her. "Besides, he's not your type. He's more, hmm, Hannah's type, I'd say."

Hannah twisted around, mouth gaping. "I do declare, what is all this talk about Gabriel Devlin? First Papa, then Grandmother, and now you two. He's a nice enough man, yes, but he's not—*divine*, as you put it, Abbie. And he certainly is *not* my type."

Abbie stilled her unbuttoning task. "Why not?"

Why not, indeed? Completely at a loss for words, Hannah yanked open the top drawer, snagged her nightgown under her arm, and marched to the washroom situated just outside the girls' bedroom. Even when she closed the door behind her, it was difficult not to hear Abbie's remark: "Well, I guess I've found another button to push when I want to get a rise out of her." Her sisters' high-pitched giggles trailed off.

K

"It's gettin' cooler these days, Pop. Cain't we hole up in a hotel somewheres tonight?"

Rufus reined in his horse, turned full around, and stared at the three hooligans following his lead. Although the sun shone through puffy clouds, there was a chilly nip coming off Lake Michigan this morning that passed right through their holey cotton shirts, a sure sign that autumn would soon come knocking. If snow fell before they found that rotten kid, they might freeze to death. The boys shifted in their saddles, Roy pushing his weathered hat back to gaze at the sky, Reuben leaning forward to rub his lathered horse on the neck, and Luis watching his father with hopeful eyes.

"We ain't stayin' in no hotel, Luis, and don't none of the others of y' come up with anymore half-baked ideas. We can't take any chances on folks recognizin' us. You saw that article in the newspapers. Least ways, y' saw m' picture. Not a one of us can read worth squat, but that picture alone tells me they's after us. Maybe that fool kid already come forward 'bout seein' us. We gots t' watch ar backs, y' hear?"

"Then, what's the point in killin' that kid, Pa, iffin' he's already tol' on us?" asked Reuben. "Seems t' me, we should jus' skedaddle and hope no one spots us on the way out."

"Seems to me we should just skedaddle." Rufus wagged his head and mocked his boy in a whiney voice, then spat at the ground, hitting the toe of his boot instead. "Anyone tell you y' got the brains of a gopher? That kid's the only witness to ar crime. Anythin' else is hearsay. Even you spoutin' off t' that painted woman down in South Bend ain't goin' t' hold water with the law if it was to ever come t' trial. Who's goin' t' believe her? That don't mean it weren't plain daft of you to go braggin' 'bout what happened, Reuben. An' if I hear tell you open your yapper again, I'll close it for good, y' hear?"

"Yes, sir, Pa. I ain't tol' nobody since." Reuben looked as scared as a hog going to the slaughterhouse. Rufus nodded, feeling satisfied.

"You think it'll go to trial, Pa?" asked Luis. Luis looked scared, too, but his fears came from his own naiveté.

"They'd have to catch us first, bonehead," said Roy. "And they ain't goin' to, right, Pa? That's why we have to stay out of folks' sight, lay low, sleep under the stars, wear ar hats down low on ar faces, split up when we can. We gots to watch our backs every second. You fellas can go to trial if y' want, but I'll die 'fore some judge stamps 'guilty' on my forehead and sends me off t' prison."

Pride welled up within Rufus for his oldest boy's cleverness. Maybe he couldn't read, but that was only because Rufus had kept his boys sheltered their whole lives. They didn't need book-learning for the kind of work they did. Robbing was plain work, living on the edge, constantly watching their tails, never taking time to enjoy the finer points of life, like a good-tasting wine, a soft feather bed, or a decent roof over their heads. No sir. They'd be living the wayfaring life the rest of their days, which, for Rufus, wouldn't be much longer, what with him getting up in years. What was he, anyway? Sixty? He'd been forty-something back when Wilma had Luis, but after her passing, the years and their numbers seemed to lose all meaning. She never approved of her husband's lifestyle, but she appreciated the money well enough when food got scarce. And, after suffering a few blows to the chin, she'd learned to quit asking how he earned it.

"Simple" best described her, which probably explained Reuben's pea brain.

A flock of gulls swooped down on them when Luis threw down a half-eaten apple he pulled from his pocket. Rufus's horse whinnied and pawed. "We'd best find a place to settle in for the day. Don't want no one catchin' sight of us. Roy, ride on ahead and see what you can find. Me and the boys'll walk the horses down to the shore for a drink. We're goin' to hang out in Holland till we can get some news on that kid. Might be we'll even find 'im hidin' out here. Someone's bound to leak some information one o' these times. Matter o' fact, I got a good feelin' 'bout this place."

"You bet, Pa," said Roy, his face beaming with importance.

"Why's he always get to go scoutin'? When's Luis or me get a turn?" Reuben whined.

"I don't want no turn," Luis chimed.

Rufus shook his head at both of them and spat a big wad, this time making his mark on a decaying log.

Not waiting around, Roy turned his horse toward town and kicked him into action. "I'll be back 'fore you can say jackrabbit, Pa. You boys do as Pa says, now, y' hear?"

When Roy galloped out of earshot, Reuben groused, "He ain't my boss."

Rufus glowered. "You best start thinkin' different, boy. Once I pass on t' glory, you'll be answerin' t' him."

K

"Rise and shine, buddy boy, we're going to church this morning."

"Hmmm." Jesse moaned and turned over, pulling a skinny leg back under the hotel bedsheet and burying his face beneath the pillow. Gabe knew that Jesse'd had another nightmare last night, for he'd had to wake him from a crying spell. As usual, though, Jesse had refused to talk about it, so the most Gabe could do for him was tousle his hair, assure him of his safety, and tuck him back under the blankets. The boy was probably tired, but that served as no excuse for playing hooky from church. Memories flooded Gabe's mind of the many times he'd tried to feign a headache or sour stomach as a kid, and his mother's unsympathetic rejoinder that if he didn't have a fever, then God wanted him in church. Her reasoning may have been a bit extreme, but it had followed him into adulthood, and he meant to continue enforcing it with Jesse.

"Hey." Gabe sat on the edge of the bed. "I've been thinking. I have the day off today, so maybe after lunch, we'll head over to the livery to check on Zeke and Slate, then walk down to the pier and watch the boats. Might see some big ones comin' through the channel. Would you like that?"

That got Jesse's attention. He turned over and wiped the sleep from his chocolate-colored eyes.

The sanctuary was filled to capacity as folks stood to sing the closing hymn. The soles of Gabe's feet vibrated with the pipe organ's resounding chords. Rev. Cooper had delivered another rousing sermon, this one about God's faithfulness, unconditional love, goodness, mercy, and certain presence in uncertain times. Gabe appreciated the reminder, especially in light of all the changes he'd undergone: acquiring a new job, new friends, a new house—and a boy! He glanced down at Jesse, who still stuck to his side like a fly to honey. In that instant, deep emotion welled up in him for the child—tenderness, affection, and untold warmth. Without forewarning, Jesse Gant had wrangled his way straight into Gabe's heart, and the notion made him squirm with uneasiness. When the time came, how was he ever going to say good-bye to this boy?

For the tenth time that morning, his eyes snaked a path to Hannah Grace, standing just three pews ahead of him, a flowery hat atop her head concealing her mass of red curls. Ralston stood next to her; on her other side stood the rest of the Kane clan. A provoking knot rolled around in his gut. Why couldn't he keep his eyes off her, and what possessed him to resent the good doctor?

He wasn't envious. He refused to be envious!

Straightening his shoulders, he focused all his attention on the portly Rev. Cooper as he delivered the final benediction.

$\mathcal{K}$

Dazzling sunshine dispelled any hint of clouds as Hannah and Ralston traveled down Water Street in his horse-drawn coupe after a lovely Sunday dinner at the home of Edgar and Alice Carlton, owners of several thriving businesses, and long-time members of St. Elizabeth's Catholic Church in Sandy Shores.

Ralston waxed verbose. "Edgar sure seems engrossed with building a new hospital someday. He's already organized a committee and hired an architect to draw up initial plans. He's asked me to serve on the planning board, too, for which

I'm thrilled. Naturally, I'll want to be a part of the project as it moves forward. I'm glad he's so interested in coordinating an investment group. Perhaps your father will want to take part. Why, there's enough wealth in this town to get a dandy start on the fund-raising. Edgar said he's approached several businessmen in the area, including a few over in Mill Point, who are eager to see this dream come to fruition."

"Is that so?" Hannah replied. "A hospital would be a lovely addition to Sandy Shores, wouldn't it?" *Not to mention a boon to Ralston's career—increased clientele, a private nurse or two, perhaps a partner,* Hannah thought. Ralston had such lofty, ambitious goals. And, of course, she admired him for them.

"Much more than that, my dear; it would provide convenience, improve health care, increase property values, and give folks a sense of peace knowing they needn't travel clear to Grand Rapids should they need specialized care," said Ralston. "Of course, Muskegon is opening a fine facility next year, but that's still a hike for citizens of Sandy Shores."

Hannah looked at Ralston and smiled. "You and Edgar must have done quite a bit of talking while Alice showed me around her flower garden. It would have been nice to hear some of the discussion."

His roundish face lengthened to a frown, his brows slanting downward, indicating her statement took him aback. "I'm afraid you would have been quite bored by all of it. Edgar went into a detailed account of the financial aspects of such an undertaking."

A brown and white dog that looked to be the twin of the one they'd found hanging around outside Kane's Whatnot raced across their path in pursuit of a big tabby cat. Ralston had to rein in his horse to give the critters right-of-way, as did an oncoming carriage.

"Bored? Why would you say that? I enjoy hearing about such things, especially when they concern my community. Building a hospital is a very big venture, and it's not as if I don't have a business head. After all, I do take care of the books at Papa's store."

"Yes, well…" Ralston angled her with a dubious look and chuckled low in his chest, as if she'd just made a humorous remark. A tiny seed of indignation that he should assume she would be easily bored by intelligent conversation burrowed itself beneath her skin.

His expression softened. "You're looking quite lovely today, did I tell you that?"

She relaxed only slightly and tried to ignore the fact that he'd brushed over their tiny tiff. "Thank you."

His arms bobbed up and down with the tilting of the wagon as he held on to the reins. A smile formed beneath his mustached lip. "Emerald green always suits you well; it brightens up your pale features."

Without knowing it, he'd turned his compliment into a jab. Yes, emerald green was one of her best colors, but did he have to remind her about her pallid skin tone?

She stewed for a moment longer as they rode for half a block, the breeze cooling her heated cheeks.

"One of the first things I'd like to purchase for us, once my practice becomes better established, is a motor wagon," he announced unexpectedly, interrupting the gentle clip-clop of horses' hooves coming and going on Water Street. Passing them on the opposite side of the street was the Clemson family, all dressed in their Sunday duds and apparently on their way home from the potluck held at the First Baptist Church. Mr. Clemson waved a greeting, and Ralston returned the gesture. "There's a company in Massachusetts that builds gasoline automobiles. I think we'd do well to look into it."

His use of the words *us* and *we*, as if he expected her to accept his offer of marriage without any further thought or discussion, created a niggling sensation that started in her heart and moved downward to her toes, which started to wiggle impatiently. Somehow, she needed to broach the subject today without causing a stir. She had certainly considered marriage to Ralston, but only with her father's blessing, and only after she grew to know Ralston better. And then, there was that matter of *love*. Would she recognize it when it hit?

"Where would you get the gasoline to run it?" she asked.

He tossed her a confident look before directing his horse away from an oncoming buggy moving down the center of the street. "As folks catch on to this modern-day necessity, someone will start supplying filling stations, perhaps even scattering them all about town."

"Filling stations? Automobiles? It all sounds so, I don't know—modern. Whatever would you need a motorcar for when you have a perfectly fine horse and carriage? As a matter of fact, yours is one of the finest conveyances in town."

He looked pleased at her compliment. "True enough, but a motorcar makes a great deal of sense when you think of the miles I have to travel making house calls twice a week."

"That's true, I suppose. What about those electric cars I've been hearing about?"

Ralston shook his head and made the turn off Water Street, passing Sherman House's three-story structure. Without thinking, Hannah raised her head to see if she might guess which window went to the sheriff's room. Perhaps she'd catch either him or Jesse gazing out over the beautiful waterfront. *Foolish notion*, she chided herself silently.

"Those won't last. They run too slow, and the few who do own them complain about how frequently the batteries need to charge." He shook his head. "Not the least bit practical, in my opinion."

"Oh." She might have argued that the gasoline contraption seemed just as foolish to her as the electric car, but she held her tongue.

Giving up on finding Mr. Devlin's hotel window, she turned her gaze out over the channel to watch a family of ducks skimming the glassy water, their graceful moves leaving tiny ripples behind them. In a matter of months, they would be waddling on frozen ponds, seeking breaks in the ice to look for food and fluffing up their feathers for extra warmth. Most flew south to a milder climate, but many stuck out the cold and survived it just fine. Hannah pressed down her skirt when it lifted past her ankles in a light gust of wind, held the brim of her hat until the breeze let up, then settled her clasped hands in her lap.

When Ralston found a spot to park his rig, he reined in his horse, Gus, pulled the brake handle into position, and shifted in his seat to face Hannah, so as to gain her full attention. The black Morgan steed, tall and sleek, lowered his royal head and exhaled a fluttering breath from his nostrils.

"Now might be a good time to discuss our future wedding, perhaps setting the date, for starters."

"A date? So soon?" Tension such as she'd not expected coursed straight up her spine. "I didn't exactly accept your proposal yet, Ralston. I still need time to think it over." *And pray about it,* she added to herself. Why couldn't she verbalize that part? *Because we rarely discuss spiritual matters, that's why,* Hannah answered herself. A tiny thread of misgiving wove through the fibers of her conscience.

Lord, have I failed to put You first in my life? The thought rankled Hannah. Yes, she made a point to read her Bible every morning, but sometimes she wondered if she didn't do it more from habit or duty than from a devoted heart.

Wrinkles of worry etched into Ralston's forehead, joined by a few gathering beads of perspiration. He wiped the dampness with the back of his hand. "Naturally, I wonder why you didn't give me an affirmative answer last night, but now I'm supposing it's because it wouldn't appear proper for a lady to accept on the spot." He flashed her a forced smile and winked. "I wouldn't presume to understand the workings of a woman's mind, but I suppose it does make sense you'd need some time." He cupped her cheek in broad daylight as swarms of folks passed by. "How much time do you think you'll need to ponder the matter?"

Hannah's throat dried up like day-old toast. "Why must we be in a rush? And, well, you haven't even spoken to Papa about it."

That put an even deeper wrinkle in his brow. "Yes, well, I fully intend to do that. It's just—we've courted for several months." *Four, to be exact.* "And I assumed the news would please him. Oh, darling, I'm sorry if I've done it all backwards. I'll be sure to make amends with him. Last night just seemed so right to me, that's all."

Darling? He'd never used the endearment before, and hearing it now set off a burning sensation in her stomach.

"Have I missed the cues you've been sending?"

"Cues?"

"Well, I thought we had something wonderful going between us—our evening walks on the pier, our weekly dinners at Culver House, our shared plans for my medical practice." *Our shared plans?* "All the hopes and dreams I've so freely exposed to you."

And what of *her* hopes and dreams? Had he ever once asked her what they were? Did he even know or care how much she loved Kane's Whatnot and the citizens who shopped there?

And then, there was this matter of her heart. Ralston had proposed marriage, yet where was the mention of love? If she did indeed love him, and he her, shouldn't a river of passion and joy be surging through her veins about now?

Oh, Lord, am I missing something important here? Have You caused our paths to cross for a reason? Is it that I love him but simply can't identify the emotion? He is dear to me, yes, but shouldn't I expect an explosion of feeling?

"*He will fulfil the desire of them that fear him: he also will hear their cry, and will save them….The* LORD *will give grace and glory: no good thing will he withhold from them that walk uprightly.*"

The passages Hannah had memorized during that morning's Bible study—Psalm 145:19 and Psalm 84:11—brought a measure of comfort but did little to assuage her confused mind.

While she tried to form a proper response, Ralston scooted closer and lowered his face, as if he meant to kiss her on the spot. It would be their first. Should she allow it? In a sudden move, she prevented it by turning her gaze skyward. "What kind of bird is that?"

Ralston withdrew his face and looked up. "Where?" He had a keen interest in bird-watching and even subscribed to *Forest and Stream*, a periodical about outdoor life, which included ponderous information pertaining to various bird species. Hannah knew no better way to distract him now than to quiz him about his feathered friends.

"It's gone now. Some kind of pigeon or something, or maybe an eagle," she muttered while giving herself a chewing out for her deceit.

He laughed, a rarity for him. "That's like comparing a hog to a stallion, my dear. In other words, no similarity whatsoever." He continued to search the skies.

"Oh." To distract him further, she asked on a whim, "Shall we walk a bit, say, as far as the pier?" The matter of his proposal needed discussing, yes, but not now, not with her mind a big muddle.

In one fluid move, he draped the reins over the brake handle and jumped down. She watched as he proceeded around the conveyance in front of Gus. The horse snorted and swished his tail. Stopping at her side, he lifted a hand to assist her. Without ado, she accepted it and stepped to the hard earth, holding her skirts with her free hand.

They set off in silence along the wide wooden path beside the Grand River channel, worn by countless footprints and lined on both sides by tall dune grass. Half a mile ahead, the Sandy Shores lighthouse stood tall and dauntless as a faithful soldier, the catwalk leading out to it situated high above the rough waters of Lake Michigan. Many citizens, also enjoying

the balmy September afternoon, strolled past, some conversing, others simply watching the sights—waterfowl, small
boats, big vessels, and the occasional diver who dared leap off
the riverbanks to the rocky bottom. Here and there, fisher-
men threw out their lines in hopes of reeling in some supper.
About thirty feet ahead of them, a woman lost her hat to the
wind, complaining loudly to her husband when it landed in
the water and began its journey upstream, pheasant feathers
protruding out of the top. A few mallards swam over to investigate the newcomer, then glided away when the thing floated
too close for comfort.

Ralston reached out and took her hand, something else
he rarely did in public but now did without hesitation. "You
don't mind if I hold your hand, do you? After all, news travels
fast in this town. I daresay, a good deal of folks have heard
about my proposal and wouldn't be the least bit shocked to
see us walking along hand in hand."

Hannah supposed he was right. What could a little hand-
holding hurt—even though the humidity, not to mention her
nerves, had turned her palms sweaty?

She opened her mouth to reply, and, at that very
moment, spotted Jesse and Gabriel Devlin some distance off.
Thankfully, Ralston's eyes seemed intent on watching the
skies. Still bird-gazing. The handsome pair stood on the riv-
erbank, throwing stones into the channel, Gabe showing Jesse
how to make them skip along the surface. The two looked
more like father and son than sheriff and stray boy. Gabe
bent down to Jesse's level and placed a hand on his shoulder,
pointing with the other across the horizon, either describing
an incoming boat or explaining the proper technique of stone
skipping. She watched in hushed fascination.

Her heart took a tumble that was completely uncalled for, and suddenly, a worrisome question surfaced.

Why am I looking at the sheriff when I should have eyes only for Ralston?

Chapter Nine

Gabe spotted Hannah before Jesse did and quickly pointed him in the other direction, back toward the pier. His mood did not dictate a desire to confront the hand-holding lovebirds. For reasons he didn't feel like analyzing, he couldn't quite stomach the idea of her marrying Ralston Van Huff. "That's about enough stone skipping for one day, wouldn't you say? How about helping me count the boats coming into the channel?"

Jesse gazed up with interest and nodded his head.

"Let's go where we can get a better view, though. Come on." He hoped that when they reached the end of the wooden sidewalk, Hannah and her beau would turn around like all the other couples tended to do, not wanting to deal with shoes full of sugary sand.

"I count seven right there," Gabe said, pointing out at the rough waters of Lake Michigan while walking at a near jog.

Jesse poked him in the side, huffing to keep up, shook his head with fierce determination, and held up ten fingers.

"Ten? Are you sure?" Gabe looked again and spotted a couple of sailboats and a barge off in the distant horizon. "Ah, I didn't see them. Your vision's better than mine, sharper than an owl's at midnight."

Shoulders drawn back, Jesse nodded, looking proud as a rooster as they marched along.

"Hey, let's head for that sand dune over there. We'd get a great view from the top." He pointed across the railroad tracks and the dirt road beside it, the same one they'd traversed between Holland and Sandy Shores some weeks ago. Dunes that looked to be miniature mountains soared upward. Homes small and large nestled in the hillsides next to hardy trees that had managed to sprout from sandy soil. Between a big two-story gable-roofed structure and a tiny beach cottage was a narrow hiking path. Gabe wondered how in the world a horse pulling a wagon ever navigated up a steep hill like that in icy conditions. *But perchance they don't have to,* he reasoned. Several families from Chicago and elsewhere didn't even inhabit these parts in the winter months.

"Hello there, Sheriff," called a cavernous voice. Gabe turned at the sound and discovered Earl and Lillian Schusterman gaining on them, Lillian holding her hat with one hand and her wayward skirts with the other, Earl dragging her along by the arm. The wind generally picked up at the water's edge, and today was no exception. With the slightest bit of dread, he pulled Jesse to a stop. He'd met the middle-aged couple at the post office a few days ago when he'd gone in to find out the procedure for having his mail delivered to his new place of residence, and he quickly learned how much they loved to talk.

When they overheard him inform the clerk of his new address, Lillian approached him, beaming with delight. "Why, you're buying the Bronson house," she exclaimed. "We live just up the street. We'll be neighbors. Won't that be nice, Earl?" She slapped her husband's arm. "Think of it, the sheriff residing close by. It'll be the safest spot in town."

They stood and talked for several minutes about the neighborhood—which folks owned the howling dogs, who attended Sunday services and who didn't, the huge potatoes Vivienne Wildersmith's garden produced, and what covered dish Mrs. So-and-So had brought to the block picnic last July that had everyone oohing and ahhing. Gabe listened with as much interest as he could muster, knowing he had to get back to his office. He nodded at the appropriate times, chuckled at Earl's attempted jokes, and thanked Lillian profusely when she insisted on preparing his first week's worth of suppers just as soon as he moved in.

He inched his way to the door, even as they kept up their friendly banter. In the end, though, it was Mrs. Mortimer who saved the day when she walked in with a package under her arm, all in a huff about the drunkard swaying in the street and shouting obscenities in front of Howard's Blacksmith Shop. He'd promptly excused himself to tend to the matter but found no such person. After questioning several citizens, none of whom had seen or heard him, he figured the offender had either ambled down some alley and passed out or had found his way into another saloon. Whatever the explanation, it got Gabe out of the post office.

Now, here he was, facing the same predicament again.

"Ain't this a fine day, Sheriff? Won't be seein' many more of these once October gets here," Earl said.

Lillian Schusterman's smile revealed a wide gap between her front teeth. She tucked a few thick, gray strands of hair behind her ear and pressed her wide-brimmed hat further down on her head until it shadowed a good share of her liver-spotted face. "I declare, if it weren't for that cooling breeze coming off the lake, I could bake my bread in the sun today."

Earl gazed skyward and furrowed his brow in a partial frown. "*Farmer's Almanac's* predictin' a cold winter, so we best enjoy that sun while we can."

"Now, Earl, don't go talkin' like that. Besides, you can't put much stock in that book. Last year, they predicted a bad planting season for the Middle West, and it was the best we've seen in years."

Over Earl's gray, balding head, Gabe spotted Hannah and her intended about fifty yards off, halting their steps to gaze up at a flock of geese flying in V formation. No longer holding Ralston's hand, she had tucked her arm through his instead.

"You're right about that," Gabe chimed, forcing his attention off Hannah and onto the gabby couple. What difference should it make to him anyway what the woman with the rusty curls chose to do with her life? He had met her only weeks ago, and now that she was apparently betrothed to the fine doctor, he'd do well to stop staring at her.

As if Lillian Schusterman had just spotted Jesse standing there, she bent at the waist to acknowledge him. "Well, hello there, young man. What's your name?"

Obviously, she hadn't heard about Jesse's mute condition. Either that, or she figured she was exactly what he needed to come out of his shell.

Jesse sidled closer to Gabe, almost stepping behind him to avoid a confrontation.

Gabe put a protective hand on the boy's shoulder. "He's a trifle shy."

Lillian nodded without taking her eyes off Jesse, then bent closer and whispered, "I used to be like that—shy, I mean. You could hardly peel me off my papa if someone tried to speak to me after Sunday services. Why, I can still remember clinging to his pant legs while peeking out from behind his big, wide body. Oh, I felt so safe there."

Jesse gave her the tiniest hint of a nod and a smile, and she straightened, looking pleased that she'd gotten that much out of him. Turning her gaze to Gabe, she said, "I thought I heard you had a youngin' staying with you."

"Yes," Gabe replied, not wanting to give details.

Before she could press the issue, a young couple with two small children—a baby in a buggy and a toddling boy— stopped to greet the Schustermans. More neighbors, he learned, who lived one street over. After a brief introduction and a bit of small talk, Gabe tipped his hat at the small gathering and urged Jesse toward the railroad tracks.

But something caught the child's eye when he angled his head backward for one last glance—something that made his face brighten like the rising sun.

"Han—" he squeaked, looking beyond the cluster of people and pointing in the direction of Hannah Kane and Dr. Van Huff.

"Huh?" Shocked, Gabe went immediately to one knee and grasped the boy by his narrow shoulders, nearly shaking him out of his shoes. "What did you just say?"

He knew good and well, but he wanted Jesse to verify that he wasn't imagining it.

Looking as surprised as a caught fox, Jesse blinked twice and stared gape-mouthed.

"It's okay, buddy," Gabe urged. "You can trust me."

Jesse kept his eyes on Gabe. Then, lifting a hand, he pointed a finger in Hannah's direction. "Hannah," he said as clear as a newly polished bell. A tiny grin formed on his lips—not a confident one, by any means, but still, it was a start. Gabe's heart took a huge dip. *Dear Lord, he speaks. Please let this be the beginning of his healing.*

If he had any dread about meeting up with Hannah and Ralston, he dismissed it. Keeping a hold on one of Jesse's shoulders, he remained crouched and raised his face to search through the mass of ambling people. Finally, he spotted her in her long green gown, carrying her matching hat in one hand and sweeping at her unruly red curls with the other. Ralston strolled alongside her, hands secured behind his back, mouth moving in conversation as he nodded at passersby.

Gabe willed her to look over at him, and, when the pair came within twenty feet of him and Jesse, she did. Immediately, he hooked his index finger at her in a "come here" gesture. She halted and stared for a full five seconds, as if she were trying to make up her mind about the proper thing to do. Ralston followed her gaze, and, seeing her point of interest, scowled, said something, then tried turning her around by the arm.

"Come here," Gabe mouthed silently, hoping she would detect his urgency. She read his lips, lifted her green skirts slightly, and stepped down from the sidewalk to trudge through the sand, leaving Ralston on the wooden walk.

Jesse's eyes gleamed when he spotted Hannah. She spread out her arms to him, and he pulled away from Gabe, taking off on a run and spewing up sand with each eager stride. Gabe stood up and brushed off his pant leg, watching the two embrace in a friendly squeeze. Something rolled over in his gut—a wave of emotion he couldn't quite define. He lowered his gaze to focus on the toe of his boot, which seemed to be grinding a hole in the sand.

Hannah's flowery scent forced his chin up moments later. "How are you?" she asked, her arm resting on Jesse's shoulder. The doctor had trudged purposefully toward them until a neighborly gentleman stopped him mid-stride and set to talking his ear off. To say Ralston Van Huff looked pleased by the interruption would have been a barefaced lie. Gabe felt an inner satisfaction well up from some deep place.

Ridiculous.

He saw this woman every day. Why, now, did his tongue choose to cling to the roof of his mouth? She tipped her face at him, obviously waiting.

"Oh. Fine. He, I just—I thought you'd want to know that he said your name."

"What?"

"Jesse. He spoke your name a few moments ago." How he could sound so casual went beyond reason, particularly since his head was still reeling over the victory.

"He said my—you said my name, Jess?" Her voice went powdery soft as she dropped to both knees to look square into the lad's face, her eyes fixed on him like those of a tenderhearted mother on her child. "Can you say it now? Just for my ears?"

Teeth that looked too big for his miniature face latched onto his lower lip while he seemed to contemplate the pros and cons of repeating the act. He sucked in a deep breath. "Hannah," he whispered, loud enough for Gabe to hear over the Big Lake's pounding waves.

Hannah gasped and pressed the fingers of one hand to her mouth, her grin spilling out the sides. Her gaze lifted, making a connection with Gabe's eyes.

"Did you hear that, Mr. Devlin? Jesse Gant said my name."

Gabe tipped back on his heels and returned the smile, barely containing his slipping, sliding emotions. "I did, Miss Kane. I did indeed."

In the days that followed, Jesse offered only a few additional words, just enough to whet Hannah and Gabe's appetites, but none sufficient to reveal where he came from or to give them any hints about his family. One morning when Gabe dropped him off at the store, they watched him gallop out to the back stoop to check on the stray dog. Gabe leaned across the counter where Hannah was tallying the cash drawer contents and commented that they might never learn the full truth about Jesse Gant. He plopped his policeman's cap down in front of her and sighed.

"I've exhausted every lead that's come across my desk, and I still can't make head nor tail of where he's from—no recent missing children accounts, no recorded kidnap attempts, no hot-off-the-wire reports of any runaways." He stopped to run a hand through his blond hair. Hannah noted the ridge made by his hat in the middle of his forehead, and she had the oddest urge to run her finger over it. "There's always a current list, mind you, but nothing there matches Jesse's size, age, or description." He cleared his throat and leaned close enough to reveal the piney scent of his shaving perfume. "I've prayed countless times about this, Hannah. I want to know who that boy is and where he comes from, and I'm asking God to give me wisdom. And leads. I need leads."

While Hannah tried to count the bills under her nose, her heart hammered back at her, tangling her thoughts. *He prayed about Jesse? Gabriel Devlin prays?* Somehow, the notion warmed her body to the soles of her feet. To think the sturdy, strapping, self-reliant sheriff would admit his need for God's wisdom—why, put simply, it bedazzled her. When had Ralston ever confessed to praying about a specific need or problem? Never, in her recollection. But Mr. Devlin—why, he simply blurted out the fact that he'd prayed about Jesse's situation, and he made no apologies for it, either. This made a strong impression on her.

"You know, it's possible Jesse himself doesn't remember the events that landed him in the street, Hannah," he said, interrupting her thoughts.

It was one of the few times the sheriff had decided to linger at the store, and his presence made her lose count at sixteen dollars and seventy-three cents—*or was that sixty-three?* "Jesse has a story, Mr. Devlin, and we will get to the bottom of it. I'm certain of it. I've been praying myself that we'd find answers."

"Have you? I'm glad to hear it. He needs our prayers."

Something prompted her to look into his striking eyes, the brilliant blue of them reminding her of how the Big Lake looked on a cloudless, shiftless, summer day. But a second was all she allowed herself before she went back to counting.

"Something terrible happened to him, and it's up to us to help him get beyond those fears so he can tell us about it," she asserted. "He's a smart boy, did you know that?" she asked.

"I've never doubted it."

"Why, he doesn't miss a word I read to him. If I so much as turn the page before I've finished, he turns it right back and points to the paragraph I missed. He's a sly one, that Jesse. And those are not easy books. *The Wizard of Oz, The Prince and the Pauper, Black Beauty.*"

"You've read all those to him?"

"I've read chapters from each. He's trying to decide which one he wants me to stick with to the end." A lighthearted giggle erupted, which she quickly stifled with her hand.

"Why'd you do that?"

"What?"

"Why'd you stop laughing? It was nice. I bet you don't even know the way it lights up your face when you do it, like one of those electric streetlights out there." He propped the bulk of his weight against the counter, and she felt his nearness as she might the trenchant heat of an iron just inches from her face.

"Well, thank you." Oh, she hated when she blushed. Those splotchy red flushes just crept up on her and took no mercy. It was that cursed red hair and pale skin Grandmother Kane had passed down to her. She lowered her face and started counting all over again, laying out the bills and collecting her bearings. "Well, getting back to Jesse. He's a lot smarter than other boys his age, don't you think? His life experiences probably add up to a whole lot more smartness than you and me put together."

"Probably true."

"And another thing—"

"Shh." He reached out and covered her hands, forcing them down. "You're not counting that money, you know."

"I most certainly am." She stared down at the big, capable hand, rough and marred, and fought off a rising shiver. Ralston's hands were smooth—almost feminine, as any doctor's should be—but the sheriff's? They seemed to have endless stories behind them. And suddenly, she wanted to hear every one of them. How many fistfights, gunfights, barroom brawls, or murders might those hands have had a part in stopping?

"How can you count and yak at the same time?"

"What?" Another blush pushed up. *Blechh!* What was a woman to do when every kind of distraction destroyed her concentration?

His grin went into its usual lopsided tilt.

"How much do you have there in your hands?"

Rattled, she looked down and realized she hadn't a clue. "So far?"

Still grinning, he peeled her fingers off the tightly clutched cash.

"No one is to touch the cash in the box except for a Kane," she warned him.

"I'll take my chances with the law."

"That's Papa's law," she put in.

"Ah, a tad riskier, then."

In silence, she watched him sort out the bills and coins faster than a bullet leaves its casing, then slap them back into the drawer in their proper slots.

"Thirty-six dollars and seventy-nine cents. Rather a lot, don't you think? Ever worry about getting robbed?"

"Not particularly. Sandy Shores is a quiet place, especially since peak tourist season has passed."

"Crimes usually occur when folks least expect them, Hannah."

"That must be your lawman side coming out."

Flaxen eyebrows raised in a dressing-down fashion, and his eyes seemed to dig deeper than the surface. "I'm serious about this. You need to stay on your guard."

"Like now, you mean?" She looked down at the hand that had just grazed hers, and a boldness came over her.

He tossed back his head and gazed out the window where Jesse and his brown and white mongrel romped.

"He sure likes that mutt."

"Are you keeping something from me, Mr. Devlin?"

He turned and fixed his blue gaze on her face, running his eyes all over it. "It's a little too early to say."

Her chin sagged. "What do you mean? Is there some trouble brewing? Do you know something about Jesse you're not telling me?"

He sniffed and dredged up a faint smile. "Nothing to worry about just yet, but I'm not fooling you when I say you should stay on guard."

"Mr. Devlin, I've a right to know if Jesse's in danger."

He drew in a deep breath through his nostrils, then let it out slowly. "Yes, you do, and I'll be sure to tell you if he is." All at once, he reached up and snagged a lock of her hair, twirling it about his index finger while they measured each other for a second or two. "You ever plan to address me by my given name? I mean, it is a little silly, you treating me so formally when we see each other every day. Or would your fiancé object to that?"

Uncomfortable, she started to step around him, intending to hang the "OPEN" sign on the door, but he seized her by the wrist as she rounded the counter.

"Or is 'fiancé' premature? Have you given him your answer yet? I've been meaning to ask."

A hundred breaths clogged her throat until she feared a lack of proper breathing might make her light-headed. "Oh, if you must know, he is not my fiancé—yet, Mr…"

"Uh-uh!" He poked a warning finger in her face.

"*Gabe*," she emphasized, shoulders sagging in resignation. "Don't you have to go to work?" she asked in a shaky voice. "There might be crimes in the works at this very minute." It suddenly occurred to her that he'd far outstayed any other of his morning visits, and it bordered on downright improper.

Just then, the back door swung open and a gasping, wide-eyed boy ran through it, sliding to a halt in front of them.

"Dusty!" Jesse exclaimed, the grin spreading across his narrow face to reveal the gap in his teeth.

"What?" both adults asked in unison.

He hooked his thumb behind him. "Dusty!"

"I know. Some of those canned goods have been sitting there a while. How about I give you a cloth and…?"

His grin turned under. "No, I *mean* my dog!" he corrected. "He's Dusty."

"Well, the dirty mutt's probably never had a bath," Gabe said.

Jesse frowned, propped his hands on his hips, and stared at them as if they'd both gone loco. "His name. It's Dusty."

Realization struck Hannah and Gabe at the same time. "You've named him, then?" Hannah asked.

When Jesse gave them a satisfied nod, they all smiled, easing Hannah's recent tension. "Well, I guess that settles it, then," Gabe said. "Dusty stays."

Chapter Ten

"Well, so here you are. I've been looking all over the hospital for you, young man. Your mama would like to see you." The tall, skinny woman dressed in white from head to toe, starting with the stiff cap pinned into her flat hairdo and continuing down to her white, spotless shoes, wore a pale, rigid expression to match the rest of her. She crouched down beside Jesse, picking up the hem of her skirt to shield it from the mound of gray dirt he'd found on the side of the three-story, brick structure.

"You couldn't have found a cleaner place to play?" she asked in a severe tone, which he easily ignored because it seemed more important to study his work of art than to listen to her lecture.

Stick in hand, Jesse continued laboring over the picture he'd been drawing in the dirt, a square house with a front door and a big window, and, on the roof, a chimney with smoke swirling out the top in little ringlets. And those little round things in the front were flowery bushes, although he'd probably have to explain that to anyone who asked.

Also in his picture were a sun and moon because it was neither day nor night at this place. He'd determined that no one ever slept here, the bright electric lightbulbs hanging from the ceiling making it impossible, not to mention all the noise those nurses and doctors made. Off and on, his mother dozed, of course, but mostly she just coughed and cried when she didn't think he saw—and grew too weak to lift her hand to his cheek.

They'd made a little bed for him next to hers, something the cranky head nurse said completely broke the rules. Where else can he go, someone had asked, unless we send him to *the home*? The way they said *the home* made his gut squeeze into a hard ball.

He stared at his stick drawing, wondering what he could do to improve upon it. He wanted it to be nice since it would be the house he'd buy for his mother someday when she grew stronger and could breathe better. A frown pulled so tight across his brow that it almost hurt. The stupid house looked crooked. Out of anger, he drew a big line through it, then several more, until it was nothing more than a pile of dirt and dust.

The nurse seemed not to have noticed, just tugged him up by the arm. "Come on, brush yourself off now. Your mama's waiting for you."

When he walked through the door, his mother's brown eyes, mournful and saggy, brightened a smidgen at the sight of him. She looked skinnier than a twig, her black hair matted around bony cheeks, and he could hear her uneven breaths from across the room. "There's—my little—man," she said, her voice seeming to come from some far off place. She pulled out a scrawny hand from under the sheet and patted the bed. "Come—sit by—your ma."

The nurse nudged him forward. The bed stood high off the floor, but he managed to climb onto it by putting one foot on a chair and hoisting himself up. Once he was situated, the nurse, looking harried and distracted, left without a word.

"What have you been doing?" his mother asked.

He shrugged and angled his eyes at the scary looking machines and wires surrounding her bed. The sight of one tube attached to her arm by a long needle made his stomach churn uneasily.

"When you gonna leave this place, Ma?" he asked, impatient. For reasons he couldn't explain, his mother made him mad. Why'd she have to go get sick when they were just starting to figure stuff out? It had always been just the two of them, ever since his pa died in that horse accident a few years ago, that is, and she'd always promised him she'd never leave him. Times were tough, yes, but they were going to make it. She said so a hundred times. Now look at her.

Sadness crept into her eyes again. "I—I don't think I'll be able to leave, Jess, so—we need to talk about some things." She swallowed and winced. "Now, you have to—listen to me." It was difficult to hear her husky voice, so he leaned closer. She opened her mouth, but for a second or two, nothing came out. Then, "I have talked—to some people at The Children's Relief Society—and..."

A burning feeling filled his throat. "No! What you talkin' about? 'Course you're gonna leave." This he spoke too loudly for hospital rules. "You got that job at the rest'rant, remember? What'll that man think when you don't show up? And what about that new apartment you said we was gonna move into on 32nd Street?" His anger rose to new levels, and he felt guilty for it, but he continued ranting anyway. "All you need's a little more medicine, and you'll be fine. I ain't going to live with anybody but you."

"Don't say ain't," she murmured between shallow breaths. "How many times I got t' tell you it's not—proper English? If you want to—go places—in this world, y' got t' talk proper."

He didn't care about proper English. Mounting fear nearly swallowed him whole. "Let's go home today, Ma," he begged. "I can take care o' you. We can go back to that mission place and…"

She rubbed his arm with shaky fingers. "Shh. We can't go back there, my precious son. I—I'm very near to dying, I'm afraid."

He didn't know what it was that made him suddenly go still as a rock, but he did. In fact, he didn't even take a breath until his lungs screamed for air—he just sat there and stared at the big round clock over her head, watched its hands move in obedient strokes, counted each noisy, endless tick, tock, tick. In all the time they'd spent together—eight years next month—he'd never heard her talk like this.

"The Lord—will take care of you," she was saying. "You must learn to trust Him. People will—fade away, but God—will always be with you."

She continued pushing out words, but none of them made sense to Jesse, whose mind was still stuck on the "dying" word.

Finally, his gaze went back to her face. He felt tears rolling down his cheeks. With every ounce of strength his mother could muster, she dabbed at the tears with the corner of her sheet. "You got to be strong—you hear me? And brave. I'm goin' to—need you to be…"

Just then, she screwed her narrow face into a frown and took a gasping breath, which set off a string of coughs so loud that Jesse had to cover his ears. A nurse he had never seen before hurried through the door, looking all business-like. He jumped off the bed and ran to a corner, where he hovered, unseen, while his mother gagged and heaved and the nurse did things to the machines like flip switches and touch the wire going to her arm and yank her up to pat her back between her shoulders.

After an interminable time, she settled down, but the air coming through her mouth sounded raspier than before. Something with the weight of a rock lay heavy in his chest.

When the nurse left, he tiptoed close to his mother once more and touched her colder-than-usual hand tucked under the sheet.

He might have thought her dead right then if it weren't for the few hushed and garbled words eking by her dry, cracked lips. "L-love you, Jesse Ray."

He didn't know how long he stood there staring at the grayish face he used to consider the prettiest sight in the world.

⌒K⌒

Dusty nudged Jesse out of his trance, a long stick clenched between his teeth, eyes pleading with him to give the twig a good toss. Seated on the bottom step of the back stoop, he reached up and rubbed the dog's velvet ear, then made a fast swipe at the dampness around his own eyes. He'd been thinking a lot about his ma lately, which always made him sad, so he welcomed Dusty's interruption.

"What you want?" he asked the brown and white pooch, giving him a friendly pat and watching dirt particles drift through the air. Dusty whined and tilted his head to one side, eyes and ears drooping in equal amounts.

"Okay," he relented, wrenching the stick from the dog's mouth and throwing it as far as his arm would allow, almost to the back alley, where horses and buggies passed in steady succession. Dusty whipped his lean body around and dashed after the stick. In the distance a train whistled, indicating its approach.

With the whistle, another memory floated to the surface, this one of the time he'd hitched a ride on a car toward the back of a train to get to the next town. When he slipped through the crack in the big doors, he was surprised to discover a roomful of freeloaders, mostly guys with long, unshaven faces, hats that shaded their shifty eyes, and ratty clothes that stank so bad he nearly retched.

"Where you off to, kid?" a toothless fellow asked, his back against the wall, legs drawn up, one bony knee sticking out of a three-corner tear. "Hain't you got no family?"

Jesse had slid to the floor, playing brave. He placed his tiny pack of supplies next to him—mostly stuff he'd found in garbage barrels—and let his eyes adjust to his new surroundings. He shrugged in nonchalance. It took every ounce of courage he could muster not to let the tears fall. "Nowhere special," he answered, settling against the hard wall, wanting to close his eyes but wondering if it was safe. His young bones were weary from running.

"Ain't you a might small for gallivantin'?" asked another drifter, this one hunched and wrinkled and looking every bit as ancient as Mr. Carver, the man who sold fruit from his kiosk on Becker Street, a four-block walk from the mission where he and his ma used to live. He'd passed the little market every day on his way to second grade at Edison School, and, if he was lucky, Mr. Carver would slip him a shiny apple to add to his meager lunch sack.

"I'm older 'n I look," Jesse said, sitting up taller.

"Yeah?" the drifter asked. "What's you got in that bag? You got anythin' good in there?"

Jesse placed a hand over his little bundle, ready to protect it from the first guy who tried to wrest it from him. It wasn't much, but it was all he had to his name.

"Leave the kid alone," boomed a voice from the back. "First one who lays a hand to him or his belongings answers to me."

At that, a hush fell over the gathering; shortly thereafter, the train started moving, then humming, over the tracks. Jesse meant to thank the stranger later, but the whirring sound lulled him to sleep, and, by the time the big locomotive crawled to a stop at St. Joseph's train station and he opened his eyes, it was too late for thanking anyone. They'd all jumped off ahead of him, leaving him the lone passenger.

Dusty loped back with the bone and dropped it at his feet. Jesse picked it up and heaved it out over the yard again, watching the dog dart away.

"That's a nice dog you got there."

Startled, Jesse leaped to his feet, an instinctual reaction he'd acquired from months spent on the run. A boy about his age and size stood at the edge of the yard, pail in hand. Jesse had spotted him on prior afternoons at the same time, cutting through the plot of land between Kane's Whatnot and DeBoer's Hardware. Until now, though, he'd managed to stay in the shadows. He mentally kicked himself for not noting the time more carefully.

"What's your name?" asked the boy, boldly crossing the yard in his direction. Dusty dropped the stick from his mouth and ran to greet the newcomer, not at all the intimidating watchdog Jesse had hoped he would be.

Jesse's mouth went as dry as the stick Dusty insisted on chasing. So far, he had spoken only to Gabe and Hannah; even with them, he barely dared utter more than a couple of words before his stomach tied into a pinching knot. Talking did not come easily to him, even though he couldn't explain why that was, exactly.

People plain scared him, and that was about the gist of it. It hadn't always been the case, but after his ma died, something snapped in him—something that got only worse when those hospital people hauled him off to a big home full of orphans. As if that wasn't enough, in May, some people put him on a train with a whole bunch of other kids to find him a new family. The last thing he'd wanted was a new family, but how could he argue with a bunch of adults who thought they had all the answers? Along the way, he witnessed fistfights on the train, his food was stolen daily by bullies, he was knocked to the ground by a big kid waiting in the food line, he listened to screaming children with runny noses, and, once, he got so sick with fever that he begged God to let him die.

At each new town, an agent urged Jesse off the train, then quickly pushed him to the side for an "inspection." Inspections usually involved orders to pull back his shoulders and fix his wrinkled collar. On occasion, the agent even spit-polished his dirty cheeks. In the end, though, the agent would frown, as if to say, "There's only so much one can do with a face like that."

Next, he'd push him into a long line with dozens of other children, each to be examined by the careful eyes of adults from the town. Some who arrived simply as husband and wife walked off as a family, taking with them a child, or, in some cases, several children.

Jesse could have tried harder to be polite in these towns, but he didn't want to imagine living with anybody but his own mother. "He's too frail for my taste," one woman said of him. "Must've had small parents." He'd wanted to spit at her, but the agent would have punished him on the ride back to New York, so he'd tried to think of other things—like when his mother was alive and they'd walked to Central Park to play on the big rocks.

Then, there was the tall, big-nosed woman with pimples who'd lifted his chin with a pointy finger and made him open his mouth. "That a cavity in there, or just a speck o' food?" she asked. "I ain't got money for takin' you to the dentist right off the bat." As simple as that, she dropped his chin and moved on, leaving him to send his tongue on a quick cavity search, only to find a tiny black bug that had somehow found its way into his mouth.

Big-Nosed Lady moved on down the line and selected a little girl with long, blonde hair. "You'll do fine," she'd said, taking her by the hand and marching off with her, as if she'd just found herself the cutest pup in the litter.

The boy now approaching him held a curious gaze, but he looked harmless enough. In fact, he looked about as dangerous as Dusty. Still, Jesse wasn't up for questions, the mere thought of which rattled his nerves. What if he asked hard questions: "Who's your real family?" "Where did you come from?" "How come you don't go to school?"

Jesse stuck his hands deep in his jean pockets and studied his shoes, which were unusually clean for a boy his age. In fact, the clothes Hannah and Gabe had given him showed nary a speck of dirt from play.

He lifted his face when the boy was within a few feet of him. The first thing he noted about him was the spray of freckles peppering his face—and then the grin that exposed a top row of crooked teeth. He wore knickers that came well above his knees and sported stain. His dirty shirttail hung out, covering the clips on his suspenders, and a tawdry cap was parked sideways on his dark brown mop of straight, poky hair. The boy reminded Jesse of how he'd looked only weeks ago, before Gabe and Hannah took pity on him.

Rather than ask permission, the boy helped himself to the top step, stretching out his lanky legs and tossing aside his dented lunch pail. Dusty's tail wagged like a flag in the wind as he licked the boy's freckles.

"Hey, it's okay by me if you rub those stupid things off'n my face, but my Grandma Hiles won't be too happy 'bout it. She says they're the diamonds God's gonna use for decoratin' her crown o' glory some day." He laughed and caught Jesse's eye, but Jesse remained silent and wary.

When it looked like Dusty might be wearing his welcome thin, Jesse nabbed him by the scruff of his neck and pulled him to his side.

"He part hound or somethin'? He's a nice dog. Hey, I hear you been livin' with Sheriff Devil."

The misuse of Gabe's last name brought up his defenses. "Devlin," Jesse corrected him.

The boy shot him a sly smile. "Just checkin' t' see if you was payin' attention. I thought maybe you was missin' yer tongue or somethin'."

Anger brewed under his skin, but he remained careful not to let his mask slip. As much as he wanted a friend, he wasn't about to let down his guard.

"My name's William Bruce Hiles, but my ma and grandma calls me Billy B. You can, too, if you want. Or drop the B. Makes no matter. I'm nine. How old are you?"

Jesse pushed his hands deeper into his pockets and shifted his position.

The boy sized him up through narrow green eyes. "That's okay, you don't have t' tell me. I'll just tell you some stuff about me. My pa, he ain't around. Ma used to tell me he was dead, till I turned five, when I guess she thought I was old enough for the truth. He's in jail, 'cause he kilt his own brother, Tom Hiles, in a barroom. I wasn't even born yet, so I never met 'im, not that I'd want to, mind you. Ma said if I didn't hear the truth from her then some ol' chatterbox 'round town was bound t' tell me." He leaned forward to look past Jesse, through the clearing of trees just adjacent to an old, unused outhouse at the back of the Kane property. "See that little white story-and-a-half over there behind that big oak tree? There's a big red bush by the front step."

Jesse squinted to see which one he meant, as there was a block of houses all similar in features.

"Yellow door?" Jesse heard himself ask.

"Yep, that's the one. That's where Grandma Hiles, Mama, and me live. Grandma Hiles is my ma's mother-in-law. I have a sister ten years older 'n me, can you believe it? Plus, she's married. Mama says Katrina shouldn'ta got married so young, but y' can't talk blood out of a turnip—or somethin' like that. In other words, y' can't talk 'er out of somethin' once she gets 'er mind made up. Mama's used to the whole thing now, though, and she likes Micah plenty. He's older than Katrina by five years, so that makes him twenty-four. Seems ancient, don't it?"

Jesse nodded, overwhelmed by all the words flying at him. Maybe he wouldn't have to worry so much about questions since Billy B seemed pretty intent on doing all the talking.

"Wanna know what we learned in science today?" Billy B asked.

Jesse's ears perked up. He'd always enjoyed science. Shoot, he liked all his school subjects and never once earned a poor grade. His ma used to call him a genius, but he'd never go that far.

He hoped his nod didn't show an abundance of enthusiasm. There was no sense in giving Billy B high hopes for earning his friendship, even though the idea seemed appealing.

Billy B scooted over and patted the space beside him on the top step. "First, you got to at least tell me yer name."

He might have known there'd be a hitch to getting a free science lesson. He sucked in a noisy breath. "Jesse."

The boy raised his thick, brown eyebrows. "That's it? No middle or last name?"

"Ray. Jesse Ray Gant," he supplied. "I'm eight."

Billy B looked thoughtful. "Yer little for your age, but you'll probably grow tall when you get in the bigger grades. That's what happened to Joe Cort, you know. Everyone says he was a pip-squeak till he got in ninth grade. Just like that, he took off and never stopped till he was eighteen. Now he's somethin' like eight feet tall."

"Huh?"

"Well, I don't know my feet an' inches that good, but when you see 'im walkin' down the street, you know it's him."

Billy B slanted his eyes down to study a loose thread coming out of his pants. He gave the thing a pull, and several more inches came loose from the fabric. It didn't seem to bother him, though, as he set to winding the excess thread around his index finger. "You'd be in my grade, third—if you come to school, that is. I'm older'n you, but I flunked first grade. Couldn't read them big readers. All the letters kept turnin' 'round on me. I still don't get it very good, but I'm good at science. And world history, too. Those are my whiz subjects. Math's pretty easy, most days. What's your whiz subjects?"

Bored, but contented enough, Dusty curled up at the foot of the steps and closed his eyes.

Overhead, the wind rustled the leaves, which were fast turning from green to oranges and golds. In the gentle breeze, several more leaves broke free of their branches and settled to the ground, adding to the already orange-brown, crispy blanket.

"R-reading, I guess. W-what about—that—science lesson?" Jesse asked, still timid.

"Oh yeah, I forgot. Okay. Mr. Middleton, ar teacher, took two balloons."

"You have a man teacher?" Jesse didn't know that men could be teachers.

"Yeah. Anyway, he takes these two balloons. One of 'em, he blows up; the other'n, he puts a quarter cup o' water in first. Then, he blows it up."

"Young or old?"

"What—the balloons?"

"No, the teacher." He was starting to like this kid.

"Oh, old. He's around twenty-nine."

"That's not old."

Billy B rolled his eyes. "You want for me to tell you about the science lesson or not?"

For the first time in a long while, Jesse felt near to laughing. "Yes."

"Okay, so he lights a match under the balloon with no water, and poof! The thing pops. Made Margaret Wilderdeek jump clear to the moon."

Jesse covered his grin with his sleeve.

"Then, he sticks a flame under the balloon with water in it—right where the water's sittin', you know, and guess what? That balloon didn't pop, even though he let the flame touch the balloon. It's 'cause the water in the balloon—what's that word?—absorbed the heat from the flame, so the rubber in the balloon didn't get too hot to break. Water is a good, um, absorber of heat. It takes a lot of heat to change the temperature of water. He told us other stuff about why water in teakettles takes a long time to boil and why the ocean helps keep land warmer in cold months, but he lost me there. Besides, I was still thinking about how Margaret Wilderdeek's face looked when that balloon popped."

This triggered an unexpected spurt of laughter from both boys, and, when it happened, the pair fused together like paper to glue.

They sobered in seconds. Billy B picked up the stick that Dusty had between his paws. When he did, the mutt leaped to his feet. Billy B gave it a toss and they both watched Dusty zoom off. "You don't have to talk to me if you don't want to," said Billy B. "Some things take time."

A thousand rivers of relief flooded Jesse's veins.

Just then, the screen door opened and Hannah stood over them, a platter in hand. "I've brought you some cookies and lemonade."

"Cookies?" Billy B jumped to his feet quick as a cricket to survey the plate of cookies, no doubt looking for the biggest. "Mmm, sugar cookies, my favorite."

Hannah laughed. "Take two," she offered. Then, dipping her face down to study Billy B's, she said, "You're Katrina Sterling's little brother. Did you know she's best friends with my sister, Abbie? 'Course, now that Katrina's married, I don't think they see each other quite as often as before."

Billy B looked thoughtful. "I know Abbie. She used to come over and tell us jokes. Gabby Abbie. That's what Kat calls 'er. She's real funny. My ma said she should be in show business."

Hannah laughed. "That's our Abbie." She glanced from Billy B to Jesse. "Well, I see you two are busy talking, so I'll just set this tray down here and leave you be."

She winked at Jesse before turning to go back inside, and the tightness he'd felt around his chest for days slowly let up.

Chapter Eleven

October had drained the last of summer's warmth, ushering in a cold start to the month of November. Rufus shivered under his thin jacket and pulled tight the flank cinch on his horse's saddle. The critter balked and sidestepped, missing Rufus's big toe by an inch.

"Hey, watch it, y' dumb brute," he sneered, coughing up a wad of tobacco juice and spitting it at the horse's hoof.

He took a gander at his boys, still hunkered over the fire and grousing about having to get up on such a cold, windy morning. He pulled his watch from his pocket. Already going on seven. From their vantage point up in the hills, surrounded by thick woods, they had no view of the Big Lake, but they sure heard its pounding surf; today, it resonated like a thousand hungry lions.

"You lazy fools," he muttered under his breath. His horse flicked its tail and bent back its ears. "I ain't talkin' to you, for a change," he said to the horse.

"I'm goin' into town on business. You boys clean up this camp. We'll be movin' on soon."

"Movin' on?" asked Roy, coming to life. "How come y' ain't told me nothin' 'bout it?"

Rufus's patience had worn thin over the past few weeks with that rotten little kid still on the loose, and he'd taken his vexation out on his boys, even backhanding Reuben last week when he had the nerve to question his decision to stay in Holland a few more days. If there was one thing he always made clear to his boys, it was that he ran this outfit; if they didn't like it, well, they could just move on, knowing that if they did, they wouldn't get far. He would make sure of it himself. He liked being the one in control, but sometimes, maintaining that position meant instilling a little old-fashioned fear.

He finished saddling his horse and prepared to mount.

"Pa!" Roy said, leaping to his feet. "What are y' plannin' on doin'?"

Irritation cut deep. He climbed in the saddle, wincing with the pain of old bones gone arthritic, and tugged on his beard. "You don't go worryin' over my every move, y' hear? You ain't in charge—leastways not yet. I tol' y' I got business in town. That ol' biddy who owns that restaurant in the center of town tol' me yesterday she saw some little straggler a few months back. Diggin' through garbage, he was. Said I ought t' come back this mornin' and talk t' some guy name of Vanderslute who comes in there pert near ev'ry mornin'. Said he might know somethin'. So there. I'm goin' to talk to him. That make y' feel any better?"

"I thought you tol' us we was to lay low, not talk to folks, just keep ar eyes and ears peeled for clues," Roy said, blatant challenge in his eyes.

"You got any clues yet, turkey brain?" It wasn't often he allowed himself to rant at Roy, his number one supporter, but every now and again, Roy needed it bad as the other two.

Roy hung his head and poked his boot around in the dirt. Good. "Now, listen up. I want this camp lookin' just as it did before we got here, wild and rustic. Put that fire out, throw dirt over it, haul some logs over top, hide any trace of us, y' hear? Chances are, no one's seen hide ner hair of us anyway, but we ain't takin' no chances."

No one appeared to be in any big hurry.

"Move!" he yelled. This got their attention. "When I get back, I want you boys ready to ride." He kicked his horse in the side, and the gelding jolted. "And start lookin' alive!" he ordered.

K

Six forty-five. Gabe had lain awake for the past hour, not wanting to disturb Jesse, who had slept soundly through the night, for a change. Something seemed different with him lately—it was like he'd turned a big corner. His words were coming out better these days, as the precarious trust he'd placed in both Hannah and Gabe grew in tiny increments. And then, there was that boy he met, Billy B—someone Hannah knew and said would be a good friend for Jesse. Gabe prayed that was so. He'd grown very protective of the lad, sometimes wondering how he would give him up if they ever found his parents, even if they proved to be good people.

"Lord, I pray You'll give me direction as to the next steps for this boy," he whispered, lying on his back and staring at a spot on the ceiling. The ceiling that needed a new paint job.

No light shone through the windows yet, but a low-burning kerosene lamp provided enough light to pinpoint its flaws.

He had lived here for three weeks, and though he enjoyed having a place of his own, it wasn't till after he'd moved in that he'd noticed the imperfections—cracks in the walls, ruts in the wood floors, peeling wallpaper, and rusty pipes. And, as if that wasn't enough, an outhouse needing a new hole! He supposed that's what he got for giving the place no more than a perfunctory look before purchasing it.

He drew in a deep breath and pulled a bare leg out from under the blankets. "All in good time, Lord," he muttered. "I thank You for the blessings You've given me, and this house is one of them."

Outside, he heard a beckoning neigh and an answering bray, and he grinned to himself. At the same time every morning, Slate and ol' Zeke the Streak let him know they expected their breakfast of oats. It appeared they'd had a bit of pampering over at the livery, but that was okay by him. He'd rested easier knowing they were in good care. They'd had some adjusting to do in their new environs—a meager shed with three stalls that was tighter and cozier by far than what they'd had in Ohio on the Devlin ranch, and then over at Enoch Sprock's roomy livery. *But they'll survive the cold just fine*, he told himself, figuring they'd probably be more comfortable in their smaller confines, what with all the straw he would provide.

Jesse rolled over and whimpered like a pup, not yet awake but fighting his way to the surface of consciousness. He had his own room, but so far, Gabe hadn't convinced him to take ownership of it, even though a thin wall was all that separated his room from Jesse's. "Look, I can give you a little knock to let you know I'm here, and you can knock back. It'd be like our own special little code," he'd said shortly after moving into the house.

Jesse had looked partially impressed by the idea, and he'd started out that night in his own bed, knocking on the wall every few minutes and Gabe knocking back. But when Gabe had drifted off to sleep and stopped reciprocating Jesse's knocks, the boy had padded into Gabe's room and crawled under the covers. It wasn't until the next morning that Gabe had discovered the mite of a boy snoring into his back. Since then, he'd given up, even though he wasn't wild about sharing his bed with a wiggly worm.

Time. That's what he needs. But a niggling thought told him it was much more than that.

Gingerly, Gabe pulled back the comforter, snagged his pants off the bedpost, and stepped into them. Coffee. He needed coffee. He'd drink a couple of cups while reading his Bible, then tend to the animals, wash up, and put on his uniform before hauling the youngster out of bed.

A kind of restless, nameless energy coursed through his body as he went about his morning chores, but it wasn't until he put a razor to his face, leaned into the mirror, and looked square into his own eyes that he discovered the reason behind it.

Hannah Grace Kane.

He was getting downright accustomed to seeing her every morning, if not anxious to do so.

K

Just before seven, the windup alarm clock pealed off its annoying clang.

"Up and at 'em, dear sisters," came Abbie's equally annoying announcement. *Oh, how did she do it? How did she manage to rise before the entire household and appear ready for anything?* Hannah wondered, rolling over on her side and taking her pillow with her, pressing it over her head to block the torturously bright lightbulb hanging directly over her bed.

"Abbie, please pull the switch on that light."

"I can't. You'll go back to sleep."

"Which I am allowed to do," she muttered with a groggy morning voice.

"You know how angry you get with yourself when you oversleep." Abbie pounced on her bed like a cat eager for play, which made Hannah groan.

Across the room in the other bed, Maggie rolled over and groused, "How can you be so chipper in the morning, Abigail Ann? It's simply not fair." Her tone, ill-humored and whiny, put a smile on Hannah's face, cueing her to cover her mouth with the corner of her blanket. She let her eyes adjust to the light while Maggie droned on about the negative aspects of morning. "It seems I just close my eyes, and minutes later ,the sun's up. Why, oh, why, can't I set aside one morning for sleeping in?"

"Oh, pooh, listen to you!" Abbie chided. "You slept in Saturday morning."

"Till eight o'clock," Maggie said. "That's *not* sleeping in."

"It is, in Grandmother's eyes."

"Aargh! Six o'clock is sleeping in to Helena Kane," Maggie grumped, pulling the blankets back over her face in one dramatic move.

Abbie made a production of bounding off Hannah's bed, sprinting across the room, and thrusting herself across Maggie's covered body. Maggie made a distant, muffled squeal beneath the weight of her younger sister. When the tickling began, it was all-out war, interspersed with fits of wild laughter and even more bellowing, the old bed springs squeaking in loud protest. At one point, all Hannah saw was Abbie upended in a whoosh of pink and white petticoats. She giggled at the sight.

As Hannah watched the two go at it, memories flooded of days gone by—days they'd played with dolls and other toys, danced to silly tunes, frolicked in the backyard, skipped rope, walked to school, and even squabbled for no good reason. She tried to picture life apart from her sisters and couldn't quite do it.

How things would change if she married Ralston. *If.* What a big word for only two letters. She knew Ralston's impatience for an answer grew daily, but she still sat on the fence, wondering what to tell him, trying to determine her exact feelings for the dear man. And he *was* dear. Lately, he'd been more attentive—asking her about her needs, inquiring about her day, complimenting her appearance, even holding her hand more frequently. There were no recent kissing attempts, but that didn't bother her in the least. His occasional pecks on the cheek or forehead satisfied her plenty.

He even spoke to her father about the proposal, and, although Ralston hadn't divulged the details about their conversation, her father had told Hannah that he would give them his blessing, providing they both prayed about it and determined the marriage to be in line with God's perfect will.

God's perfect will? How did one ever ascertain such a thing? Hannah read her Bible dutifully, a chapter from the Old and New Testaments and two Psalms daily. Moreover, on her morning walks to the Whatnot, she thanked God for all His blessings and prayed for her family and friends, particularly Jesse. Most of her prayers were for others, though, as it seemed rather selfish and presumptuous to mention her own needs, much less express the many questions she had about determining His will. It all seemed so complicated and unattainable. She imagined a huge Being sitting upon His throne, issuing out instructions on matters of war and poverty, certainly not matters pertaining to simple little Hannah Grace Kane.

Maggie and Abbie saw things differently, believing God cared about the everyday things of life. If ever anyone walked passionately and intimately with Him, it was Hannah's sisters. Quiet, sweet, resolute, and dedicated Maggie served the Lord with tireless determination, always looking for one cause or another to sink her teeth into; boisterous, outspoken Abbie was ever fervent in her faith.

While her sisters continued romping and wrestling on the bed, Hannah did some mental wrestling of her own. Did Ralston Van Huff strive to bring out the best in her, build her confidence, and encourage her on matters of faith and prayer? Her stomach clenched uneasily. Could she even be certain Ralston possessed a wholehearted faith?

Quite unexpectedly, the image of Gabriel Devlin's face popped into her mind. Now, there was a man not afraid to show his faith—*why, he spoke out, unabashed, about how he prayed for Jesse.*

She shook herself back to reality. Tonight, Ralston would take her to Culver House for dinner. Perhaps this evening would prove the defining moment in their relationship, particularly when she asked him where he stood with God.

"Stop it! Stop it this instant, Abigail Kane, or I will cut your hair off the next time I catch you sleeping."

"Ha! If you do, I'll paint your face black while *you're* sleeping."

Hannah narrowed her eyes on her scuffling sisters, hearing enough. In one fast maneuver, she tossed back her blankets, leaped from her bed, and ran across the room, throwing herself atop the pair and creating an even bigger fracas.

⌒ *K* ⌒

Rubbing his freshly shaven face, Rufus McCurdy surveyed the little restaurant for an available table. He hoped his new duds, complete with tweed trousers, Western shirt and bow tie, and brand-new socks and shoes would conceal his identity. A new wool coat hung loosely over his arm, his handsome new hat dangling off his hand. The same hand that had made a clean sweep over his smooth face now combed through his fresh haircut as he took a deep breath, trying to appear calm.

A few heads turned when he closed the door behind him, the "Open" placard that was hanging by a chain flapping against the glass. Out the corner of his eye, he noted whether any patrons appeared overly interested in his presence, then quickly relaxed when they all returned their attentions to their breakfasts.

"Table over in the corner," a man behind the serving counter ordered, pointing with his spatula. *The cook?* It must have been, for he wore an apron bearing witness to splattered grease, catsup, and mustard. Rufus nodded his thanks and made a path through the densely arranged tables. Now and then, someone acknowledged him with half a nod or a silent, disinterested glance. He pulled back a spindly chair and sat down, glad to have a corner table where he could keep an eye on customers coming and going.

Where is that scrawny old thing who owns this place? Eva somethin' or other. As if she'd heard his private thought, Eva appeared from behind a closed door, three heaping plates balanced on her skinny arms, and maneuvered her way to a table near him. Plunking the plates down in front of three men in business attire, each one smoking a pungent cigar, she promptly headed for the coffee pot, then came back to refill their cups. The one with his back to Rufus thanked her profusely, then drew her down to him and whispered something in her ear. She slapped him on the shoulder and snickered. Without delay, she moved over to Rufus next. He had wondered whether she'd noticed him. *Must have eyes in the back of 'er head*, he ruled. Setting down the coffee pot on the empty table next to him, she removed a pad of paper from her pocket and a pencil from behind her ear.

"What ken I get y', mister?" she asked, gaze fixed on her pad.

"Is that feller here you was tellin' me 'bout yesterday?"

She jerked her head up and angled him a beady stare. "I cain't recall ever talkin' to you. Not yesterday, anyhow."

It gave him a powerful rush to know that his disguise had worked. He sat up a little straighter, pride welling up, and thumbed the navy suspenders that helped hold up his tweed trousers. "Guess I clean up good, huh?"

She stepped back and tilted her face, giving him a hawk-like stare. Then, she lowered her pointy chin in confusion. "When was y' in here?"

"Yesterday, 'round two. Had me a big bowl o' bean soup."

Looking skeptical, she asked. "What's yer name?"

"S-Smith," he stammered, caught off guard. *Drat! I couldn't come up with somethin' more original?* "Gomer Smith." At least the first name had a unique ring. "I come from up in Iowa." *Is Iowa up?* "I tol' y' I was on the lookout for my cousin's kid. Seems he disappeared a few months back, and they's, uh, there's a whole bunch of us out searchin' for 'im, includin' the law."

It was downright difficult keeping his speech half decent, not to mention his lack of know-how hidden.

She sank her second finger into her hollow cheek, as if waiting for something to register. Suddenly, her little brown eyes popped. "Ah, you! Now, I remember." She tilted her face and studied him further. "Yep, you plumb changed, all right, got yerself a haircut and—and what else? Y' shaved! Well, I'll be."

He nodded, wanting to get on with things. Her loud, raspy voice rallied a few customers, causing their heads to raise and turn. His nerves set to jangling.

"Y' want some coffee?" she asked, pouring before he had a chance to say he'd rather have tomato juice. He'd already had three cups of stiff, black brew back at the camp.

"So, yer lookin' for that kid, eh? Yeah, Vanderslute's here t'day. Right there, matter o' fact." She turned her body and pointed. "Hey, George! Man here wants to talk t' you."

Two tables over, the fellow with his back to Rufus, the one who'd whispered something in Eva's ear, swiveled on his chair, a half-smoked cigar hanging out from under his pencil-thin mustache. "What's that?" he asked, sticking the cigar in an ashtray.

"This feller's got some questions for y' 'bout that kid that was hangin' 'round here way back in August."

"Oh yeah? Don't know as I can tell you anything. That was a while ago." The man pushed back in his chair, rose, and came directly to his table, perching over him with owl eyes.

"George, this here's Gomer Smith. Hails from Iowa. What city did you say yo'r from?" she asked.

Horse hockey! City? I don't know no stinkin' cities in Iowa.

George leaned forward, looking keenly interested.

"Well now—I didn't tell you—and for good reason," he blurted, fishing in his shallow head for the good reason.

Both Eva and George stared at him intently and waited while nothing but the sounds of gabbing patrons, shuffling newspapers, and grating forks and knives came between them.

Before Rufus made an even bigger fool of himself, George grabbed his hand and gave it a hearty shake. "Well now, Aunt Eva, it's not important what city he comes from. What's important here is ar good manners." His mouth slanted into a grin, and, quick as a steal trap, he pulled out a chair and sat down. Rufus wasn't sure if he should relax or keep his guard up good and high. He clasped his hands in a tight knot and plopped them in the center of the table, then quickly thought better of it and stuck them in his lap. *Tarnation! I wouldn't know good manners if they up and bit me in the backside.*

"Aunt Eva, bring this here man a big plate of bacon and eggs. That suit you, uh, uh—?"

Rufus had to think a minute. "Gomer," he supplied. Then, to Eva, he affirmed, "Yeah, that's fine."

Eva hobbled off as fast as her wrinkled old body would take her.

"Ah, sorry 'bout that, Gomer. Rememberin' names is one of my bad points."

"Yeah, I know what y' mean."

"Now then, what's your interest in that little fugitive?"

Rufus proceeded to weave a tale he'd only half thought out ahead of time. Dim-witted, he was, for not plotting out his words more carefully. *What must this George fella think of me?* he wondered. But George's questions fueled his lies, lending him confidence to continue, and, by the time he finished, his zigzagged story seemed to stretch about as far as the Mississippi River.

"Well, I'll tell y' what," George finally said, leaning back in his chair to stretch out his legs, hands fastened behind his head. "I do believe that kid was here, all right. 'Bout so tall, dark-haired thing, skinny little mongrel. Eight or nine, mebbe. Dirty and scruffy, too. What's the kid's name?"

"Name don't matter. That's him, though. You described him to a tee," Rufus said, sure of it, heart pumping blood faster than his veins could handle.

George shook his head, deflating his hopes. "Can't say where he might've taken off to, though. Humph." His head kept up a constant back and forth shaking until finally he paused and lowered his chin. "Unless..." He straightened, put a finger to his cheek in deep thought, then started nodding. "Yeah, that could be it," he said, talking to himself.

"What?" Rufus asked, nearly coming off his chair with nervous excitement.

"I don't want to get your hopes up." George chewed on his lower lip and gazed across the table at Rufus. For just an instant, Rufus felt baited, but he didn't care.

"What? What was y' goin' to tell me?"

"Well, there was this stranger comin' through town. Think he said he was moving to Sandy Shores. He, uh, took a job at a—a lumbering outfit. Yeah, that's it. Lumbering. Anyway, he was asking questions about that boy, and, come to think of it, once that stranger moved on, I never did see that boy again."

Just after eleven o'clock that morning, Rufus rode into camp. "Mount up, you big lazybones. We're headin' fer Sandy Shores."

The boys all scrambled to their feet, wiped the slumber from their eyes, and stared gape-mouthed at Rufus.

"Pa! What happened to y'?" Roy asked, voice wavering with shock.

"What do y' mean?"

"You look all—all spiffed."

"Y' hardly look like y'rself, Pa," Luis whined. "What'd y' go and do t' yerself?"

"Where'd y' get them new clothes?" Reuben groused. "I thought you said we didn't have no money t' waste. And y' got a new coat an' hat." Envy shone in his clouded eyes.

Rufus sneered. "It was all fer a good cause. Stop y'r bellyaching, all of you. Now, mount up, and I'll tell you all about it on the way. Things is lookin' up, boys. I got a good feelin' this time."

Under his breath, but just loud enough for his father to hear, Reuben muttered, "Yeah, that's what you always say."

Chapter Twelve

F our stories tall, Culver House Hotel represented all that was the best and most progressive in the hotel world, particularly for a modest town like Sandy Shores.

Having been destroyed in the fire of 1889, along with at least fifty other businesses and homes in a five-block area, Culver House rose from the ashes to reopen just two years later, perhaps not as large or flamboyant as the first building, but every bit as tastefully elegant. Sandy Shores' citizens were nothing if they weren't full of grit and gumption, so soon after the fire, they had gathered for town meetings in City Hall to plan their strategy for rebuilding. Nothing happened overnight, but now, four years later, the ordinary visitor would have no inkling that a fire had wiped out a good share of the northeast section of the downtown area.

Ralston and Hannah passed through the veranda on the Third Street side and entered Culver House's welcoming lobby through the glass double door. A blast of warm air greeted them, a welcome relief from the chilly night. Leather easy chairs and potted plants graced the room, where, suspended from the ceiling, three oversized chandeliers gleamed and glistened, their light reflecting off the elegant marble floor. Ralston put his hand to the center of Hannah's back and guided her across the large room toward the dining area, past the broad, massive oak staircase, the Western Union Office, a cigar room, a barbershop, and several small conference rooms with shiny oblong tables and matching chairs. It was a lovely place, and Ralston insisted on bringing Hannah here every weekend. She would have been just as happy to eat at the Lighthouse Restaurant, but it fell far beneath Ralston's standards. And, because of his high standards, it never bore mentioning that Marie's Ice Cream Parlor would be a wonderful place to stop after dinner.

Hannah's sturdy heels click-clacked across the marble floors, the sound echoing off the walls and high ceilings. She removed her heavy shawl and bonnet and lifted her yellow satin skirts past her ankles to take the two steps up to the restaurant level, Ralston's firm hand cupping her elbow and nearly squeezing the lifeblood from it. She was thankful when he finally released it.

"Good evening, Dr. Van Huff, Miss Kane." Dressed all in black, a white towel draped over one arm, the maitre d' greeted them, friendly only insofar as his professional status would permit.

"Good evening, Peter," Ralston said, his tone cool and cavalier. "We'd like our usual table, please."

"Certainly, sir."

Of course, Ralston never inquired whether Hannah would like a switch in scenery; he presumed to know her preferences. A tiny knot of resentment tightened under her rib cage as Ralston pointed her in the proper direction.

When they arrived at their customary table in the corner, Peter pulled out Hannah's chair and retrieved her napkin for her, spreading the snowy linen cloth across her lap. Hannah smiled up at him, but he kept his gaze averted, as if he feared stepping over the boundaries of propriety. Hannah thought his aloofness a bunch of silliness, and she yearned to tell him so, but it wasn't her wish to humiliate the middle-aged man whose dark muttonchops reached clear to the chin line. The thought occurred to her that Ralston might intimidate him. Whether purposely or not, Ralston did tend to set people on edge. Perchance once they married (*if we marry*, she reminded herself again), she could make a few subtle suggestions as to how he might make folks feel more comfortable.

After filling their sparkling glassware to the rim with ice water and assuring them that a waiter would be along shortly, Peter gave a half bow and hurried off, every ounce of his demeanor painstakingly businesslike.

Ralston retrieved a shining silver knife and held it up to the light, inspecting it for spots, as usual. The knot in Hannah's chest squeezed even tighter.

"Too bad Peter can't relax a bit more. He's so stiff and formal."

"What's that, my darling?" Ralston asked, barely looking at her. And that was another thing. Lately, when addressing her, he'd been calling her "darling," as if proposing marriage entitled him to do so. It would be one thing if she'd accepted, but she had yet to give him her answer.

"Peter. He seems so—so ceremonial around us. It's not as if he doesn't know us. Goodness, he sees us every week. You'd think he'd be friendlier."

"Friendlier?" Satisfied with his knife's cleanliness, Ralston set it down, folded his hands before dropping them into his lap, and finally looked her in the eye. "Ah, Peter. He's a member of the serving staff, dear. One wouldn't expect him to be too familiar."

"He's an ordinary person, no different from you or me."

A slighting look washed over Ralston's face, and he tugged at his well-trimmed goatee the way he often did when he seemed bothered.

At least he doesn't have muttonchops, she mused, something else to stroke and pull at when deep in thought.

"I hardly think a physician and a restaurant maitre d' compare, Hannah Grace."

No "darling" this time?

"Why not? We're all created equally in God's sight."

Rarely did she have a wish to argue with Ralston. In fact, most times she was happy to comply. Somehow, she wasn't tonight.

"Well, that's true, but Peter doesn't have years of education under his belt as I do."

"Nor do I, Ralston. Does that make you superior to him? To me?"

That brought him up short. "You, of course, are a woman. Most women perceive a college education as unnecessary due to their wishes for having a family. I assumed you felt the same."

She chewed on his words, noting how he'd dodged the real question. Pulling back her shoulders, she said, "I would like a family someday, yes, but that doesn't mean I wouldn't also like an education. Perhaps I'll earn a degree in accountancy, since I would like to take over Papa's store someday."

He tipped his chin at her and smiled, arched eyebrows quirked in amusement. "Darling, believe me when I say that there will be absolutely no need for you to work after we marry. My financial status will be more than sufficient to meet your every need."

"My every need, Ralston? What about my need to stay busy outside of the home? Granted, I want children someday, but until then, I'd love the chance to continue working at the store, perhaps even raising my children to take it over one day."

"What? That's a preposterous notion, Hannah Grace. Imagine a physician's children running a general store."

"And what about a physician's wife? What if this is something I desire to do? Do you even know about my hopes and dreams, Ralston?"

"Shh. You're causing a stir, my dear." Ralston raised his napkin to his chin in a nervous gesture and glanced about the room. "Where is all this coming from?"

She grasped the table's edge with both hands and leaned forward. "Why do you wish to marry me, Ralston?"

"What? Well, I thought I'd made that clear enough. We seem well suited, don't you think?" He looked uncomfortable. "I, well, now you've caught me quite off guard, dearest."

Dearest? If she were his dearest, shouldn't his reasons for wanting to marry her be right there on the tip of his tongue?

He reached across the square table and seized her hand, cupping it between his smooth ones and raising it to his soft lips for a gentle kiss. When she might have felt pleasure at his touch, she felt nothing. In fact, a memory she had no business recalling pulled at the edges of her mind; Gabe's hand coming to rest on hers when she was counting the store's petty cash; rough-hewn, strong, and powerful hands, so very different from the doctor's effeminate ones.

Feigning the need to wipe a smudge from her cheek, she withdrew her hand and took a handkerchief from her clutch purse. A scowl marched across Ralston's face as he heaved an impatient sigh. "Oh, Hannah, you have so many strong points. I—I don't even know where to begin."

She smiled. "Can you name them? For instance, what first attracted you to me?"

"Well…" He looked perfectly tongue-tied as he fumbled with the rim of his nearly empty water glass. The notion that he couldn't name even one appealing thing about her created a ball of irritation that tumbled around in her stomach. Her backbone bristled, and, without warning, she remembered the day Gabe had accused her of being stubborn and bristly. *Ugh!*

"You can't think of anything?" she asked, her voice rising above a whisper.

"Hannah, shh—of course, I can. You've many wonderful qualities."

"Name some."

"Well," he hemmed. "You're very friendly with others— yes, cordial. You've a big heart and a lovely smile."

"I do?"

"You are a wonderful listener and encourager. You never seem to grow weary of listening to my dreams for my practice."

I don't?

She bit her tongue and stared at him. "May I ask you something personal, Ralston?"

He drew back slightly. "Of course. Anything."

"How old were you when you made a commitment to follow Christ?"

The question must have thrown him, for his head jerked backward and he gave a nervous chuckle. "Good grief, you're jumping all over the map tonight, aren't you?"

"If I'm going to marry you, I would like to know more about your personal faith. Surely, you must agree that it plays an important part in a relationship. For me, I was a mere child, perhaps six or seven, when Grandmother sat all three of us girls down and asked us if we wanted to accept Jesus into our hearts. I don't recall a moment's hesitation about inviting Him in. How about you, Ralston?"

"Well…" He cleared his throat and frowned. "Naturally, I've attended church my entire life. Growing up in the town of Holland, one wasn't worth much if he didn't go to church." He fidgeted with his water glass, stirring the few remaining ice chips with a spoon.

"Yes, but surely you're aware that just going to church isn't enough. Salvation requires an act of faith, believing Christ died for one's sins, and asking Him to cleanse and renew the inner person."

A tense jaw betrayed instant displeasure. Gathering a tight breath, he leaned across the table and whispered, "This is not the time, much less the place, for this conversation, sweetheart."

"Then when, Ralston?" she asked, trying to contain her own frustration. He opened his mouth to reply, but the waiter arrived, pad in hand. Ralston sighed with blatant relief.

"Ah, it's time to order, darling. What shall we have tonight? Shall I choose for you? How does the chicken almandine sound to you? Hmm?" He cast her a very brief look before giving the waiter his full attention. "I believe we'll have the chicken almandine, and please, go light on the almonds. Oh, do bring more water. I'm parched."

He picked up his glass and drained it right there.

When their food arrived, they ate in silence, Ralston concentrating on cutting his chicken into perfect little pieces, sipping his water between bites, and taking long glances at the door as if he couldn't wait to go through it. Hannah picked at her food and brooded over the fact that she still hadn't come one step closer to learning whether Ralston even had a genuine personal faith.

It wasn't until they stepped outside and the doctor took her by the arm that he finally spoke. "Forgive me, darling. That was a completely ruined dinner for both of us." He leaned close to nuzzle her ear. "If it's any consolation I've had the chance to mull over several of your wonderful qualities. Would you like to hear them?"

She couldn't keep her eyes from going as round as tonight's full moon. That was what he'd pondered over during the meal? Her wonderful qualities? What about the question of his faith? Had he shoved that one aside?

A weak smile trembled on her lips. "Suddenly, it's not so important, but thank you, anyway."

He shrugged. "Well, suit yourself, then." They started walking up Third Street in the direction opposite her house.

She stopped. "I really should go home, Ralston. It's been a very long day for me, working at the store and watching over Jesse."

She turned and walked the other way, and he ran to catch up, snagging her by the hand. "Oh, that boy. You really shouldn't be spending so much time with him, you know. He's not your responsibility."

She glanced at the starlit sky and pulled her collar closer with her free hand to keep the strong breezes from biting her exposed skin. "I love that little boy."

"Love? Hannah, really, he's a waif. What in the world would possess you…?"

Around the corner, a loud commotion had dogs barking and horses whinnying nervously, drowning out the end of his sentence. *Probably some scuffle at one of the saloons*, Hannah thought. She shivered against the brisk winds threatening to steal her bonnet. "Clearly, the sheriff isn't getting anywhere in locating his parents," Ralston was saying. "Seems to me he ought to start thinking of a permanent placement for that boy—an orphanage or something. Orphanages can be found in just about every state."

She could hardly believe her ears. "An orphanage is the last place on earth…! Why, he needs love and care, two things an institution cannot offer. I would think that you, as a physician, would have more compassion, Ralston." She pulled abruptly away from him and started marching toward Ridge Street.

"Hannah, stop this instant!" he demanded. "I didn't mean…"

From behind, the approach of horses' hooves bore down on them. "Doc!" someone bellowed, breathless. Instinctively,

Hannah whirled in her tracks. "We been lookin' for you." It was Ike Bergmann, owner of the White-n-Bright Laundry, and his teenage son, Ben, reining in their horses, creating a regular dust cloud.

"What is it, Ike? Is someone sick?"

"There's been a drowning down at the pier," Walter volunteered. His face was as white as one of Ike's freshly laundered sheets.

"Oh, no," Hannah heard herself utter. "Heavenly Father, please help that poor soul."

"Too late for prayin', ma'am," Ike said. "I'm afraid he's done drowned. The ambulance wagon's bringin' the body up to your office, Doc, so you can pronounce him dead—or whatever it is you do. Pete Kloosterman and Vernon Graham worked on him for some time, but it didn't do any good. Appeared by the look of that fellow, he'd been in the water a while."

"Who is it?" Ralston asked, genuine concern in his voice.

Ike shook his head. "Talk is, he's unidentified."

"He don't go to ar school, that's for sure," Ben was saying. "There was other kids up there, and nobody recognized him."

"But that's awful. He must belong to someone around here. I'll go with you, Ralston," said Hannah.

"No, you go on home. You don't want to see the body of a drowning victim, I can tell you that."

"It's not pleasant, ma'am," Ike echoed. "Believe me, I got a close look."

Hannah thought she detected a hint of pride in his voice for having had the experience. She felt her face pull into a painful frown. "Just the same, I'm going with you. Maybe I can help in some way, particularly if the boy's parents show up. Ben, would you mind going to fetch Reverend Cooper?"

"Don't need to, ma'am. Sheriff Devlin's already sent for him."

That said, everyone hurriedly headed south on Third Street.

K

Gabe wished he didn't have such a procession following him up to the doctor's office. He felt like the grand marshal in the Independence Day parade. He and Jesse had been enjoying a quiet evening—playing checkers and sipping hot cocoa—when Gus van der Voort, one of his deputies, showed up at his door to inform him of the drowning. Naturally, he had to go, but what to do with Jesse? "You'll have to come with me, Jess," he said, spending all of one minute pondering it. He bent down to his level. "Promise me you'll do as I say when we get there."

Jesse's big brown eyes moved over Gabe's face. "Okay," he said. "But I'll stay by you."

"That depends, Jess. I won't let you look at anything scary, you hear me? You've had more than enough nightmares. I don't want to be the cause of any new ones cropping up."

Gus stood by the door, listening to the exchange. Out of the corner of his eye, Gabe saw his weight shift from one boot to the other. "You want me to go saddle up Slate for you?" Gus asked.

"No, Jess and I'll do that. You ride on ahead; we'll be along shortly. The pier, you say?"

"Yep, feller must have fallen right off the south side of it 'cause his body drifted up on the south shore. 'Course, he could've been pushed, I s'pose." He gave a glance at Jesse. "A crime scene ain't no good place for a little squirt."

"The boy comes with me," Gabe said. "I won't have him staying home alone. And let's not call it a crime scene, Gus—not yet."

Duly reminded of his place, Gus gave a half nod and backed out the door.

All the way there, Gabe prayed the Lord would intervene where Jesse was concerned. He also prayed for wisdom regarding the drowning victim, asking God to grant him a clear head and an intuitive sense about things—whether it was an accident or a deliberate action.

Now, heading toward Van Huff's office, Gabe thanked the Lord the boy hadn't seen the washed up, swollen body of the young man stretched out on the shore, ice-cold waves washing over him, seaweed tangled in his mouth and hair, eyes wide and round as cat's eyes. After a sight like that, he'd have had nightmares, for sure.

As soon as he'd reined in Slate at a hitching post not far from the scene, helped Jesse dismount, and then jumped down himself, he'd spotted Minnie Durham walking her toy poodle. She waved and hurried across the dirt-packed road. "How about I take Jesse up to Marie's for a dish of ice cream—just until you're finished with business here, Sheriff?" she'd suggested, her expression awash with understanding. Jesse clung tight to Gabe's hand, not knowing the elderly woman in the navy blue dress and heavy wool shawl, wide-brimmed hat covering her friendly eyes.

"Why, that'd be mighty nice, ma'am," Gabe had said, nudging Jesse forward. "I'll stop by Marie's to fetch him when I'm done."

But Jesse would have none of it, so Gabe excused himself to speak to Jesse privately. "She's safe, Jess," he'd explained, crouched at his side. "Besides, she has a dog, and folks with dogs usually turn out to be real nice people. Trust me, okay?"

He'd looked half convinced, but then shook his head. "I'll go with you."

"Sorry, buddy, not this time. I've got important work to do. Mrs. Durham is—"

"Hi, Jesse! Hi, Sheriff Devlin." The familiar female voice had both of them craning their necks. Maggie Rose Kane and a group of her girlfriends were making their way toward them.

"Maggie, hello," Gabe said, standing, nodding at the others. God's perfect timing never ceased to amaze him. "I was just trying to convince Jesse here to go with Mrs. Durham to Marie's Ice Cream Parlor."

"Really? We're on our way there now," Maggie said. "We need a little cheering up, if you know what I mean."

The remark had Gabe giving the young ladies a closer assessment, and, when he did, he noted tear-streaked faces and knew they had come upon the sordid scene at the pier.

He nodded his understanding. "I sure do." He wanted to ask them more about what they saw, but not in Jesse's presence.

Just then, Maggie's face brightened. "How about I take Jesse up to Marie's and then over to my house? You can pick him up later."

As far as he knew, Jesse had yet to utter more than a few words to Maggie, but he looked relieved to see her, anyway.

Maggie extended her hand to Jesse. "Come on, handsome, we'll all go together."

Jesse took her hand, and the entire group, including Mrs. Durham and her poodle, headed for Water Street.

Now, Gabe's deputies lifted the sheet-covered body from the ambulance wagon and carried it into Ralston Van Huff's examining room, stretching it out on a sterile table. Ralston pulled back the sheet and examined the young man's head, turning it this way and that, no doubt looking for abrasions.

"He has a bump here," Ralston said, feeling a spot slightly behind the temple area, concealed by his thick head of hair, now frizzled and matted. Gabe helped hold the body in place so Ralston could inspect the wound more closely. "It's quite a gash, but my guess is he hit a boulder when he went under. Probably knocked him out as soon as he hit it. Bet the kid never even had the wherewithal to gasp for breath—which could be a blessing when you think about it."

With Gabe's help, Ralston started removing the boy's shirt. He was a skinny thing.

"I wonder who he is," Gabe mumbled while Ralston continued his examination, starting at the neck and moving downward. One of the deputies was looking pale and excused himself, and that's when Gabe discovered Hannah sitting in a chair in the corner.

"Hannah, you shouldn't be here," Gabe said, his throat clogged with unexpected feeling.

"I told her to go home," Ralston mumbled, completely absorbed in his work. Gabe couldn't help but appreciate the doctor's thoroughness, even if his bedside manner was sorely lacking. "Humph," he tacked on.

Gabe pulled his eyes off Hannah, who was twisting a handkerchief in her hands. "What is it?"

"Humph," he repeated. "It's a tattoo right here on his left arm. See it?"

Gabe bent over the body for a closer look. A snakelike figure wove itself around inky blue letters. "Luis M.," he muttered, louder than he intended. A strange sensation, almost like mounting dread, started at his feet and scuttled upward.

He knew of a Luis M. *But it can't be the same one*, he told himself. Highly unlikely, in fact. *But what if…?*

"Luis M.," Ralston said, as if Gabe hadn't just announced it to the room. "Well, there's a little clue, anyway." He went on with his perusal, seemingly unmoved by the name.

The rest of the room remained in rapt silence. Standing next to the closed door, Stewart Stuyvesant, a reporter for the *Sandy Shores Tribune*, held a pencil and tablet in hand, and presently, his hand couldn't seem to write fast enough. *Great. How did he get past the door?* Gabe wondered.

He looked at Hannah. Her face was tilted down, her eyes studying her tightly clenched hands.

Lord, please protect Jesse and the people of this town, Gabe silently prayed.

Chapter Thirteen

The temperature dropped in the next two hours, the wind slowing to a chilly breeze. Hannah shivered and hugged herself as she and Gabe trudged up the hill to Ridge Street, where the house at the top seemed to await their arrival. Ralston, engulfed in his work, had gladly accepted Gabe's offer to walk Hannah home, especially when he explained he had to stop by the Kane house anyway to retrieve Jesse.

Death by drowning had been Ralston's determination. With no sign or proof of foul play, they could only assume the boy had fallen on the slick dock, resulting in the deadly plunge.

"I have a lot of paperwork to do, Hannah. You don't mind, do you?" Ralston asked.

"Of course not," she'd said, humiliated at how quickly he'd given in to Gabe's suggestion. Could he not have spared a minute to walk her home, or was it that their argument remained fresh in his mind? He and Gabe carried the body on a gurney to Ralston's basement, where he maintained a makeshift morgue. After filing a report for the courthouse, Ralston planned to start the embalming process. He hoped some family member would step forward and identify the body before it was buried. Until a funeral director moved to Sandy Shores to set up practice, Ralston would continue acting as both physician and mortician, having studied to become both at the university. Pete Kloosterman and Vernon Graham operated Sandy Shores' one and only ambulance company, but even their first aid training proved limited, making their operation less than reliable.

"You cold?" Gabe asked, breaking the silence between them, his voice gravelly.

She drew her shawl more snugly around her. "I'm quite fine," she fibbed.

He glanced down at her as they walked. "Oh really? Then, why are you shivering?"

"I wasn't—"

"Hush." Without a second's delay, he removed his coat and wrapped it around her shoulders, the warmth from his body remaining in its creases.

"Now you'll get cold," she said, moved by his kindness and made even warmer by it.

"I'm pretty warm-blooded." As if that should explain his generosity, he set his eyes on the road ahead. "What made you come to the doc's office tonight?"

She grasped the front edges of his coat, glad for its added warmth. "Ralston and I had just finished dinner at the Culver House when the news arrived of the drowning. I insisted on coming along, thinking maybe the family would show up and need some consolation."

"Reverend Cooper was there for that."

"I know, but I thought if the young lad's mother were to come by, I could be there for her. Oh, I do hope they find that poor boy's family."

Gabe nodded in the darkness. All at once, two cats shrieked, then darted across the road. Hannah lurched with surprise, and Gabe put a steadying hand to the center of her back. "Just a couple of ornery cats," he assured her. She wasn't sure what startled her more, the snarling felines or that strong hand at her back.

After they resumed their steady pace up Third Street, Gabe said in a low voice, "I do admire your compassion, Hannah." She wondered if he could sense her uneven breaths, her skittish heart. Yes, the cats had played a part, not to mention the events of the evening—her quarrel with Ralston; seeing the lifeless body of that poor, unidentified boy—but Gabe's close proximity plucked at her nerves more than anything else.

"Thank you. I—don't like to see people suffer."

"That's very evident."

She dared give him a slanted glance. Wasn't this the man who'd once called her bristly and bullheaded? She decided not to bring up their rather bumpy start and dwelt instead on the question of why Ralston couldn't have noticed this particular quality in her, especially after four months of courtship.

"Frankly, you've been a godsend to Jesse. I doubt he'd be speaking yet if it weren't for the way you love and accept him. He feels safe with you."

"No safer with me than with you. I daresay, you're the one who's made the greatest impact on his life, opening up your house to him as you have, treating him as if he were your own son."

He dipped his face close to her ear and whispered, "Ah, but it's you he has the mad crush on."

A nervous giggle bubbled out of her. "And I on him!"

"Uh-oh, a mutual crush. Does Ralston know about this?"

He'd intended the remark in jest, but it touched a tender nerve, and she had to bite her tongue to keep from revealing Ralston's ridiculous remark about sending Jesse packing. *And to an orphanage, of all places.* She shrugged and feigned nonchalance. "I don't think a childish crush poses a threat to him."

They'd reached the path leading up to the front door. One lone porch light made for a dim entry. Gabe stopped her midway up the footpath, just a few yards from the first porch step, and turned her to face him. "Apparently, I don't pose much of a threat, either, or he wouldn't have been so free to let me walk you home."

His words rang painfully true. She focused on his middle shirt button, the one that came within perfect eye range. Trouble was, he lifted her chin, forcing her to look into his eyes, tripping up her heart.

He lowered his face until his damp breath made contact with her earlobe. "Would he be threatened by this?" A chill of a different kind moved over her skin, prickling, tingling, waking her nerves, as she started toying with thoughts she'd never entertained before, not even with Ralston. Thoughts that included embracing, kissing—*loving. Gracious!*

Nearly frantic, her heart pounded out a desperate prayer. *Lord, what is happening to me? My very soul feels as if it's teetering on the edge of some cliff and is about to topple.*

Remember what you read from My Word this morning in 1 Peter 5:7: "Casting all your care upon him; for he careth for you." And in Acts 22:14: "The God of our fathers hath chosen thee, that thou shouldest know his will…and shouldest hear the voice of his mouth."

She gulped a deep breath of air. Never had a still, small voice ever made itself so audible. She wanted to ponder it further, but Gabe's warm breath upon her face unraveled her wits into tiny pieces, making it quite impossible to think clearly.

When his lips brushed her cheek and headed for her temple, she gasped and ducked, stepping out from under the circle of his arms. "Wh-where exactly do you come from, Sher—ur, Gabe?" she suddenly asked, surprised her voice even worked.

He released a quick breath and blinked twice, arms falling to his sides. "Pardon?"

"You know, where did you live as a child? You once mentioned your father and brother, but, well, do you have any sisters? And were you a sheriff in your other—wherever you lived—before?"

Surely, she sounded like a blundering idiot the way her questions tumbled out one after another, but he'd forced her into this predicament with his impending kiss.

A gentle wind shook the trees, causing more leaves to break from brittle twigs and flutter to the ground. His chest heaved with a breathy chuckle. "You're a scamp, you know that?"

"Me?" She promptly put a little more space between them and gathered her wits. "If anyone's a scamp, it's you. You know very well Ralston's proposed to me. I can't—I wouldn't even think of…"

"Kissing me?"

"It wouldn't be appropriate, seeing as I'm already…"

"Already what? I don't see you wearing any token of commitment—like a ring or locket," he challenged. "Are you betrothed to him—officially?"

"Well—not in so many words."

"Ah." Their eyes clashed for long seconds. "Is that because you're not ready, or because you're unsure about your feelings for him? Which is it?"

She tried to speak, but nothing came out, and she blamed her loss of words on shock at his surprising directness. He touched a finger to her nose. "Hannah, if my question has you that stumped, you shouldn't marry him, believe me."

She had an inexplicable sense that he spoke from experience.

"You have to know beyond a doubt that you're marrying for the right reasons and that you and God are in agreement."

"Now you sound like—Abbie." *And everyone else.*

He chuckled. "I like the way that girl thinks." Another long pause passed between them, his probing gaze stirring her emotions. "You have prayed about this, I presume."

Somehow, she hadn't expected words like these coming from the sheriff, but there they were, transparent and real. *Lord, he truly is a man of faith.*

"Yes." Had she? "I mean, I've tried to—I guess. But then, I wonder if I'm being selfish, praying for my own needs."

"Selfish?"

"Ralston is a good man," she said.

"I'm not arguing with you on that."

"And he's highly respected."

"I don't doubt it."

"He attends church with me every Sunday."

He rocked on his heels while she talked.

"He would always provide well for me, and he's—he's dependable."

"Whom are you trying to convince—me or you?"

That annoyed her. "You don't like him."

"I like him fine," he retorted, voice raised. He heaved a couple of long breaths and set his gaze on something overhead—a moving branch or a falling star? Suddenly, he shot her a piercing stare. "How does asking God for wisdom for your future equate to selfishness? Don't you know that God cares about every aspect of your life?"

As if he had the right, he reached up, snagged a lock of her curly hair, and twirled it around his finger. A chill ran the length of her, but she couldn't find the inner resources to step away from him.

"Would you say you care about the details of Jesse's life?" he asked.

Almost immediately, she got the point. "Of course."

"How much more your Heavenly Father wants to be a part of your life! Every aspect of it. It's not an imposition to Him when you ask for guidance."

They looked at each other, faces illuminated in the moonlight. A dog barked, a twig snapped, and, in the distance, faint sounds of twangy music coming from the saloons drifted on the cold, night breeze.

He hadn't yet dropped her lock of hair, and she was growing quite accustomed to the delicious chill his gentle tugging wrought. He gazed down at the top of her head. "I almost married once. For all the wrong reasons, mind you. She was a pretty thing, had me wrapped around her finger for the first while."

His admission nearly knocked her over. "What happened to change your mind?"

"I started seeing through her, realized her beauty didn't go much past her skin when she started asking about my father's money." His face brought forth a lazy smile. "She wanted to be certain she'd get a piece of the pie, you see, and was quite shocked to discover I wanted to make my own way, apart from my father's hard-earned money. Don't get me wrong, my dad's a generous man, and he'd give me the shirt off his back if he thought I needed it, but I don't. My parents raised my brother and sister and me to have strong Christian values and an honest work ethic. I've lived with much and with little, and I prefer the simpler life by far. When I saw Carolina's shallowness—learned she'd been faking her love for me, not to mention her Christian walk—well, let's just say it didn't take me a long time to renege on my marriage proposal." He chortled. "Looking back, it was a silly relationship. I praise God for helping me see the light. Well, I also gotta add some praise for my brother. He caught Carolina going through some papers on my father's desk when she thought no one else was home."

"Oh my!"

He grinned and gave his head a gentle toss. "We'd just returned from a picnic and I was rubbing down the horses. She said she was thirsty and needed a drink, so I sent her in the house. Turns out she was thirsty for information instead."

In some peculiar way, Hannah almost felt empathy for this woman. Her own father's success had resulted in a certain level of affluence for the Kane family, and she realized she'd become accustomed to creature comforts. Not that they swam in money, but poverty simply didn't exist in their world, and she'd grown accustomed to the security of prosperity. It impressed her that Gabriel Devlin chose to walk away from a carnal life of materialism.

She pondered this thought in private until he blew out a loud breath. "Well, I guess you weren't expecting a big confession out of me, but there you have it, and all because I wanted to make the point that you better know for sure you're marrying for all the right reasons, and that they align with God's will for your life." There it was again, that question of finding God's perfect will. How *did* one go about it?

Behind Gabe's broad shoulders, she noted the cats darting off across the road again, their distant yowl combining with the rustling breeze. To her dismay, she realized she'd memorized his woody scent, as even now it wafted through the air, a mixture of musk and mint. Ralston's scent was usually spicy, applied to the point of overpowering. Gabe's was subtle and earthy.

They stood close in the brisk, breezy night, her long skirts whipping at her ankles, fine shards of moonlight reflecting off the brim of Gabe's hat. She held his warm, woolen coat closed at her throat and felt pleasantly comfortable.

"Come on. Let's sit on the porch swing a while." He put a hand to her elbow and gently led her up the steps.

"Oh, I shouldn't."

"Of course, you should. Besides, you asked me some yet unanswered questions about my family and former job, remember?"

Oh, well, he had her there. He brushed past her to take a gander through the front window. "Jesse's sound asleep on the couch," he whispered. "Look at that boy, would you?"

She sidled up next to him to peer through the glass. Sure enough, Jesse lay still as a fallen log, Grandmother's handmade quilt thrown over him, a lone light glowing in the kitchen and casting a peaceful aura about the house.

"You can let him stay here for the night if you want. Seems a shame to disturb him."

"I better not. He'll need me if he has a nightmare."

She glanced up to find him watching the boy intently, and she took the opportunity to study his profile—the straight plane of his nose and forehead, now overshadowed by his hat; his rigid cheekbones and strong mouth; the broad set of his shoulders. Ah, there went that silly heart-tripping thing again.

As if sensing her watchful gaze, Gabe granted her a wistful smile. "I never thought I'd grow so attached to that boy."

"But you have. What do you think will happen to him—if you don't find his family, I mean?" Ralston's suggestion of the orphanage continued to grate at the edges of her mind.

"He'll stay with me." He straightened to his full six-foot-something frame and pulled her to the swing on the other side of the porch.

"Really? You've already decided that?" He'd said it with such matter-of-factness.

He swept an arm out in silent invitation. Fascinated, she dropped into the swing without argument. Gabe cozied in beside her, removed his hat, and tossed it across the porch, aiming for the rocker, hooking it easily over a spindle. "Well, it's not something I'm spreading around, mind you, but I sure won't send him anyplace unless someone steps forward to claim him. And whoever does had better be good and worthy."

With a touch of finesse, he pushed off with one foot. The familiar creak of rasping, rusted chain links rocked her into a peaceful state, and within minutes, she found herself relaxed, even with his arm situated behind her as it was, grazing the top of her shoulder.

"So, you still want to hear about my family?" he asked.

The soles of her shoes grazed the porch floor, while his stayed firmly planted, his wide thighs moving slightly with the swing's gentle sway. "Yes," she said, earnestly.

For the next several minutes, he told her about his home in Delaware, Ohio, where he'd not only grown up, but where his father held the office of county judge and his mother ran an efficient household. He spoke about his sister, Elizabeth, and her husband, Karl, a successful rancher and landowner, and their three children, all under the age of seven. Then came Samuel, Gabe's older brother by two years, a lawyer like his father. He'd married his high school sweetheart, Charlotte, and the two of them were busy raising Sarah, three, and Vance, one.

Without even meeting them, Hannah liked his family. Chagrined, she realized she knew very little about Ralston's upbringing, just that his family hailed from Vriesland, Michigan, not far from Holland, that his parents died in a train derailment two years ago, and that he had six older siblings, all married and scattered across the country, none of whom she'd met. He'd attended the University of Michigan Medical School, had done a one-year study in Berlin in 1897, and had turned down an invitation to accompany an expedition to the North Pole in 1898 as the group's physician in favor of starting his own practice in Sandy Shores. She had been formally introduced to him at a church supper in '01, but he hadn't asked to court her until this past spring. Naturally, she'd accepted, mesmerized that the town's only physician had paid her one minute's heed.

"To answer your question about where I worked before this, I was the Delaware County sheriff." Gabe cocked his head to one side and grinned. "Delaware's on the outskirts of Columbus, in case you're interested."

"And Columbus is the capital of Ohio," she said, smiling up at him.

A glimmer of moonlight cast a gentle glow over his arched brow. "Ah, I see you paid attention the day the teacher taught about states and capitals."

She flicked an imaginary piece of lint off her lap and grinned. "I'll have you know I was a good student who never gave my teachers an ounce of trouble."

"I find that hard to believe," he murmured.

She sent her elbow into his side for a swift poke, and he clutched the place with his free hand and leaned over with contrived pain. So relaxed had she become that she actually let the laughter flow when he reciprocated with a teasing poke of his own.

They sparred back and forth for a few seconds when, suddenly, he leaned forward and kissed her square on the lips. Drawing back, he paused to look at her, perhaps to gauge her level of shock, then, before she could resist, kissed her again, this time with thoroughness and feather-touching warmth, his breath fanning her face. His arms did not encircle her, but the hand that rested on the back of the swing came down to draw her close. Tingling heat wrapped her in a blanket of bliss.

Dear Jesus, help me, she prayed, even as she felt her body floating into some unnamed paradise.

But seconds later, paradise clashed with reality when the front door opened.

"Sweet land of liberty, what have we here?"

Hannah scrambled for composure, and, fast as one withdraws a hand from a hot flame, she made it to her feet, smoothing her dress, patting her hot cheeks, fixing her flyaway curls, and glaring at her younger sister.

"Abigail Ann, you were spying."

"No, I wasn't. I just came down to check on Jesse when I heard a noise."

"Well, everything's fine. Go back upstairs."

"What—and miss the fun?" She pulled her sleeping gown close at the throat and leaned in the door frame, mischief rampant in her brown-as-chocolate eyes.

Apparently, Gabe saw no reason for alarm, for he maintained his relaxed posture on the stilled porch swing, his legs stretched out to their full length and crossed at the ankles. He folded his arms and clutched his armpits.

"Does this mean we can kiss ol' Huffy g'bye?" Abbie asked.

"Abbie, I'm warning you," Hannah said.

"I'm just asking."

Gabe cleared his throat. "I'd say that's exactly what it means." His voice, though deep, rang crisp and clear with meaning.

Hannah sucked in a cavernous breath, puffed out her cheeks, and blew at her forehead. She pointed an accusing finger at Gabe. "You did that on purpose to manipulate me. You know very well I'm considering Ralston's proposal."

"Not anymore, you're not." His smile was every bit as intimate as the kisses they'd just shared.

A bristly chill scampered up her spine. Oh, how could things have moved so quickly from confusing, to wonderfully comfortable, to downright convoluted? And who did he think he was making such a forward statement in Abbie's presence—as if he held some claim to her? One kiss did not give him special rights—no matter that Ralston had yet to kiss her anywhere but on the cheek or forehead.

Abbie remained fully entertained, if the engrossed grin on her face indicated anything. "Oh, stop it," Hannah ordered, giving her foot a gentle stomp and glaring at Abbie as she might a naughty four-year-old.

Abbie upturned the palms of her hands and shrugged, her expression turning innocent. "What? I didn't do anything wrong."

"She has a point there," Gabe agreed from behind, only fanning the flames.

She whirled on him. "You stay out of it."

He turned down his mouth to avoid smiling, she just knew it, and the notion that the whole incident amused him fueled her the more. How could he sit there with his arms folded and feign such indifference? Abbie had caught them in the act of kissing, for goodness' sake! Shouldn't he share in the mortification of it all?

After a five-second stare-down, she spun on her heel and headed straight through the door, failing even to bid him good night. "I'll leave you to see to Jesse," she said, brushing past Abbie.

"Could I have my coat back?" he called after.

"Aargh!" She yanked it off and tossed it to Abbie, who barely had time to snag it before it hit the floor. "Thank you for loaning it to me, Mr. Devlin," she said, imagining the smirk on his face. "And for seeing me to the door."

"Gabe," he corrected on her way to the stairs. "My pleasure."

Chapter Fourteen

Roy and Reuben McCurdy moped and poked at the dying fire, both bearing puffy, blotched faces and red, swollen eyes. Rufus doubted they'd slept a wink the whole night. He cursed under his breath. He didn't feel any better than they did, but life went on, and he had to convince his boys of that.

"Time t' start breakfast," he said, unbuttoning his pack and removing a slab of bacon and the dozen eggs he'd bought at the market the day before.

"I ain't that hungry," Roy said.

"Me neither," said Reuben.

"Y' gotta eat, jus' the same."

Roy dug a hole in the sand with the toe of his boot and stared at it. "I shouldn'ta let him walk out there," he said for the hundredth time. "I'm the oldest. I should have been lookin' out for 'im."

Rufus rolled his eyes, annoyed that the subject kept coming up.

"I done tol' you, it wasn't yer fault. Luis shoulda knowed himself not t' go out there in the wind. Them waves was splashin' right over the pier."

"How would he have known that, Pa? He ain't been on a pier before," Reuben said, his tone lined with something cold and bitter—hatred? Whatever it was, it sent a frosty nip up Rufus's spine. "And why didn't you warn him? You're his pa."

"Luis was fifteen years old. It weren't my job to run 'is life." Anger welled up against the blame he saw in Reuben's eyes. "'Sides, I was sleepin'. You was the ones who let 'im go out there."

Seconds of silence ticked away. "You goin' to the funeral, Pa?" Roy asked, throwing a hefty stick into the fire and watching it sizzle before bursting into flames.

"You kiddin'? I ain't goin', and neither are you." He sneered at both of his sons. "That'd be ar ticket to jail right there. Three unknowns walkin' into a funeral service? You don't think folks is gonna know right off who we are? You boys need to grow some brains between them ears o' yours."

Roy scowled, eyes hidden in the shadows. Reuben kept up his hateful stares. "And stop lookin' at me like that," Rufus yipped. "It was an accident, it happened, and we need to get our focus back, remember our reasons for bein' here in the first place."

He knew he sounded cold, but what other choice did he have? If he gave in to the moping like these two sorry sloths, they'd get nowhere. Truth was, an unclaimed dead boy might raise suspicion. They didn't have time to lose or emotions to waste on feeling sorry for themselves, and the quicker they tended to business here in Sandy Shores, the quicker they could get out of there.

"He looked plain awful layin' there on the shore," Roy said.

"I hope to the heavens you blended in with the crowd," Rufus groused. "I tol' y' not to go down there."

"It was dark, Pa. No one noticed me. 'Sides, everyone was more fascinated by Luis's dead body. They was arguin' back 'n forth, 'He's breathin',' 'No, he ain't. It's yer 'magination.' 'He's whiter'n a sheet,' someone else said. 'He ain't got no blood left in 'im.'"

"Did he lose all his blood?" Reuben wanted to know.

"Jig-swiggered if I know," Rufus said.

"Don't talk 'bout it no more," Reuben said, covering his ears.

"That's the smartest thin' I heard come out o' your mouth since y' quit drinkin' off your mama's—"

"So, what do we do next?" Roy asked, jumping to his feet as if someone had just poked him in the rear.

"We go lookin' for the kid. At least we know he's here."

"And livin' with the sheriff. I don't know 'bout you, but I ain't goin' knockin' on the sheriff's door lookin' for no kid," Reuben said, still crouched at the fire and staring at its flames, ignoring the fact that his brother and father had started rounding things up.

"We ain't that stupid," Rufus said. "We look for the opportunity to nab him when the sheriff ain't around. For now, we just scout things out, learn the routine, watch an' wait. And we spread out. I don't want you two hangin' together, you got that? Wear yer hats down low on your faces."

"When we gettin' new coats like you, Pa?" Reuben asked.

"What's wrong with the one y' got?" Rufus asked, perturbed that all his middle son could think about was new duds.

Reuben held up his arm to reveal several gaping holes.

Rufus grumbled under his breath. "She-oot, that ain't nothin'. Stop in that Whatnot store t'day and buy yerself a needle and thread."

"Buy?" Reuben asked. "When was the last time we bought anythin', Pa?"

Rufus chuckled in spite of himself. "Y' got me on that one."

Reuben pulled himself up. "Maybe I'll jus' see if there's any coats in that there Whatnot store. I can walk out o' there with a coat easy as I can a needle an' thread."

Roy chortled. "See if they got any of them licorice drops in there while you're at it. Grab me a pocketful."

Rufus sniffed, happy to see his boys rousing. "You jus' don't do nothin' dumb that's gonna get you noticed or caught, y' hear?"

Reuben glared in his usual way. "Nobody's catchin' me without my say-so."

Rufus nodded, satisfied.

They were going to be all right. Might even be easier traveling with one less.

When Gabe dropped off Jesse at Kane's Whatnot the next morning, Abbie greeted them from behind the cash register, all smiles and full of good humor, no doubt recalling the night before when she'd caught Gabe kissing her sister. No better words than *devilish imp* came to mind to describe this youngest Kane girl.

"Grandmother Kane allowed Hannah to sleep in this morning." She cleared her throat and smoothed back her flowing black coiffure, then cocked her head jauntily to one side. "Due to a headache, you see."

"Oh." Gabe wasn't sure what to say. He knew enough about people to know when they were baiting him, and Abigail Ann Kane was a baiter. And a conniver, albeit a pretty one.

"'Course, you and I both know..." She leaned slightly forward, batting black lashes that shaded mischievous eyes.

He lifted his brows, waiting while the sentence dangled.

"Well, I mean, there she was, lying in bed with one hand draped over her eyes. I know what her problem is—she didn't want to face the morning—more likely, you."

The little imp giggled, her deep brown eyes gleaming with brightness—like the first rays of sunlight. She was nothing short of a firecracker, and, truth was, he liked her.

"She'll be along a little later, that's my guess," spoke Maggie Rose, who was standing to the side and folding men's shirts. "No doubt you're anxious to see her." Her eyes twinkled with meaning, and Gabe knew instantly that Abbie had clued her in on the events of the past evening. Without warning, his cheeks began smoldering. *Blast!* He didn't normally embarrass easily. What was it with these Kane women?

"Well, then…" He turned his hat in his hands.

Jesse, who'd run through the store and out the back door as soon as they entered, came bounding back inside, dog pan in hand. "Dusty needs water," he announced, running past Abbie and him to get to the water closet situated on the other side of a curtain in the room behind the counter. It seemed Jesse Gant felt plain at home in Kane's Whatnot, dashing behind the counter as he did, helping himself to the faucet, even speaking in sentences.

"I'll be going now, Jesse," he called.

"Bye," Jesse hollered back, failing to show his face behind the curtain. Gabe heard water pouring down the drain and imagined the boy stretching to his full height to reach over the sink.

He took a couple of backward steps to the door. "You ladies have a good day, now."

"Oh, we will," they chimed in unison, both wearing the grins of Cheshire cats.

At the door, he took a breath and paused. "Oh, and one more thing. Pay close attention to anyone coming and going today, and the next several days, for that matter. After that drowning incident, and with us not knowing who the victim was, I just want everyone to be on the lookout for anything suspicious. And keep a close eye on Jesse."

He noticed how quickly their smiles vanished. "Is everything okay, Gabe?" Maggie asked.

"No need to worry. I'm just asking you to take precautions, that's all."

He'd never seen Cheshire cats sober up so abruptly.

Across the road, he opened the door to Kane and Perkins Insurance Agency and spotted Ernestine Middleton, a middle-aged roundish woman in spectacles who seemed to act as the agency's secretary or bookkeeper, he couldn't tell which. She greeted him with a wide smile, her eyes crinkling up and nearly vanishing. Without cause, she started pressing down the gray bun at the back of her head and adjusting her high collar. "Why, Sheriff Devlin, what brings you here? Looking for some insurance on that new house of yours?"

He might have told her his "new" house required a heap of work, but for lack of time, shook his head. "Jacob set me up with a fine policy already, thank you. And speaking of Jacob, is he around?"

"Oh, he sure is. I'll let him know you're here."

"No, don't get up. I'll just go back myself, if you don't think he'll mind the intrusion."

"Intrusion? Why, heavenly stars, you'd be no intrusion atall. Help yourself," she said, gesturing an arm with a billowing sleeve toward the back of the long, narrow building. "Straight down that hall there and second room on your left; but then, I'm sure you know the way."

Gabe tilted his head in a polite nod and advanced down the hall.

Jacob sat behind a cluttered oak desk, marred from years of use. It looked as if he'd buried himself in paperwork. Gabe cleared his throat, and Jacob jolted.

"Didn't mean to startle you," he said, one hand on the doorknob.

"Well, well," said the smiling Jacob, who tossed down his reading spectacles, pushed back his chair, and motioned

Gabe inside. "Come, come, sit down and tell me what brings you here."

"I won't keep you," Gabe said, sitting down in the chair to which Jacob pointed—after removing a pile of folders and stacking them on the edge of Jacob's desk.

"Excuse the mess. Ernestine is forever scolding me to clean up this office, but it seems I never have a spare minute to do it."

"And here I am taking more of your time."

"Nonsense. Maggie Rose is coming in later this week to organize things. She does that every so often. She's my systematic one. Practical yet passionately driven. What a combination, huh?"

"Ah." Gabe hadn't come to talk about the beautiful Kane sisters, but Jacob's remark made him curious. "I suppose each of your daughters has her own special quality."

Jacob chuckled and settled back in his chair, stroking his beard as he thought. "Besides systematic, Maggie is kind to a fault—always looking for something or someone to dedicate her time and attention to. She's prudent, wise beyond her years, and genuinely thoughtful. Of course, that's not to say she doesn't have that Kane streak."

Gabe lifted questioning brows.

"All the Kane women have it, you know, including my dear mother, and it's known as tenacity. Actually, 'shameless spunk' might be a better descriptor."

Gabe couldn't hold back a sudden peal of laughter. "I think I know what you mean."

"I'm certain you do. Hannah Grace displays it perfectly."

Gabe felt warm behind the collar at the mere mention of her name, and the realization struck him that a week ago he wouldn't have had the same reaction. *It was that blasted kiss!*

He wondered if Jacob might be fishing, so he aimed for casualness. "Just out of curiosity, what would you say about your other girls?" He pulled his ankle up and rested it on his knee.

Jacob's gray eyes glittered with merriment. "Ha! They're all different as peanuts and peas, but listen, my boy, you've hit upon a subject for which I never tire talking. Are you sure you want to get me started, or would you rather clue me in as to the real purpose for your visit?"

Gabe wove his fingers together and clasped his hands behind his head, sinking back against the chair's worn leather. "I'll clue you in a little later. Go ahead and tell me about those daughters of yours."

Jacob took up a pencil and started tapping out something like a message in Morse code on his desktop. He glanced across the room, pondering. "Well, there's Abbie Ann, of course. What can I possibly say about her that you haven't already figured out?" Laughter erupted between them.

"She is rather an open book," Gabe said.

"That and much more. She's spunky, yes, but the mind in that little brunette head of hers is always turnin', don't be fooled. Of my three girls, she just might be the most determined, enterprising, and straightforward one. She's definitely the most melodramatic, I'll give you that."

Gabe grinned, but before he could say a word in response, Jacob started in on Hannah. "Now, Hannah's a girl with spark and initiative. Someday she'll take over the Whatnot, you wait and see. And I'll hand it over with confidence. She's capable and smart, that girl. Tender and compassionate, too. Look at how she dotes on that boy of yours."

Interesting he would refer to Jesse as *his*. "Sensible, too," the man added.

And prettier than a flower, Gabe might have put in.

Jacob tugged at his beard and flexed his shoulders against the back of his chair. "But I hope she exercises more than her sensible nature with regard to Ralston Van Huff's marriage proposal."

It took some effort to keep his voice steady. "How do you mean, sir?"

"Well." Jacob grunted. "Ralston's a fine young man and a faithful church attendee. I'm sure you've noted him sitting at the end of our family pew every Sunday." For no good reason, Gabe gritted his teeth against the image. Simply put, *that kiss* had ruined his image of Hannah with Ralston Van Huff—or with anyone else, for that matter! "And if one were to look at their relationship from a purely practical, sensible stand-point, then, yes, they probably complement each other." *No!* "But I want her to think beyond sensibility, of course, and to make this marriage proposal a matter of utmost prayer." He tilted his head in thought and cleared his throat. "Which I'm sure she will do."

The seconds ticked loudly from Jacob's desk clock. "Well." He looked Gabe square in the eye and blew out a loud breath. "I'm certain you didn't come here to listen to me spout about Hannah. I mean, you appear to be decent friends, the two of you—when you're not bickering, that is." This he said tongue in cheek, eyes twinkling. "But whether or not she marries the doctor probably doesn't much matter to you." He paused for effect—certainly long enough for Gabe to reply. "Am I right?"

Gabe tried to keep a light tone in his voice, but he still stammered seriously, "I—would have to say—it's of great concern to me, sir."

Jacob's eyes lit up like a pair of firecrackers. "Is that so? Well, all right, then. Perhaps you should jump into the game."

Gabe couldn't help the laugh that rolled out of him. "Yes, sir."

"Now then, what was it you came to tell me, young man?"

K

Hannah dismissed Abbie from her post at twelve-thirty. "I thought you'd never get here," Abbie whined. "Katrina's expecting me for lunch. Look at the time. I'm going to have to ride like the wind. I hope that ol' nag I reserved from the livery is up to the task."

"I'm sorry, sister dear, but I was helping Grandmother with the wash, which included *your* soiled sheets and towels, not to mention your dainty little unmentionables."

"Well, goodie for you. I've done yours plenty of times. I'll have you know that I've slaved at this store all morning long, when it wasn't even my day to work, so you should be greeting me with a thankful tone, not a snappish one. And what about your headache? You couldn't have worked too hard at the wash with your head pounding as it was this morning."

The look on Abbie's face, clever and calculating, had Hannah fighting for self-control. After all, what would folks say if she clawed her baby sister's eyes out? "It improved as the morning went on, thank you," she said, pushing past her sister and proceeding to the cash register to count the morning's receipts.

"I'm sure it did, particularly once you knew Jesse had arrived safe and sound without your having to face the sheriff."

"Oh, please. Where is he, by the way?"

"I'm sure he's dreaming about kissing you when he should be out looking for criminals."

Hannah pursed her lips and mentally counted to ten. "I meant Jesse. Where is he?"

"Where do you think? Out back with that dirty little mongrel with the same name."

"Dusty, you mean."

"Precisely."

Hannah focused her eyes on her task, even as Abbie drilled holes straight through her. Suddenly a giggle spilled out from across the room.

"What is so funny?"

"Oh, Hannah banana, you are the berries. Look at those rosy cheeks of yours. Admit it. You like the sheriff."

"Stop it."

Abbie giggled the harder. "Don't worry, darling sis, your secret's safe with me."

"And Maggie, I daresay. I'm sure you told her all about the kissing incident."

"Well, of course. We couldn't leave her out, now, could we?"

Hannah prayed her cheeks might return to their normal shade.

"What about me?" Maggie called from the top of the stairs.

"Nothing," both girls replied in unison.

"Be off with you!" Hannah ordered through clenched teeth, putting on her sternest face.

Abbie tossed back her head of charcoal hair and smiled, throwing open the door, then holding it so old Mrs. Gurley could pass. "Tootles, sweet sister," she called over the woman's flowery hat.

Upstairs, Maggie started singing the popular song by Harry MacDonough, "I Can't Tell Why I Love You, but I Do." Naturally, she sang every other note off-key.

Mrs. Gurley pointed her gaze toward the stairs and said, "Someone really ought to tell that girl she can't sing."

Hannah nodded in agreement.

Later, Hannah was helping Fanny Von Oettingen find the perfect pair of salt and pepper shakers with matching cream and sugar bowl for a couple whose wedding she planned to attend in Mill Point, a little town just across the river, when a young man she'd never seen before sauntered through the door. Fanny appeared more interested in studying the selection of ceramic ware than in the stranger's entrance. However, some sort of warning bell sounded in Hannah's head, though she couldn't say why—his tawdry appearance, perhaps, or the fact that Gabe had warned her to be on alert. He caught Hannah's eye the minute he entered and gave her a cold-eyed, humorless slant of a smile. A shiver climbed her spine.

"I think I like this set with the yellow flowers, dear," Fanny remarked, holding the creamer out at arm's length and turning it at an angle. "It's much daintier, don't you think?"

"Yes, that's my favorite." She only half glanced at the pretty little pitcher, while following the new customer out of the corner of her eye. "Shall I wrap it for you, Mrs. Von Oettingen?"

"Oh, would you? That will save me time. I so love shopping here. You girls always make a body feel welcome, and you offer such nice prices." She leaned forward and cupped her mouth with her palm. "I much prefer the Whatnot over Dirkse's."

Dirkse's wasn't truly a competitor, as the store predominantly featured dry goods, but folks liked to think they had a choice when shopping. "Well, thank you, ma'am."

They walked to the register together, the cold-eyed stranger wandering up and down aisles, handling merchandise along the way, raising his head every so often to glance at Hannah. She felt his frigid stares like she would a spider crawling over her skin. Mrs. Von Oettingen didn't seem wary of his presence, so Hannah told herself to stop being so paranoid. Still, the notion of being alone with him in the store didn't set well. Just ten minutes ago, Maggie had closed the library and taken Jesse for a walk down to the channel to watch the barges bring in supplies to be transported further by train. "Won't be many more days of beautiful sunshine," she'd explained. "We'd better take advantage of it, right?" Of course, Jesse wanted Dusty to tag along, so they tied a rope around the pooch's neck, buttoned their jackets to the neck, and donned their hats before setting off. As usual, November air coming off Lake Michigan had a strong nip to it.

It took a full ten minutes for Hannah to wrap the wedding gift, taking care to swathe the individual pieces in thin paper before setting them in a larger box, then wrapping the bigger box in foil paper and tying it with a strand of silk ribbon. The whole time, the stranger did nothing but scope out the entire store. While ringing up Fanny's sale, Hannah asked him if he needed anything in particular, but he shook his head and kept wandering about.

"He seems an odd sort," the woman murmured across the counter, finally noting his presence. She drew in her double chin and tilted her head to the side. Then, batting her hand in front of her nose, she hissed under her breath, "Doesn't appear he's had a bath in a month of Sundays, either."

Hannah had to agree. The stench permeated the room, even though he stood a full thirty feet away.

With the transaction complete, Fanny thanked her and headed for the door, no doubt grateful for the chance to escape. Hannah sucked in a breath for courage and approached the young man, who, upon closer inspection, didn't look any older than she.

"Where's yer winter coats?" he asked.

"I'm sorry, we don't have any in yet. We do expect a shipment in the next week or so. You might check back." Now, why had she invited him to do that?

He gave another of his icy looks and shot her a twisted grin, revealing decayed top teeth. Inclining his head, he asked, "Can I count on you to help me?"

More warning bells. She stepped back, for not only did his body odor nearly knock her over, but his breath smelled worse than dead fish.

"Hmm?" he inquired, pushing forward the more she moved away. A frayed wool coat, baggy, worn trousers, and a shabby cap, not to mention his odor and grimy, whiskered face, revealed his shoddy lifestyle. Where did he come from? More important, when was he leaving? She started to turn, but he snagged her by the arm, gripping so tightly that a pulsing knot formed in her stomach.

"Unhand me this instant!" she yelled, surprised by the firmness of her voice, sensing the importance of remaining calm. *Dear Lord, give me courage, and please lend Your protection in this hour.* It was one of the few times she recalled praying with such urgency.

He snorted, unleashing another wave of rancid-smelling breath. "But we're just getting to know each other."

She struggled to wrench free of his grip. "I don't know you at all. Who are you?"

"Wouldn't you like to know?" he sneered.

Just then, the door opened and her father sauntered in. A sigh of thankfulness tumbled from her chest. Immediately, the stranger dropped her arm and stepped away, turning his attention to a nearby display of sewing notions. He picked up a spool of thread and a package of needles then tossed them back in their bin.

Jacob stood at the door looking at the stranger. "Everything all right here?" he asked, his eyes now moving over his daughter.

"Everything's fine, Papa," she said, pressing for composure and quickly moving to the counter, glad to break away from the man's clammy touch. She looked at her jonquil-colored sleeve and found he'd left a soiled mark there. Oh, how she wanted to rush home and have Grandmother throw her dress in the wash.

"I'll be back later to check on those winter coats," the scruffy fellow said, passing her and walking to the door.

"I think perhaps it's best if you don't show your face around here again, young man," her father said, standing tall, blocking the man's efforts to pass.

"Oh, yeah? Ain't this a public place?"

"It is, but as the owner of this establishment, I have the right to decline my services to anyone I choose." Her father's smile matched that of the stranger's, minus any feigned friendliness. "I hope I make myself quite clear."

Hannah had never seen Jacob Kane look more serious, not even when taking his young daughters aside and scolding them for some infraction or another. Usually one stern look put them back on the straight and narrow. Would he have the same effect on this young man?

Jacob stepped aside to allow the scoffing ruffian to leave. He muttered something indiscernible on his way out, and she wondered if her father had made out the words.

Jacob shut the door emphatically, making the bell above it gong rather than jingle.

He leaned against it briefly and shook his head. "Are you all right, Hannah Grace?"

"Of course, Papa. Don't look so worried. He's gone now." She moved from around the counter and walked to her father, who looked to be breathing heavily.

"What brought you over here, anyway?"

"I've been watching the comings and goings of folks all morning. I noted the time that fellow walked through the door. When he didn't leave shortly afterward, I figured something wasn't right."

He eyed her gravely. "Do you happen to know his identity—or the nature of his business in Sandy Shores? What did he want from you? Did he ask any questions about anyone in particular?"

"Papa, no. He was just looking for a coat and making a pest of himself. Acting like a bully, in truth. Why? What's wrong?"

Jacob swallowed hard. "Sheriff Devlin stopped in to see me early this morning. Seems there are some criminals on the loose. He's suspicious that the kid that drowned is somehow connected with this—this group of crooks."

"But—what would they be doing in Sandy Shores?"

"I'm not sure, but we need to stay alert."

The deep lines etched in his brow revealed worry. "I'm not saying that the fellow who just left is one of them, but it doesn't hurt to remain particularly cautious. I hope he heeds my words and stays away. I don't want some devious character snooping around my store, much less ogling my daughters." He ran a hand through his normally neat head, mussing the part.

"Where're Maggie and Jesse, by the way? Upstairs?"

"No," she replied. "They went for a walk to the docks to watch the workers remove cargo from the barges and load up the freight cars. Things like that fascinate Jesse so. They should be back most any time. Why, what's the problem, Papa? Does Gabe truly think Sandy Shores is in danger?"

Even under his thick beard, she saw his jaw clench. He studied her with thoughtful eyes. "I'd say so, Hannah. Gabriel Devlin is a perceptive man, and my instinct is to follow his instructions very carefully."

"What do you mean, 'instructions'?"

He heaved a loud sigh. "He's concerned for Jesse's safety, in particular."

No sooner had he uttered the words than the bell above the door tolled, and in raced Jesse, Maggie, and the scruffy pooch. "Hannah," Jesse squealed with bulging eyes. "You shoulda seen the big barge in the harbor! It was plain amazin'!"

Chapter Fifteen

G abe pored over the most current files, the latest bulletins, and the most detailed summaries of wanted felons, looking for some hint regarding the drowned victim, something more than a silly snake tattoo. He knew he had to base his hunch on more than just that—a hunch. Nothing new came to the forefront regarding the McCurdy gang, only that the South Bend police department was still actively seeking them, following up on leads but always coming up short.

Then, there was that local reporter who'd barged into his office earlier. "Luis M. could be Luis McCurdy, you ever think of that?" the bushy-haired fellow with the wire-rimmed spectacles had asked while leaning his heavy frame over Gabe's desk. Of course, that was what he was thinking, but he didn't want to voice it just yet, particularly not to some newspaper reporter he barely knew.

"What makes you say so?" Gabe asked, curious.

Removing his glasses, he rubbed the bridge of his nose and squinted. "A hunch."

Gabe couldn't help the chuckle that erupted. "That's about all I've got to go on myself, friend."

Stuyvesant gawked. "You serious?"

"As a dead duck."

The two conversed further, Stuyvesant asking Gabe to relay what he knew of the McCurdy gang and Gabe posing further questions of his own. Between them, it wasn't much, but enough that Stuyvesant thought he had a story worth writing.

Gabe groaned. "Promise me you'll stick to the facts. I don't want this town whipped into a frenzy thinkin' there's a murderous gang lurking about."

Stuyvesant lifted one sly brow. "But what if there is? The people have a right to know. Don't worry, sheriff; I always state the facts. 'Course, it's easier when folks give 'em to me straight."

The lead tip on his pencil broke off from all his tapping as he watched Stuyvesant exit his office a few minutes later. He couldn't decide if he liked the guy or not.

Later, one of his deputies, Gus van der Voort, stopped by with some incident reports, a Peeping Tom on River Street, a drunk who'd fallen asleep on a park bench and needed reviving, a domestic dispute on Jackson Avenue, and a cat that had scampered up a tree three days ago in Bill and Evaleen Elwood's backyard and refused to come down.

"A cat?" Gabe asked, laying down his paperwork to rub his tired eyes.

"Yep. Evaleen insists we come over and handle the matter."

"Tell her to summon the fire brigade. They've got the ladders for that."

"I did that," Gus said. "But she's determined this is a case for the sheriff's department."

Gabe hated to ask. He arched his brow and slanted Gus a curious stare.

"Says her husband Bill ain't got all his rocks in a row up here." Gus pointed at his temple area. "Lately he's been polishing his gun and talking about killing that critter if it keeps him awake one more night. According to old Mrs. Elwood, the feline carries on from dusk to dawn. Trouble is, she says while he polishes the barrel, he lists off all his enemies from as far back as '75, some who still live in Sandy Shores. She says he's saying things like, 'Long as I've got my gun out, I may as well put it to good use.'"

Gabe shook his head, let out a long breath, and dragged his hand down over his face. "I suspect you'd better go pay a call on the fire chief yourself, then go to the Elwoods' place and kindly ask Bill to hand over his gun."

"What if he don't give it to me?" Gus looked mildly concerned. "He is a mean ol' cuss."

Gabe grinned. "If I was you, I'd figure out a way to take it off his hands. You never know, you could be on his hit list."

Gus considered that with grimness, his brow furrowing into several crinkled lines. "There was that time in '93," he said, turning and heading for the door. "And '88, and now that I think about it…" He walked out just as Kitty peeked inside, silver hair askew.

"Somebody's here to see you. Name's Vanderslute."

His mind had gone in so many directions today, he had to concentrate to rein it back in, then focus his attention on Kitty. "Vanderslute? Who is he?"

Her round shoulders shot up, held, then slumped. "Never seen 'im before. He says you'll know 'im right off."

"I will?" He looked to Kitty as if she held the key.

Kitty's patience looked like it was wearing as thin as the skin of an onion. "You want to see him or not? He rode the train from Holland, if that tells you anything."

Gabe snapped his fingers. "I met a fellow in a restaurant there. I think he went by the name of Vanderslute. Wonder if it's the same guy. I'd seen Jesse scrounging around in a waste barrel before I went inside, and then again from my table by the window. This guy sat across from me, and I asked him if he knew anything about the boy."

Kitty's shoulders squared and her face softened. "Did he?"

Gabe shook his head. "'Fraid not."

"Well, maybe he'll have some answers for you today. You want me to send him down?"

Gabe pushed back and stood to his feet. "Absolutely. You've got me curious now."

As soon as Vanderslute walked through the door, wearing a string bow tie over a white, ruffled shirt, a woolen coat, and baggy tweed trousers, Gabe recalled the first name of the man with the pencil-thin mustache.

"George, right?" Gabe walked around his desk and extended his hand. Vanderslute took it, his handshake firm and hearty.

"Excellent memory, my friend."

"What brings you here?" Gabe asked, gesturing at the chair across from his desk.

Instead of sitting, though, George tossed his bowler hat on the chair and started wandering around Gabe's office. "I ran across an interesting tidbit a couple of days ago. Thought I'd take the train over and tell you about it."

"Well, I'm anxious to hear what that might be."

George took his good ol' time removing his spectacles from his shirt pocket, tugging the wires around his ears, and leaning in to look at an old James Whistler print, facing away from Gabe. "I've always liked this one," he murmured, studying the details of *Man Smoking a Pipe*. "Whistler had a knack, didn't he? Look at that moth-eaten hat and the old guy's dark, weathered skin." He was in his own world as he viewed the masterpiece, tilting his head in several directions. "I've always wondered about that left eye, haven't you? Looks like a glass eye, if you ask me." He took a closer look, hands clasped behind his back. "You think they had glass eyes back then?"

"I wouldn't know."

"Humph, definitely somethin' wrong with it. I'd guess Whistler painted this in, say, 1860, what do you think?"

"I've never been much of an art buff." Truth was, he'd barely noticed the painting, except to set it aright once when he'd brushed against it in a mad rush. The muscles along Gabe's neck went taut, and he massaged them with care, even as his impatience mounted.

Vanderslute stepped back from the painting and Gabe grew hopeful. "Want to have a seat?" he asked.

"Sure." But then, Vanderslute noticed the old Seth Thomas wall clock with chimes and ran a quick hand over its side. "You ever dust?" he groused, squinting at his hand.

"Sorry about that," Gabe said, grabbing yesterday's *Tribune* and offering it over the desk.

Vanderslute looked down his nose at the paper, then looked up at Gabe. "I can't wipe my hands on an inky newspaper. Shoot, I wear gloves when I edit my newspaper work. Newspapers are notorious for leaving ink."

"You're right. What was I thinking?" He didn't recall the fellow being so persnickety upon their first meeting. All he could recall was the cigar hanging out of his mouth.

While Gabe rifled through one drawer after another, looking for a piece of cloth on which Vanderslute could wipe his dusty hand, the guy flipped his wrist at him. "Never mind. A little dirt and grime never hurt anybody, right?"

Gabe would be sure never to invite him to his house. Ever since he and Jesse moved in, he had yet to take a broom to the wood floors, even though he could feel the sand grind beneath his boots. No telling how many layers of dust lay on the shelves and bed stands. In that very moment, it occurred to him how much he needed a wife—and, just as quickly, Hannah Grace's face flitted past his mind's eye.

Next, Vanderslute's eyes scanned the floor-to-ceiling bookcase filled with law manuals, leather-bound classics, and even a few dime novels, mostly detective-type and mysteries. He pulled a title from a tight slot and blew the dust off its top, handling it with care.

"Tate's collection," Gabe offered. "So far, no one from the family's stepped forward to claim it, so there it sits."

"Humph," Vanderslute mumbled, "I heard tell Watson Tate was a good one for reading on the job—that and nodding off."

Gabe had heard the same. Also, that folks liked him plenty despite his rather idiosyncratic manner of maintaining the law.

"Well." Vanderslute replaced the volume, brushed his hands together, and faced Gabe head-on. "I s'pose you're wondering about my visit."

Nervous laughter spilled out—the kind that won't stay contained. "Haven't you heard it's wrong to keep a sheriff hanging? I'll tell you, my head's whirling with all kinds of thoughts."

Vanderslute smiled. "Didn't mean to do that to you. I s'pose that was rude of me, snoopin' around soon's I walked in, leaving you wondering what in the world I'm even doing here. Want me to walk out and come back in for a fresh start?"

"Nothing doing," Gabe said with a tight grin. "Take a seat."

"Well, now, that sounded like an order." The middle-aged man walked to the wooden chair with the worn upholstery, picked up his hat, and released a groan as he sat, stretching out his legs. "I'm an inquisitive sort, though my wife would say I'm nosier than a coon." He chuckled at his own joke.

For some reason, Gabe had pictured the man living alone. "Nosiness is crucial in the newspaper business. You're just doing your job."

He nodded several times. "Well, I must say I surprise myself with the facts I recall. Line editing will do that to a person. Take the other day, for example. I was sitting there at Eva's Place—you remember Aunt Eva—jawing with some cronies, when I hear this feller wants to talk to me. I may just be a copy editor, but I told you that night I met you that I didn't miss much when it comes to the news. I read it before anybody else does, and certain tidbits stick at the inside of my head like a feather to tar."

Gabe shoved down the thought that Vanderslute might be about to reveal some very valuable information.

"I'm sure you being in the law business and all, you've heard of the McCurdy gang—thieves, murderous scum, rotten to the core."

Gabe started thumping his boot heels on the floor, then shifted his body. "I've heard of them," he said, tone straight as he could make it. "Haven't run into them—yet."

"Yeah, well, I'm sitting at Eva's when she tells me this here guy has some questions for me about that little stray kid who was hanging around Holland a couple of months ago. You remember the boy, right? Because you asked me about him. Funny thing—he up and disappeared that same night you were in town."

Gabe nodded, his pulse quickening. "The little rascal climbed under my gear in my wagon and rode into Sandy Shores with me. Been with me ever since. I don't mind saying I've grown attached to him. His name's Jesse Gant."

"Is that so? Where're his parents?"

Gabe shook his head. "Haven't figured that out yet. He doesn't appear on any missing children's reports, and if he knows anything, he's not saying. We've only recently gotten him to start uttering his first words."

"We?" There went that probing look again, the silent inquiry famous to reporters.

"A young woman and myself. She's taken quite an interest in Jesse. Between her and her sisters, Jesse's well cared for every day while I'm on duty."

"Ah, that's good to know." Vanderslute laid a finger to his chin while propping an ankle over his knee and sitting back. "I can't tell you why exactly, but I'm not surprised the boy's with you. Sort of figured he'd followed you, which makes my reasons in coming here all the more important."

Gabe's boot heels clicked the harder. "Why is that exactly?"

"Well, I'm getting to that. See, I go over to this guy's table and sit down, and, right away, he seems familiar to me. Couldn't put my finger on it at first—something in the eyes, I think—or maybe just gut instinct. He'd shaved off his beard, bought new clothes, and tried to look spiffy, but you know what they say: 'You can't put a sock on a rattlesnake and expect folks to think it's just a sock. At some point, that snake's going to slither out.'

"Anyhow, this fool started weaving a tale about his cousin's missing boy and how everyone, including the authorities, were out looking for him. When I asked him why the boy was running, he gave me two different answers; one, that he was a rebellious little cuss; two, that he'd stolen some goods from a farmer, and they needed him to come home and confess to the crime. He kept saying he didn't intend to hurt his cousin's boy when he found him; he just wanted to take him home, said things would go better for him if he found him ahead of the lawmen.

"Not five minutes later, he changed his tune and said the tyke was a good little kid who'd been traveling with his family and accidentally got off at the wrong stop, probably around Dowagiac, thinking his parents were ahead of him. They failed to discover his absence until they'd gone thirty miles further south.

"The more questions I asked, the more his story changed. And here's the funny part. The fool had no clue. I tell you, he didn't know which end was up, and I wouldn't have been surprised if he'd mixed a little brew with his coffee that morning, if his breath and clothes were any indication."

"Why are you telling me all this?" Gabe cut in, leaning forward in his chair, taking up a fountain pen to drum its tip into an ink blotter.

"Because, Sheriff"—Vanderslute pushed forward, eyes sparking with animation, fingers tapping on the chair's arms—"I'd bet my eyeteeth I was talking to Rufus McCurdy, and he wants to get his hands on that boy."

Gabe had suspected the same, of course, which would fully explain Jesse's terror at having seen Rufus's picture in the newspaper.

While a bitter taste pooled in Gabe's mouth, he took a calming breath and asked, "What do you think McCurdy wants with Jesse?"

"Humph, that's easy," Vanderslute said, sitting back and clasping his hands over his chest. "The boy witnessed something Rufus ain't happy about, and he's of a mood to rid himself of the worry over it."

Exactly.

Gabe sat mute for a full thirty seconds, digesting the exchange. Next steps. He needed to think.

Lord, give me wisdom. Protect Jesse and Hannah. Matter of fact, Lord, I'm asking again for Your protection over the whole town of Sandy Shores. The thought that McCurdy and his sons could be sneaking around out there sends a cold sense of dread through my veins.

A flashback from shooting down Smiley Joe Hamilton back in '01 froze in his brain, the vexing eyes and vicious smile, the challenge in his expression when he drew his gun, and the split-second decision Gabe had made to pull his own gun and bring the man down—and then the blood shooting from Smiley's nose and mouth as he lay there, soundless and unmoving, his body sprawled on the bank floor.

Gabe had come to Sandy Shores to escape additional bloodshed. Petty crimes, he could handle—but another gun-fight? *Lord, am I equipped for a face-off with Rufus McCurdy?*

"God is our refuge and strength, a very present help in trouble." The first verse of Psalm 46, which he had read in its entirety that very morning, washed over him with fresh assurance.

"I heard you had a drowning here a couple of nights ago," Vanderslute said, breaking into Gabe's musings.

Gabe nodded, placed the pen back in its well, and started sorting several papers into various stacks. He looked at Vanderslute. "Yeah, the victim couldn't have been more than fourteen or so. He had a tattoo bearing the name Luis M."

Vanderslute's face seemed to lose some of its color. "Luis McCurdy had a tattoo on his—let me think—left arm. A man in Chicago put it there. In fact, if you ever catch up with the rest of the McCurdys, you'll find their names etched into their left arms, as well—some kind of snake figure twirling around the letters."

The hairs on the back of Gabe's neck shot straight up. "What? How would you know this?"

Vanderslute shook his head and grinned. "When you're in my business, sometimes you get an inside line on things. A guy who runs a little business on the outskirts of Chicago confessed to having tattooed every member of the family. They paid him big bucks to keep his mouth shut. He didn't come forward with the information till after that murder down in South Bend, when he learned they were suspects. Says they were drunker than skunks when they came in—'cept for the youngest. Apparently, he didn't want the tattoo, but Rufus forced him into it."

It angered Gabe no end that something so important hadn't made it into the most recent police files. Not that it would've made any difference.

He pushed back in his chair, its legs squeaking in protest against the polished wood floor. He stood and extended a hand over his desk. On cue, Vanderslute rose. "I appreciate your coming, George. This information could be invaluable, if not lifesaving."

The two shook hands before Gabe ushered Vanderslute to the door, opening it ahead of him. In the doorway, he paused and looked up at Gabe, who had at least six inches on him. "You watch your step, young man. Rufus McCurdy's the devil in disguise, and I'm convinced those boys of his—well, the two remaining ones, anyway—are under his spell. They'd probably duel with a grizzly if their pa demanded it. He's evil, I tell ya."

Gabe nodded, his stomach churning, his mind congested with thoughts and questions. *McCurdy and his boys are in town. I've got to get to Hannah and Jesse. Can I keep them safe? I must speak to Ed Bowers. I'll send a wire to Pa and Samuel—no, I'll phone them from the office—and the South Bend Police Department. I may need reinforcements.*

"*The* LORD *is the strength of my life; of whom shall I be afraid?*" Again, the psalmist's words came back to refresh his soul, calm his spirit, and get him back on track. *I am with You, My son. Trust My promises.* The assurance bolstered his courage.

He pulled his hat over his head and followed George Vanderslute out the door. Hannah Grace might not be pleased with the idea, but the first thing on his agenda involved getting her and Jesse out of that store.

Chapter Sixteen

W hat do you mean I can't work in the store anymore? That seems a little extreme. Papa, tell
him I'm needed here."

Jacob sighed. "I'm afraid the sheriff's right, Hannah. You
and Jesse need to stay out of sight, unless you're with Gabe, of
course. Too many people come and go from this place."

She lifted arch-shaped brows. "You want us to stay con-
fined, like prisoners?"

"Be reasonable," Jacob said. "It's for the best—at least for
now."

Yes, be reasonable, indeed. Gabe and Jacob had spent the
better share of ten minutes trying to convince the willful
little imp of the importance of keeping a low profile for Jesse's
sake.

"It's not a life sentence, Hannah," Gabe put in, feeling the
urge to grab her by the shoulders and give her a shaking, but
with Jacob standing next to him, he counted silently to ten
instead. Had he really kissed her full on the lips last night?
It seemed like an eternity ago considering how quickly she'd
managed to raise his ire today.

She shot him a distrustful look. "Who are these so-called criminals again?"

He clenched his jaw and tried to hide his growing impatience by taking a few steadying breaths. "We now know the boy who drowned is Luis McCurdy, the youngest son of Rufus McCurdy. Rufus and his two living sons are in Sandy Shores, no question."

Her chin poked out to acknowledge her cussed stubborn streak. "I've never even heard of them."

"Then you don't read the papers!"

"You don't have to yell about it," she said.

"I am *not yelling!*"

"You most certainly are!" If her chin went out any further, he could balance a thimble on it. She turned and left the two of them gape-mouthed, as she busied herself straightening several new pieces of artwork on the wall behind the register. "Aren't these pretty?" she remarked. Gabe and Jacob exchanged glances. "They just arrived in a shipment last week. There's another case of them in the back room. Oh, and several big cartons of goods I haven't even cracked open. There is so much work to do in preparation for the winter season; speaking of which, I ordered a whole shipment of Christmas décor some weeks ago. Those could be in one of the cartons out back and would need arranging in our Christmas corner. I always put the tree over there."

"I know exactly where you put it—and the display of decorations, as do your sisters. Between the three of us, we'll see to the important things," her father said.

She sniffed and wiped her hands on the sides of her skirt, turning full around. She lifted her impertinent gaze to Gabe.

"What did they do, anyway, these McCurdys? And what could they possibly want with Jesse?"

"They're wanted on possible murder charges in South Bend." He hesitated in giving her the details, but only for a second. "Jesse may be a key witness."

She opened and closed her mouth, then quietly muttered, "Oh my."

"Yes, oh my," Gabe echoed. "That louse who paid a visit to your store a while ago might very well have been one of the McCurdys. Did he appear to be scoping the place out, looking for something—or someone?"

"He wanted a winter coat, seemed plenty perturbed we hadn't received our winter shipment yet, although for all I know, they could be among those still-sealed boxes. I told him to come back later, but I think Papa discouraged him from doing that. He had a pockmarked face, if that helps."

"When I get back to my office, I'll review his physical traits. We don't actually have a picture of Reuben, but I'm assuming it was he, the younger of the two boys, only because he's prone to making the most mistakes. His hot temper and easy-flowing mouth often get him into trouble."

"So, if he heeds Papa's warning about staying away, he probably won't be coming back, right? Which means—"

"Which means you're still not staying here. No telling what the other McCurdys might decide to do if they discover Jesse's at the store. Come on, gather up whatever things you need, and I'll walk you and Jesse up the hill," Gabe said, issuing the order in much the way he might speak to one of his deputies.

"Yes, sir," she sassed sarcastically.

Another look passed between the men, and, this time, Jacob shrugged his shoulders. Apparently, the Kane patriarch didn't have the best handle on Hannah's obstinacy—obstinacy Gabe was sure came more from personal reasons than logical ones. Again, *the kiss* had wreaked some havoc, and it seemed her intention to make everyone pay for it!

K

Gabe attempted conversation on their way to the Kane house, Jesse between them, Dusty at their heels, his nose held high to sniff the many scents coming from Thom Gerritt's Meat Market, the Star Bakery, and Van Poort's Grocery Store.

"Looks like it'll be a nice night for raking the leaves in the backyard, Jess. Maybe afterward, we can toss the ball. Would you like that?"

"Yep," Jesse answered, eyes focused on his black lace-up boots.

Over Jesse's head, Gabe looked at Hannah, but sheer stubbornness kept her from acknowledging him. The notion of staying locked up in her own house still had her worked into a lather, even though she knew it made sense, particularly if it involved keeping Jesse safe. Somehow, though, giving in to Gabe's demands didn't sit quite right with her.

Lord, forgive me for my appalling attitude, she prayed.

"Why we goin' to Hannah's house?" Jesse asked, looking up at Gabe when they crossed the street at Third. Jesse gave Dusty's leash a yank when the mutt insisted on chasing a darting squirrel.

"I've already told you, Jess—Hannah's grandmother has some odd jobs for you, jobs that could take several days to finish." His voice hinted of slight frustration, and Hannah knew her morose mood lent to it. Out of the corner of her eye, she caught a glimpse of his square-set jaw, watched it tense and flicker.

"What kind of jobs?"

Gabe shot Hannah a floundering look. She quickly refocused her gaze on the road ahead.

"I don't know. Maybe polishing silver or—"

"I don't know how t' do that."

"I'm sure Hannah will be happy to teach you, right, Hannah?"

She gave an irritable tug at her coat sleeve. "I'd be delighted."

If Jesse sensed her sarcasm, he didn't let on. Gabe, on the other hand, looked as cross as a boxed-in bear, and who could blame him? She'd been anything but accommodating, revealing a rebellious attitude for which she now felt guilty.

It was that dratted kiss that did it, she finally ruled in her head, and she had herself to blame for allowing it to happen. Ever since experiencing the tantalizing taste of it, she couldn't get it out of her mind, especially since she had nothing else to compare it to. *Oh, bother!* Now, she'd have to wheedle a kiss out of Ralston—a *real* one—to see if it produced the same kind of reaction in her deepest, innermost parts. Perhaps the next time she saw him....

"What about Billy B? He's goin' to wonder where I am," Jesse mumbled, his words bringing her back to the present.

Gabe shrugged. "I don't know, bud. I suppose Abbie or Maggie will tell him where you are."

"He can come over after school and play. How about that? The school's only four blocks from our house," Hannah said. "Oh, and I heard the teachers are having meetings all day Tuesday, so there's no school. How about I send Abbie over to invite him to spend the day with you?"

This caused a smile. "Goodie!"

After that, the words between them fell away. In the distance, a dog barked, and Dusty responded with a low growl. Gabe made a quick survey of the area as they hurried up the hill, glancing over his shoulder and from side to side, face clouded with uneasiness.

With a pang of guilt, she realized the gravity of the situation, and she put a gloved hand around Jesse's shoulder to tug him close.

With Jesse and Dusty in the fenced-in backyard, Gabe briefly explained to Helena the plan for putting Jesse to work on several minor tasks so he wouldn't grow suspicious about why they stayed away from the store. Helena nodded. "I have plenty of things he can do. Why, there's a whole box of children's books in the attic just waiting to be sorted." She winked at Gabe. "Books from when the girls were this high." She gestured with a flat palm positioned three feet from the floor. "That should take a day or more." She rambled on, listing off a slew of jobs to keep a boy busy—polishing Jacob's shoes and boots, dusting all her knickknacks, organizing canned goods in the cellar, helping her bake cookies and bread for the shut-ins and elderly, and so on.

"How did I know you would have it all figured out, Helena?" He flashed her a smile, which prompted Helena to fuss over the already perfect bun at the back of her head. Grandmother's bun never fell out as Hannah's did. Even now, Hannah's peripheral vision saw several clumps of red curls cascading down her temples.

"Well, I suppose I'm thinking about that boy's welfare. You're not the only ones whose hearts he's affected. And now that you tell me he might be in danger, why, I'll do whatever I can to help. Besides, it might be nice to have a little boy around the house." She crinkled her brow and dipped her hands into her apron pockets. "'Course, I'm not saying the same for that mongrel of his. He'll have to stay outside."

As if the dog meant to make her pay for her remark, the back door opened, and in he came, dirty paws and all, dashing between Gabe's legs like a streak of lightning.

"Oh, merciful Molly!" Helena declared, even as Dusty darted past her, ran under the table, leaped over a chair, and sprinted through the living room, sniffing everything in sight.

When he made another pass through the parlor room where they were all congregated, Gabe reached for the rambunctious canine but failed. Hannah joined the chase, extending her hand and using her harshest voice. "Dusty! Come here! Stop!"

All to no avail.

"How did—what—shoo! Out! Scat!" Helena ordered in a drill sergeant voice, flinging her arms and turning on her heels in an attempt to keep track of the action.

When Dusty raced into the kitchen, Hannah and Gabe followed, intending to corner him, but he proved cunning by slipping right through Hannah's grasp and running to the stairs, continuing up to investigate the second story.

"Oh, mercy me!" Helena bewailed. "Now he's gone upstairs."

On cue, Jesse walked out of the water closet, his wool coat hanging open as he buttoned up his pants.

"Why'd you let Dusty in?" Gabe asked him, clearly exasperated.

"Don't yell at him," Hannah said.

"I'm not yelling, I'm asking," Gabe said, lowing his volume slightly just the same.

"I had to go—bad."

"You couldn't have left him outside?"

"He followed me in." The boy's face looked stricken by Gabe's impatient tone, and it occurred to Hannah how much he looked up to the man.

"He's not to come in the house," Gabe instructed him.

"Would someone please get the dog?" Helena cut in.

Without ado, Jesse walked to the foot of the stairs and looked up. "Dusty!"

Immediately, four feet came bounding back down. At the bottom, the dog's eyes searched Jesse's face expectantly. "Go!" His firm voice and pointed finger proved sufficient. Tail between his legs, Dusty sauntered toward the kitchen, through the pantry, and straight to the back door.

Three pairs of adult eyes watched in awe as the dog succumbed to Jesse's authority.

"My!" Helena exclaimed, raising her hand to her throat. "That was amazing."

"Remarkable," said Hannah.

"How'd you do that?" Gabe asked.

Jesse shrugged, a look of pride replacing his earlier chagrin at Gabe's abruptness. "I guess he knows who's in charge." With that, he retrieved his stocking cap out of his coat pocket, pulled it over his ears, and walked to the door, where Dusty was waiting patiently.

After Jesse closed the door, Helena sniffed. "Well—I suppose it wouldn't hurt for the dog to come inside once in a while—so long as Jesse gives him the occasional bath and makes him behave. He certainly has a fine way with him."

"Grandmother, you've gone soft as a poached egg!" Hannah exclaimed. "Moments ago, a tornado on four legs ran all over your beautiful rugs, and now you're saying he's welcome to come back in!"

"Well, there was that stipulation of keeping him under control, of course."

"Of course."

For the first time, Hannah and Gabe exchanged a glance containing a hint of a smile. No question about it—Helena Kane had fallen prey to Jesse Gant's charms.

Later, while Helena hummed a hymn to herself as she rattled pots and pans in the kitchen sink and Jesse played out back, where Helena could watch him from the window, Hannah held the door for Gabe, warding off a sudden awkwardness at having been left alone with him. Damp and chilly air mingled at her ankles.

"Sorry you have to stay cooped up. I guess I did come off a little ironhanded back there. It's just—I'm concerned for Jesse's safety." He leaned forward, his body half in. "And yours."

The way his voice dipped low caused a warm blush to spread across her cheeks. She held the door in a death grip, as if she expected it to blow away on her. "And I overreacted. Of course, I want what's best for Jesse."

"I know that." He rubbed his nose with a knuckle and held back a smile. She saw it when he shot a quick glance at a rabbit scampering across the front yard. Arching one of his sandy brows at her, he asked, "You're not still sore at me, then?"

Why did he have to be so charming? She thought about Ralston and his utter lack of magnetism, then quickly berated herself for comparing them. Of course, both were sophisticated in their own realms—Ralston, intellectual and world-trained; Gabe, pragmatic and worldly-*wise*. But when it came to adventure and diversion, Ralston fell flat. Why, they'd courted for months, and not once had he even attempted to kiss her on the mouth. Gabe, on the other hand....

"Well?" He'd planted one foot on the lower step, putting their eye levels within close range.

"I was never—sore at you," she fibbed. "Just irritated."

Tossing back his head, he gave a hearty chuckle. "There's a difference?"

Flustered, she pushed a strand of hair behind her ear, his gaze following the move. "I mean, you bossing me around like that, giving me what for without my getting a word in edgewise—that irritated me."

He grinned, his eyes moving over her face. "Pardon? If I recall, you got plenty of words in edgewise. '*What do you mean I can't work? Who's going to unpack the cartons? Papa, tell him. Isn't this extreme? Am I a prisoner?*'" In his attempt to mock her, his voice lifted several decibels.

She gave him a playful gut punch. "Oh, stop it. And I didn't say, 'Am I a prisoner?'"

"Well, something close to it, then," he replied with light laughter.

"And I wasn't nearly that dramatic, either." In spite of herself, a string of giggles bubbled up. "You see why you irritate me?"

When the laughter dissipated, she glanced behind her. The kitchen had grown quiet. As if on signal, Helena announced, "I'm going out back with Jesse. I may as well get to know that mongrel of his." They heard her wrestle with her coat before opening and closing the back door. Outside, a solitary blue jay bellowed a harsh jeer.

Hannah swallowed and shifted positions, hanging tighter to the door, one hand gripping the doorknob, shivering more from his closeness than from the cool air nipping at the hem of her skirts.

Gabe brushed the fingers of his closed hand across her cheek and sobered. "Hannah," he whispered. She stood frozen to the floor and stared at that eye-level button again instead of those appealing blue eyes.

No more kisses, she told herself. *None. Not until I square matters with Ralston. Why, it wouldn't be right—or even fair to him*, she argued.

Her heart pounded heavily and soared weightlessly at the same time.

She'd always considered herself a loyal and truthful individual, but how were courting one man and kissing another compatible with those character traits?

He stepped closer, but still she kept these thoughts safely hidden, even as his hands gently cupped her face.

"I'm giving you the chance to step back," he muttered, as if reading her thoughts, his head half-bent toward a kiss. Her heart hammered at full tilt.

He expected her to dictate the next move, but as a gentleman, he figured he should take responsibility. *Oh, bother.*

Leaning forward, he kissed the tip of her nose, then brushed a gentle, velvety kiss across her forehead before journeying downward to kiss both cheeks. *Oh, but his lips are soft—much softer than Ralston's, she decided, and savory—yes, that was it—savory, not to mention smooth as polished stones.*

Lord God, have mercy on my soul. What's happening to me? I'm not going to swoon, am I? What could be more mortifying? Oh, I do so hate to swoon. Remind me how to breathe, Lord.

His hands slipped up her arms and tugged her to him, and because of her wobbly stance, she couldn't find the strength to move her legs, so she simply sagged into the warmth of his embrace. *Double bother!*

"Hannah Grace Kane, what am I going to do with you?" he whispered against her lips.

Ralston never whispered such things, never fanned her face with his breath, never made her skin tingle. Why, he'd never even kissed the tip of her nose! And who would have known such a kiss could feel so lovely?

Repositioning his hands at the hollow of her back, Gabe locked them tight around her, and so she followed suit, her trembling limbs clinging. She tried to say he would be the death of her, but when she parted her lips, he chose that moment to smother her words, if not her breath, with another moist kiss, one that seemed to carry her to places she never knew existed. Ralston never took her anywhere but Culver House!

Warmth rippled through her veins while the kiss lingered, urging her to do her part to make it worthwhile, which only made her heart hammer harder and her senses swim. Ralston never made her senses swim, never made her—Ralston. *Oh, my!*

Ralston! Oh, for goodness' sake, what am I doing?

Guilt-ridden and shocked for having yielded to Gabe's kisses—again—Hannah wriggled away from his embrace, reality striking her with astonishing clarity.

"You are a masterful manipulator, a—a proficient persuader!" she accused.

Looking as dazed as someone who'd just been whacked in the gut, he gave his head a stunned shake. "What?" She moved away from him, at which time he invited himself back inside and closed the door. "I am neither of those, Hannah Grace, and, if you'll recall, I gave you plenty of time to stop me."

"Plenty, my sore foot! You barely gave me a chance to think."

A mouthful of air hurtled out of him and he scraped a hand through his hair. "You knew it was coming." He grinned in that crooked, beguiling way. "Face it, Hannah, something's going on between us, and you're having just as hard a time resisting me as I am you."

She dropped her jaw and sucked in a raspy gasp, pulling her shoulders straight as pins. "Wh—I can resist you just fine."

Now he tossed back his head and let the laughter flow.

She saw no humor whatsoever in the situation, and she opened her mouth to tell him so, but a deafening boom—gunfire?—drowned her attempt. He jolted with shock, then immediately leaped into action, snagging her by the arm and pulling her into the kitchen. "Stand there and don't move," he ordered her.

She was inclined to obey. Next, he bolted for the back door, but Grandmother and Jesse rushed inside before he even got there, slamming the door shut after Dusty galloped in behind them.

"It came from that direction," Helena panted, pointing east up Ridge Street.

"Was that a g-gun?" Jesse stammered. "It—it sounded like that time I…" But he left the sentence hanging, his milk-white face creased in worry.

Gabe crouched beside the boy and rumpled his head of black hair. "Like what?" he asked, his voice uncommonly controlled. "Have you heard gunfire before? When was that, buddy? Can you tell me?"

Rather than respond with words, Jesse threw his arms around Gabe's neck and buried his face in its solid cushion. Gabe put a hand to the back of his head and drew him close. "It's all right," he assured. "Everything's gonna be fine. We'll talk later." Over Jesse's head, Gabe looked from Helena to Hannah.

"Poor lamb," Helena whispered.

Jesse clung for several seconds, but finally Gabe peeled him off, angling him with a steady gaze. "You're going to have to be the man here," he explained, arms on his narrow shoulders. "Can you do that?"

Jesse straightened to his full height and hiccupped a jagged sigh, then gave a slow, solemn nod.

"Good. I knew I could count on you." Then, to Hannah and Helena, he said, "I want everyone upstairs and out of sight. Do not come down until I give the word. Do you understand?"

Helena gave three rapid nods, her face long and serious. "Absolutely. Come on, Jesse." She extended her hand. "I want to show you something."

"What?" he asked, taking the hand she offered, Dusty herding them toward the stairs.

"You do like to read, right?" Helena asked.

"Yeah."

"Well, then you'll be amazed by my book collection."

Their voices faded as they mounted the stairs.

"What's happening, Gabe?" Hannah asked.

Gabe left her standing in the kitchen and made for the front door, taking out his revolver and checking its cylinder for ammunition. Satisfied, he stuffed it back in its holster. "I don't know, but I'm about to find out." His professional air somehow left her feeling deflated. She wanted the same reassurance he'd just doled out to Jesse.

She moved toward him and looked at his gun. Did he expect to shoot someone? "Go upstairs, Hannah," he issued. "I don't have time to talk."

"But—"

"Go!"

He pushed the door open, paused, then turned and kissed her on the cheek. It held about as much passion as one of Ralston's pecks.

When she didn't budge, he reached up and gave one of her curls a gentle tug. "Listen, Hannah, I don't want to worry about you while I'm trying to sort out who's shooting who, you understand?" The stare-down lasted a few seconds before he dropped the curl and turned around. "Go upstairs."

Leaving her standing there, he pulled the door shut behind him, then looked through the glass at her while pointing at the stairs.

Another gunshot sounded, jolting her body. "Go!" This time, the command held no friendliness.

In haste, she picked up her skirts and dashed across the room, taking two steps at a time up the stairs, just like she used to do when she and her sisters had played hide-and-seek in the big house.

Chapter Seventeen

Fully aware of his surroundings and having no idea where the shots were fired from, Gabe advanced down the porch steps with caution, his trained mind focused now on nothing but scouting out his environs, attentive to every sight and sound. He wished for his horse, but he'd walked Hannah and Jesse home, so it appeared he had no choice but to walk, which was just as well. This way, he could cut between houses, if need be, and crouch from bush to bush.

Sensing danger, or at least excitement of a different kind, neighborhood dogs barked and howled, interfering with his ability to focus. A black squirrel skittered down a tree and darted across Gabe's path as he headed east on Ridge. Cold air forced him to secure the top button of his coat.

"Lord, please protect this town and guide my steps. I need Your direction right now." This he whispered as he hurried up the pebbled road, hand poised on his revolver. Out of the corner of his eye, he noted several folks peering out their front windows, drawing back the curtains far enough to watch him pass. One block over, he saw a man on horseback.

He was about to warn him to back off when the fellow reined his horse into a thicket of trees, disappearing from view.

A squeaking door opened. "Psst! Sheriff!" hissed a voice. It was Herb Horton, who came out in his long underwear and stepped to the edge of his porch.

Gabe approached him. "You best get back inside," he warned.

"If I had my guess, I'd say that was old Bill Elwood shootin' off his gun. I seen the fire wagons go up Fourth a while ago. I was over t' Bill and Evaleen's place last night tryin' to help get a cat out of their tree. 'Fraid I made matters worse, though. Fool thing kept hissin' and goin' higher. Bill's about lost most of his marbles, if you know what I mean, and this cat ain't helped matters."

"I appreciate that, Herb."

"You know where the Elwoods live?"

"I have a good idea."

"Turn right on Fourth an' take that one block t' Oak Avenue. My guess is, them fire wagons are parked outside."

"Thanks, Herb. Now, you best get back inside."

"I'm a goin'." After yanking open his squeaky door, he gave a holler. "Ol' Bill ain't really dangerous as he seems. He's just fallen off his rocker."

Old Bill was off his rocker, all right. In fact, when Gabe rounded the corner on Oak Avenue, he saw Bill standing on the edge of his porch, rifle aimed and at the ready, several members of the Sandy Shores Fire Department and a few unidentified citizens hiding out behind trees and wagons, too afraid to move. Crouching down, Gabe crept to the side of the house, unseen by Bill, but catching the eye of his deputy,

Gus van der Voort, who had found a spot behind a skinny maple.

"Throw your gun down, Bill," Gus shouted out. "You don't want anyone gettin' hurt, now, do you?"

Gus looked at Gabe, who gestured for him to continue talking. Gus gave a helpless shrug and raised an inquiring brow.

Gabe mouthed the words, "Keep talking." Gus nodded.

"Come on, Bill. Throw down that rifle. None of us here means you any harm."

"Shut yer trap!" Bill retorted, his words resounding through the quiet little neighborhood, setting off a couple of dogs. A black cat darted across the neighbor's yard, and a woman opened her door in haste, inviting the feline inside. As soon as the cat skittered in, the door closed with a whop.

From his hiding place, Gabe took a moment to study Bill Elwood. He had to be in his late seventies, but he still had a hefty build, probably the result of his career in logging. Too bad his brain had fallen behind.

"Didn't I tell you to send for Mort McPherson?" Bill hollered like a wild man. "What you waitin' for?" He fired off another warning shot into the trees. Gabe felt the hairs on his neck stand straight up, saw the men Bill held captive jolt to attention. "I ain't puttin' my gun down till he gets his hide over here. He and me got a score t' settle."

Gus shot Gabe a forlorn look, which Gabe answered with an encouraging nod. Gus sucked in a fortifying breath. "I already told you, Bill, Mort McPherson's dead."

"Would you stop sayin' that? He's not dead. Shoot, we played cards not two weeks ago." Bill waved his gun in a frantic fashion as he talked. "Good-for-nothin' scoundrel didn't win fair and square, though. Took my last dime, and I mean to get it back."

"I'm afraid that's not possible, Bill. He died last spring, when the pneumonia took him. You were one of his pallbearers, if I recollect right."

"Huh?" Bill rubbed the back of his neck and scowled, his eyes closing for the briefest time. When he scraped a hand through his thinning white hair and started to pace, Gabe took advantage of the moment by advancing around the corner of the house, skulking like a prowler to stay out of sight, then hunkering down behind a mostly bare forsythia bush a couple of feet from the porch. Thankfully, Bill never detected his presence. Through the thick brush, Gabe watched the old man process Gus's words.

Wincing, Bill gave his head a couple of fast shakes. "No, you're lyin'."

"Come on, Bill, why would I lie about something like that? Mort's dead. That's all there is to it. Now, put the gun down, would you?"

Bill held on to his head with one hand and waved his rifle in the air with the other, his finger on the trigger.

Gabe swallowed hard, waiting and praying for that perfect moment to overtake Bill Elwood.

Just then, Evaleen Elwood pushed open the door and hobbled out onto the porch, a blood-spattered towel pressed to her forehead. "You put that cussed gun down, ol' man."

Before she even had the sentence out of her mouth, and well before Bill had time to react, Gabe leaped over the forsythia and landed on the porch, yanking the rifle from Bill's grasp.

"I'll take that, Sheriff," said Gus, who'd materialized at Gabe's side and relieved him of the gun. With the squirming Bill in a firm hold, Gabe looked up as men emerged one by one from their hiding spots, relief evident on their faces.

"He's plain loco," one of the firemen muttered.

"Belongs in the nuthouse," another spouted.

"And all that over a blasted cat," yet another fireman groused. "Dumb thing nearly killed me with his claws when I finally got him down." He extended his arms to reveal several tears in his jacket sleeves.

"It's over now, folks," Gabe said. "Thanks for your patience. Glad everyone's safe."

Still murmuring among themselves, the men made their way back to their wagons. Riding by on his scraggly looking horse, the same fellow Gabe had spotted just moments ago another block over slowed as if to size up the situation. His hat was pulled low on his head, shading his face from view. He lingered long enough to rouse Gabe's curiosity, then nudged his horse into a canter and disappeared around the next block.

"Who was that?" Gabe asked his deputy, nodding up the road.

Gus, who'd been looking after Evaleen's head wound, squinted in the distance. "Got no idea. Probably just a curious neighbor. Much as I'd like to, I still don't know all the citizens of Sandy Shores."

A strange sense came over Gabe that he had seen him before, but with the wiggly Bill in his grip, he had little time to recollect where.

"You all right, ma'am?" Gabe asked Evaleen, concerned about the blood on the towel from the cut on her forehead. "You'd better take a seat there."

She mumbled under her breath and wobbled to the wicker settee, making sure to whop Bill in the side with her free hand as she passed. "That's for hittin' me with that rifle butt, you ornery cuss."

"He hit you?" Gabe asked.

Bill looked stunned. "I didn't hit you, woman."

"You sure shootin' did too. 'Course, you called me 'Howard' when you done it. He's plumb lost it, Sheriff." She tilted her head at Gabe and squinted. "You are the new sheriff, right?"

Bill jerked his head around. "Huh?" His hawk-like eyes looked Gabe up and down. "What you talkin' about—new sheriff? What happened to Watson?"

It would seem poor Bill Elwood had some catching up to do.

K

"This is a fine place, Pa. How'd you say you found it again?" Roy asked, running his fingertips over the piano's keys as he walked by it for the third time.

"How many times I gotta tell you t' leave that thing alone? You're goin' to wake the dead, runnin' your hands up an' down that keyboard."

"Don't say dead. This place is creepy enough as it is," Reuben said, his eyes as big as a Kansas moon as they roved about the roomy house, which was lit by a meager amount of candles.

"It ain't creepy. Look at this place. Sittin' up high on a sand dune overlookin' the Big Lake, shut off from everything, and ritzier than any hotel. Why, it's the pleasantest place I ever been in," argued Roy, walking over to the long divan and yanking a protective sheet off its lush velvet upholstery. He threw it to the floor in a heap, then plopped onto the sofa and sighed with pleasure.

Reuben scoffed. "That's 'cause all you seen in days is the back end of a pony, lunkhead. Anything'd look good to you by now." He walked to the window and pulled back the heavy drapery, looking into the black of night. "How you know the people what own this place ain't comin' home, Pa?"

Rufus had had about all he could take of these two. "I told you, I heard talk down at the saloon 'bout the folks who live here. They only come here two months out o' the year, July and August. Rest of the time, they're in Chicago." From his place in the paneled doorway, he gazed at the mahogany fireplace mantle, the fine oak desk in the adjoining study, the massive walnut staircase, and the long dining table of an unfamiliar, finely polished wood. "Stinkin' rich buzzards," he muttered, angry how some folks just seemed to have the knack for growing money while he had spent his life scrounging for it, starting out stealing for his ma and pa when he was no more than a little squirt.

Roy settled back and stretched out his arms on the back of the sofa, a cocky grin on his face. "You get yerself a new coat today, Reub?"

Reuben snapped the drapery shut and whirled on his heel. "Oh, shut yer trap 'fore I throw you into the drink. You already know I didn't."

"Thought you was goin' to get yerself one at that Whatnot store," Rufus said, pushing away from the door frame and walking to a chair, a big leather job with a cloth draped over it. Like Roy, he removed the cloth and threw it on the floor beside the chair.

"They didn't have any yet. The girl told me they'd be gettin' some in next week or so, said I should check back later."

"'Cept there won't be no checkin' back, right, Reub? He got kicked out o' there, Pa, thrown out on his nose." Roy grabbed his stomach and rolled over with laughter.

Reuben shot his older brother a hostile glare. "Didn't I tell you to shut up?"

Rufus's mood veered from annoyance to anger. "And didn't I tell you boys not to be makin' any trouble? Last thing we need is for folks t' start recognizin' us. You shouldn't be talkin' to no one, y' hear? How'd you get kicked out, anyhow?"

"He was playin' up to the shopkeeper's daughter, who, I'm findin' out, is friendly with the sheriff," Roy said, still grinning like a monkey, all teeth and no warmth.

"I knew I shouldn't o' told you nothin'," Reuben grumbled.

"Shut up, both o' you!" Rufus ordered, digging his fingers into the chair arms, thinking about that fifth of whiskey he stole from the saloonkeeper when his back was turned away from the marble-topped bar. Soon as these boys found themselves a bed upstairs, he'd let that sizzling liquid do its job; but for now, he had to think, had to figure out next steps. Both boys fell silent, sobered by his no-nonsense tone.

"All right, now, who is this—this storekeep's daughter, anyway?"

"I don't know—just some young skinny thing with a mass o' red hair. Testy little woman, too."

"Fine lookin', if y' ask me," Roy cut in.

"You'd a' thought I was some big ol' bear the way she jumped when I snatched her by the arm."

"You what?" Rufus bellowed.

"I was just tryin' to earn some respect, is all."

Rufus stood up, ready to knock some sense into his younger son. "You're dumber than an ol' mule lookin' for a second gate. It ain't enough that you've etched yer mug in that girl's mind; now her pa's goin' to be searchin' for you 'round ev'ry corner."

"And he's respected about town, too, not someone to tangle with," Roy put in, tapping on the back of the sofa, grinning like some know-it-all. "Owns an insurance agency across the street from Kane's Whatnot. Spends most of 'is time in the office while his lovely daughters tend the store, but he checks on things often. The oldest, Reub's new girlfriend, is there most days, and there's a library upstairs that the girls take turns overseein'."

Rufus's anger at Reuben quickly yielded to sudden interest in the research Roy had just disclosed. He unclenched his fists and turned a slow gaze on him. "What made you so smart?"

Roy brought a hand down to study his dirty fingernails. "Why, you, Pa. I learned my tricks from you. I just walks in that saloon on Columbus Street, that grungy one hardly nobody patronizes, and starts drinkin' my beers, mindin' my business. Pretty soon, I finds me a boozed up stewie sittin' in a dark corner talkin' to hisself, so I make my move! Ain't you always tol' us to go lookin' for the ones what keep to themselves?"

Rufus stuck his chest out. "Most times they're the ones who spill the information you're after," he said. "'Specially when they're wallowin' in the brew."

"Exactly. I got me an earful, too."

Rufus plunked down at the other end of the sofa and looked at Roy, hungry for information. After a second, he slapped him in the arm. "So, what'd you learn?"

"Well, let's see here." Rufus bit back a curse while Roy took his sweet time. Roy loved hording information from everyone, especially his own pa. He scratched his head, then folded one leg over the top of the other and played with his bootlace. "The oldest daughter, name's Hannah Grace, watches over the kid during the day while the sheriff works, but after Reuben's well-timed visit to the store, that might end. I saw the sheriff walkin' 'er and the little snot up the street to the Kane house. I hid out behind some brush while they all went inside. Wouldn't surprise me none if he starts takin' the kid there ev'ry day.

"There was a to-do up at some ol' codger's house. Fool went loco shootin' off his gun. The sheriff headed up there to investigate, and I followed from a block over. 'Course, he never knew I watched the whole commotion from a distance. Afterward, I got real brave and rode right by there. Sheriff just throwed me a casual glance. I got me a good look at him, too. He don't look like much."

"Huh." Rufus was impressed. "You looked straight at him?"

"Sure did. Here's what I figure." Roy slid forward on the couch, his eyes blazing with crude excitement. Rufus didn't much like the way he took the lead, but curiosity kept him from saying so.

"There's goin' to be a graveyard service on Tuesday—for Luis." An uncomfortable, burning knot formed at the pit of Rufus's stomach at that bit of information. Roy truly had done his homework. "Figure the sheriff'll be busy with that," Roy went on, not missing a beat. "Fact is, he'll probably be scoutin' the area lookin' for some clues about Luis's identity, maybe hopin' some family members will show up at the cemetery.

"I'm thinkin' while the service is goin' on, we'll snatch the boy. He'll be at either the house or that store, but I'd try the house first. We can bring him up here for a day or so while we decide the best way to, you know, dispose of him. After the deed's done, we'll be on our way."

Roy sat back and gazed, cold-eyed, at Rufus. "Well? What do y' think?"

Rufus licked his lips, fighting back a sudden wave of nausea. "Yeah. Yeah, it's good," he muttered, hiding the fact that for the first time in his life, he felt swallowed up in mud, and, worse, bested by his own son. "What about the woman? How you think yer gonna snatch the kid without a fight from 'er?"

Roy chuckled and the sound made even Rufus squirm. "Could be fun, y' know? Might be we'll end up bringin' her along for some excitement. There's a grandmother in the house, too, but she'll be easy enough to handle."

Roy shot his brother an icy look, his mouth twitching in the corner. "What's the matter with you, brainless?"

A squeamish expression had washed over Reuben's countenance. He shook his head. "You want us to nab the kid on the day of our brother's funeral?"

Raw hate seeped from Roy's eyes. "It's the best time to do it, dimwit, and we ain't goin' to the ceremony, if that's what you think. We show up there and we're goners, for sure."

Rufus took a long gander at Reuben. If Reuben's eyes had been daggers, Roy would have been a goner in that instant.

K

"You okay, buddy?" Gabe asked, pulling back the comforter on the bed, dropping to the mattress, and removing his boots. Ever since arriving home, Jesse had uttered little more than a couple of sentences, and he'd only picked at the meager supper Gabe had put together. Of course, who could blame him? Cooking for two wasn't exactly his forte.

"I told you those gunshots you heard were nothing to worry about. An old fellow losing track of reality went a little berserk, that's all. He's staying in the jail for the night, and Doc Van Huff is giving him some medicine that will help his mind."

At least, that's the plan, Gabe thought. Sedatives might make the old guy sleep more, but they wouldn't help him regain his faculties. It wouldn't surprise him if, down the road, Evaleen Elwood committed her husband to the state asylum. In fact, any more physical assaults and Judge Bowers would personally see to it.

Jesse pulled back the covers on his side of the bed and crawled in, taking one of the wooden toy soldiers Hannah had given him and tucking it under his chin. He looked as sober as a brick.

Gabe slipped out of his uniform and into his pajama pants, threw it in a heap on the chair beside the bed, and crawled in on the other side. Nights were getting nippier. In preparation for the winter months, he'd ordered a ton of coal to be delivered the week of November 21. Until then, he'd conserve what supply he did have. That meant not always firing up the furnace on chilly evenings like tonight but doubling up outerwear instead.

Dusty turned several circles on the braided rug beside the bed before finding the perfect place to plop his furry brown body. Gabe hadn't wanted to start inviting the dog inside, but it seemed the natural thing to do tonight, in light of Jesse's somber mood. Until tonight, the mutt had been fending for himself outside, and doing a fine job of it, as far as Gabe knew.

"Your dog seems to have made himself right at home," Gabe said, turning down the bedside light before settling in. A harvest moon cast its shadow across the room, giving off enough light for Gabe to make out Jesse's profile—his rumpled hair that called for another trip to the barber, little pug nose, round cheeks, short chin, pouting lips, and wide eyes, gazing up at the ceiling.

Gabe turned on his side and stared at the soundless boy. He could almost see his little mind turning over one troubled thought after another.

Lord, help him trust me enough to tell me his story. What can I say that will draw him out? It's been more than two months. He sighed while sending up the prayer.

Tell him he's a fine boy, and that you care about him.

What? It seemed too simplistic to Gabe's mind. What would that accomplish? Besides, hadn't he said as much by getting him off the streets, providing for his needs, spending all his spare time with him—letting his dog sleep in his house, for Pete's sake?

I once was lost but now am found. Where had he heard it? Oh yes, from Maggie Rose while she was singing her off-key rendition of "Amazing Grace."

A lost boy needs to know someone loves him, wants him, will never leave him. Don't you remember getting lost in your father's cornfield when you were about Jesse's age? How you started screaming his name, and how he managed to find you after looking a full half hour? Remember your sense of fear? Like it was yesterday. One hot August day, he'd been chasing down field mice, putting them in his pockets while going deeper and deeper into the maze. His banshee-like screams, when he discovered his predicament, put his father on a mission—one he wouldn't have abandoned for the world. To this day, Gabe remembered that blessed relief of falling into Joseph Devlin's strong arms and savoring his words of assurance.

A lost boy needs to know someone values him.

As if he'd been knocked alongside the head, Gabe got it. Sometimes actions weren't enough. Words. Jesse needed words.

Gabe swallowed a hard knot of emotion and raised up on his elbow.

"You're a fine boy, you know that?"

Chapter Eighteen

I'm nothin' special," Jesse mumbled into the sheets. "An' I'm gettin' dumb, too, 'cause I been missin' so much school."

"What? You're smart as a whip. Missing a little school isn't going to hurt you any," Gabe quickly countered. "I don't know many boys who can read like you. Shoot, I think you're better at it than me."

Jesse pondered that one. "Did your ma teach you?"

"To read, you mean? No, I think I learned that in school. How 'bout you? Did your mama teach you?"

A blanket of silence fell over them, save for the clock ticking on the bedside stand. Jesse pulled his covers up tight around his chin. "I guess. Ma read to me every night until she…"

"What, Jess? Until she what?"

"Died."

If someone had hit him square in the face with a brick, he would not have been more stunned than he was right now. Bit by bit, the wall of secrecy Jesse had built around himself had started crumbling. *Lord, I need to tread softly here.*

"I'm sorry to hear that, bud. You must have been very sad."

Jesse nodded in the shadows. He pulled out his soldier and looked at it. "Pa died, too." This he said with chilling matter-of-factness.

"Were they—in some sort of accident?"

Jesse shook his head. "My pa was, but not my ma. Pa fell off a horse and hit his head, I guess. I don't remember him very good, 'cause I was just little when he, you know, got kilt. My ma got put in a hospital back in—hmm, I don't know when, but it was startin' to get warm outside. She couldn't breathe good."

Pneumonia, maybe? "You mean last spring?"

"Yeah, springtime."

"So, you were on your own since then?"

No answer, just a slow up and down nod as he handled his special toy soldier.

"Where did you and your ma live—before she got sick?"

"New York."

"New Y—Jess, how did you wind up in Michigan?"

Silence like a black cloud draped them again. Was he pushing too hard? *God, I don't want to blow it.* Feeling his pulse thud hard in his gut, Gabe fought to keep his voice at an even keel. He touched a finger to the boy's forehead and rubbed lightly. "I care about you, Jess. Very much. You know you can trust me, right?"

Jesse turned his head and looked at Gabe in the shadows, studying, processing. At last, another slow nod. "Yeah."

He breathed a sigh. "Then, tell me how you got here."

In the moments that followed, Jesse loosed a slew of words, more than Gabe had dreamed possible—everything from what the crowded little mission was like that he and his ma had lived in, to the city school he'd attended, to the way his mother had looked as she lay dying. Little by little, he got to the part about how he'd come to arrive in Michigan, but the details wound up sketchy, at best. Gabe guessed he'd blocked out a good share of it, and who could blame him? What kid wants to recall nothing but bad memories? The best he could tell, he'd arrived at some children's facility after the death of his mother, lived there for a time, and then left on an orphan train to join a family in the Middle West. That would explain the tag Hannah had found sewn into his shirt. But after that, the story fell apart. What had happened to prevent his moving in with this new family? Had he simply balked at the whole idea and jumped off the train at some remote station? Somehow, the McCurdy gang played into the scenario, but in what way?

"You think you can tell me how you happened to wind up in Holland, you know, the place where you crawled onto the back of my wagon?"

In the shadows, Gabe detected a growing frown. "I think— I jumped on the back of a train or somethin'. I did that a lot. I don't know. It's hard to remember it all."

"I know, I know, but…" He swallowed hard and prayed for just the right words. "You saw something, Jess, something that scared you plenty. Do you think—now that you know you're safe with me—do you think you could tell me what you saw?"

The boy sucked up most of the air in the twelve-by-twelve bedroom, then slowly let it back out. "I—don't like guns."

It seemed a random thing to say, but it held a great deal of meaning. Gabe whistled through his teeth. "Boy, I know what you mean. I don't either."

Jesse jerked his head in Gabe's direction. "How come you wear one, then?"

"Well, it goes with my job, buddy. People see me wearing it, and they know they have to tow the line. It represents justice, and it gives them a sense of security knowing I'm watching over them. Guns are dangerous, yes, but they can serve a good purpose. In some ways, they help to keep a place peaceful. I don't like having to wear one, but I wouldn't want to be caught in a bad situation without it."

"'Cause you might have to kill somebody?" Jesse asked.

The words slammed against Gabe with intense power. He'd managed to block out the worst of the memory of that day he'd confronted Smiley Joe Hamilton, but every so often, it came back with force. It did so now.

"Only when absolutely necessary, such as in cases of self-defense or if I believe another's life is in grave danger. Usually a cop aims to injure, not kill." He believed the best approach with Jesse was the straightforward one.

"Did you ever have to kill any bad guys?"

"Once." He swallowed down a bitter taste. "And I didn't like it. I hope I never have to do it again."

Jesse thought on that while he played with his toy soldier, tipping it at different angles in the moon's shadows. It took great self-discipline on Gabe's part not to prod him into talking, knowing it best to let him move at his own pace.

"Sometimes soldiers have to kill if it's for a good cause."

"Well, yes, that's very true."

"Like in the Civil War. Ma said my grandpap had to fight in that war. He was on the South's side, but his side didn't win. Ma says he died of drinkin' too much after the war ended. He probably had to kill somebody, huh?"

"It's possible."

Still propped on his elbow, Gabe watched the boy with interest, shocked by his sudden impulse to talk.

"It's a sin to kill people just 'cause you want to, but it's not a sin if you're a cop or a soldier, and y' have to do it."

"See, I told you that you were smart."

The ticking clock and Dusty's low-throated snores filled up the next minute or so.

Outside, a dog barked, the wind rustled the dead leaves around, and someone on a late-night journey galloped past the house, the horse's hooves pounding on the pebbled street.

Jesse took a deep breath and let it out slowly. "Those people what wanted to adopt me was murdered by bad guys," he said with surprising calm. Gabe's heart pounded out of control. "I know, 'cause I saw 'em do it."

"Jesse."

"I watched through the window. There was four of 'em, an old guy and three younger ones. The old guy, that one I saw in the newspaper, he shot 'em both. I didn't really want to live with them two people, but I didn't want to see 'em get shot, neither."

"Of course you didn't," Gabe answered in a breathy murmur.

"They met me at the train station in South Bend where that agent lady left me, and they were pretty nice." Gabe listened with heart-stopping intentness, praying God would give him the right choice of words when it came time to speak. "They took me to their house. It was way far out from the town, and there was a barn with two horses, and some cows and pigs." He grew quiet, contemplative. The clock ticked, and Gabe stopped breathing. "But I only stayed there two nights," he continued. "'Cause they got, you know, shot dead. I never saw blood before that day. My ma didn't bleed when she died, but that one lady in South Bend had blood comin' out o' her nose an' ears. I didn't like it. I didn't like it at all."

Erratic shivers ran through Jesse's body, so much so that the blanket covering them started quivering.

"Oh, Jesse, I'm so sorry you had to witness that." He brushed his hand over the lad's forehead and found it damp with perspiration.

"That one guy saw me and started yellin'. That's when I runned like there was no end t' the day. I mean I runned even faster than a train, I think. And I think—I think—I'm still runnin'."

Gabe's heart pooled like a melting block of ice in July. "No, buddy, you're not running. Not now, and not ever again. You're with me, and nothing is going to happen to you, do you hear me? Nothing." Without forethought, he took the small-framed boy into his arms, pulled him close to his chest, and felt the tremors travel clear to his heels. Squeezing shut his burning eyes to hold their moisture at bay, he rested his chin on Jesse's matted head of hair and rubbed his bony shoulders.

All at once, as if a river's dam had broken loose, its powerful waters surging the banks, Jesse started sobbing, deep-throated sobs that spilled and spewed, wracking his body, making him go limp from exhaustion.

"It's okay, Jesse," Gabe crooned. "You've been holding in that river for too long. Time to let it out."

A loud, hiccupping sigh tumbled out of Jesse, followed by several minutes' worth of earth-shaking wails, some so pitifully dismal Gabe thought his own heart would split in two.

There is was—finally. The truth. And, oh, how it did pain a soul to come out after hiding for so long. And yet how absolutely freeing.

He clutched Jesse so tight he feared he might be cutting off his air supply, but then another pathetic, high-pitched howl pushed out, and he knew his oxygen intake was adequate. Dusty got up from the floor to investigate, sticking his wet nose in Gabe's back and then padding around to Jesse's side of the bed. When it looked like things were under control, the mutt turned several circles and plopped back down again, this time next to Jesse. Gabe raised a hand to dab at his own watery eyes. *Shoot!* He couldn't remember the last time he'd shed tears, unless it was when his grandfather went to be with the Lord five years ago.

An eternity seemed to pass before the crying spell wound down, and, when it did, a hundred wracking sighs followed on top of each other, each one ending on a hiccup.

Gabe loosened his hold, and Jesse settled into his shoulder, his nightshirt drenched with sweat that moistened Gabe's bare chest.

"I love you, Jess, you know that?" The effortless words drifted out like a song. "And so does God. He's had His eyes on you since the day you were born, and when your mama died, He decided to send you to me, even if you did take the long way to get here." He grinned over the boy's head.

Jesse sniffed. "My ma tol' me God would take care of me."

"And she was right."

He sniffed again, this time hard and loud. Then he dragged the blanket up to his face and blew his nose.

Gabe groaned. "Oh, Jess, did you have to do that? I got a whole slew of handkerchiefs in my top drawer."

Jesse giggled—a giggle wrapped up in relief and unspoken joy. Gabe sucked in a lungful of air and chuckled himself.

Seconds passed. "Are you g-gonna be my pa?"

The question lunged out at Gabe like a snake from a closet. Here he was, inexperienced in every way concerning parenting, but wanting the label of father more than he could imagine. "I'd like to be, Jesse, if you wouldn't mind."

"Wouldn't we need a ma, too? Like maybe Hannah?"

The snake lunged again. "I'd have to wrench her out of Dr. Van Huff's grasp first."

From under the blanket came the little wooden soldier. Jesse studied it in the moonlight. "I think she likes you better."

"Really? What makes you say so?"

"'Cause she's always lookin' out the window waitin' for you to come. And then she says, 'Here comes Gabe,' all excited-like, and runs to the mirror to fix her hair."

Gabe pulled his arm out from under Jesse and positioned himself on his side again, propping himself up on his elbow. "So, you think that's a good sign, then?"

Jesse turned his head toward Gabe, then gave him a light bop on the arm with his toy soldier. "You better learn about women."

The statement caught him like an uppercut on the chin and made him laugh.

Later, after their banter had died down, Jesse slept soundly beside him, breaths light and peaceful. Gabe lay in a bed of mixed emotions. On the one hand, it gave him great joy to watch Jesse's wall of secrecy collapse in a heap, to be the one to assure him of his safety. On the other, knowing Rufus McCurdy's presence in the town threatened everyone's well-being, especially that of Jesse and Hannah, placed a huge burden of responsibility on his shoulders, filling him with a sense of dread and inadequacy.

"God, I'm going to need Your divine intervention here," he prayed, having slipped out of the sheets to kneel beside the bed in a spirit of humility. "Without You, I'm no good. In fact, I'm nothing. But with You, I can do all things. I'm leaning on Your promises, God, depending on You to give me the strength, courage, and wisdom I so need to keep this town safe.

"And thanks, Lord, for making a way for Jesse, for breaking down those barriers in his young life, giving him the freedom to trust me.

"Now, if You could just provide a way for Hannah and me..."

"*Son, be of good cheer,*" came the words of Matthew 9:2. Then, the command from Hebrews 10:35 to "*cast not away therefore your confidence, which hath great recompense of reward.*" Gabe had read these words that very morning, followed by

Hebrews 11:6: "*Without faith it is impossible to please him: for he that cometh to God must believe that he is, and that he is a rewarder of them that diligently seek him.*"

As for strength for the day, the Lord seemed to say, *did you not just say you are nothing apart from Me? Therefore, lean unto Me, for My strength is made perfect in your weakness. Trust Me, My son. Trust Me.*

Comforted, Gabe returned to his bed and slept like a rock.

K

Despite November's biting chill, every pew in Sandy Shores Church held Sunday morning worshippers with hardly a space in between. The morning singing had been lively, Mrs. Overmyer's organ music especially skillful, and the portly Reverend Cooper's sermon timely, if not inspiring. Hannah held her Bible open to the primary passage of the morning's message, Psalm 37:1–4, silently rereading it and committing portions to memory, even as the pastor delivered his final few thoughts. "*Fret not thyself because of evildoers, neither be thou envious against the workers of iniquity. For they shall soon be cut down like the grass....Trust in the* LORD, *and do good....Delight thyself also in the* LORD; *and he shall give thee the desires of thine heart.*"

Over and over, distinct phrases seemed to lift themselves from the feathery pages and wash over her like fountains of mercy, as if each word held special significance for this particular time in her life. She continued to read Psalm 37: "*Commit thy way unto the* LORD....*Rest in the* LORD....*Fret not....For yet a little while, and the wicked shall not be....The wicked plotteth against the just....but the* Lord *upholdeth the righteous....He is their strength in the time of trouble....He shall deliver them from the wicked, and save them, because they trust in him."*

What it all meant, she couldn't say for certain, but somewhere in the depths of her soul, she sensed the need to cling to these truths from God's Word.

Not for the first time, her eyes traveled to the back of Gabe's blond head, spanning his broad-shouldered frame, his strong arm resting on the back of the pew, and his large hand cupping Jesse's narrow shoulder. He was sitting just a row ahead of her and across the aisle, his eyes trained on the preacher. The pair nestled close, looking suspiciously like father and son. Her heart warmed to near melting. As usual, Ralston sat next to her, and, every so often, she glanced up at him, as well. Whereas Gabe seemed focused on the minister's message, Ralston looked distracted, even bored. He fidgeted throughout the service, probably thinking about his patients and his beloved medical practice, tapping his fingers on his knee, crossing and uncrossing his legs, seeming impatient for the service to reach its conclusion. With chagrin, Hannah realized this was nothing new for him. If she were to marry him, would he even persist in attending church with her?

Her eyes were drawn once more to her Bible, where she returned to Psalm 37:4: *"Delight thyself also in the* Lord; *and he shall give thee the desires of thine heart."* This time, the words fairly popped out at her, prompting her to pray silently, *Lord, I long to delight myself in You. Please help me to focus on learning Your perfect will for my life.*

Ralston reached over and took her hand without warning, bringing it to his lap and clasping it between his smooth palms. The tiniest frown etched across her face, and she had to make a conscious effort to erase it. He'd held her hand on other occasions and she hadn't minded, but now she had the strongest urge to yank it away.

Her eyes traced another path to Gabe. As if he sensed her gaze, he turned his head, and, just like that, their eyes locked. Suddenly, her hand in Ralston's made her feel self-conscious, for she remembered the kisses she and Gabe shared the day before, ones that rocked her to the soles of her feet. *Masterful manipulator!* Gracious, had she really called him that? Thinking back, she could blame only herself.

Dragging her eyes to the pulpit, she tried her best to digest the reverend's words, but they sank into oblivion as she worried in secret. Perhaps she did find Gabriel Devlin irresistible.

In which case, to be fair, she must quickly find a way to end matters with Ralston.

Sneaking another peek at Gabe, she was surprised to find he had angled his body just so, putting her in perfect view. His sapphire gaze held her captive for several seconds until he reared back his head a few inches and lowered his eyes to Ralston's lap, delivering her a most disapproving frown.

Mortified, she snatched her hand away and started fumbling for a handkerchief in her little brown clutch purse.

After the service, rather than mingling outside, as folks did in warmer weather, people stood in crowded clusters in the church's small foyer, laughing and exchanging greetings and discussing everything from the preacher's timely message of hope to the rising prices of bread and milk. Ralston always enjoyed this part of the morning, as it gave him the opportunity to rub shoulders with a few of the upper crust, the folks he tended to migrate toward because they offered potential financial support for the hospital project. Strange—it hadn't bothered her until now the way he snubbed the "common folks," many of whom he treated in his office, in favor of ingratiating himself with the elite.

Ralston steered her elbow in the direction of Mr. Roland Withers, president of Sandy Shores Bank and Trust, and his wife, Ruby, who were standing in the entry with another finely dressed couple Hannah didn't recognize.

"Hannah!" The small voice from behind rose above the murmur of conversations taking place around her. *Jesse*. To Ralston's consternation, she halted her steps and turned, seeking the source of the voice.

"Come on, Hannah," Ralston urged, directing her through the shoulder-to-shoulder throng. "I want to catch Roland Withers before he leaves."

"You go ahead," she said, straining through the crowd to pinpoint Jesse's whereabouts. She couldn't possibly leave without giving him a hug.

"Oh, all right." He sighed and grimaced. "But meet me at the door." *Why have I always tolerated his almost militant manner?* she wondered as she watched him turn away and head in the direction of Roland Withers, vanishing from sight within seconds. She certainly didn't appreciate it coming from Gabriel Devlin. In fact, more than once she'd outright defied his directives, even when they made perfect sense. Could it be that with Gabriel, she felt free to be herself, to act in a manner befitting of her true character—and that, conversely, with Ralston, she'd professed early on to be someone she wasn't for the purpose of winning his attention? *How shallow and small-minded of me*, she suddenly concluded, *to have fallen in love with the idea of marrying a physician but not love the man himself*. But then, Ralston hadn't exactly expressed his love for her, either. He'd proposed marriage, yes, but had never professed his undying love. Perhaps to him, she represented a convenient solution and nothing more—someone to help him in the advancement of his career.

A new sense of urgency tugged at her heart. Certainly, they had reached a threshold in their relationship. The time had come to settle matters—tonight at her house after their supper date, at the very latest.

"There you are." She turned at the familiar, deep-timbred voice. As much as she wanted to conceal her elation at seeing Gabe, she knew he couldn't possibly have missed the heated flush of her cheeks. He smiled down at her, hand resting protectively, as usual, on Jesse's shoulder. "We thought we'd say hello."

Allowing herself more than a second or two to peruse Gabe's handsome features would have been improper, but, oh, how she wanted to feast her eyes on his fine charcoal-gray, almost black, wool morning suit with the grosgrain trim, his starched white shirt with the winged collar, and the silk Windsor tie, all of which fit his broad frame to perfection.

"Hello," she offered, forcing composure upon herself. Goodness, she had nearly given him a complete, top-to-bottom perusal before catching herself. And Jesse looked as dapper as ever in his blue button-down shirt tucked into his baggy brown trousers, navy suspenders holding everything in place; his black hair, sufficiently greased down and parted on the side, was as shiny as a wet paintbrush. With his coat draped over his arm and his brown cap in hand, he smiled up at Hannah with a look of contentment she had never seen before.

She bent at the waist and tweaked his earlobe. "Jesse Gant, you are, by a country mile, the finest-looking boy in all of Sandy Shores."

He scrunched up his nose and lifted a corner of his mouth. "Thanks. Gabe makes me dress up when we go to church."

She couldn't help but think what a doting guardian Gabe had become—and what a transformation from the man who'd once considered Jesse a regular nuisance.

"I think it's a fine idea, looking your best when you come to Sunday service," she said, touching the tip of his nose and straightening her posture.

Jesse gave her a good assessment himself. "That's a nice dress and hat you're wearing."

A feather-light giggle rippled through her. "Why, thank you, fine sir."

Then, angling his gaze up at Gabe, he asked, "Don't she look pretty to you, too, Gabe?"

Gabe tipped back on his heels and kept up his perpetual grin, pleased to see, she was sure, the crimson blotches appearing on her face and neck. Oh, how she hated that her fair skin made it impossible to hide the faintest blush. "I don't think I've ever seen a prettier sight. That a new green dress you're wearing there?"

It was strange that he would notice the dress she'd ordered from a catalog and worn for the first time today, when Ralston hadn't so much as uttered one word about it. "Why, yes, it is." In a self-conscious act, she touched her throat and felt the lump there when she swallowed. Why did she suddenly feel so nervous in his presence, while he appeared so confident in hers?

Gabe's grin spread wider. "I thought so. You have another green one similar, but I think that one's got some frilly stuff going on around the neck and cuffs." He made no bones about looking her over. "This one seems more, hmm, I don't know, *tailored*."

The way he said the word made her eyes widen, so that she felt compelled to look at the floor, then at Jesse's plastered down hair, then over at Mrs. Hack, who had just let loose a loud burst of laughter over something Mrs. Gallup or Mrs. King had said. The three women huddled close, standing not ten feet away from her, their conversation lively and animated.

"Am I right—about the dresses?" Gabe asked, leaning toward her, hands behind his back, a rascally glint in his eyes.

"You're very observant," she said. "I'm quite impressed."

"You want to come to the beach with Gabe and me today?" Jesse suddenly asked. "We're going to climb sand dunes."

"The beach?" The question took her by surprise.

"Yeah, why don't you join us? It's a nice, sunny day. A little brisk, maybe, but clear as blown glass. We're hiking up Five Mile Hill—when you get to the top of the dune, you can see for five miles in every direction."

She knew the hill. What resident of Sandy Shores didn't? Folks came from all over just to climb the hill. A far-fetched rumor had it that, on an exceptionally clear day, one could actually see Wisconsin across the glossy blue waters of Lake Michigan.

"I really…"

"Come on, Hannah." Jesse tugged at her long sleeve. "Gabe wants you to come. In fact, he's the one who told me to ask you."

"Jesse," Gabe scolded, scowling. This time, his cheeks flushed a nice shade of pink, a satisfying sight for Hannah.

She folded her hands in front of her and focused on Jesse, too afraid to gauge Gabe's true feelings on the subject. Had he really put Jesse up to asking her? The notion nestled nicely in her mind. "Well, I—suppose I could consider it, but I'd need to be back by six, as Ralston is…" She left it at that. She had no obligation to explain her supper date.

"Ah, yes, Ralston," Gabe said, knitting his brow into an even deeper scowl. "Don't worry, we'll have you back in plenty of time for your _beau._" He peppered the word with a healthy dose of sarcasm, then looked at his watch. "Can you be ready by one?"

"One?" It was just after noon now. "I—I suppose I can."

"Good." He steered Jesse away. "We'll bring a picnic lunch. All you have to bring is your appetite."

"A pic—really? You're packing a lunch?"

Gabe winked. Her heart tripped over itself. "Dress warm. We'll come by for you at one."

The two sauntered off, passing Ralston, whose face bore an expression of annoyance.

"What was that about?" Ralston asked Hannah, hooking a thumb over his shoulder at them.

She could hardly lie—and yet, to tell him the whole truth just now struck her as awkward. Tonight she would be forthright about her feelings for him. Her *fading* feelings, that is.

"Oh, that. Jesse is always so excited to see me."

Ralston grimaced and shook his head. "Pathetic little urchin," he mumbled. "Come on, I better run you home. Roland Withers has invited me out to the site of the property the hospital committee's considering for future purchase."

With relief, Hannah noted he failed to include her in the invitation.

Chapter Nineteen

A bracing wind coming off Lake Michigan served only to invigorate the trio making their way up Five Mile Hill, Jesse seeming the most enthusiastic of all, taking seriously his mission of reaching the top ahead of Gabe and Hannah. Although Jesse had fifteen feet on them, at most, Gabe never took his eyes off the boy, unless it was to observe the other hikers coming and going. The McCurdys' unseen presence kept him wary and watchful. Even so, he didn't consider the trek up the hill a dangerous venture— not today, at least, with the sun beating on their shoulders and a multitude of other people out and about, basking in its brilliant rays. The McCurdys never did their dirty work with throngs of people present, not if it meant risking getting caught.

"Jesse's having a grand time," Hannah said, picking up her heavy skirts as they scaled the hill, the toes of her boots digging into the trail for traction. "He seems different today, happier than I've ever seen him. You must have reassured him in some way. Do you think those McCurdy fellows have moved on?"

"I wish I thought so, but no. They're around."

"How can you be sure? You haven't seen them, have you?"

He might have seen one of the boys—Roy?—yesterday on his horse, but he decided to keep that tidbit to himself. "It's a hunch, I guess. I think they'll stay around until after the funeral service Tuesday. I'm hoping we'll catch at least one of them lurking around the cemetery. They're in town because they want Jesse, but they're not getting their hands on him without plowing through me first."

"Or me," she stated, sticking out her chin. "Remember, he's under my care while you're on duty."

He admired her grit, but she'd need more than grit if it ever came to facing off with Rufus McCurdy or one of his boys. His stomach roiled at the very idea of it.

"I'll be checking in on you often, and I expect the South Bend police department to arrive most any time to help conduct the investigation, so that will give us some added protection. The sooner we have those McCurdys in custody, though, the quicker I'll relax." Gabe noted tension in Hannah's eyes and was sorry he'd put it there. "Don't worry," he quickly tacked on. "Things will be fine."

Rather than responding, she grew contemplative as they tramped ever upward. Finally, she asked, "Like I said, Jesse seems different. Has something changed?"

Gabe trudged along beside her, his arm brushing against hers every so often. "You're a perceptive woman, you know that? Yeah, he's changed. Jess and I had quite a talk last night, starting with that shooting incident that got him all riled up. It stirred some unpleasant memories for him."

Hannah's head shot up and a frown creased her pretty brow. "What did he say? Any news on his family?"

He sighed. There was no easy way to say it. "Jesse has no family."

She came to an abrupt stop and stared up at him, eyes wide and shielded from the sun by her hand as the small brim of her hat was not sufficient for the task. "No family—are you sure?" Looking at her now, he was convinced he'd never seen a more beautiful sight—the sun in her face, her red flyaway locks flowing out from under her hat and glistening like hot copper, her freshly licked lips shining like two diamonds.

He chuckled, interlocked his fingers with hers, and nudged her onward up the hill. "Come on; I'll tell you on the way."

And he did, starting with Jesse's having lived in New York, the loss of his parents in two separate incidents, and Gabe's deduction that Jesse had arrived in South Bend, Indiana, by orphan train.

"Orphan train. I've heard about those trains. They carry homeless waifs to various parts of the Middle West in search of new homes. Maggie Rose has done some research on them, talked a lot about moving to New York someday to work in the orphanages. Of course, Papa balks every time she brings up the subject, saying New York is no place for a lady. I wonder if Jesse lived in an orphanage after his mama died."

"Oh, I'm sure he did," Gabe said, enjoying actual conversation with her, the kind that didn't feel like it would end in a yelling match. He also liked the way her small, slender fingers interlaced with his larger ones. "Someone put him on an orphan train, and I'm thinking it was an agent from one of those children's charities."

She frowned as they marched along, head down, watching her feet kick up tiny mounds of golden sand. "Keep talking," she insisted.

He gave her a summarized version, for they reached the top of the hill before he had time to spill all the details. It was just as well, though. She'd gotten the gist, and she knew that Jesse had witnessed the McCurdys' gruesome deed.

"Oh, dear Lord, it's so terrible," she said under her breath. "No wonder he went so long without talking. He had no idea whom he could trust, if anyone. For all he knew, we were the bad guys." This she said on a tiny sob, and, more than anything, Gabe wanted to take her in his arms, right there at the top of Five Mile Hill, and shout to the world that he'd fallen hopelessly in love. When a few glistening tears gathered at the edges of her blue-green eyes, he reached up and dabbed them with the pad of his thumb.

"Hannah, Gabe, come look! You can see forever up here." Gabe sighed. Leave it to the boy to bring a halt to his lovesick meanderings.

Later, they found a flat, secluded spot on which to spread the tablecloth Gabe had thought to pack in the knapsack slung over his shoulder. Besides that, he had packed tin mugs and plates, chicken sandwiches, apples, and a jug of sweet tea. They piled sand on the four corners of the tablecloth to hold it in place, then made themselves as comfortable as possible on the ground, legs crossed and drawn up close, or in Gabe's case, stretched out in front. He couldn't cross his legs to save his life, which Jesse found enormously funny and giggled about for five minutes straight.

"How come you can't?" Jesse kept asking. "Everybody knows how t' cross their legs."

"Not me. My legs are too big and bulky, I guess."

Jesse laughed again, a carefree sound that had Hannah and Gabe casting smiles at each other over Jesse's cap-covered head.

After Gabe offered a quick prayer of thanks for their lunch, they set about distributing food, then conversing between bites and enjoying autumn's crystalline sunshine.

Midway into their meal, Hannah took a sip of tea, wiped the corners of her mouth with a cloth napkin, and looked at Jesse. "Did you know there's a treasure of stolen loot buried somewhere up here?"

"Huh?" Jesse stopped chewing, dark eyes brimming with rapt interest. What boy wouldn't want to hear about some hidden fortune? Or what man, for that matter?

"Yes sir. Two satchel cases full of gold coins and diamonds, buried in these hills."

This was news to Gabe, and he found himself as engrossed as Jesse.

"Where are they, the gold and stuff?" Jesse asked.

Hannah shrugged. "No one knows for sure. The story is that many, many years ago, there was a robbery in Kalamazoo. One of the crooks took off with his share of the loot and made for Sandy Shores. He arrived here late one afternoon, but knowing the police were chasing him, he came up here and buried his treasure—supposedly by the biggest tree at the top of the hill and directly across from the lighthouse—which, everyone knows, would be that one over there." She hooked a thumb over her shoulder and pointed at a huge, ancient oak tree surrounded by dune grass, its trunk almost as massive as a redwood. "He planned to come back later, of course, and dig it up, but he got himself involved in another crime and ended up in the Jackson Penitentiary."

Caught up in her storytelling, Jesse planted himself in the sand like a statue. Even Gabe had to remind himself to chew and swallow.

Hannah surveyed the two with amusement in her eyes before biting into her sandwich, then took another slow swig of tea. *The little baiter!*

"Hurry up, Hannah," Jesse said. "Tell the rest."

"Yes, the rest," Gabe said, eyeballing her over his tin cup.

"The rest? Well…" She fixed a teasing grin on her face. "There's not that much to tell, really. Rumor has it that the crook lay dying in his prison cell some years later when he asked for a visit from a Sandy Shores official. He claimed he wanted to make a deathbed confession. We had a town coroner at the time—a Mr. Joseph Grayling. Mr. Grayling is the one who paid a call on the villain and returned with the whole story of the buried treasure."

"Did they try to find it?" Jesse asked.

"Oh, many have tried and failed. Some say it's probably shifted after years of sand erosion." She leaned close to Jesse and dipped low, eyes crinkled at the corners. "We might be sitting on it, for all we know," she said in a throaty voice.

Jesse quickly chewed down the rest of his sandwich, then leaped to his feet. "I'm gonna go look for clues," he announced.

"Don't go far," Gabe called after the running boy, hauling up a knee and resting an arm across it. Then, tilting his head at an angle, he set his gaze on Hannah's oval face. She had a pair of the nicest lips he'd ever seen, and he'd already learned their softness. He found himself studying them until she twisted her head around to search out Jesse. "He's fine," he said to the back of her head, where an array of copper ringlets had escaped her brown woolen hat and were blowing in the wind.

"That was quite a story you told."

She swiveled back in place and turned shining eyes on him. My, but she had the knack for making his head swim. "It was true, every bit of it," she said, poking out her chin.

He chuckled. "Yeah? And you believe it?"

"Everyone does, as far as I know."

"Really, now? I'll have to ask around."

"You do that."

He reached across and snagged one of her stray curls to finger its silkiness. She didn't even move, but he did hear her quick intake of breath. "I know, I know," he teased. "You have a *beau*." He inclined his head and said on a whisper, "I'll try to watch my step."

Only a hint of a smile played around her lips, her eyes connecting with his in a way quite foreign to him—thoughtful, inquiring. "You're somethin' else, Hannah Grace."

He scooted forward, fully intent on planting a kiss on her forehead, but Jesse's ill-timed interruption foiled his perfect plan. "Hey, you guys!" he called. "Let's go exploring!"

Gabe sighed and Hannah giggled, already rising to her feet.

He followed suit, looking over her shoulder to discover Jesse starting to climb another slope behind the big tree. Hannah gazed down at the remains of their picnic.

Gabe shrugged. "We'll come back for it later." He watched the boy ascend the dune and heaved another breath. "I hope you know you started something with this hidden treasure story, madam."

She covered her mouth to hold back another spurt of laughter.

"Come on," he said, taking her by the hand and pulling her along. They laughed on their way.

At the top of this particular dune, they had an even better view. They saw a few ships and barges leaving the channel to enter rough waters, moving south toward Chicago, and a lone sailboat about a mile offshore, dipping and rising with the white-capped waves. Directly in front of them stood the lighthouse, tall and serene at the end of the catwalk like a beacon of hope.

"What a beautiful sight," Hannah said, looking out over the waters, palm shading her eyes from the lowering sun, her skirts billowing in the chilly breezes.

Gabe's eyes focused on something else as he bent close. "Yes, beautiful," he murmured in her ear, mesmerized ever since she'd removed her hat to allow the wind full liberty with her hair.

They stood there, the three of them, each wrapped up in private thoughts. Suddenly, Jesse broke into their silent musings and asked, "Who lives up there?"

Hannah and Gabe's eyes traveled to where Jesse's outstretched finger pointed at a two-story, mansion-like structure built into the side of a hill, wooden steps leading down the steep incline to the beach.

"No one, now," Hannah replied. "Hard to believe, but that's just a summer cottage. It belongs to Harold and Nora

Morrison, who live in Chicago. They come up here only in July and August."

At first, Gabe thought little of Hannah's remark, except to muse that the cottage looked like something his own parents might build if his father would ever consider giving up the ranch and lessening his hours as county judge. He knew his mother would enjoy a summer retreat. However, something else caught his trained eye, some sort of movement inside the house—a fluttering curtain, a shadowy figure. And then, there were the horses tied outside, their heads barely visible over the crest of the hill.

Gabe went stone still for a full ten seconds while he pondered the unspoken possibility, surveyed the house and its surroundings, tried to see through thick drapes that covered a wide picture window by beading up his eyes. He removed his hat and scratched the back of his head, then set it back in place, all the while staring at the house, then at the horses out back.

"What is it?" Hannah asked. Jesse had already lost interest in the house and had bent over to study a few blades of dune grass and an ancient piece of driftwood.

Gabe looked down at her. She hadn't seen the horses, probably because she was too short to spy their heads over the summit. Nor had she detected any movement inside the big house. Gabe decided it was best not to alarm her over something for which he had no ready answers. His job as sheriff sometimes meant holding back information until he'd investigated a situation fully. Now was one of those times.

"Nothing," he said, keeping his tone light while touching her elbow. Looking at his watch, he breathed a sigh. "Well, we best get back down the hill. After all, you do have a date with the cavalier doctor tonight, right?"

She grimaced, as if resenting the reminder.

Good. He wanted her to put the man straight out of her head.

"Come on, buddy," he said to the squatting lad with a handful of dune grass. "Time to go back."

K

"That was a fine supper, Hannah," Ralston said that evening when they returned from Culver House. He led her to the dimly lit front parlor of the Kane residence.

Helena busied herself in the kitchen; Jacob retreated to his upstairs quarters. Maggie Rose set off on a brisk walk with a friend directly after supper, and Abbie Ann was spending a couple of days with Katrina Sterling so she wouldn't have to be alone while her husband was away on a business trip with his father. The Sterlings were big-time farmers in the area, mostly dairy, as far as she knew.

"Well, Grandmother made most of it," she replied. Ralston extended an arm, inviting her to sit on the divan.

Once they settled in, Hannah wracked her brain for a good topic of discussion before launching into the inevitable one in which she'd break the news she'd decided not to marry him. She prayed God might pave the way.

"Did you have a nice meeting with Roland Withers today?" she asked, smoothing out her flowered skirt.

He ran a hand along the back of the sofa, and she hoped he wouldn't drop it to her shoulder. "Absolutely. We walked the property where the hospital will one day stand. It's quite exciting to envision it—a two-story, L-shaped, brick structure with plenty of hospital beds; fine, state-of-the-art medical equipment; and a number of physicians and nurses running the place with cool efficiency. Withers already said they'd consider me above all others for chief. How about that?

"Of course, there's much to consider before any of this will come to fruition, the finances, for one thing," he rattled on, giving her not a second to put in a word. "But it's looking like even that will work itself out. Several government grants await our applications, not to mention the potential monies available from numerous other untapped resources Withers is only now learning about."

His brow went into a temporary frown. "I meant to speak with your father about all this over dinner, but your grandmother seemed bent on spending the entire time talking about that shooting incident over at the Elwood place, and how the sheriff had sent you all upstairs on the chance you might be in danger." He shook his head and sniffed. "Doesn't take much to stir up this little town, does it? All that hoopla over a man who's fast losing his buttons. Harmless ol' coot." He chuckled, which reminded her that the only times he ever laughed were when he made a remark that he found humorous.

"I thought I'd catch your father after the meal, but I notice he escaped to his room straightaway. Well, no matter, there's plenty of time later for seeing whether he wants in on the ground floor of this hospital project. This is an exciting time for Sandy Shores, you know. I'm certain Withers wants to keep its citizens abreast of our plans, and particularly the business owners."

"Yes, you're probably right about that." His opinion that her grandmother—and everyone else, for that matter—had overreacted to the shooting incident galled her plenty, but she decided to let the matter pass. "I wanted to talk to you about something, Ralston," she inserted. "Something else altogether."

"Really?" She detected his smile from the corner of her eye. "And I have something on my mind, as well." As feared, he put a hand around her shoulder and tugged her close, so close his coffee breath lingered near her nostrils, making her cringe. "Do you want to go first, or shall I?"

Please, Father, give me the proper words, words that won't jab or be hurtful, but will nonetheless get the job done.

"I suppose—"

"Well, I'll start, then," he said, intentionally cutting her off. "I proposed marriage some weeks ago, Hannah, and I'd truly like to get on with our plans." He turned her chin until their gazes met. His eyes were nothing like Gabriel's azure ones—Ralston's were brown and sadly drab, shaded under heavy lids and thick brows, too thick when compared with his thinning hair on top. Gabe's eyes were a melting blue and virtually magnetic.

"I've been thinking a June wedding would suffice. The Reverend Cooper will perform the ceremony, of course, and we'll have a fine reception at Culver House. I've the resources, you know, to make this a dandy affair."

He leaned ever closer, his breath falling on her neck and making her skin prickle.

"I never actually told you this, Hannah, but a very large sum of money awaits me on the day of my marriage. Very large," he restated. "In fact, my lawyer will be among our guests. When Mother and Father passed, one of the stipulations of the will was that each of us children must marry before receiving his or her inheritance. As you know, I'm the last of the lot to accomplish that goal."

Goal? She hardly had the wherewithal to speak. Had he purposely kept this news from her in the hopes it would serve as additional ammunition, should the need arise; that it would make his proposal that much harder to refuse? She scratched an itchy spot above her temple and stared at him, barely able to move. "Let me get this straight, Ralston. Your goal is to marry me so that you may obtain your inheritance?"

He gasped and spewed a nervous laugh. "My goal—well, no, yes—no! Oh, my dear, you misunderstand me. I suppose it did come off sounding like that, didn't it? Truly, what I wanted was for you to see what awaits you by marrying me. Don't you see? You'll never want for another thing as long as you live."

"But I don't want for anything now, Ralston."

"And you never shall," he emphasized. "Think of it, never having to work in that—that dusty general store again."

"That—dusty general store is all I've known, Ralston. It belongs to my father and—I believe it will one day be mine for the asking."

"Precisely!"

"What?"

He looked heavenward, then settled himself more deeply into the sofa cushions.

"All right," he stated, as if he'd just received a marvelous breakthrough. "Think about it this way, Hannah Grace." His eyes, though normally dark and distant, rose to a sparkling chestnut color. "With the money I'm to have in my possession, I shall be able to take you to parts of the world you've never seen, much less heard about. I could show you the pyramids of Egypt, the cathedrals of Rome. Or, how does deep-sea fishing sound to you?"

"Dark."

"Whales! We'll catch the whales and sea lions off the deep southern coast."

"You actually catch them?"

"Or even Africa. How does an African safari sound to you?"

"Far away," she answered in a whisper.

"Think of it. The untamed wilds of Africa."

His eyes gleamed with self-indulgence, having not heard a word she'd said.

Her heart sank, not for herself, but for his wasted energies. "But Ralston, I'm happy right here in Sandy Shores."

He scoffed. "Nonsense. That's because you've never gone anywhere. Why, there are places out there that will make you swoon, Hannah, high mountains, low valleys…"

"I dislike swooning, Ralston—I've told you that. I hate that dizzy, sweaty feeling it leaves me with."

"…rivers so wide, you'll think they're lakes," he continued, never missing a beat, oblivious to the sentence she'd inserted.

Ralston Van Huff was a terrible listener—he didn't even know her passions, her desires to one day make Kane's Whatnot her own. He didn't know, or even care, how much she loved Jesse Gant. And then, there was the matter of Gabriel Devlin, but more important, her faith in Christ.

Her faith in Christ! How often she'd put the Lord in the background of her life, even making a mindless ritual out of reading the Holy Scriptures. She'd been praying and asking Him to guide her and reveal His divine will to her, but how could He do that if she refused to listen for His still, small voice? Well, enough! Time to stop making decisions that didn't include consulting God.

She opened her mouth to explain her newfound revelation, but Ralston blocked her chance with a sudden kiss. A kiss! One that totally lacked emotion and pleasure and pressed hard against her mouth—so hard, in fact, she might have described it as painful. Why, if Gabe hadn't kissed her beforehand, she would have considered the whole act of kissing a most unpleasant pastime.

In haste, she wedged both hands between them and pushed on his chest. It took some persuading, but he did unloose his lips, leaving hers numb and tingly. "Ralston." Breathless, but not from any thrill from his touch, she immediately put space between them.

A puzzled expression washed over him. "Did I do it all wrong?"

Lord, please give me the right words. She gave a deep sigh and repositioned herself in front of him. "No, but, well, I—I'm sorry to disappoint you, Ralston, but—I simply can't marry you."

"What? Then when?"

"No. I mean, I can't—*ever*—marry you. I don't love you, Ralston, just as you don't love me."

"Hannah, that will come in time. Lots of couples marry without all the essential feelings in place. You're simply not thinking straight right now."

She smiled. "Actually, Ralston, I'm thinking straighter than I have in a very long while. I've decided I need to spend more time with the Lord, concentrate on reading His Word. I mean *really* reading it. I haven't been doing that as I should. All my life I've read the Bible very dutifully, almost ritualistically. And in all that time, I haven't truly allowed the Word of God to speak to me."

"What?" The very nature of his question indicated his lack of spiritual depth and understanding. "It's that sheriff, isn't it?" he complained, as if he hadn't heard a word she'd said. "Ever since he and that—that orphan came to town, things haven't been the same between us."

She swallowed that bit of truth, pondering it in her mind. "You might be right about that, but lest you think I'm calling an end to our relationship strictly because of the sheriff and my love for that little boy, let me clarify something. I don't love you, Ralston, and I can't marry someone I don't love. Therefore, I can't marry you. Moreover, I've thought for the longest time that marriage would bring a certain sense of completion to my life, but, really, God alone can truly complete me. Right now, I want to focus my attentions on living my life for Him, learning what it means to be content."

Ralston Van Huff clearly didn't get it. Dumbfounded best described the look he gave her. "But I—I truly *need* a wife," he whined. "It's the matter of my inheritance. If I—we…" The poor man looked near tears.

She patted his arm. "Yes, I know you wanted to marry me to get to your inheritance"—the notion should have angered her deeply—"but there are other women out there,

Ralston—women who will probably jump at your proposition. And a proposition is exactly what that was, by the way—a proposition, not a true marriage proposal. Next time, clarify your intentions, and perhaps you'll find a woman just as money-hungry as yourself."

He didn't argue her suggestion, nor did he even take offense by it; he merely nodded absently.

"Well then, I guess this is good-bye," he said with little emotion.

How awkward, and yet how simply freeing. They actually smiled at each other before he pushed himself up and headed for the door. She watched him snatch his coat off the rack and put it on. What a truly pathetic scenario. He had used her, really, and, for a time, she'd actually fallen into his scary, black trap. *Thank You, Lord, for pulling me out of that. May I never again jump into something without first seeking Your perfect, divine purposes. And that includes Gabriel Devlin. Give me a clear head where he is concerned, Lord. Let me seek You first, above all else!*

Hand on the doorknob, Ralston gave her one last look. "For what it's worth, I did enjoy your company."

She sat with hands folded. "And I yours." It was, after all, partially true.

Chapter Twenty

G abe wouldn't say Hannah treated him with a particular chill the next morning, but neither did she lavish him with a blanket of warmth. Rather, she greeted him cordially and with a sort of serene aloofness, as if she could easily take him or leave him. The whole thing caught him off guard, stole his sense of confidence. He'd thought they'd made progress yesterday, especially after spending a delightful afternoon together. And now this—this strange civility.

Unfortunately, he'd had no time for socializing at the door, nor had she, by the look of her flour-covered hands. In haste, she ushered Jesse inside and told him Grandmother Kane anticipated his arrival up in the attic. Eager to learn what awaited him, Jesse made a mad dash for the stairs, and Hannah, granting Gabe a smile that was friendly enough, thanked him for bringing Jesse by and promised to have him ready and waiting when five o'clock rolled around. She then curtly wished him a good day and closed the door. Any other time, he might have stopped the door with his foot, but he'd had South Bend detectives waiting for him at his office, so he'd walked away feeling baffled, if not slightly rebuffed.

Four plainclothesmen were waiting in the courthouse lobby when he walked through the front entrance, all looking eager to know what he could tell them about the McCurdy gang and their alleged presence in Sandy Shores. After a brief round of handshakes and introductions, they went to his office, where they made small talk while Kitty delivered tall mugs of steaming coffee and Gus and a few other deputies gathered enough chairs for everyone to sit in. Once they were situated, Gabe told them about the drowning victim, Luis McCurdy, and the graveside service they'd scheduled for tomorrow afternoon; about the young stranger in Kane's Whatnot he suspected was a McCurdy; and about his recent visit with George Vanderslute. He also brought up the matter of Jesse Gant—his being a witness to the South Bend murder—and his strong suspicions that the McCurdys meant to capture and kill the boy.

"You think any of them will show up at the cemetery tomorrow, maybe lurk in the shadows?" asked Howard, who seemed to be the one in charge, thumbs hooked in his suspenders, cigar drooping out of the corner of his mouth. He'd crossed a portly leg over the other and tried to look comfortable.

"I seriously doubt it, but I intend to be on the lookout, just in case," Gabe replied from behind his desk. "In the meantime, I have another lead worth checking." He proceeded to tell them about the horses he'd spied in the backyard of the massive summer cottage just yesterday and the movement he'd detected on the other side of the drapes.

The one called Harry, middle-aged and skinny as a twig, shrugged. "Could be the folks who own the place are here on a brief visit. Just because they normally come only in the summer don't mean they can't break with tradition. Maybe they had some maintenance to tend to and didn't want to leave it till summer."

"You're absolutely right," Gabe said. "But I wouldn't want to ignore the fact that someone's up there, owners or not."

"I agree," said the fellow introduced as Shorty, who hardly lacked in stature. In fact, Gabe surmised he had to be pushing six and a half feet. And he wasn't skinny, either. Of the four men who'd ridden the train into town from South Bend, Shorty was the one he'd most want on his side. "How 'bout a couple of us ride out with the sheriff to do a little pokin' around after we're done here? Might be we'll learn a thing or two. You do have extra horses, right?"

"At the livery," Gabe said. "Enoch'll have 'em ready and waiting for us as soon as we come through the door. He's expecting us, in fact."

"I'll be happy to tag along," chimed the fellow known as James, a man about Gabe's age. He had a full beard and a husky build, looking more like a woodsman than an officer of the law.

"Good idea," said Howard. "James, Shorty, and me will go with Sheriff Devlin here. Harry, you stay back and scout out the town, drop in on a few establishments, chat with some bartenders and shopkeepers, see what you can learn. Might be you'll get somethin' out o' someone that ain't been discovered yet."

"How 'bout us, boss? What should we do?" asked Gus van der Voort, speaking for himself and two other Sandy Shores deputies. The two who'd worked the night shift, Randall

Cling and Fred Van Dam, went home for some rest, knowing they might be summoned back on duty.

"Gus, I want you to take a ride around the outskirts of town," Gabe said. "See if you spot anything unusual—fresh camps, suspicious tracks of any kind. If you happen to see anyone out and about, ask if they've noticed anything peculiar—for instance, strangers poking their noses where they don't belong. We're looking for anything that might give us some new insights."

"You got it, boss."

He turned to his other deputies. "Clyde, you stay here and tend to office calls." Clyde nodded. "And Van, I want you standing guard out at the Kane house. If anybody comes nosing around, stop 'im in his tracks. I'm putting a twenty-four-hour watch on the place, meaning no one's to come within twenty feet of that house, you understand?"

"What if I know 'em, boss?" he asked, ever the conscientious soul.

Gabe held his patience intact. "Use your head, Van. Common sense will be your guide."

With a snap of his head, Jarvis "Van" Vandermueller straightened his narrow shoulders and pulled back his jacket to lay a palm to his gun handle. "You can count on me, Sheriff."

Gabe nodded, hoping he was right. His deputies were good men, meticulous and hardworking, although Van sometimes worried him with his sense of self-importance. He wouldn't say any of his men was accustomed to hauling out his gun, either, except for a thorough cleaning, another point of concern. Gabe whispered a silent prayer that God would fit them all with supernatural armor, strength, and wisdom.

The men finished their coffee, dialogued a bit longer, then sauntered out the door, boot heels pounding against the hardwood floor and making them sound like a herd of buffalo tramping down the hall. Kitty shot Gabe a curious-as-a-cat-on-the-prowl look when he passed her desk, and he knew she wanted nothing more than for him to stop and give her all the details. Instead, he tipped his hat at her and said, "I'll be back later, Kitty. Help our friend Clyde hold down the fort, okay?" He winked at Clyde.

"Sure, but..." She lifted a hand to protest, but he closed the door behind him without letting her finish.

The big house at the top of the hill appeared quiet and peaceful, if not completely deserted. Not even a trace of horse droppings littered the surrounding area, making Gabe wonder if he'd dreamed what he'd seen yesterday. A thick blanket of dead leaves made it impossible to even distinguish horse tracks.

They dismounted their steeds and set off in various directions, guns at the ready. Howard headed for the barns, James to the front yard overlooking Lake Michigan's unusually still waters, and Shorty in the direction of some outbuildings. Gabe made for the house, where he intended to do some window gazing to check for any evidence of break-ins.

An eerie sense crept up his spine. Something didn't feel right, and he meant to find out what that was before leaving the premises.

⌒ K ⌒

Although Hannah had thought boredom might set in, Grandmother put an end to that worry by lining up enough jobs to take her into 1904—everything from sweeping the cellar and taking an inventory of canned goods to scrubbing floorboards, cleaning out the fireplace, and dusting under the lid of the family's old upright piano. By afternoon, she was stretching her aching back muscles and longing for work in the Whatnot.

She had seen Jesse at lunchtime, when he'd appeared just long enough to wolf down a sandwich and gulp a glass of milk. As suspected, Helena had put him to work sorting old books, arranging them in alphabetical order.

"Grandmother Kane says I don't need to hurry none. Says there's enough books up there to take me a month of Sundays." While he chewed, he started rattling off a running list of the titles he had come across—leather-bound volumes by Shakespeare, *Black Beauty*, *The Prince and the Pauper*, and even Beatrice Harraden's *Ships That Pass in the Night*—all books Helena had given her granddaughters to read.

"You've heard of these books?" Hannah asked Jesse, bending over the stovetop to scrub it clean.

She heard him drain his milk glass and place it on the table with a clink. "Ma read most of them. If she wasn't readin' her Bible, she was reading some book or another."

"No wonder you're such a fine reader. You inherited your love of words from your mama."

"Yep. May I be excused now?" he asked in a rush.

Before she'd even finished nodding, he'd bounded up the stairs again. Now, according to Helena, he'd found a spot under Grandfather Kane's moth-eaten army uniform to lose himself in a tattered copy of *Alice's Adventures in Wonderland,* one of Hannah's old favorites, and fallen asleep with his head on an old quilt.

Hannah first discovered Jarvis Vandermueller while she was dusting off the front windowsill. She paused in her work and wondered what Gabe would think if he knew his deputy was napping under a tree, legs crossed at the ankles, unsmoked cigarette hanging from his mouth. His horse, on the other hand, looked to have been busy for hours nibbling at a tree and nearly stripping it of its bark, as well as grazing on some shrubs. Grinning to herself, she walked to the kitchen. What that poor man needed was a plate of cookies and a tall glass of lemonade to wake him up.

A cold blast of air assaulted her ankles when she opened the door and made her way down the porch steps, platter of cookies and pitcher of lemonade in hand. Van never heard her approach, but when she called his name, he jumped to attention like a soldier caught with his pants down, stuffed the unlit cigarette in his coat pocket, and cleared his throat.

"Oh! I didn't mean to startle you."

"Miss." He tipped his wide-brimmed hat at her and stumbled over a twig. "'Case you're wonderin' what I'm doin' here," he said, gathering his wits while dusting off his pants, "the sheriff sent me over to keep an eye on things."

"Ah, well, isn't that nice? Though quite unnecessary, I'm sure. I've seen no activity, have you?"

"Not a thing," he said. "But the sheriff, he don't want to take any chances with strangers comin' around stirrin' up trouble."

She might have asked him how he planned to stop them while napping under a tree, but she decided not to embarrass him further. "Your horse—he's been eating my grandmother's shrubs." She nodded at the big black galoot behind him.

Van twirled on his heel. "Bartholomew, you ol' thief. You can't be eatin' off other people's property." The horse raised his head and snorted. "Sorry 'bout that, miss. I trust they'll grow back."

She laughed, even as the horse went back to feasting on the greenery as if it were a bed of oats. "I wouldn't worry about it. I'm sure they needed a good fall trim, anyway. I just hope he doesn't get sick."

"Pfff, Bart? He'd eat the tar off a roof if he could reach it. What's you doin' out here on such a cold day?"

She extended the platter of confection and the jug of lemonade with the upturned tin mug on the spout. "I've brought you a snack."

"What? Well, ain't that nice of you. Hope you didn't go to any bother."

"No trouble at all. These are Grandmother's chocolate mountains, in case you wondered."

"Oh, my, the real deal? I confess I bought a dozen of 'em at last summer's fair. My wife made oatmeal raisin, don't you know." He leaned forward and whispered, "Don't tell my Rosie, now, but I daresay Helena Kane's chocolate mountains beat out hers by a long shot. Why, they were the talk of the town for days."

Hannah laughed and shivered at the same time. "Your secret's safe with me, Van." Giving a slight turn, she said, "Well, you looked like you could use a break."

It was facetious of her, but she simply couldn't help herself.

His sunken chest swelled as far as it could go, which wasn't saying much for Jarvis Vandermueller's narrow frame. He raised his proud chin as she'd expected him to do. "Well, it does take a mite out of a man standing watch by the hour, never quite knowing when danger might strike."

"Absolutely." She pursed her lips to keep from smiling.

Not even the slightest breeze raised the hem of her skirt, but she wrapped her long-sleeved arms about her waist to hold in the warmth. A cold nip in the air meant a strong chance for Sandy Shores' first snowfall, early as it was in the season.

"Well, you enjoy those cookies, Van. I best get inside before my nose—"

"Hannah!" Jesse took a giant leap off the side of the porch and ran to her. He wasn't wearing a hat, but at least he'd thought to put on his winter coat, which was more than she could say for herself.

"Well, lookie here," said Van. "You're growin' right tall since you moved to Sandy Shores, young man. You think it's the drinkin' water what's doin' it?"

Jesse angled the deputy with a curious look. "He's just teasing you, Jess. Say hello to Mr. Vandermueller."

Jesse raised a hand. "Hello, sir. I seen you before—and your big horse." Jesse's eyes meandered to the giant Morgan. "He must really like to eat—bushes."

"He likes to eat most anythin', I'm afraid."

One corner of Jesse's lip shot up. "I bet he wouldn't go for Gabe's cookin' that much."

"Jesse Gant, you take that back," Hannah scolded, barely controlling the urge to laugh. "It can't be that bad. You eat a nice hot meal every night, don't you?"

He tipped his head to one side before nodding, nose wrinkled, one eye tightly shut. "Sometimes it's burnt, though."

Van laughed for both of them. "Sheriff's told us he can't cook worth a mound o' dirt, miss. By the look o' those lunches he brings into the office, I'd say he might be right."

"Gabe needs a wife," Jesse shot out, looking directly at Hannah when he said it. "He even said so hisself."

"Did he now?" Van asked with apparent interest. He downed another cookie. "He say he has anybody in partic'lar in mind?" he asked between chews.

Despite the bite in the air, Hannah felt a certain heat rise to her cheeks. Now would be a good time to turn tail and head for the house, but, oh, how she wanted to see how this conversation played out.

"Yep!" Jesse said, taking a cookie when Van stuck the plate under his nose. He bit off a good-sized chunk and chewed thoughtfully. "But I'm not supposed to talk about it."

"Oh. Must mean he has someone in mind, then," Van said. "My wife's been beggin' her cousin Corinne to come visit from Saginaw. I'm pretty sure she wants to hook the two of them up. I s'pose I should tell her to lay off, huh?"

Jesse wiped his crumb-covered mouth with his sleeve. The lad had a ways to go in the manners department. He lifted his gaze so his eyes met with Hannah's square on. "Yep, you best tell her he's got someone else in mind."

Hannah shivered from head to toe—a full-out shudder—and she couldn't blame the cold entirely.

"Well, good day, Van. I should think you could leave any time now," Hannah said, preparing to turn.

"Oh, no, miss. Not until my shift ends. There's to be a twenty-four-hour watch on your place."

"Twenty-four—but that seems like such a waste of the department's time."

"How come you're watchin', anyway?" Jesse asked.

The sound of horse's hooves coming up the hill had all of them turning, and Van quickly set the platter of cookies and pitcher of lemonade on the ground. He rose to his full five and a half feet. "Hey, boss. Any news on the home front?"

Rather than a friendly greeting, all any of them got from Gabe was a stern look. To Hannah, however, the look was scalding. "What are you doing outside?"

She tried to relax, pasting a smile on her face despite her annoyance. "Enjoying the brisk air."

"Jesse, you and Hannah go inside right now," he ordered.

"But I just got out—"

"Go."

His tone did not allow for arguing, so neither of them tried; they just swiveled on their heels and made for the door.

Hannah's insides tensed as she laid a hand on Jesse's shoulder and guided him toward the house. Had Gabe found the McCurdys—or, worse, had someone else drowned or come to an entirely different cruel fate? When she glanced back at Gabe, he had dismounted his horse and was giving poor Van the what for, something about having told him to make sure they stayed inside.

Lord, give me patience with that man, and most of all, take away this growing love I have for him if it's not part of Your greater plan for me.

⌒𝒦⌒

"What we goin' to do now, Pa?" Roy asked, stoking the flames in the little brick fireplace.

"We're goin' to sit tight for the night, plan out ar strategy," Rufus said, sitting back in a grungy old chair, the only piece of furniture in the whole place save a rickety table and a couple of empty crates. Not even a single cot graced the one-room shanty.

"Why'd we have to leave that nice house in such a hurry?" Reuben asked.

"I told you, blockhead," Roy answered for his father. "I saw the sheriff on that bluff looking up at the house. He was with your girlfriend from Kane's Whatnot and that bratty little kid we're trying to get ar hands on."

"She's not my girlfriend, and I doubt he even saw you, you idiot."

"Shut up. He saw me, all right—looked me straight in the eyes. 'Fact, whatcha want to bet he came snoopin' around up there first thing this mornin'? Won't find nothin', though, right, Pa? We spiffed that place up right fine. That was smart thinking, throwin' the horse dung over the cliff." Roy laughed and spat on the dirt floor of the run-down hunting shack they'd found in the middle of a deserted piece of land a few miles east of town. A covey of pine trees out back shielded the horses from any passersby.

"I ain't stupid," Rufus said, belching after a supper of sausage and sauerkraut before guzzling down the last of his bitter ale. He stared at the crooked ceiling and hoped it wouldn't rain tonight, knowing they'd get wet if it did.

"So, what's ar plan?" Reuben asked.

Rufus tossed the empty bottle to the floor and wiped a hand across his mouth. "I'm thinkin' on it." He hated that he didn't have a true game plan and hoped it didn't show in his face. Fact was, the ale he'd been drinking lately had made it hard for him to put two thoughts together, let alone a sensible plan. "I need a smoke," he complained, wishing his boys would quit looking at him like he was some kind of monkey in a cage. He felt his pockets and panicked. Where were his smokes?

Roy reached into his hip pocket and threw him a hand-rolled cigarette. "It's my last one," he said with a begrudging tone.

"It ain't like you don't got any time on your hands for rollin' more, you big horse's rump," Rufus said.

"So, what *is* your plan, Pa? You got one?" Roy asked, ignoring the remark.

"Would you stop askin' me? I told you, I'm thinkin'!" Rufus let loose a powerful curse and a sharp pain hit him square in the chest, nasty enough to steal his breath away.

He snatched hold of the spot with both hands. It wasn't the first time he'd experienced pain in his upper torso, but this time seemed more pronounced. He dug deep for a decent breath of air.

"What is it, Pa? You look like you just seen a spook," Reuben said.

Gradually, the pain started to let up. "Nothin'," he said, glad when he could breathe again. "Just a little indigestion, is all. It ain't nothin'."

Any concern either of his boys may have had for him was short-lived. Both retrieved their bedrolls, Reuben unrolling his first and tossing it in front of the fireplace.

Roy scowled. "You can't sprawl out there and block all the heat. Move over."

"I ain't blockin' it." To appease his older brother, Reuben made a slight shift to the side.

"You only moved two inches."

"Did not."

Roy kicked Reuben's bedroll over another two feet.

"Keep your grubby boots off my bed."

"Would you two stop bickerin'? Yer yappin' reminds me of a couple of stupid girls."

A semblance of peace settled over them while Reuben and Roy situated their beds. Rufus lit his cigarette and took a couple of satisfying puffs.

"You got any ideas about how we're goin' to nab that kid tomorrow?" Roy asked again.

Rufus rolled his eyes to the ceiling and took another long drag, then blew it out slowly. "'Course I do. I'll tell you mine after you tell me yers."

Roy's face split into a cold, hard grin as he lifted a brow and sat down, legs tucked under him. "So, we each come up with a plan and then vote on the best one, is that it?"

"Seems fair."

"Wait, I don't got any plan," Reuben said in a huff. "I figured Pa'd come up with one."

"'Course you don't have a plan, jarhead. You never do," Roy said.

"Shut yer face," Reuben muttered through his teeth, dropping onto his makeshift bed and turning his back to both of them. "We oughten t' be doin' nothin' on the day of ar brother's funeral. It's plain disrespectful, if y' ask me."

"Well, we ain't askin' you, are we?" Roy sneered. "Besides, we been over this already. Tomorrow's the best day. We'll catch the whole town unawares by doin' the deed right durin' the ceremony."

Out of nowhere, that same stabbing pain recurred like a vise, pressing in and crushing Rufus's chest. He clutched the point and sucked in a tight gasp, but neither boy noticed as Roy proceeded with his perfectly laid out plan, casting Rufus only an occasional look. "We start out together just before noon but split up a half mile east of town so's we're all enterin' from a different street. The last thing we want t' do is draw attention to ourselves.

"The service starts at one o'clock, so while that's commencin' we'll take the back roads to the Kane house. You listenin' to me, Reuben?"

"I'm listenin'," Reuben grumbled, face to the fire.

"Stay clear of Water Street and Third. Approach the house on Ridge from every direction but north. In other words, stay away from the center of town and keep outta sight.

"When you come within a block o' the house, dismount and tie yer horse in some inconspicuous place, 'hind a cluster of trees or in a deserted shed. We'll meet up at the Kane house soon's we can, got that? If you see anybody lurkin' about, though, hang back and lemme handle it. Whatever you do, don't move in till the coast is clear."

Roy put great emphasis on every word, eyes trained on his brother's back. It was a good thing, too, or he'd have noted Rufus writhing in pain. Roy droned on while Rufus took several slow breaths, letting his cigarette waste away between his fingers.

"Pa'll stand guard outta sight while I knock on the door— and too bad for the woman that answers it." A black-hearted chuckle rose from his chest.

"Whatcha goin' t' do to her?" Reuben wanted to know.

"Thump her out cold, what else? It'll happen fast, believe me. Reuben, after I whack 'er, you'll stand watch over the body. If she starts comin' to, show 'er the butt of yer gun." He laughed again. "One more good wallop should do the trick.

"While Reuben's standin' watch, I'll run through the house and find the kid. When I find him, I'll tie 'im up and gag 'im."

"Thought you tol' us there was two women in that house," Rufus said, doing his best to sound attentive.

"Exactly," Roy answered. "Dependin' on which one's left, I'll deal with 'er when the time comes. If it's the younger one, I might tie and gag her, too, and bring 'er along for some fun."

Rufus jerked his head up. "You best not go messin' with the sheriff's lady friend."

"He ain't nothin' t' brag about," Roy said. "I can take 'im." He puffed out his chest like he was something special, then gave a quick shrug. "Who knows? Maybe we'll find the boy playin' all by himself outside. In that case, we'd gag him and haul 'im off and no one would be the wiser."

Reuben made a scoffing noise. "I don't like it. Sounds like a silly plan, if y' ask me, something a half-wit kid could dream up."

It took a lot to make Rufus McCurdy cringe, but Roy's string of ear-splittingly vulgar curses, which followed Reuben's remark, did just that. Of course, he wouldn't let on that his boy's crude mouth and hideous manners affected him. After all, he'd taught him everything he knew. Resting his head on the back of the wooden chair, he took another drag off his dying cigarette and closed his eyes.

After a minute, Roy asked, "You got a plan better 'n mine, Pa?"

Eyes still closed, Rufus clutched tight at the chair arms to control his tremors and mumbled, "Mine was pretty much the same as yers."

Chapter Twenty-one

Tuesday morning's sky showed the probability of rain—or perhaps even the season's first snowfall— if heavy, drooping clouds were any indication. Icy, damp air clawed clear to the bone as Gabe made his way to the station on Slate after dropping off Jesse at the Kane household, clicking off a mental checklist of the day's duties. First on the agenda: return his father's phone call of yesterday afternoon—Kitty said he sounded anxious. Next, meet Ed Bowers in his office at eight-thirty. It would stand to reason that the judge would insist on an update regarding the McCurdys. Around nine, he planned to sit down with the South Bend detectives for another review of each man's appointed responsibilities, and, after that, he'd drop by Ralston Van Huff's office to draw up the final plans for transporting Luis McCurdy's body to the cemetery.

From what he'd heard, Baker & Baker Furniture and Funeral Store had donated a coffin from their most basic line for the burial service, and the city had rented a funeral wagon from the livery. *Very generous,* Gabe thought, *considering the kid's criminal background and no-good reputation.* But then, he was finding that out about the residents of Sandy Shores—they were a kind and bighearted group of people. They could have taken a less expensive route, like cremation, but city officials had voted to give the boy a decent burial, some arguing he'd probably never stood a chance, having Rufus McCurdy for a father.

Gabe had wanted to keep matters concerning the boy's identity secret for as long as possible, but Stewart Stuyvesant hadn't missed a single morsel of information the evening of the drowning, and he'd made it more than clear he intended to print his findings. Joining the parade of curious spectators marching up the street to Van Huff's office and sneaking past the door with the medics and deputies, Stuyvesant had kept a watchful eye on the proceedings while Van Huff examined the body, and he'd documented all of it in his handy notebook.

Thankfully, Stuyvesant had printed the facts as he knew them and kept any speculative hunches to himself. That is, until his good friend George Vanderslute met him for supper the same day he came to see Gabe and filled him in on the rest of the story. After that, the reporter leaked enough information for the citizens of Sandy Shores to realize that their lives could be in danger. *Maybe it's just as well*, Gabe reasoned, *as long as folks keep their heads about them and don't panic*. For now, they traveled in pairs, stayed off the streets after dark, and kept a closer eye on their properties. Almost without ceasing, Gabe prayed things would reach a peaceful conclusion.

Gabe gave Slate's reins a gentle tug to the left, routing him up Fifth Street in the direction of City Hall. Slate snorted, and a cloud of mist shot out from both nostrils. As they made their way into town, Gabe's thoughts went to Jesse, tucked away safely at the Kane house and awaiting the arrival of his friend, Billy B. What might have happened to him, had he not jumped into the back of Gabe's rig that night in Holland? Very likely, he would have wandered aimlessly, perhaps eventually hooking up with the wrong set of friends—people much like the McCurdys. Not for the first time, Gabe thanked the Lord for bringing the two of them together, as well as for the providential manner in which Hannah had entered their lives.

Hannah. He'd missed seeing her this morning, and he'd hoped his disappointment hadn't been too obvious to Helena, who had come to the door instead. She welcomed Jesse with a grandmotherly hug. Gabe must have looked confused, for over Jesse's head, the older woman lifted a curious, if not impish, brow at him, then said, "She's upstairs collecting the day's laundry."

"Oh." Was his disappointment that blatant?

Apparently so, for she'd chuckled and shaken her head. "I declare, you two are the berries! Seems to me you both come from the same berry bush, just landed in different baskets. The trick's going to be to get yourselves onto the same plate." In some roundabout way, he understood her mixed-up symbolism.

His father answered on the second ring after Gabe situated himself in the chair behind his desk and dialed his number. It didn't surprise him when their connection crackled and he had to yell into the mouthpiece. Sometimes these telephones proved more troublesome than good. "What's that? Yes, I'm fine, and you?"

"We're fine here," his father answered. "Mother sends her undying love, and Elizabeth tells you to hurry home for a visit—those rascals of hers miss their uncle. Sam's past his neck in clients but praising the Lord for the way his law practice has grown. Looks like he might be bringing in a partner come spring.

"But listen, I've something important to tell you, which has nothing to do with any of this."

"Yeah?" Gabe pressed the receiver tightly to his ear, noting the sudden seriousness in Joseph Devlin's tone. This would not be a social call. "What is it?"

More crackling on the phone line.

"Howard Twining called me yesterday afternoon with some interesting information." Howard was one of his father's old cronies. He'd worked for years in the Columbus Police Department and had served as a sort of mentor to Gabe when he got his start in law enforcement. "You know, he's been following that South Bend murder case, gathering facts and details as they come across his desk."

His agency isn't the only one interested, Gabe said to himself. Ever since news had seeped out about the apparent identity of Sandy Shores' recent drowning victim, inquiries had come in from around the country—people wanted to know if there had been any McCurdy sightings. In the eyes of the press, Stewart Stuyvesant had done a bang-up job of reporting.

In Gabe's eyes, he'd created something of an uproar.

"I'm all ears," Gabe said.

"Yesterday, some young woman showed up at the South Bend headquarters claiming to have left a Jesse Gant with that couple who was murdered. She works as an agent for the

Children's Relief Society in New York, chaperoning orphans to homes in the Middle West.

"After visiting with the couple back in August and affirming they were good people, she left Jesse in their care and took the train further west to find homes for two remaining orphans. Apparently, this young couple had decided, quite on impulse, to foster Jesse, and since they lived a ways from town, no one else even knew about the arrangement. Therefore, they knew nothing about Jesse."

Gabe strained to take in every word, his heart pounding with elation, not for the unraveling of one of the saddest stories he'd ever heard, but for the way it validated Jesse's earlier claims that he had witnessed the couple's murder.

He sucked in a bottomless breath and gathered his fast-moving thoughts. "What took this woman so long to come forward?" he asked, glad to discover an improved connection, if only for a brief span.

"I wondered the same thing, but, apparently, her mother passed on unexpectedly, prompting the woman to leave the agency on a temporary basis to tend to family affairs.

Her intention was to check on Jesse's welfare on her way back to New York.

"Until yesterday, no one, not the agent or anyone from the society, knew anything about Jesse's missing status. It goes without saying they're on a frantic search for him right now. As you might know, this doesn't bode well for them. These orphan trains have already taken a hit from some of your Middle Western politicians who feel as if New York is taking advantage of their pleasant little farming communities by shipping them the dregs of society."

Anger such as Gabe had never known bubbled up within him like a geyser. "Dregs of society? These are orphans we're talking about—children without parents."

"Not all of them are orphans. Some have parents who've simply abandoned them to society. Many of these unfortunate little souls have learned to make their own way, and, once the orphan train leaves them at a destination, they run away, particularly the older boys. Some of them find themselves in a heap of trouble with the law, too, and this is what has some grandstanders in a dither, but enough about that. My suggestion is you put in a call to New York and let them know Jesse's in good hands."

"I'll do that. And, while I'm at it, I'll tell them I'm adopting him," Gabe said, surprised by his offhanded announcement.

An awkward pause ensued. "Well now, you mean without a wife? Your mother and I support you, Gabriel, but adoption? That's quite an undertaking for a single man." Another long pause followed a convenient string of static. "Are you still there?"

Over the pop and crackle, Gabe sneaked in a promise to call his father later, successfully evading his question about a wife. Hanging up the receiver, he stretched back in his chair for one brief moment and allowed himself a giant sigh.

⌒*K*⌒

"Hot-diggity, this here's somethin'," said Billy B, scoping out the Kane attic in the same way Jesse had the first time he saw it, eyes wide open, mouth gaping. To get to the attic, one had to walk through the Kane sisters' bedroom, as the attic was an extension of their room, separated only by a curtained doorway. It was a long room with a ceiling that sloped so low that Jesse had bumped his head a few times. Crates and sealed boxes lined the short wall, and, at the end of the room where the ceiling was highest, clothes bars extended from one side to the other, holding coats, long dresses and skirts, and an array of frilly-looking things. Under the clothes were cubbies of women's shoes and boots in every style imaginable. At first glance, one might have thought he was in a boutique.

"What's in all them trunks?"

"Stuff," Jesse said. "Pillows, blankets, old artwork, picture albums, Grandfather Kane's army uniforms."

"You looked in all of 'em?"

"Not all. Mostly Grandmother had me sorting through those books over there." He pointed at a floor-to-ceiling bookcase at the opposite end of the room, its shelves lined with volumes of all sizes, from encyclopedias to children's books. "There's another room downstairs they call the library. There's a big desk in there and more bookcases with glass doors. The only place I ever seen more books was at my school library in New York."

Billy B gave him a sideways glance, and Jesse suddenly realized he'd never told his friend about his former home, much less talked about his mother, or the mission where they lived, or the orphanage where he was sent after she died.

"New York?" Billy B moved away from Jesse to roam about the cedar-scented room, stroking the fabric of a long wool coat as he passed it, then bending to pick up a stray work boot and place it with its mate. "Ain't that a long ways away? I'm not very good at my maps."

Jesse rubbed the side of his nose with his sleeve and nodded. "Yep, it's a long ways from Michigan."

"How'd you get here if you ain't got parents?"

It was a fair question, and one Jesse gave Billy B credit for neglecting to ask a lot earlier. He looked at the big cedar chest sitting next to the bookcase and pictured all the quilts inside it—quilts Grandmother Kane said survived the trip across the ocean when she and Grandfather Kane left England those many years ago. She said every quilt had its own special story, just as he had his. Jesse liked thinking about his life in that way.

He walked to the big chest and plopped on top of it. "You want to hear my story?"

A flicker of light flashed in Billy B's eyes, accompanied by a lopsided grin. "If y' want t' tell it to me."

K

Hannah hung the last of the wash on the clothesline at half past twelve and hoped it would dry before the rain came. The air was heavy, not at all a good day for doing the wash, but Grandmother insisted she stick to her routine. Tuesday was wash day, rain or shine—it always had been and always would be, even when it meant a two-day drying period.

In the dead of winter, at least they hung their finer things on clothes racks in the kitchen.

She bent to lift her empty clothes basket. "Howdy, Miss Hannah."

Startled, she turned at the voice, then quickly relaxed at the sight of Jarvis Vandermueller's head peering over the wooden privacy fence. She wasn't sure when he'd arrived to relieve the fellow who had stood watch all night, but he'd been there when Gabe had dropped off Jesse that morning.

She knew, because she had run to the window to gaze down, hoping for a peek at Gabe. And when she'd seen his muscled frame loping down the porch steps, her heart had lurched, just as she'd suspected it would. *Drat!* There simply was no denying that she'd fallen head over heels for the bossy sheriff.

Before mounting Slate, Gabe had stopped for a moment to speak to Van, gesturing with his hands as he spoke, probably telling the deputy to keep the women of the house locked up tight. She could see keeping Jesse under lock and key, but why her?

"Well, hello there, Van." Clothes basket resting on her hip, she walked to the fence, pulling her coat collar close to her throat to ward off the icy chill in the air and putting on a smile for the friendly, if not slightly quirky, deputy. "You must be plumb tired of guarding our house."

Ever the gentleman, he removed his hat as she approached. "No miss. I'm just doin' my duty."

"I appreciate your dedication, then. Would you like something to eat?"

"Oh, no, thank you, ma'am. The wife packed me a fine midday meal. In fact, I just finished it not ten minutes ago."

"How about some coffee, then?" It seemed a shame to make him stand outside by the hour with nothing hot to soothe the nip in the air.

He gave a nervous glance in all directions, as if expecting trouble. "I better not. Fact is, the sheriff told me you mustn't be out wanderin' around."

She shifted the clothes basket on her hip. "I'm not wandering around, Van. I'm standing in my fenced-in backyard."

A sheepish expression washed across his narrow face. "Well, I s'pose that is different."

"Of course it is. I don't know what the sheriff thinks is going to happen. It's been very quiet around here."

"Yeah, almost too peaceful, if you ask me."

It did seem deadly quiet for the noon hour, now that she thought about it. Most weekdays, Ridge Street bustled with folks heading toward downtown on horses or in buggies to attend doctor appointments, make bank deposits and withdrawals, mail letters at the post office, and pick up items at the grocery store. She wondered how business fared at Kane's Whatnot.

"I only seen a few folks pass by in the last hour. I guess that article Stewart printed in the *Tribune* has Sandy Shores livin' more cautiously these days."

Hannah had not read the article, but she heard talk of it over the supper table. Naturally, the subject was taboo in Jesse's presence. "You're probably right. I'm hoping that awful bunch of scoundrels has left the area altogether. Has anyone actually spotted any of them?"

"Can't tell you that for sure, miss. All I know is, the sheriff's one smart man. He wouldn't be issuin' all these orders if he didn't believe some kind of danger lurked."

She wondered what other orders he'd doled out besides the ones intended to keep Jesse safe. A shiver shimmied up her spine. "You sure I can't interest you in some coffee?" she asked, turning back toward the house.

"No, Miss Hannah, but I thank you for askin'. You best get back inside now, 'fore you catch your death." His choice of words gave her pause, prompting her to lift a brow at him.

"Oh, sorry, I meant 'fore you catch a *cold*," came his quick revision.

K

"You s'pose folks is still expectin' some of Luis's family members to show up at the cemetery, Pa?" Roy asked as the threesome made their way down a narrow path carved parallel to the main drag leading into town. At the fork, they'd separate, then meet again at the Kane house, just as Roy had recommended. Earlier that morning, over a breakfast of dried bread and hot coffee, they'd rehashed their plan, then wiled away the rest of the morning in nervous anticipation.

"I'm sure they're hopin' so."

"Don't see what it would hurt for one of us to pay ar respects. I'd gladly go. It ain't like anyone knows who he is, or who I am, for that matter. I'd stay way in the background," Reuben said.

He had been spouting offers to attend the funeral all morning long, and Rufus's patience had long run out. "How many times Roy and me gotta drill this through your grapefruit-sized head, Reuben? You ain't goin' to no funeral."

"He's my brother," Reuben whined.

"I don't care if he's the king of Siam, you ain't goin'. We got no idea what folks is sayin' about us. Just 'cause we ain't heard no talk don't mean there ain't been somethin' in the newspapers. Shoot! If one of you jackrabbits could read, we might have some idea what we're dealin' with here."

"You can't read, neither," Reuben blurted.

"Both of you shut your faces," Roy said, taking over Rufus's job as authority.

Rufus spat a wad of tobacco juice out of the side of his mouth and clammed up, the ache in his chest still there, but not as pronounced as it was the night before. He heaved a few deep breaths and studied the darkening sky. "What happens if it rains?"

"Nothin'. We proceed as planned," Roy said, sounding increasingly like the leader of the pack.

Thirty or so yards ahead, they spotted the fork in the road. Something like a heavy rock settled in the pit of Rufus's stomach, making his throat dry up and his chest constrict.

"Here's where we part ways," Roy said, voice strangely calm. He looked from Reuben to Rufus. "Everybody remember his job?"

"Yeah, yeah," Rufus said, feigning confidence, even though his heartbeat fluttered in an unnatural rhythm, sometimes stealing his breath.

Roy checked his pocket watch, then shot them both a menacing glare. Rufus hated that Roy had taken advantage of his weakened state and had taken over. "Don't nobody do anythin' stupid, y' hear?" He looked straight at Reuben. "If everything goes as planned, we'll split out of this half-cracked town before sunset."

K

A few sprinkles of rain fell on Gabe's sleeve. He watched them shimmer on the seasoned leather of his coat. A loose twig dropped from a nearby tree. Startled, Slate shifted his stance and tossed back his head. Gabe calmed him with a gentle whisper and a pat to his withers. The cemetery, situated several blocks from downtown on Lake Avenue, couldn't have been more eerily quiet as folks—mostly men, along with a few women in furry hats and long woolen coats—started to gather for Luis McCurdy's funeral service. Whether from sheer curiosity or genuine compassion, they came in hushed clusters, tying their horses to hitching posts at the cemetery entrance before coming in. Gabe couldn't fathom why they'd come unless the kid's notoriety played a part.

He tipped his hat at those who passed: Mr. and Mrs. Gerritt, Peter Van Poort, Josh Herman, and, hobbling along behind them, good old Enoch Sprock.

Gabe lifted his gaze to meet that of Harry, one of the detectives from South Bend. Harry would stand guard at the west entrance to the cemetery, watching for any suspicious behavior. Beside him on horseback sat Arend Fordham, one of Sandy Shores' oldest citizens. Every day, like clockwork, Arend watched the masses from his roost on the second floor of Dirkse's Dry Goods. A confirmed bachelor, he'd lived in the upper story apartment for the past forty years, and he rarely missed a thing around town. He knew virtually every citizen, just as they knew him. That's why Gabe had selected him to assist Harry as a sort of watchdog, an appointed deputy.

And the oldster wasn't the only one he'd chosen. As a matter of fact, once word got out that Arend had a "job" helping to find the thugs, several other citizens volunteered their services, claiming they could spot a newcomer a mile away. Apparently, many citizens already had seen strangers; they just hadn't come forward to tell about it. One man finally divulged that he'd spoken with a young fellow in Sparky's Bar over in Columbus. Evidently, the fellow had asked a lot of questions about the drowning victim's funeral, then wanted to know about the Kanes, the sheriff, and the orphan boy and his whereabouts. Several bartenders admitted they had served a number of newcomers, not suspecting anything unusual, but after reading the article in the *Tribune*, they realized that a couple of the new customers had borne a tattoo on the left arm—a snakelike figure weaving around a name.

Area merchants also claimed to have seen the criminals. With the help of Hank Groding, South Bend's chief officer, Gabe considered each report, wanting to be thorough and, at the same time, levelheaded. Yes, Gabe could swallow Cora Hesselbart's claim that Rufus McCurdy had visited Peter Van Poort's grocery store and purchased a slab of bacon and a dozen eggs, and even Eustace Buford's account of having seen one of the McCurdys come out of the bakery with a sack of donuts. But when Minnie Durham swore that old Rufus had come into her hat store looking to buy one of her lovely, feathered concoctions, he'd had to draw the line. That woman would stop at nothing to draw attention to her business.

Besides stakeouts at the cemetery, Gabe and Groding positioned their deputies and volunteers at strategic places around town, giving them authority to act on their best judgment. They told them to consult supervision when possible, but to exercise independence, including the decision to use firearms, if faced with an emergency. Key street corners, access roads into town, saloons, markets, and restaurants all had someone's watchful eye covering them and their surroundings. Even churches received extra notice due to the notion that the thugs might consider them safe places for hiding out. Still, anyone with sense knew that it was impossible to cover every square inch of a town, no matter how many folks showed up to try.

Gabe sighed and drew his collar close, wincing against the icy pellets of moisture hitting his face. How could he even be sure the crooks would make their move today? Sure, he'd hoped the funeral service would fish them out of their hiding place, wherever that might be, but it was a gamble. How long would he be able to hang on to his volunteer posse after today?

"Lord, You promised in Your Word to give wisdom when we ask for it, and I'm asking for it right now. The citizens of Sandy Shores are counting on me to keep them safe," he murmured under his breath, even as he nodded at Alvin and Carlotta DeBoer as they hurried past him toward the main gate of the cemetery, apparently deciding the elements were not worth battling. And who could blame them? *Blast!* He wished the rest of those gathered around the freshly dug grave would follow suit. Any moment now, he expected the skies to start spitting big snowflakes.

Certain the cemetery was filled with plenty of vigilant eyes, and noting nothing out of the ordinary, Gabe turned Slate around and headed east on Lake toward Sheldon. From there, he would head back toward town and make his way to the Kane house to see how Van was faring with his guard duty, and to assure himself that all was well with the people he loved.

Chapter Twenty-two

Rufus dismounted his horse in an empty lot two blocks away from the house at the top of Ridge Street. He wanted to inch closer, but doing so would put him within view of several snooping neighbors. This way, he could tie his horse to a tree at the back of the wooded lot, and no one would be the wiser. He took a gander at the Kanes' two-story house and wondered if his old ticker would hold out long enough for him to climb the hill. He looked at his watch. *Five minutes till one. Good.* He was ahead of schedule. He would park himself on that old tree stump over there, try to keep warm, and wait things out. Maybe a few minutes' rest would ease the awful pain building in his chest.

K

Hannah gazed out the front window to watch the first hint of winter fall from the sky: tiny, fragile snowflakes, barely visible to the eye.

"Wow! Snow! Billy B, come quick!" Jesse shouted. Hannah realized that an eight-year-old probably spots snow quicker than a goat eats grass.

Billy B bounded into the front room behind Jesse, Dusty on his heels, and all three of them, minus the dog, crowded around the window, waiting to see if the flakes would stick.

"The ground is still too warm for that," Hannah voiced when Jesse suggested they might build a snowman the following day. "We need several days of freezing weather, followed by a wet, heavy snow, the kind that balls up when you roll it on the ground."

Hannah's mind drifted back to those innocent days of childhood—waging snowball fights with her sisters, building snow forts in the front yard, and sledding with Papa down Duncan Hill, then coming home to Grandmother's cinnamon biscuits and hot cocoa.

It occurred to her then that she'd like nothing more than to do those things all over again, but this time with Jesse and—dared she hope—with Gabriel Devlin? *Lord, I am waiting for a clear sign from You.*

"Ain't that guy awful cold?" asked Billy B, pointing at Jarvis Vandermueller, whose lanky body was propped against the old maple tree, hat low on his head as he hugged himself. "He was there when I got here this mornin'."

"Why's he have to stand out there, anyway? What's he waitin' for?" Jesse asked.

While Hannah tried to come up with a convincing response, Billy B beat her to it. "He's standin' guard so no bad guys can come on yer property, don't y' know? My ma tol' me she's heard talk about some criminals on the loose—right here in Sandy Shores. Says there was a big article 'bout it in the newspaper. 'Course, I can't read good enough yet, so I ain't got all the details. But I do know there's lawmen keepin' watch all over the place."

"Well, I wouldn't worry too much," Hannah cut in, hoping to change the subject. "How about I bring out the checkerboard? Anyone up for a game of checkers? Or we could play a game of caroms. Which do you prefer?"

"Who are the bad guys?" Jesse asked, pulling back the curtain and pressing his nose against the frosty windowpane. A wave of frustration washed over Hannah at being ignored.

"Don't know, exactly," answered Billy B, stuffing his hands in his pockets and puffing out his chest. "But my grandma calls 'em depraved and rotten to the core."

"Checkers, boys? I'll make some hot cocoa, too, if you like. How does that sound?"

"The only reason Ma let me come over today was 'cause she knows the sheriff's watchin' over things. Even the school board said no kids is to walk to school anymore without a big person bringin' 'im."

Hannah sighed, not missing the sudden worry that sullied Jesse's cheery countenance. Had they been wrong to shield him from the truth? She might have known Billy Bruce Hiles would spill the beans.

"I'm sure the school board is just taking precautions," she said. "Let's talk about something else, shall we?" She took them both by the hand to steer them out of the room.

Just then, Helena exited the library, dust cloth in hand, a rare black smudge streaking her cheek. "Well, my stars, it is snowing," she said, voice uncommonly cheerful for the boys' sake as she bent to gaze out the window. "Would you look at that?"

"I'm just trying to talk these boys into a game of checkers or caroms. Which do you think is the better choice, Grandmother?"

Helena tilted her face in serious deliberation. "Hmm, I'd vote for caroms, if it were me."

"You want to play?" Billy B asked her with high-pitched enthusiasm.

Hannah regarded her grandmother, who, despite her plastered-on smile, looked as weary as a war veteran—and who could blame her? It had been a hairy few days.

"Ah, well..." the older woman's brow furrowed.

Hannah stepped forward and stole the dust cloth from Helena's hand, then took her by the arm. "Actually, I'm going to insist that Grandmother go upstairs to lie down for a while."

"What? Oh, goodness me, I couldn't do that. Why, I haven't napped since...let me see, the summer of 1891, maybe...or was it '92?"

Hannah laughed. "I didn't say you had to sleep, but a little rest would do you good. How about you go upstairs where it's quiet, and I'll bring you a nice cup of hot tea?"

Helena's face turned pensive. "I suppose I could resume reading that book of memoirs on Jane Austen's life, and, I must say, reading during working hours does sound perfectly luxuriant. Almost like taking an afternoon bath. Can you imagine?"

The two walked arm in arm toward the stairs. Behind them, Billy B muttered, "What's lux-uriant?"

"Some kind of soap, I think," answered Jesse.

K

Billy B had a loud, boisterous laugh, the kind that made a person want to join in, and that's exactly what Jesse did, but in the back of his mind, he couldn't stop thinking about the bad guys roaming Sandy Shores. Even Dusty barked with enthusiasm when Billy B whooped his excitement over dropping yet another carom into the pocket.

"How many times have you played this game?" Jesse asked.

Billy B shrugged. "A couple." Stick in hand, he bent over the board and took careful aim, one eye pinched shut.

"More than that."

"Okay, a dozen."

"More."

"Shh, you're breaking my concentration."

Jesse let a few seconds lapse. "Don't miss!" he said, right at the pivotal moment, throwing off his friend's aim.

"Hey, no fair!" Billy B whined, dropping his stick and narrowing his eyes at Jesse in feigned anger. "I'm gonna get you for that."

Jesse laughed. "No, you're not. I'm faster than you." And just like that, the two set off on a run through the house and into the dining room, Dusty barking and nipping at their heels.

Hannah entered the room with a tray of cookies and two mugs of hot cocoa. "Okay, you two, time to settle down," she warned, not in a harsh way, though. Hannah didn't have a harsh bone in her body.

When Billy B saw the platter of goodies, he immediately stopped the chase. "Hmm, yum," he said, running to the dining room table and pulling out a chair. "That cocoa smells good."

Hannah set the items on the table. "I'm going to put Dusty in the backyard while you have your snack, then I'm going upstairs to check on Grandmother and to tend to some chores. You can call him back inside in a few minutes. No more running through the house, though, okay? Remember, Grandmother is trying to rest."

"Okay," Jesse said.

Billy B nodded. He was too busy shoving cookies down his throat to make an audible reply.

K

Rufus huffed all the way up the hill, the pain in his chest mounting with every step. He pulled his wool collar closer, then clutched at the place where it pained him the most, the upper left side. He groaned aloud and winced at the inconvenience. He had a job to do, and he certainly had no time for dealing with a bothersome ache. Trying to ignore it, he trudged along, hoping no neighbors were watching from their closed up houses.

When he was still several yards away from the Kane residence, Roy's familiar bird whistle stopped him in his tracks as he sought out the source. "Over here," Roy hissed through his teeth. Crouched behind a tree, he motioned for Rufus to join him. "I don't see that brainless brother of mine anywhere," he muttered when Rufus staggered over to the tree. "He's late. So help me, if he went over to that cemetery, I'll wring his skinny neck. He's gonna get us all kilt."

Rufus had better things to worry about, namely staying in an upright position.

"You drunk?" Roy asked, eyes narrowing in suspicion.

"No, I ain't drunk. It's that stupid indigestion I been havin'."

"Oh." Roy's icy gaze lingered but a moment before he turned his attention back to the Kane house. "There's some weasel standin' guard out front. I wasn't countin' on that. We'll have to figure out a way to get past 'im. I'll shoot 'im if I have to."

"Shootin' will draw attention."

"I ain't worried 'bout that. By the time the authorities get here, we'll be long gone."

"We gotta get back to ar horses. How you figure we'll be long gone? And how you gonna haul some squallin' kid down that hill without makin' a stir? This plan don't seem to be comin' together like it ought."

"Stop yer worryin', you ol' fool. I got it all figgered out."

Any other time, Rufus would have slapped his son's mouth. "What about Reuben?" he mumbled instead.

Roy cursed and spat. "Far as I'm concerned, if he ain't here when the deed's done, we're leavin' without 'im."

Nausea swirled in Rufus's gut as he realized how hard he had to work to snag a breath.

"I'll circle 'round back," Roy hissed. "If that coot looks like he's gettin' suspicious, throw somethin', a stone or stick, to distract 'im, but whatever you do, don't let 'im see you."

"You're gettin' awful bossy, you know that?"

"And if Reuben happens to show up, tell 'im to wait for my signal."

"You'd think you was in charge."

A snide grin spread over Roy's face. "Just practicin' up, that's all."

"Pfff. You think you're somethin'."

Ignoring the taunt, Roy poked his head around the tree, slinking low, then quickly darted across the street and disappeared behind a house situated three doors away from the Kane residence. The so-called guard was leaning against a tree, completely oblivious to the goings-on.

When Rufus hunkered down behind the tree, preparing to watch for Roy's signal, a sudden cramp seized his chest. He'd known pain, but this one pierced him to his toes, slicing straight to his core. In an instant, his squalid world tumbled and turned and tipped on its axis.

And before he breathed his last, he cursed the pain, cursed his wretched life, and cursed the God he'd never once acknowledged.

⌒*K*⌒

Dusty barked, but it wasn't an ordinary bark; this bark was tinged with fuss and fury. "He must be chasing a squirrel. He'll never get it through his head he can't catch one," Jesse said between cookie bites. He took a few sips of cocoa to wash down his cookies, but his hand slipped unexpectedly on the handle and at least half the mug's contents spilled down his shirtfront.

"Yow!" he squealed, leaping off the chair, his skin stinging from the hot liquid, but not nearly as much as his pride.

"You okay?" Billy B pinched his lips together to keep from laughing. "You made a fine mess."

Jesse looked down at himself. "Oh, man, Hannah never gets mad at me, but this might be the first time." Brown liquid soaked through his light blue, button-down shirt, running the length of his pant legs and seeping into his shoes. He pulled the cotton fabric away from his skin and made a face. "Yeeeeuck!" Now Billy B gave a full-out laugh, and Jesse couldn't help it—he followed suit.

Outside, Dusty's barking came to an abrupt stop, but neither boy seemed to notice.

"Would one of you let Dusty in?" Hannah called from the top of the stairs.

"Oh boy, wait till she finds out what I did," Jesse whispered. "It's even on the rug."

Billy B's laughter settled. "It'll be okay," he muttered between chuckles. "Go wash yourself up while I get the dog. Then we'll try to clean up the mess before she comes down."

"Deal."

K

Hannah worried that the boys' incessant laughter would disturb her grandmother, but when she checked in on her, she found her sleeping soundly and snoring lightly with an afghan tucked under her chin, a peaceful half-smile on her face. Well, would wonders never cease? Helena Kane was napping. Hannah smiled and closed the door as soundlessly as possible, then went back to dusting the upstairs study area. Beyond the small study, which housed a rolltop writing desk, an office chair on castors, and a tall bookcase, was a set of glass-paneled French doors leading out to a second-story terrace, which formed a roof over the rear entryway. A white balustrade encased the small balcony, making it a safe and cozy place to lounge with a good book on a warm, sunny day. She paused and glanced out the window at the backyard, where the dry autumn leaves still lay in small, half-burned piles, the family's efforts to rake them up having ended abruptly one week ago, when a rainstorm moved in.

Since Dusty's barking had ceased, she assumed the boys had brought him back inside, but why, then, did she not hear the crazy mutt running helter-skelter through the house? And what of the boys' high-spirited giggles?

An odd, clamoring sound, almost like a yelp, came from the backyard, followed by a string of muffled words: "Hey! Stop! Let go!" More tussling, more muted talk, and some kind of cracking sound had her wrinkling her brow in apprehension. Had Dusty's play gotten too rough? But then, she'd clearly instructed both boys not to play outside, so who would be yelling at Dusty? Van, perhaps?

She hurried to the glass doors and flung them wide open, then darted to the edge of the terrace to look down at the yard. Dusty, sprawled and dazed-looking, was struggling to get to his feet, but Van, not five feet away from him, lay perfectly motionless next to a two-by-four board—the kind Papa had used for a recent woodworking project. Hannah's stomach twisted with raw fear, but when she looked to her right and spotted a man dragging Billy B by the arm toward the front gate, her fear advanced to all-out hysteria. "Billy!" she screamed. Then, to the man, she shouted, "What do you think you're doing?" stomping her foot and pointing wildly. "You unhand him this instant!"

Surprised by the interruption, the man paused for a second, stared up at her, then drew something from his pocket. Billy B yowled and tried to wrestle free, kicking and squealing like a banshee, but to no avail. Frantic, Hannah turned, preparing to make a beeline for the stairs, but then it happened—a loud, splintering crack fired through the air, and, after that, a jolt to her body knocked her sideways, sending her reeling and teetering until she landed with a thud on the terrace floor. For the life of her, she couldn't figure out why she'd fallen—until searing pain as she'd never known it clutched her in the left side. Glancing down at the point of pain, she noted a red splotch darkening her dress.

A scream she barely recognized as her own bellowed from her throat.

"Lord God, help me," she gasped between sobs. And then, "Billy. Jesse. God, please—send Your angels of protection."

Another scream tore out of her, and she did not stop screaming, then whimpering, until everything went black.

Chapter Twenty-three

Gabe choked down fear as he kicked Slate into a full-out run down Sheldon. Only a block from Ridge, he'd heard the gunshot clear as day, and, somehow, he sensed with dread that it had come from the Kane household. "Lord, Lord, Lord," he prayed as Slate galloped up the street. Out of the corner of his eye, he saw folks emerging from their homes but took no time to acknowledge them, maintaining focus on his mission.

At the corner of Ridge, he reined in Slate to appraise the situation. As much as he wanted to continue barreling ahead and to insure everyone's safety, his years of training and experience warned against such action. *Best to move in with a plan,* he thought, ever wary of brash action on impulse.

"It came from up there, Sheriff." Gabe glanced around to find Herb Horton standing on his porch in his long underwear, pointing up the hill.

"Herb! Did you see anything suspicious beforehand? Notice anyone passing by your place?"

The man pulled at his graying beard and shook his head. "The wife and I was just sittin' in ar living room reading yesterday's paper when we heard the blast. Sounded like gun-fire, if y' ask me, and this time, it ain't comin' from ol' Bill Elwood's place."

Slate snorted and danced, impatient to keep moving. A few other neighbors poked their heads out, some coming to stand on their porches. "What's going on, Sheriff?" someone asked.

"No time to explain, folks. Go back in your houses and out of harm's way."

Most of them heeded his words, however reluctantly, but one woman who looked to be in her thirties, supporting a toddler on her ample hip, walked out her front door and came straight down the steps in Gabe's direction. He quickly hustled Slate forward to meet her halfway.

"Ma'am, you'd better get back inside. It's bitter cold out here, not to mention dangerous."

"I saw them, Sheriff—two men," she spat out. "The younger one darted across the road and behind the Kane house." She pointed with her head. "I watched them from my front window. That young one had evil on his mind, I could tell, the way he ran across the road all hunkered down, look-ing every which way. The older one, he's layin' out flat behind that tree over yonder, drunk or something. See 'im?"

Gabe swiveled in the saddle and strained to see where she gestured. Sure enough, several yards ahead and across the road, a body lay motionless beneath a tree. *Rufus McCurdy?* "I see him," he replied. "You best get back inside now. Thanks for your help, ma'am."

She gave a nod and pushed a few strands of hair behind her ear. "I hope you get those awful men, Sheriff. Sandy

Shores has always been a quiet place. We all want it to stay that way."

He tipped his hat at her and watched her scurry inside, her little son staring over his mother's shoulder at him. Turning Slate around, Gabe steered him in the direction of the body under the tree. To stay on the safe side, he retrieved his holstered gun and prepared to use it if necessary. "*God is our refuge and strength, a very present help in trouble,*" he murmured, recalling the first verse of Psalm 46, which he had read in his Bible that very morning. Just repeating the verse calmed his adrenaline-surged pulse.

Up ahead, two of his deputies, Gus van der Voort and Clyde Oertmann, approached on horseback. They either heard the gunfire or somehow received word of impending trouble at the Kane household. Gabe motioned with an outstretched palm, and they nodded, pulling in their mounts and easing to the side of the road to await further instruction. He inched Slate closer to the motionless body, lying face-up to the elements, and found it clad in dirty denims, new-looking boots, and a fine wool coat. Unblinking eyes that had glazed over stared skyward, even as snowflakes landed on the weather-worn face. Beside the body lay a Colt revolver. Gabe leaned forward and read the monogram on its handle grip—RJM. He needed no other proof. Sandy Shores had claimed the life of another McCurdy.

With no time to ponder what to do with the body, he guided Slate toward the house, ears and eyes keenly tuned to every sight and sound—each snapping twig, each rustling leaf, a darting squirrel scurrying up a tree and out on a bare branch. Even the snowflakes, which were falling more steadily now, seemed to resonate when they hit the ground. In the distance a dog barked, a horse neighed. And that's when he heard it—a verbal skirmish taking place behind the Kane house. "Let him go!" came the male voice.

Signaling at his men to move in, he advanced more quickly. Just then, Helena Kane opened the front door and waved hysterically, her face a picture of silent anguish. He and his men quickly dismounted and approached the house.

"They're in the backyard," she said in a frantic whisper. "Two men. One has hold of Billy B, and, oh, dear, I don't know what's going on, exactly. I told Jesse to stay put upstairs. It's awful, and, worst of all, Hannah's been shot! By the time I got to her, she'd passed out. Somehow, I managed to drag her inside when those fellows had their backs turned. Jesse's watching over her now."

"Shot?" Like an axe, the single word sliced straight through Gabe's core, making his blood run hot and cold. "Is she…?"

Helena shook her head. "I think it's just a surface wound, but only Dr. Van Huff will be able to tell us for sure. Just—just hurry!"

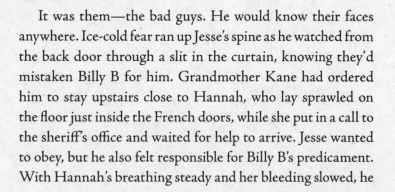

It was them—the bad guys. He would know their faces anywhere. Ice-cold fear ran up Jesse's spine as he watched from the back door through a slit in the curtain, knowing they'd mistaken Billy B for him. Grandmother Kane had ordered him to stay upstairs close to Hannah, who lay sprawled on the floor just inside the French doors, while she put in a call to the sheriff's office and waited for help to arrive. Jesse wanted to obey, but he also felt responsible for Billy B's predicament. With Hannah's breathing steady and her bleeding slowed, he bustled down the stairs anyway. At the ground floor, he spotted Grandmother, crouched by the front window with rifle in hand. Quiet as a mouse, he tiptoed past her to the open gun cabinet and grabbed a rifle for himself, then made a beeline to the back of the house.

Hunkering down, hand to the doorknob, he turned it slowly, pulling open the door an inch or so, waiting for the perfect time to make his move, not even sure he'd recognize it when it came.

Dear Jesus, my ma told me You'd keep watch over me, said You had a plan for my life. If that's true, would You please help me right now? Billy B's in trouble, and it's all because of me. I need to help him get out of this awful mess, so would You show me how? And while You're at it, Lord, could You make me brave?

"Let 'im go, Roy. So help me, I'll shoot you right here," yelled one of the men.

"No, you won't. You ain't got the guts, little brother."

Jesse's heart pounded through his drenched shirt, which still smelled like cocoa even though he'd cleaned it vigorously with a washcloth. He peered through the slit in the door. The bickering brothers were pointing pistols at one another. Billy B fussed and wriggled, and the one called Roy tightened his hold. Beyond the two men and Billy, Jesse spotted Dusty trying to get up, his legs wobbly and his eyes glazed over. When he plopped back down, Jesse wanted to sob in anguish. Then, there was that fellow lying a few feet away from Dusty, and poor Hannah upstairs suffering from a gunshot wound. "God, please don't let any of them die. Please."

"Stand still, you little twerp. I finally got you where I want you, and I ain't lettin' you go. He's comin' with me, Reuben.

Pa's waitin' out front, and we're hittin' the road. Are you comin' or not?"

"I'm not goin' with you. I'll go to jail first," Reuben said. "It's the end of the line, and if you can't see it, well, then yer dumber than I thought. Takin' the kid is not the answer, Roy. The town's onto us."

"What you mean by that?"

"I heard talk at the city park. After we parted ways, I went and sat a spell tryin' t' decide if I should go to the cemetery. That's when I heard there's a big posse out lookin' for us. Some folks who passed by me was talkin' about it. Your brilliant idea about catchin' the town off guard, well, it didn't hold much water, Roy. You take that boy, and there'll be a lynching, fer sure. If we give arselves up, though, we at least got a chance at a fair trial. It was Pa what done the murderin', not us."

"Yeah, and me who just shot that woman up there. I ain't stickin' around."

"I am," Reuben said. "I'll testify against you—and Pa, too."

Roy sneered. "You traitorous slimebucket. I ought to do you in right here." He raised his gun.

Praying for courage, Jesse shoved open the door and stepped outside, rifle aimed at Roy—as if he had a clue how to fire it. "I'm the one you really want," he announced, surprised by his confident tone, especially with the way his heart pounded in his chest. Caught off guard, both men whipped their heads around and stared.

"Who are you?" Roy asked.

When he might have known sheer terror, a newfound sense of courage boiled up from the soles of his feet. *So, this is how it feels to trust God with all my heart.*

"I'm the one who saw you in the house the day your pa murdered those people."

Reuben actually laughed at Roy. "Oh, so now you've gone and done it, you imbecile. You don't even have the right kid."

Roy's face went as gray as a storm cloud, and his shifty eyes, narrowed in suspicion, darted from Jesse to Billy B.

"Let 'im go, Roy, 'fore you get into worse trouble," Reuben said.

Yanking Billy B closer yet, he twisted his upper lip into an ugly grimace. "He's lyin', the little fiend. This is the kid I saw that day."

"How d' you know? They look alike, same hair color, similar in size. Seem near 'bout the same age."

A smidgen of doubt crept onto Roy's face. Clutching a fistful of Billy B's hair, he jerked his head backward. "You'd tell me if you wasn't, right?"

Billy B stared daggers up at Roy. "I ain't sayin' nothin' to you, dirty scoundrel."

Wow, Jesse thought. He wondered if Billy B had prayed for courage, as well.

Propelled by obvious anger, Roy suddenly poked his gun in Billy B's temple. "So, little man," he chided, staring Jesse in the face. "If I got the wrong kid here, how 'bout we make a nice little trade before I blow this one's head off?"

Jesse froze, his sense of assurance quickly draining from his veins.

"I wouldn't do that," came the clear, determined voice dripping with power. "Drop your weapons, boys—slow and easy."

Gabe emerged from the side of the house, pistol aimed, looking like a hulking giant in Jesse's opinion. "Pa!" he exclaimed, the name slipping out as natural as breathing. Two deputies came around the other side of the house, rifles directed at their targets. Reuben dropped his gun and raised his hands over his head.

"You dumb coward. What's Pa goin' to think of you now?" Roy growled, taking his sweet time about lowering his gun.

"Not much, I'm afraid," Gabe inserted. "Your pa's, hmm, shall we say, belly-up—under a tree a block or so back. My guess is, he's in a warmer place about now."

Thanks to the sudden confusion Gabe's words wrought, Roy lost his focus, allowing Billy B the opportunity to wrangle free from his grasp. Roy swore and reached out to snag him, but in that instant, Gabe hurtled his body at Roy and tackled him to the ground, knocking the gun from his hand and pinning him facedown. The tussle couldn't have lasted more than a few seconds, with Roy the clear loser, Gabe wrenching the felon's hands behind him to snap a pair of handcuffs in place. Clyde kept a gun on Reuben while Gus stepped forward to lend Gabe a hand. Clutching Roy by the collar, Gabe dragged him to a standing position.

That's when Jesse and Billy B bounded off the porch and ran to Dusty. The poor pooch bore a wound to his head, but he wagged his tail and lifted himself up on his haunches. A few feet away, the so-called guard moaned and opened his eyes.

"What's goin' on here?" Van stammered, giving his head a shake and raising it up to look across the yard.

Jesse heard what sounded like a stampede of horses galloping up to the house. "Must be those fellows from South

Bend finally got word of our whereabouts," Gus muttered, rolling his eyes.

"Nice you could make it," Gabe said when the whole lot of them rounded the corner, guns raised. "You wanna take these good-for-nothings off my hands?"

K

"I think we should close the store for a few days," Jacob was saying.

"Is Hannah going to be all right?" Jesse asked in a broken whisper.

"She'll be good as new before you know it," said Ralston. "I'll keep her sedated for a few days to help ease the pain and give the wound time to heal. I had to do a bit of digging to find the bullet. Mostly we'll be watching for infection, but I've no cause to believe there'll be that complication."

"I'll keep watch over her tonight," said Grandmother Kane.

"I think it'd be better if you got a good night's rest," argued Abbie Ann.

"Oh, pooh! I'm fine as duck's down."

"I'll stay with her," Maggie Rose inserted, a determined edge to her voice.

"You worked at the store all day, and all I did was sit upstairs in the library and read. I'm probably the most rested of all, so I'll stay," Abbie countered.

"I should be the one to stay. After all, I *am* her father."

"It's really not necessary for any of you to stay," Ralston put in. "She's my patient, so I'll be looking in on her often throughout the night. Besides, I expect she'll sleep for the next several hours."

Hannah struggled to open her eyes, but her weighty eyelids blocked all attempts. Everyone seemed so near, and yet so far away. If this was a dream, she needed to awaken from it. *I'm not sleeping!* she wanted to scream.

Someone cleared his throat. "I'd just as soon stay." This particular voice carried a deep-timbered quality lined with uncompromising authority. *Gabe.* With all her heart, Hannah wished to muster the strength to rouse herself.

"Yeah. She's gonna be my mother, so we should both stay," chimed Jesse.

Mother? Dreams of this caliber were rare. *Lord, help me open my eyes.*

"Jesse Gant, for crying out loud. Nothing's official yet." Gabe's tone bordered on scolding.

The atmosphere in Ralston's little office grew painfully quiet, so quiet, in fact, that an ant could have dragged a crumb away and everyone would have heard it.

But Abbie Ann took care of that. "Oh, my stars in a bucket! Are you truly marrying my sister, Sheriff? But that's great news! No offense, Dr. Van Huff."

Ralston chuckled. "None taken. This morning, when Mr. Devlin stopped by my office to talk about moving that young man's body to the cemetery, he brought up the matter of his feelings for Hannah Grace. Seems he wants to make her his bride and was eager to determine where I stood. Since I put an end to the relationship Sunday night, well, I gave him my best wishes, of course."

"Well, I'll be a yellow-nosed toad!" Abbie squealed.

As will I! Hannah longed to say. Why, the nerve of that Ralston Van Huff, announcing to her family that *he* was the one who severed the relationship.

I know the plans I have for you, My child, the Lord whispered. *Do not trouble yourself over trivial matters.*

Trivial? But, Lord…

And do not allow your foolish pride to keep Me from accomplishing My purposes in your life.

Oh, but she had so longed to know His divine will.

A great deal of hugging seemed to take place then. Someone patted her leg, another touched her hand. *Lord God, help me see my way through this fog.*

"Sir, uh, Mr. Kane, this is rather awkward," Gabe was saying. "I fully intended to speak to you properly beforehand, but it seems the cat's been let out of the bag by this little man here. I hope you'll give us your blessing."

Papa cleared his throat. She felt his nearness, recognized his gentle touch on her shoulder. "Nothing would please me more."

More hugging, oohing and ahhing. Surely, she would awaken in moments and find herself tucked snug beneath her down comforter, Maggie Rose in the bed next to the attic door and Abbie Ann sleeping soundly by the dormer window.

Agonizing pain shot an instant hole through her side and a groan she barely recognized as her own rumbled from her chest.

"She's awake!" Abbie shrieked.

Am I?

"I don't see how that's possible," Ralston said. "I gave her the maximum dose of laudanum. Perhaps I should administer a bit more. She mustn't move. I don't want that wound disturbed."

"Hannah." The velvet murmur of his voice right next to her ear eased the pain, brought indescribable comfort. "It's Gabe. Can you hear me, sweetheart? Jess and I are right here, along with your family."

Sweetheart?

"Yeah, we're here, and guess what? Gabe's gonna adopt me, but we need a mother to make it all complete."

A mother? Well, now, that settled it. She was definitely stuck in the sweetest of all dreams.

Chapter Twenty-four

Gabe flipped the page of his wall calendar to December just as Kitty sauntered through his open door to drop a stack of mail and the *Tribune* on his desk. "You're a little late with that. It's already the tenth."

"How'd that happen?" Gabe asked, turning toward the woman who'd somehow become his secretary without his asking. Every morning without fail, she brought him a fresh cup of coffee, straightened his desktop, raised the window shades, and emptied the trash. Then, like clockwork, and even before the lunch whistle sounded from the firehouse, she delivered the mail and daily paper.

She shot him a mischievous glance, leaned back against the edge of his desk, and folded her arms over her ample waistline. "I'm not sure, unless it's that love simply has a way of making time take wing."

Like an awkward adolescent, he felt heat steal into his cheeks. She'd been making crafty little remarks like that one ever since word had leaked to her via Jesse of his intentions to ask Hannah Grace to marry him. In fact, since Jesse had started back to school—walking the few blocks to Central Elementary with Billy B and a host of other youngsters, the fully recovered Dusty escorting them halfway there before turning around to come back home and sleep the day away in the barn with Zeke—he wondered who else had heard the news.

"Have you proposed to her yet?"

"What? No."

Kitty stared at him as if he'd just stolen someone's last dollar. "Well, gracious me, what are you waiting for? When you take Jesse as your legal son, wouldn't it be nice to have a marriage certificate to file away with those adoption papers?"

Relentless woman!

"Every time I go over to the Kanes' house, Hannah's holed up in her room. I think she's avoiding me. About all I get are reports that she's resting and making a nice recovery."

"And so you just leave it at that? You don't inquire further?" Kitty scowled, and that silly schoolboy feeling returned.

"What am I supposed to do, barge upstairs to her room?"

"No, but you might send a message with one of the women that you'd like to see her when she feels up to it."

"Oh."

"Have you never courted a woman?"

"I'll have you know, I nearly married one last summer. Praise the Lord for rescuing me from that disaster." Gabe strode to his desk, picked up his mail, and started thumbing through it, tamping down annoyance for the way Kitty mothered him—and for the way he secretly enjoyed it.

She unfolded her arms and straightened her plump frame. "Well, what do you know about that? Why did you never mention it?"

"Didn't know I needed to," he said, pushing back a grin. "Believe me, I'm better off without her."

Finding nothing of importance in the stack of mail he held, save some correspondence from the South Bend Police Department, Gabe tossed it down in favor of the newspaper. Opening the *Tribune* to the front page, he read aloud, "McCurdy Brothers Convicted on Several Charges."

Kitty hurried around to his side of the desk. "What's it say?"

"Nothing I didn't already know," he answered, skimming over the lengthy article.

"Sentence pending final hearing in Sandy Shores. Humph, I thought that Roy character already pled guilty to shooting Hannah Grace and clonking poor Van and that pooch with a two-by-four," Kitty said, reading over his shoulder.

Gabe continued scanning. "He did, but both brothers need to appear before Judge Bowers. Roy will spend the rest of his life behind bars. I suspect Ed will go lighter on Reuben. In the end, he did try to save face by intervening on behalf of Billy B and Jesse, but make no mistake—Ed will see that he gets plenty of jail time. Those sentences, piled on top of the ones they'll get for their part in the murder in South Bend… those boys will be lucky to ever see the light of day again. Sure, Rufus was their ringleader, but they could've turned in that snake of a father at any point—or just plain walked away."

"How do you know that? Maybe he threatened them, made them think themselves worthless and incompetent. I mean, really, what chance did they have, a life of crime being the only thing they ever knew? I swear, parents who don't have the first clue about raising youngsters shouldn't be allowed the privilege. Just think what might have happened to those fellows had someone stepped in to rescue them when they were mere boys."

She had an excellent point, and it grieved Gabe to think he needed the reminder.

The McCurdys, though he liked to view them as the earth's scum, had souls in need of saving. *Law enforcement sure has a way of making one's heart grow callous*, he mused.

He breathed a hasty prayer of repentance and asked the Lord to send a messenger of hope to the remaining McCurdys.

"I guess that's why Maggie Rose is so bent on going to New York City to work in one of those orphanages," Gabe said. "Jacob told me he's about to give in to her wishes just so she'll stop her nagging. Of course, meeting Jesse fueled her fiery passion the more. She's determined God's calling her to go."

"Then Jacob best not stand in the way of God's call."

Outside, the wind howled like a freezing cat. Gabe tossed down the open newspaper and walked to the window. Overhead, angry clouds threatened another fresh batch of snow to add to the already four or so inches blanketing west Michigan's frigid earth. It looked like a white Christmas was surely in store.

"Well, this looks interesting," Kitty mumbled.

He swung around. "Hmm?"

"This." She tapped her index finger repeatedly on a heading in bold typeface. "There's to be a Christmas concert at the Sandy Shores Opera House this Friday night. Says here a host of talented musicians will be performing vocal and instrumental pieces. Following the concert, folks are to gather in the large lobby area for a sampling of fresh-baked cakes and cookies. It lists several places selling concert tickets, Kane's Whatnot being one of them."

"That so?"

Kitty waggled her head and closed her eyes. "My, what woman wouldn't enjoy an invitation to attend? Why, perhaps I'll hint to Hubert over supper that I'd like to go myself. Other than Sunday mornings, I haven't had a real occasion to dress up since…well, let me see here…why, I believe it was Henrietta Morgan and Horace VanEck's wedding last July. Yes indeed, a Christmas concert would be just the thing to usher in the holiday festivities."

Sly woman! He would thank her later for planting the idea in his head.

K

Hannah stared at her drab reflection while her sisters fussed over her cinnamon-colored, velveteen, two-piece gown, purchased a year ago but never worn. It pained her still-healing wound to lift her left arm much above her head, so arranging her hair was a bit of a chore.

"Here, let me," Maggie insisted, coming up behind her to snatch the brush from her hand and take up the task of piling her rust-hued hair into a loose bun, allowing several coiled strands to fall around her face at will. "Are you sure you're strong enough to go out? You look a little pallid."

Hannah frowned. When wasn't she pallid, compared to Abbie's olive complexion and Maggie's rosy cheeks? "Thank you for the boost in confidence."

"No, I didn't mean it that way, silly." Maggie bent forward to give Hannah's shoulders a gentle squeeze. "You're pretty as ever, but you've been through an ordeal, sister dear. My goodness, you've barely left your bed for the past three and a half weeks. Do you realize how physically taxing tonight could be for you?"

"Or how relaxing," Abbie put in. "Don't worry, Mags, Gabe will take good care of her."

The mere mention of Gabe's name sent Hannah's mind to whirling. As often as she'd tried, she couldn't dismiss that childish dream of Gabe announcing his wish to marry her and precious Jesse saying he needed a mother. Imagine such talk in her family's presence, and while she lay recuperating. She'd heard that pain medications could make the mind hallucinate, so that would explain the foolish reverie. Besides, if there'd been any such announcement made in Ralston's crowded little office, Abbie Ann would never have kept quiet about it.

"No hat tonight," Maggie was saying as she stuck one last pin in her hair.

"What? But it's cold outside," Hannah argued.

"Gabe is renting a covered carriage from Enoch Sprock. You'll be plenty warm enough without one. Besides, Grandmother wants you to wear the comb she brought over from England, and a hat would simply cover it."

"I know, but that thing is so—glimmery."

"And quite lovely. You'll hurt her feelings if you don't wear it."

"Exactly." Abbie Ann shoved off from Hannah's bed to join her sisters. In the mirror they made quite a picture—Abbie still in farm overalls after helping Katrina and Micah Sterling deliver twin calves that afternoon, Maggie in the soiled blue work dress she'd been wearing since dawn, and Hannah in nothing but her underclothes. Even shabbily clad, her sisters looked regal when compared to her, and it simply amazed her that the handsome sheriff would invite her to such a public event. It would be her first outing since the shooting, and there were sure to be curious stares. Shivering from a bad case of nerves, she waited for her sisters to help her into her velveteen gown with the round décolleté neckline and flowing skirt.

Hannah slipped into the dress, put her sparkling comb in place, and applied a scant amount of rouge to her cheeks, adding just the right amount of color to her lips. Helena then made her grand entrance, skirts swishing in their usual way. "You'll wear these pearls as an accessory," she announced, extending a dainty hand from which the ancient strand of perfect pearls dangled.

"Oh, Grandmother," Hannah gasped. "I couldn't possibly wear those. What if something happened to them?" The flawless necklace had been in the family for generations, originally belonging to Helena's grandmother. Many had been the days when the girls played dress-up with Grandmother Kane's jewelry—but not with "the pearls." No, those remained locked away in a blue velvet box, never touched—and scarcely even seen.

"Nonsense. Nothing will happen, and, even if it did, people are far more important than earthly possessions. What's the point of letting these silly things continue to collect dust in my jewelry drawer? Gracious me. Now, let me look at you before I fasten them."

Helena stepped back to give her eldest granddaughter a top-to-bottom perusal.

"How do I look?" Hannah asked, biting her lower lip and feeling awkward.

"Stunning," Helena said while wiping a tear with her apron hem.

"Never prettier," said Abbie Ann, eyes round as moons.

"Like a princess," said Maggie.

"Rather beautiful, I'd say." Jacob stood in the doorway, stroking his silvery beard. Everyone turned at his voice. A faint light twinkled in his eyes before he walked across the room to place a feathery kiss on Hannah's forehead. "Lovely as a shining star." Then, looking around, he said, "Ladies, could I have a moment?"

Without a word, they filed out, Grandmother leading the way.

When they were alone, Jacob rested his hands on Hannah's shoulders. The twinkle in his eyes remained, but now they also brimmed with something like pleasure and pride. "I have never told you this, but of all my girls, you resemble my Hattie the most."

"But, Papa, Mama was Italian, dark, lovely. I always thought Abbie, with her smooth, golden skin and black hair—"

He shushed her with two fingers. "Perhaps she most resembles her physical traits, but your mannerisms—that spirited personality and tender, generous heart—are so much like your Mama's. I see her in you most every day. It is when you come floating into a room, all smiles and good cheer, that I miss your mother the most.

"When you suffered the gunshot wound and I realized how gracious God had been in sparing your life, well, it almost felt as if He'd given a part of Hattie back to me."

"Oh, Papa." Hannah swiped at a tear.

"A while back, when I thought I might be giving your hand in marriage to Ralston, I couldn't quite decide why I didn't fully approve, but now I see it.

"When your mother and I fell in love, she fairly glowed, and I suppose I did, as well. With you, though, that special radiance seemed to be missing, at least with Ralston."

He lowered his chin and studied her with moist eyes. "But I believe I've detected a bit of a glow since Gabriel Devlin and Jesse Gant came to town."

"Papa." The moment held a poignancy that sent a shiver up her spine. "I've been praying to know God's will for my life."

He cupped her cheek with his palm. "If you desire it deeply, daughter, and have a yielded heart, the Lord will reveal it to you in His good time. Be assured, He will never lead you astray. Perhaps you try too hard to figure things out, when really, your job is quite simple. Trust and obey."

He made it sound so effortless. *Trust and obey.* Yes, that is exactly what she needed to do.

⟣ K ⟢

The concert was halfway through when Gabe finally mustered up the courage to reach for Hannah's hand. "Are you feeling all right?" he whispered, leaning close enough to catch her blossomy scent. He gave her dainty fingers a gentle squeeze. "We can leave at any time."

She skimmed his face with tentative eyes and whispered, "I'm fine. It's—very nice."

He nodded, and his fresh-shaved chin caught on his high white collar and thick, knotted tie. When had they become so shy in each other's company? Mere months ago, they would argue over the proper care of an orphan boy, making no bones about their noisy disagreements; now, they sat like two sculptures, hardly daring to move. Hadn't he planted several bold kisses on her tasty lips just weeks ago? Now he had to drum up the guts to even hold her hand. *Lord, I've turned to mush— useless, countrified mush!*

He tried to give his full attention to the excellent choral and orchestral troupe from Chicago—they were performing a fine rendition of "Joy to the World," but his heart wasn't in it. Even the interspersing of several dramatic sketches throughout the evening, some amusing, others reflective and Christ-focused, hadn't been enough to stem his nervousness. He knew he was a goner from the second he'd laid eyes on Hannah in that gauzy gold gown she was wearing, the string of pearls gracing her creamy neck, and the dazzling comb planted in her burnished red curls. Even Jesse had seemed especially struck when she entered the room. He had come to the Kane house so that Maggie could watch him during the concert. "Man, you look pretty!" he'd blurted. Regrettably, it had taken a stab in the side from Jesse before Gabe had managed to find his tongue and stammer, "Yes, yes, you surely do."

Applause brought him back to the present and the house-lights came up. Intermission. All around them, folks shuffled in their chairs, rose to their feet, stretched stiff knees and achy bones, then greeted their neighbors and gushed over the show.

And yet they sat amidst all the rising, Hannah's fingers still woven with his and resting in his lap. He looked at her and saw weariness. It was a good idea, his inviting her to this holiday concert, but he needed to get her home before she wilted. Besides, there were things that needed to be said, a question that needed to be asked—and he didn't want her fading on him before he had the chance to get it all out.

He gently pulled her up with him and found her light as a feather. "Come on, darling girl."

She gasped, her hazel eyes as round as pie shells. "What? Where are we going?"

"Follow me," he shouted above the clatter and commo-tion of intermission mingling, snagging both their coats off the backs of the chairs and throwing them over his arm, then grasping hold of her hand to lead her through the masses.

Bumping bodies, he muttered a few apologies as they meandered down the row and out to the aisle. Wall-to-wall people gathered in groups, most of whom he didn't know. A few familiar folks nodded and waved as they passed, but thankfully, Gabe managed to keep them moving through the crowd and toward the vestibule minus any snags in their progress.

Away from the deafening throng, Gabe put his hands on Hannah's shoulders and turned her to face him. Someone heaved open the big doors, admitting a billow of bitter cold air. "I'm taking you home."

"I'm fine," she insisted, even as she winced and heaved a little sigh, her shoulders drooping under the weight of his hands.

He smiled. "Uh-uh." He held open her coat, and she slipped into it without a word of argument.

K

They entered a house that was dead quiet, save for a few snapping embers coming from the fireplace and the gentle ticking of the antique wall clock. Had Grandmother anticipated their early return and instructed everyone to retreat to his or her quarters? But if that were the case, where was Jesse?

The Christmas tree, bedecked in a variety of ornaments—some from England, some purchased during her childhood, and others handcrafted—stood like a splendid prince in the corner of the room, beckoning them inside. Pine bows and fresh-popped corn strung along the branches made for an aromatic mix.

Gabe closed the door and helped her out of her coat, hanging it with his own on the rack in the hallway. In the adjacent room, the cozy fire smoldered, in need of another log; shadowy figures cast themselves across the fresh-polished floor, a single low-beam lamp in the living room giving off a dusky glow to the front half of the house.

A note propped against an unlit oil lamp on the buffet table caught both their gazes at once. Hannah reached it first and read it aloud. "We've all gone next door to the Bartons' house for Christmas punch and cookies and a bit of caroling. You are both welcome to join us if you like when you get home. Papa."

"Well, so that's where everyone is," Gabe said. "Do you want to go over?"

Hannah looked into silvery blue eyes the color of new smoke and felt another ridiculous shiver run over her spine. Yes, weariness filled every bone in her body, and her side ached, calling her to sit down, but more than that, a river of pleasure from simply being alone with this man rippled through her veins. She gave him her answer by way of a shake of the head.

Suddenly, he snatched her dangling hand and brought it to his chest. *Oh, Lord, what is happening here? I feel his pounding heart. Is it possible…could it be we share common feelings for each other? Papa said You wouldn't lead me astray. I trust You to show me what to do about my own bursting heart.*

Her heart heard a whispered response: *My daughter, breathe deep of My love and relax.*

Gabe pulled her into the living room and sat her on the sofa in front of the dwindling fire. When he dropped down beside her, their knees touched, setting off another round of nervous breaths from her quivering lungs.

The seconds ticked away loudly on the mantel clock as they watched the smoldering flames, his hands clasped and set between his parted legs, hers in her lap.

"I should put another log on the fire," he said.

"I wouldn't bother. The embers are nice to watch."

More seconds. "I hope you don't mind that we left the concert early. You looked so tired."

"I was—am—but I'm fine now. Truly." Oh, why did she have to sound so vague and insecure? She could scarcely believe this was the same man she'd had an aversion to upon first meeting. In fact, she could barely recall the feeling.

"I thought it might be good for you to get some fresh air, but I see now it was selfish on my part. I've really missed seeing you these past weeks. As a matter of fact, it's made me a little stir-crazy." A low chuckle rolled out of him. "When I heard about the concert, I thought it might be something you'd enjoy. I'm glad you accepted my invitation, even though it came to you through Abbie."

All these admissions. She hardly knew what to say. She smoothed down a couple of tiny wrinkles. "I'm glad, too." Had he truly missed her? "The fresh air was purely wonderful. And I did enjoy the first half of the concert, but thank you for sparing me the second half. I'm not sure I could have endured sitting there for another hour."

Gabe looked down at his boots, still wet from trudging through fresh-fallen snow. It prompted Hannah to look at her own, which poked out from beneath her flowing skirt. She ran fidgety fingers over Grandmother's pearls.

He cleared his throat and tilted his blond head in her direction. "Does it still hurt—your side, I mean?"

"It's a bit sore to touch yet, but I'm so much better than—when it first happened. My goodness, there's so much I don't even remember about that day." *Except for that silly dream.* She concentrated on a piece of lint in her lap.

"I feel responsible, you know."

Confused, she peered at him. "Responsible? For what?"

"I never should have left Van in charge that day. He's not the most reliable guy when it comes to big jobs—he doesn't think on his toes. In retrospect, I should've had him fielding calls back at the office and put someone like Fred Van Dam or Randall Cling at the house. I keep thinking none of this would've happened if I'd used my head, you know? I just didn't anticipate the McCurdys actually coming here the day of the funeral, and that was careless on my part. I'm the lawman; I'm supposed to stay three steps ahead of the bad guys. I had my feelers out at the cemetery, not at the house."

With everything in her, she wanted to reassure him. "Gabriel…"

"I guess you don't need to ask how ridiculous I felt once I learned that Roy had actually watched me bring Jesse here. Blast if he didn't ride by Bill Elwood's house that day Bill fell off his rocker and look me straight in the eye! Now, that's embarrassing."

She rested a hand on his upper arm and felt the tensing of muscle beneath the crisp material of his black evening suit. An urge flooded her to look him full in the face, so she gave in to it. Her heart tripped at the compelling blue of his eyes, his jaw thrust forward and clenched, his blond hair falling across his forehead in manly wisps.

"You needn't worry that I, or anyone in the town, for that matter, blames you for anything that happened that day. Mercy, you organized a posse and stationed them at key locations. Between you and the South Bend force, I don't know what more you could have done to prepare yourselves for what happened. You're not mind readers. The whole town's just thankful you showed up when you did. I shudder to think what could've happened if you hadn't.

"Maggie and Abbie both say the word about town is that you put an end to the matter very quickly when you jumped on Roy's back and wrangled that gun out of his hand, then pulled him back to his feet like he weighed little more than a turkey feather."

Gabe chuckled and seemed to mull over her words in his mind. Then, he jabbed her gently on her arm with his shoulder, leaning dangerously close. "Well, you might say Helena's a mighty fine motivator."

Chapter Twenty-five

How did my grandmother play into the picture?"
Hannah asked.

"She told me you'd been shot, and suddenly I
had a singular mind: dealing with the McCurdys so I could
get to *you*! 'Course, when I discovered Jesse with a gun in
hand trying to defend Billy B against those hoodlums, saw
Van knocked out cold, and saw Jesse's poor pooch struggling
to stand, a good-sized cut on his head, why, that just got my
blood to boiling all the harder."

"Jesse had a gun?" Hannah covered her face with both
hands and peered at Gabe through the spaces. Where'd he
get a gun? How did he…?"

"I'm afraid that in her haste to snag a weapon for herself,
Helena left the cabinet door unlocked, so Jesse helped himself to the biggest rifle he could find when he sneaked down
the stairs against Helena's orders. I guess he figured it was his
mission to protect Billy B and the women of the house."

"Oh, gracious, that's sweet but—irrational. Imagine a little
boy thinking he could take on those criminals. Things could
have turned so ugly, Gabriel. Think of it—I am the only one

who suffered any real harm, and I am healing fine. Praise the Lord for His bountiful blessings. I have been thanking the Lord every day, in fact. Jesse, Billy B, Van, and even good ol' Dusty have suffered no long-lasting effects, and, best of all, those awful men can't hurt anyone else, especially the worst of the bunch, Rufus, whose body is cooling nicely in one of South Bend's cemeteries."

"Might be his body's cooling, but I'd guess his soul's not."

Hannah brushed off his remark, her hazel eyes brightening. "And since I mentioned Jesse—look how far he's come from that traumatized little urchin we first met. Why, you'd never guess he came to us a mute, given the way he talks a steady stream now. I'm so happy to hear he's doing well in school."

A grin tugged at his mouth. "Mr. Middleton says he sometimes talks too much in class."

Her jaw dropped. "No! That hardly seems possible."

The more they talked, the more the tension lifted. He pressed a hand over hers, giving her long, narrow fingers a gentle squeeze. It pleased him mightily that she didn't pull away. "You've had a lot to do with that boy's recovery, you know, taking care of him during the day like you have. He sure thinks the world of you." *And loves you almost as much as I do.* The fire sizzled and popped, mesmerizing both of them.

She flicked her free hand. "It was more you that made the difference than I. You came into his life at a most critical time. It scares me to think what might've happened if he hadn't jumped onto the back of your wagon that night."

He rolled his head to look at her. "I wasn't sure what to do with him when I found him. The little rapscallion gave me a run for my money in those first weeks." He put his face close to her delicate ear and took in her lavish, feminine scent. Turning just so, he lifted a hand to finger a coil of her hair. "'Course, so did you, if I remember right."

"Me?" A pink blotch, detected only by the fire's dim glow and the lone lamp, traversed up her cheek. "You weren't the most pleasant character yourself—calling me bristly and bull-headed." Eyes centered on the fire, she stuck out her pert chin. He gave her curl a playful tug, and her mouth twitched.

Were they flirting with each other?

"Did I really do that?" he asked in a gravelly whisper.

"Absolutely. And worse, you failed to identify yourself as the new sheriff when we first met and had me believing you were a neglectful father." A miniature smile now danced on her lips. "That was quite deceptive, if I do say so, leading me on like that."

He recalled that initial meeting in Kane's Whatnot and chortled. "And you were all set to report me to the authorities—only, I *was*…"

"You *were*…"

"…the authority!" Their simultaneous statements had them laughing at once.

"Oh, my!" she said, holding herself.

"If only you'd seen the look on your face when you discovered who I was," he said between laughing spurts. "You were madder than a wet cat."

"That was a nasty trick!"

"Sorry, but you made it hard for me to resist."

She jabbed him lightly in the arm, and their playful banter continued. When it finally settled and their breaths leveled off, Gabe released her hand and put his arm on the sofa back, slowly dropping it to her shoulder. Her quick intake of breath didn't deter him from tugging her up close to his side. "Hannah Grace, you are the berries."

A nervous giggle spilled forth. "I suppose I am, whatever you mean by that."

This produced another spurt of laughter, after which he leaned over and kissed her cheek. "I mean the sweet kind, of course, not the tart."

"Oh."

After her cheek, he traversed upward, touching his lips to her temple. "I'm glad Ralston saw fit to end your relationship."

She pushed back and quirked her pretty brow at him, tilting her face. "I—he, oh, never mind; it's not the least bit important. Yes, it's over and done with, thank the Lord."

He smiled and kissed the top of her head, just above the shimmery comb. He'd have liked to pull the contraption loose, along with all the pins holding her bun in place, and watch her fiery curls fall helter-skelter, but common sense overruled—that, and a God-given dose of self-control.

She'd started turning the white button on his shirtfront; indeed, flirting with him. His heart thumped hard against his chest. *Lord, I didn't know I could love someone this much.* "Of course, you know what that means," he said.

"Hmm?" she murmured, tilting her head up until their gazes met.

"It means you're free to accept another marriage proposal."

"Oh, is that right?" She tried to look flippant, but he knew better. Quickly, her gaze went back to her button-turning task. Much more and the thing would pop right off and poke her in the eye.

"Yes, and, in fact, I have a full confession to make." She stilled, and he took the opportunity to lift her chin with his index finger. Eyes neither green nor blue stared back at him, glistening in the corners like diamonds. Her hands dropped to her lap. "Are you ready for it?"

She gave a simple nod and he ran a gentle knuckle across her quivering lips. Leaning forward, he whispered, "I've fallen madly, unreservedly, irreversibly, head over heels in love."

"Really? With anybody I know?"

The little imp. Two could play this game. "You might. I'll give you some hints." Now his lips brushed her forehead. "She's prettier than a lily, lovelier than a sunset, sweeter than a gumdrop, and as precious as gold."

She shook her head. "Doesn't help—unless you're referring to one of my sisters."

He repositioned himself so they faced one another, then folded her hands in his and looked directly at her. "I'm referring to the prettiest of the three, which, simply put, would be you. Not that I'd want you telling them I said so, mind you."

He watched a little red spot on her cheek blossom like a rosebud. "Hannah, I love you. What do you say to that? I want to be with you, sweetheart. I want us to be a family—you, Jesse, and me." He lifted one of her curls and twirled it around his finger. It had become one of his favorite things to do, lately.

"I want to sit with you and Jesse in that Kane family pew. I want us to worship Christ together as a family, keeping God as the focal point of our lives and the decisions we make. I want to spend Sunday afternoons with you—when I'm not on duty, that is—and take long walks with you, and find out everything there is to know about you, learn your thoughts and feelings about things, have endless conversations with you—like that day the three of us climbed the dunes and shared a picnic lunch.

"But I don't want Jesse with us every minute," he hastened to add. "I'm just selfish enough to want you to myself, now and then."

She smiled, so he took that moment to catch a breath and gauge his next move.

"You might say you love me back," he urged. "Better yet, tell me you'd consider marrying me and being a mother to Jesse. Will you?"

K

He loves me, he loves me, he loves me! Hannah's heart sang the words while a blanket of awe smothered her ability to speak. Gracious, he'd even called her the prettiest of the Kane sisters. What a blessed little secret to hold close to her heart! And hadn't Papa said she most resembled Mama in mannerisms and generosity? Why, he'd even said he thought of Mama whenever she, Hannah, entered a room. What higher compliment could anyone pay her? Suddenly, it mattered little that she was tallest, skinniest, and pastiest of them all; that she had thick, spirally hair the color of a red, setting sun; or even that her blushing cheeks often revealed emotions she'd rather keep hidden. The sheriff loved her—considered her beautiful. On top of that, God loved her even more and had a beautiful plan in store for her!

She put a flat palm to the side of Gabe's cheek and he turned into it. The beginnings of beard growth prickled like the finest grade of sandpaper, and a curious swooping tugged at her heart.

"So I wasn't dreaming that day in Ralston's office?"

A hint of confusion shone in his eyes. "Dreaming?"

"I heard you all talking that day. Jesse was there, and you and Papa…" She gave her head a quick shake and a large tuft of hair fell over her cheek.

Gabe smiled, lifted a hand, and gently tucked the thick strand behind her ear. "I don't know what you remember about that day, sweetheart, but what's important is that you know God preserved your life for a reason. I believe that reason involves Jesse and me. He knew how much we would need you. Do you know I stopped by nearly every day to see how you were doing? Every day was the same, though—you were holed up in your room, healing from your wound, and I was growing as impatient as a baby bird to see you."

She giggled lightly. "Grandmother told me you kept stopping by, but I thought you were just doing your job."

He leaned close and smiled wider. "I'm not the parson, Hannah; I'm the sheriff, and I happen to love you." He started rubbing the upper part of her hand with his thumb, his eyes piercing to her soul. "So, what do you say? Will you be my wife?"

It's simple, Papa had said. *Trust and obey.*

Ralston saw her faith as mere religiosity, not something personal and tangible. No wonder she hadn't determined God's will for her life earlier. Simply put, her unequally yoked relationship with Ralston had kept her from knowing it completely! Papa's words came back afresh. *If you desire it deeply, daughter, and have a yielded heart, the Lord will reveal His will to you in His good time.*

Somewhere along the line, she had begun to shiver—and laugh—and cry. "Yes! Oh, yes! I love you, too, Gabriel Devlin! More than life itself."

She surprised herself by leaning forward and kissing him first—on the mouth—and gave him quite a shock. But then he quickly reciprocated, lavishing her with another sweet kiss—and another—and another. She swiveled to face him on the sofa and doubled her arms around his neck, massaging the back of his head where his hair met his starched white collar, then moving her hands to his broad shoulders, kneading the muscles where his shirt pulled and stretched. They'd kissed before, of course, but then, she had kept her guard up, not sure how or what to feel. Now, she kissed him with self-assured fervor.

When the long kiss ended, Gabe drew her to his solid chest, and they sat, enfolded in rapt silence and sweet thoughts—until the front door opened and a flurry of activity and high-spirited voices exploded through the still air.

"That was fun!" squealed Jesse. The whole family paraded through the door, removing coats and scarves and talking nonstop about the Bartons' new pump organ, their nicely decorated tree, and the delicious red punch that Norma Barton had concocted.

"I asked for that punch recipe, but do you think Norma would give it to me?" Helena was saying while handing off her coat to Jacob. "I swear she threw in a pinch of cinnamon."

"And that wonderful nut bread," Jacob said.

"Well now, that recipe came from the Lewis sisters. They brought it to the church supper last summer."

"I wish we had one of those pump organs," said Maggie. "It would help my singing voice immensely."

"Sorry, Mags, but it'd take more than a pump organ to fix your vocal chords," Abbie said, bending to untie her snowy boots.

"And what is wrong with my vocal chords?"

"They're—slightly warped."

"What's *warped* mean?" Jesse asked. "Is that like cracked, or something?"

"Did you notice Norma's lovely new divan? They ordered it all the way from California," Helena interrupted, rubbing her palms together.

Gabe and Hannah sat in the shadows listening to the mélange of conversation, Hannah covering her mouth to hold her giggles at bay.

Gabe cleared his throat, and the room momentarily stilled—then suddenly came to life with Jesse's shriek of delight. "Pa! Hannah! You're back." He skipped across the room, and Hannah scooted over, making a space for him to fit between them. It then occurred to Hannah what a fine little family they made.

"Well, my stars, you're sitting in the dark," Grandmother said, turning up the light on the sideboard.

"And awfully close," chimed Abbie with a devilish grin.

The entire family swept into the living room, their faces fairly blazing with expectancy.

"Well?" Maggie asked, hands clasped at her tiny waist.

"Yes, well?" Abbie echoed.

"Did you ask her, Pa? Did you?" Jesse's eyes lit like miniature firecrackers.

Over Jesse's head, Gabe and Hannah exchanged a loving glance, and, for the span of a few seconds, she doubted anyone even breathed. At last, Gabe nodded. "I did, and she said yes!"

Whoops of joy, hugs, and kisses, as well as hearty handshakes between Gabe and Jacob, went on for several minutes, with Jesse leaping around the room like a frenzied little frog, and all the ladies talking at once about wedding cakes, dresses, flowers, and colors. "This calls for a celebration," Jacob announced above the clamor. "Mother, didn't I see some pumpkin pies on the pie shelf?"

Helena smiled with a gleam in her eye. "You certainly did. I had a sneaking feeling there might be cause for celebration tonight, so I whipped up a batch of cream topping, as well. I'll put the kettle on for some tea. Girls, come and help me. Oh, my, just think—a wedding!" Helena bustled into the kitchen, all aflutter, while Maggie and Abbie bent to give Hannah and Gabe one last hug.

"Come on, little man." Maggie straightened and extended her hand to Jesse, who was spinning circles in the middle of the room. "Help Abbie and me get out Grandmother's finest china." He bounded off with them, leaving Gabe, Jacob, and Hannah in the living room.

Jacob sat down in the upholstered chair facing them, folded one leg over the other, and propped his elbows on the chair's arms, his thumbs circling one another as they often did when he was weighing important matters. "So, you're going to marry my daughter, are you?" Even in the low-lit room, his eyes flickered warmly.

"I'll treat her like a queen, sir," Gabe said, hauling Hannah's hand to his lap in a possessive squeeze. Then, looking directly at her, he added, "I love her." Just like that, Hannah's heart catapulted into a perfect somersault.

"I have no doubt you do," Jacob said. "That's why I'm happy to give you my blessing. Being that Hannah is my first-born, I'm a bit partial, you see." This he whispered, even as his thumbs kept circling.

"Oh, Papa."

His gaze held steady on Gabe. "I had a strong feeling Ralston wasn't right for her, so I stepped up my prayers. My daughters don't know this, but I've made it my business to pray for their future husbands, and something about Ralston just didn't sit right with me." His eyes danced with merriment. "And then Gabriel Devlin rode into town."

Hannah giggled. "Oh, Papa, you are the berries."

His eyes roamed from one to the other, quickly sobering, and his thumbs quit circling. "And now there is this deep peace in my heart, and I have only the Lord to thank for putting it there."

Gabe nodded, Hannah's eyes welled up with joyful tears, and several moments of sweet, awe-filled silence passed between them—until Jesse's squeals of pleasure from the other room had them all smiling. They rose at the same time and Jacob stepped forward to clap Gabe on the back. "Welcome to the family, young man."

"Thank you, sir. I'll be proud to be a part of it."

In the kitchen, Abbie's giggles nearly raised the roof when Maggie's off-key rendition of "Deck the Halls" splintered the air.

Jacob shook his head and angled Gabe an admiring look. "You're a brave man."

K

Reverend Cooper married them on a sparkling Saturday in early March. A layer of fresh snow blanketed the earth, coming on the heels of a winter thaw, and nearly half the town had trudged through it to get to the one o'clock ceremony, Gabe's entire family included. Of course, Hannah had met them in January, when Gabe took her and Jesse to Ohio by train, so the initial awkwardness had passed, if ever there was any. Right from the start, the family welcomed them. The adults treaded gently with Jesse, knowing his history; the children, on the other hand, saw him as one more cousin, and practically threw themselves on him with eagerness. And Hannah—my, how they lavished her with love and acceptance, not one of them stingy with embraces.

The Devlin ranch was anything but lowly, with barns aplenty, a two-story guesthouse and servants' quarters, and acres of land that stretched further than the eye could see. But the folks who lived in the main house, Joseph and Thelma Devlin, were some of the sweetest and most unassuming Christians Hannah had ever met.

Hannah's Tambour lace dress and long train had called up a number of oohing murmurs from admiring women as she made her way down the church's center aisle on Jacob's steady arm, her sisters already standing at the front next to Gabe, Jesse, and Samuel, Gabe's brother. The pipe organ shook the floor with Mendelssohn's *Wedding March*. At first, she had trouble deciding where to plant her eyes, loving both Gabe and Jesse so much, but in her final steps to the altar, just before her father handed her off to her groom, it was Gabe who won her full attention.

"Beloved, we are gathered here together in the sight of God..."

Both longed to look at each other, but they had to content themselves with the warmth of clinging, squeezing hands while Reverend Cooper performed his part and they theirs. Off to the side, Jesse shifted in place, scratched his neck, and pulled at his starched collar. At last, the reverend issued permission for them to turn and face each other. They did so with tender smiles and sighs of great relief. "Repeat after me," he said, and so they did.

"Do you, Hannah Grace Kane, take this man?"

"Do you, Gabriel Devlin, take this woman?"

"...to have and to hold, from this day forward, for better, for worse..."

"I now pronounce you man and wife."

"With this ring, I thee wed..."

It seemed forever and a day before Reverend Cooper finally announced, "You may kiss your bride." And what a kiss it was, done to the greatest satisfaction of everyone present. Gabe's hands gently framed Hannah's face, and he mouthed the words "I love you," easily discernable to those seated in the first three pews on the bride's side. Even Dr. Ralston Van

Huff, who sat on the aisle, fourth pew from the back, nodded a semblance of approval when the couple finally came up for air and faced their guests.

"My, she's a beautiful bride," Norma Barton said in whispered awe to her husband, Ambrose, when the happy couple swept down the aisle past them. Jesse was in the middle, linking hands with his new parents, followed by a procession of Maggie, Abbie, Samuel, and the reverend. "Which daughter do you think Jacob will give away next?"

Ambrose gave a thoughtful shrug and leaned down. "Maggie Rose is off to New York to work at some orphanage, and Abbie Ann's still on the young side, don't you think?"

Norma nodded and smiled for the length of five heartbeats, then looped her arm through his. "You're probably right. It'll be a good long while."

Outside, balmy sunshine did its job of melting the snow on roof peaks and sidewalks, turning Water Street into just that—a pool of water and slush. Out of nowhere, a brave, lone robin alighted on a branch just outside the church doors and chirped a hopeful tune.

There was no doubt about it. Winter in Sandy Shores had met its end—a sure sign of new beginnings.

About the Author

Born and raised in west Michigan, Sharlene MacLaren attended Spring Arbor University. Upon graduating with an education degree, she traveled internationally for a year with a small singing ensemble, then came home and married one of her childhood friends. Together they raised two lovely daughters. Now happily retired after teaching elementary school for thirty-one years, "Shar" enjoys reading, writing, singing in the church choir and worship teams, traveling, and spending time with her husband, children, and precious grandchildren.

A Christian for over forty years and a lover of the English language, Shar has always enjoyed dabbling in writing—poetry, fiction, various essays, and freelance work for periodicals and newspapers. She remembers well the short stories she wrote in high school and watched circulate from girl to girl during government and civics classes. "Psst," someone would whisper from two rows over, always when the teacher's back was to the class, "pass me the next page."

Shar is an occasional speaker for her local MOPS (Mothers of Preschoolers) organization; is involved in KIDS' HOPE

USA, a mentoring program for at-risk children; counsels young women in the Apples of Gold Program; and is active in two weekly Bible studies. She and her husband, Cecil, live in Spring Lake, Michigan, with their lovable collie, Dakota, and Mocha, their lazy fat cat.

The acclaimed *Through Every Storm* was Shar's first novel to be published by Whitaker House, and in 2007, the American Christian Fiction Writers (ACFW) named it a finalist for Book of the Year. The beloved Little Hickman Creek series consisted of *Loving Liza Jane*; *Sarah, My Beloved*; and *Courting Emma*. Faith, Hope, and Love, the Inspirational Outreach Chapter of Romance Writers of America, announced *Sarah, My Beloved* as a finalist in its 2008 Inspirational Reader's Choice Contest in the category of long historical fiction.

To find out more about Shar and her writing and inspiration, you can e-mail her at smac@chartermi.net or visit her Web site at www.sharlenemaclaren.com.

Loving Liza Jane
Sharlene MacLaren

When Liza Jane Merriwether rode into the town of Little Hickman Creek, her first thought was, *Oh, Lord, what have I done?* Soon, the petite schoolteacher is beloved by all… including Benjamin Broughton, a handsome widower struggling to raise two young children. Liza Jane's teaching contract explicitly states that she is to have "no improper contact with the opposite sex." Together, they may discover that with God, all things are possible.

ISBN: 978-0-88368-816-8 ♦ Trade ♦ 368 pages

WHITAKER HOUSE

Sarah, My Beloved
Sharlene MacLaren

Sarah Woodward steps off the stagecoach to find that the man who had contacted her through the Marriage Made in Heaven Agency has fallen in love with and wed another woman. Sarah feels that God led her to Little Hickman Creek for a reason. She refuses to leave until she finds out what that reason is. Rocky Callahan's sister has died, leaving him with two young children to take care of. When he meets the fiery Sarah Woodward, he proposes the answer to both their problems—a marriage in name only. Will Sarah and Rocky find true love from the hand of the ultimate Matchmaker?

ISBN: 978-0-88368-425-2 ♦ Trade ♦ 368 pages

WHITAKER
HOUSE

Courting Emma
Sharlene MacLaren

Twenty-eight-year-old Emma Browning has experienced a good deal of life in her young age. Proprietor of Emma's Boardinghouse, she is "mother" to an array of beefy, unkempt, often rowdy characters. Though many men would like to get to know the steely, hard-edged, yet surprisingly lovely proprietor, none has truly succeeded. That is, not until the town's new pastor, Jonathan Atkins, takes up residence in the boardinghouse.

ISBN: 978-1-60374-020-3 ✦ Trade ✦ 368 pages

WHITAKER
HOUSE